Death Cake

For Donna,
with best wishes,
Jeri Fitzgerald Board
2022

Death Cake

JUST DESSERTS

Jeri Fitzgerald Board

ISBN-13: 978-1-7375618-0-4

Printed by Ingram Spark

Book design by Aaron Burleson, Spokesmedia

In loving memory of Mark Schweizer, who dared me; and Alan Leonard, who insisted the law not interfere with a good story. And for Andy Haynes, my partner in crime.

Death Cake would not have been possible without the technical and creative assistance of Aaron Burleson, Spokesmedia; and, the insightful suggestions and support of Kathleen Wright, Lisa Laidlaw, Tony Rothwell, Marilyn Grube, Warren Board, and Carolyn Langston.

Death Cake

PROLOGUE
October 8, 2019

After her husband Tripp tried to kill her, my best friend Bobbye spent three days in an Atlanta hospital. The back of her head, which had been cracked open, was covered with a large bandage. When I went to see her that first evening, I fed her pudding from a spoon because her right arm was in a sling. "He's going to kill me," she'd mumbled between bites. "I know he's going to kill me."

The following evening when I went to visit, Bobbye asked me to buy her some clothes, as the ones she'd been wearing the night of the assault were stiff with dried blood. On the third night, I took those new clothes with me to the hospital and, as soon as the doctor released her, I helped her put them on. When we got to my car, she said nothing about where we were going, only that I should head south out of the city.

I'm Stacey Parks and if I'd done things differently, some of this might not have happened. But I went along when I shouldn't have and stood by while a complicated situation evolved into a deadly one—a situation in which two people destroyed each other, even as they loved each other to distraction.

Bobbye was seven years old when her dad left. A few months later, her mother abandoned her. My mom was killed in a car accident when I was six so, growing up, neither of us was blessed with a mother's love. But our friend Tripp MacAvoy was. Tripp's mother, Caroline, was what newspapers call a "society woman." Tripp's dad, Ed, owned several textile plants. The MacAvoys lived in a big white house in a fancy neighborhood that was only a quarter of a mile, as the crow flies, from Bobbye's house and mine. If economic and social factors had played a role in our little triangle, Tripp might as well have lived on another planet. But he became our best friend anyway.

Tripp was always the brains behind our fun and games, the creator of our imaginative deeds—good and bad—and the money that made it all possible. Like other kids, the three of us had had no idea when we met what our future held. We were just three youngsters who ended up in the same sixth-grade band class at Inman Middle School.

One day when Bobbye and I were alone, she told me she'd lived in three different foster homes before she'd been adopted by Russell and Janice Warren. Mr. Russell was the janitor at Inman Middle School, Miss Janice worked in the cafeteria, and they lived in a blue Cape Cod that sat on the edge of the school grounds. Behind it was a detached one-car garage and a large grassy area where Bobbye, Tripp, and I played carefree games on warm summer nights while lightening bugs turned that big empty field into a fairy land.

Many years have passed since then and, when I look in the mirror these days, I see fifty. The skin under my chin is starting to sag, spidery wrinkles frame the outer corners of my eyes, and there's a furrow between my brows that grows deeper every year. My dad would have shrugged such things off, would have blamed them on what he called *day to day living*. But I know it's more than that. It's what comes from standing on the sidelines watching as childhood games morph into clever lies, personal vendettas, artful deceit.

Some people thought that when it came to Bobbye I was blind, but that wasn't true. I'd always been intimately aware of the roller coaster life she'd led—the ups and downs, the fits and starts, the disappointments and longings that sharpened her ability to change colors like a chameleon. By the time we'd entered high school, Bobbye had mastered the art of embracing the unsavory opportunity, of shaping it to fit her needs, of stepping into whatever part was necessary to get what she wanted. And what she wanted was Tripp MacAvoy.

The death of Tripp's first wife, Lark, had the haunting elements of a Greek tragedy. When her body was discovered one August morning back in 1999, the state medical examiner reported he'd found neither internal nor external injuries, and concluded that at age 37, Lark Loflin MacAvoy had died of natural causes. But I knew better.

You may wonder *how* I know so much about this sordid story. Well, my source was the horse's mouth herself—Bobbye Revels MacAvoy. And I've been blessed with good ears, can hear flies stomp. And over the years, I've done things I shouldn't have. Like the time Tripp told Bobbye and me we had to take our friend Meredith to another state to have an abortion. But I'm not going to start this story with Tripp because he's too complicated. I'll start with Bobbye, who spent the first seven years of her life in a trailer park in Roswell, Georgia.

Part One

Certain ingredients, if exposed to
damp, will not produce desired results.

Mastering the Art of Cake Baking
Betsy P. Elmore, Editor

The Flower Garden Trailer Park was anything but. Located on a red clay knoll about three miles west of Roswell, Georgia, it contained only one paved street lined on either side by a half dozen well-worn mobile homes. Shaded in summer by old oaks and maples, it was as clean and respectable a trailer park as one could find in north Georgia, because every one of its metal houses boasted a gravel driveway alongside a little patch of runty grass. Dora and Clem Williamson, the middle-aged couple who owned it, were Bible thumping Baptists who hated drink and loved kids. Every April, Miss Dora, as she was known, bought two baskets of red and purple petunias and hung them on the white picket fence at the entrance to their property. Those baskets were overflowing with blooms on a bright June day in 1973 when Esther and Rick Revels brought their baby girl home from the hospital. Roberta Ann Revels was twenty-three inches long with a thatch of raven hair and eyes as dark as huckleberries. An even-tempered baby who seldom cried, she proved to be a delight to her daddy who nicknamed her Bobbye.

Two boys, Mark and Jed, followed in rapid succession. By the time Jed was born in the fall of 1976, Rick was working construction, building expensive houses in a new subdivision that had been laid out on old farmland northwest of Atlanta. Soon, Esther was working three days a week hauling debris from the work sites and cleaning the finished houses before the inspector arrived. Esther and Rick made enough to own a decent truck, TV, and washing machine.

Miss Dora, who loved looking after Mark and Jed while Esther worked, took the toddlers up to her house where she taught them Bible verses and fed them lunch. Most days, their big sister, Bobbye, got on the school bus with a couple of Miss Dora's sugar cookies in her pocket. Dora and Clem Williamson were head-over-heels in love with the three Revels kids and often invited them, and their parents, for home-made ice cream on Sunday afternoons. The Williamsons were an especially nice gift for the Revels' household as there were no other children in the park.

Rick Revels had grown up in a neighborhood on the outskirts of downtown Atlanta where his dad drove a beer truck and his mom waited tables at Mary Mac's Tea Room. He had a brother, Tim, nine years older, who'd left home the year Rick started school. Since he was raised an only child, Rick was the apple of his mother's eye and the son in whom a father put all his hopes and dreams. He was a handsome young man with a narrow face and high cheek bones and hair so black it looked blue. While he was a lack-luster student, he was a fine athlete who won awards in track and field and played on the varsity baseball team. When Rick dropped out of school at 16, his parents were broken-hearted, but gave him permission to join the Army. During training, he performed well on the rifle range and, upon graduation, received a citation commending his ability as a marksman. His commanding officer also noted that he could out-run, out-climb, and out-jump any man in his company.

In the spring of 1968, Rick completed an eight-week crash course for Army infantry known as "shake-n-bake," and in June, was sent to Vietnam. After just four months, he was promoted to the rank of Staff Sergeant and given command of the Eastern Sector Reconnaissance Patrol. His parents never knew it, but over the next sixteen months, Rick led small, select groups of specially trained soldiers across enemy lines for covert operations along the Mekong Delta. Rick never wrote his parents about his work, never told them how he earned the ribbons and insignias on his uniform. And no one outside his company ever knew that he'd been captured by the Viet Cong and had escaped by jumping off a thirty-foot cliff into the roiling river. In October of 1971, he was back in Georgia where he began working construction.

* * * * *

Esther Barbee, the daughter of a successful plumber and his stay-at-home wife, was tall, slender, and pretty with hazel eyes and shoulder length auburn hair. An honor roll student, she dreamed of going to college and becoming a kindergarten teacher.

One winter night her senior year she met Rick Revels at a Dairy Queen and soon they were an item. She took him to the prom the next spring where all her girlfriends swooned over the tall, handsome Vietnam vet. The fall after graduation, Esther began taking classes at the local community college. But during the Christmas holidays, her dream of becoming a teacher took flight when she suddenly realized she'd missed two periods in a row.

Early in January, Esther and Rick ran away to Valdosta where they were married by a Justice of the Peace. They lived with Esther's parents until Bobbye was born. By then, Rick had been promoted to construction supervisor and they'd saved enough money to move up to Roswell where they'd rented a trailer from the Williamsons.

While their life was not exactly American middle class, the little family had plenty to eat and a warm place to sleep when winter winds brought sleet and freezing rain to the clay-covered hills around them. For a while, Rick and Esther had steady work and a solid income. But the summer Bobbye turned six, things changed.

It all started one sultry afternoon in late August when Rick was helping a new home-owner get her washer and dryer installed. Seems his boss walked into the laundry room to check on the installation and discovered Rick and the woman agitating mightily atop the new washer. The boss fired Rick on the spot, warned him not to ask for a reference, and told him that if he had his way, Rick would never work construction in the Atlanta area again. Rick turned around, zipped up his pants, and turned back to wallop the guy in the jaw. The boss slumped to the floor and was out long enough for Rick to flee.

He went straight to the He's Not Here Lounge & Pool Hall and tied one on. When he got home about three the next morning, he didn't have the guts to tell Esther he'd been fired, so he told her he was sick of construction and was going to look for a new job. Then he dropped a bombshell telling her he wanted to move. He spent the next two weeks looking for a job and just before Labor Day, a friend told him about a high-rise condo project being built on Marco Island, Florida. Rick had no idea where Marco was, but he got out a map and figured he could drive down in one day and take a look. He was hired the afternoon he arrived and called Esther to tell her he was living in a motel room on Pirate's Island and not to worry, he'd make good money and send her some.

A couple of weeks later, Rick's older brother, Tim, showed up at the trailer park with an envelope containing $200 in cash. Esther had never known it, but Tim lived only three miles away and he and Rick had been seeing each other regularly for the last couple of years. This caught Esther by surprise, but she didn't let on. She just took the money and thanked Tim.

Since Esther had lost her cleaning job because Rick was fired, she needed work and she needed transportation. So, she went to Dora and Clem Williamson and asked them to help her get a car. Clem offered to take her to town the next day to visit a couple of used car dealers. They came home with a used Pinto that cost $675, which they'd registered in Clem's name. Esther agreed to pay him $40.00 a month to cover the car payment, plus the liability insurance, which was also in Clem's name. As soon as she had wheels, Esther began cleaning houses in Roswell five days a week. The $200 Rick sent each month paid the rent on the trailer plus the $40.00 she owed Clem for the car and insurance. The money Esther earned cleaning houses she used for the electric bill, gas for the Pinto, and occasionally, to buy clothing or a pair of cheap shoes for one of the kids.

But there was nothing left for food. So, Esther went to the office of Social Services and told the people there that her husband had lost his job and she had three hungry children to feed. They helped her fill out the application for food stamps. Then she went to the office of the Board of Education and filled out a form so Bobbye could get free lunches at school.

One Monday in October, Tim came to the trailer with some official looking papers and told Esther to sign them. Rick wanted a separation and he wanted it now. Esther was stunned. She'd been sure that Rick was going to send for her and the kids any day. She protested, but Tim told her that if she didn't sign Rick had said he wouldn't send her any more money. Esther burst into tears and continued blubbering while she scratched her name on the papers.

After Tim left, she went to the nearest liquor store and bought a fifth of bourbon and a pint of gin. While her mom wallowed in bed with her stash of booze and a box of tissues, Bobbye fed her brothers cereal and canned soup. This went on for three days. On Friday morning, Bobbye took Jed down to Miss Dora's before she and Mark went off to school, and Jed spilled the beans telling Miss Dora that his mommy was sick in bed.

That evening, Dora and Clem came over to the trailer with supper. They were upset at what they found—the stench of vomit that assaulted them when they opened the door, empty cereal boxes, candy wrappers, and chip bags all over the floor, filthy clothes lying around, a sink piled high with dirty dishes. Dora opened the refrigerator and found nothing but a jar of pickled okra. She walked back to the bedroom to talk with Esther, but Esther wasn't there. She'd fled to the bathroom and locked the door.

Dora lost her temper. "Esther," she hollered, "if you don't straighten up and take care of your precious children, I'm gonna call the cops. You've got till tomorrow at noon, and I'd better see some big changes when I come back, or Clem and I will have you evicted."

When Dora came over the next day, she found Esther cleaning the toilet. The kitchen was spotless, the beds had been changed, and the washer was running. The children sat on the floor in front of the TV watching cartoons. Esther apologized and begged Dora to forgive her. "Rick has sent separation papers from Florida," she whimpered, "and I have no choice but to sign them. I can't pay you rent if I don't agree to a separation because he won't send me money anymore."

Dora knew that Rick had been fired from the construction job and she knew he'd been in Florida working, but she'd had no idea that he planned to leave Esther and his kids. "Sorry dog," she spat, as she took the younger woman in her arms. "I've got some extra food in my freezer and I'll run get some for you and the kids."

Tim continued to come by with an envelope every month and while she tried not to, Esther continued to drink. Every night after she'd warmed up a can of beanie weenies for the kids, she hurried to the store to pick up a six pack which she polished off before bedtime. Bobbye was the one who got her brothers up in the mornings, fed and dressed them, and took Jed down to Miss Dora's before she and Mark caught the school bus.

One morning, Esther came to her senses when Bobbye woke her and told her there was nothing to eat. Esther borrowed five dollars from Dora and bought enough food to tide them over for a couple of days. She threw out the last of the beer, forced herself to eat dinner with the kids, and got back to cleaning houses. She made friends with two single women who worked in a convenience store in Roswell where she stopped for coffee most mornings. The three of them occasionally went out for a drink at a local bar or caught a movie at the mall cinema. And one night, Esther realized that, like her two single friends, she now had the freedom to date if she wanted to. One of the men who'd worked construction with Rick had called her three times to ask her out. She'd declined all three times.

But when he called one night and said he had tickets for an Allman Brothers concert at the Atlanta Civic Center, she decided to go. After all, she reasoned, it wouldn't hurt one bit to spend a few hours in the same place with Greg Allman. The guy took her out for a steak dinner beforehand and all she could think about was the way his bottom lip curled up like a prune when he took a sip of beer and the clacking noise his dentures made when he chewed his steak. She loved the concert though and spent most of it on her feet screaming and gyrating around. At intermission, she excused herself to powder her nose.

Just outside the rest room door, she ran into Skunk Rollins, a guy she'd known in high school. Skunk had become the hero of Cameron High the day he'd hidden a live skunk in the desk drawer of a certain math teacher, a man roundly despised by his students. Esther was struck by how much Skunk had changed. His shoulders were broad, his hair thick and wavy. And he was wearing expensive cowboy boots and a silver lariat studded with turquoise. He burst into laughter when he saw Esther, grabbed her around the waist, and lifted her off her feet. When he set her down again, she touched him on the cheek and said, "Skunk, it's so good to see you!"

He frowned. "I ain't Skunk no more, pretty girl. Haven't been called Skunk since high school. Don't you remember my name?"

Esther looked down at the floor searching her memory. "I'm so sorry," she apologized," but I can't remember."

"It's Jack...John Henry Rollins. But everybody calls me Jack. After we finished high school, I got a good job at the Fresh Mart and when anybody asked me my name, I told them it was Jack. People don't know about Skunk and I'd appreciate it if you'd call me Jack."

Esther promised she would and the two of them talked for a few minutes about old friends. Then she told him that Rick was gone, they were separated, and she was single again. He pulled a match book from the pocket of his plaid shirt, wrote her number on it, and said, "I'll call you next week, honey, and see if you want to go out dancing."

* * * * *

On Wednesday evening, while Esther was washing dishes, the phone rang. It was Jack Rollins. "Hi there, beautiful," he began. "If you don't have any plans Friday night, I want to take you to the Wild Bird Saloon in Marietta. The Fire Cracker Band is playing and I just love doing the two-step. Don't you?"

Esther had never done anything called the two-step, but she wasn't about to turn down an opportunity to see Jack. She told him she'd just love to, and he said he'd pick her up at nine. He didn't mention dinner beforehand, but she didn't notice. She was too excited about going out with Jack Rollins.

The next morning, she went straight to the convenience store and told her friends that she had to learn the two-step before Friday night…that she had a date with a guy named Jack Rollins. They laughed and laughed and told her what a fool she was to go out with Jack. One of them said, "Jack Rollins? Do you mean *Skunk* Rollins? If you're going out with him, you'd better watch yourself." But that warning was wasted on Esther, who went right out to the phone booth in front of the store and called the local dance studio. Yes, she could have a lesson that very afternoon to learn the two-step. It would cost $35.00. Esther hurried off to the house she had to clean that day and rushed through it in half the time it usually took so she wouldn't miss her dance lesson.

Then she headed to the mall where she bought a new outfit. Denim shorts and a cute little vest embroidered with red and yellow flowers and a pair of high-heeled yellow leather boots that came up to her knees. When she tried them on, she felt sixteen. On her way out of the store, a pair of sterling silver and turquoise earrings caught her eye. And in less than two hours, she'd blown the entire contents of Rick's last envelope. But this was her big chance, and she was gonna make the most of it.

Jack was a fabulous dancer who whirled her around the floor as if she weighed nothing. When the band took a break, they sat down at a table with some of his friends. Jack drank Wild Turkey straight from a bottle, smoked one cigarette after another, and told a string of dirty jokes that kept everyone laughing. No one asked her about where she lived or what she did or who her parents were. Jack ordered a basket of fried shrimp and fed them to her one by one. Esther had not had shrimp in ages and relished every bite. But it was the attention that Jack paid her that really mattered. He kept asking her questions about how she was doing and if she wanted another beer or something else to eat? She just smiled and shook her head. She was just fine, thank you. She was having the time of her young life and she didn't want the night to ever end.

When they left the bar, Jack drove straight to his house, a duplex on the east side of town. Esther knew he had a good job, knew he made good money as the assistant manager of a large grocery store. But she had not known that he owned a duplex until that night.

"The rent from the other side almost pays the whole mortgage," he said, as he'd unlocked the door. Esther was impressed by the large living area where a matching sofa and love seat sat in front of a brick fireplace. Jack led her down a hallway where there were two bedrooms and a bath. Everything was neat and clean and nothing like what Esther had expected to see in a bachelor's pad. She thought about the trailer with its moldy corners, rusting pipes, and cramped little rooms. Why couldn't she live in a nice place like this?

Jack went back to the kitchen and poured each of them a large whiskey. He added some ginger ale to Esther's and drank his straight. They went into the living room and settled on the couch together. Jack lit a cigarette and put his arm on the back of the sofa behind Esther.

"I'm so glad we saw each other at that concert," he said. "And I can't tell you how happy I am that you wanted to go out with me tonight. I had such a big crush on you when we were in high school and you were the prettiest girl in our class." He took a long draw from his cigarette. "I always wanted to ask you out, Esther, but I was afraid you'd turn me down."

Esther moved closer to Jack and told him that he should have asked because she would've gone out with him in a minute. But she knew it was a lie. She'd never paid much attention to Jack Rollins in school and always thought of him as just another loser...a scrawny poor boy from the other side of the tracks. But she saw no reason to dredge that up. "Oh, Jack," she crooned, batting her long lashes at him. "I'm so glad you asked me out."

Jack cupped her chin in his large hand and leaned over to kiss her. She kissed him back parting her lips and pushing her chest toward him. He began unbuttoning her blouse, something he'd longed to do when they were in school, and slowly slid his fingers inside. When he pinched her left nipple, she caught her breath. It wasn't long before her denim shorts and cute little embroidered vest were on the floor along with her panties and bra. Esther believed she could resist Jack's advances, but she was as helpless as a baby when he removed her new yellow boots, pulled down her pantyhose, and began kissing the tips of her toes. Soon he'd worked his way up to her thighs, running his tongue over her goose-pimpled flesh every inch of the way. That's when she knew she was in trouble. Rick had always been a straight-forward, rather unimaginative lover. In and out, that was Rick.

But Jack Rollins was another animal entirely. He drew the breath right out of Esther's body and filled it with a raging fire. She moaned and writhed and called his name as he entered her. And when she reached her first climax ever, she screamed. Then she began to sob as if her heart would break. She went on and on until Jack held her whispering, "There, there."

They made love not once, not twice, but three times in a span of two hours. Those hours raced by and when Esther glanced at the clock on the wall above the TV, she was surprised to see that it was almost four in the morning. She'd never left her children alone all night and felt a twinge of shame when she realized she hadn't even thought about them. All she'd thought about was finding a way to hold onto the fire that was burning deep inside her. She'd heard the term *sex appeal* all her life, but until now, it had had no meaning.

When Jack began to snore, Esther got up and went to the bathroom. Taking a clean cloth from the shelf above the toilet, she wet it with cold water and began washing her face all the while praying, Oh, Lord, don't let me get pregnant. She thought about her diaphragm and realized she had no idea where it was. I'll find it first thing when I get home, she thought, and put it in my new red purse to keep it handy.

She pulled the curtain back from the window and looked out toward a streak of soft gray light rising in the east. Then she went back to the living room and dressed. As much as she hated to, she had to go home. She knew she had to be in her own bed before her kids woke up. Sitting down on the side of the bed, she gently touched Jack's shoulder. He woke immediately and, without a word, got dressed and took her home.

* * * * *

On Halloween, Jack came to the trailer earlier than usual carrying a big plastic bag that contained costumes for the kids—Bat Man for Mark, a cowboy outfit complete with pistols and holster for Jed, and a frothy pink ballerina dress and rhinestone tiara for Bobbye. As soon as the kids were ready, he gave each of them an orange plastic pumpkin with a handle for collecting their loot. Then he and Esther put them in his truck and took them into Roswell where they made big hauls in the upscale neighborhoods west of town.

Later, Jack helped Esther put the boys to bed. After they put Bobbye on the sofa in the living room, Esther made a quick trip to the bathroom to insert her diaphragm and hurried down the hall to the bedroom where Jack was resting on the bed in nothing but his birthday suit. His burnished hair shown like brass in the light of the lamp and his steel blue eyes danced with delight when he saw her standing in the doorway. He held out his hand and she giggled as she threw off the towel she was wearing and fell head long across him. At two o'clock, Esther told Jack he had to leave. She didn't want the kids, or Dora and Clem, to think he'd been there all night.

Two days before Thanksgiving, Tim came by with a small turkey he'd won at a shoot. He told Esther he'd not heard from Rick lately but assumed all was going well because the envelopes kept coming. He gave her a curious look and asked, "Are you seeing that no-good Skunk Rollins?"

This caught Esther off guard, and she hemmed and hawed trying to think of the right answer. Finally, she said, "Jack is an old friend from high school. He takes me dancing sometimes, that's all." Tim made a little sound in his throat like *humf* and she knew he'd seen right through her. "Ya'll have a good Thanksgiving," he sneered, as he drove away.

It proved to be the best Thanksgiving ever. Jack brought a ham and a pumpkin pie from his grocery store and Esther cooked a turkey breast with all the trimmings. For the three Revels kids, it was quite a feast. The wind was blowing from the south which made for a pleasant, warm day and Esther sent the kids out to play after dinner. She washed the dishes and cleaned the kitchen while Jack watched football.

At half-time, she sat down on the sofa beside Jack and said, "Will you help me put up a Christmas tree next weekend?" Jack broke into a grin. "Lord, girl, I haven't put up a Christmas tree in years. Not sure I even remember how. Tell me what you want, and I'll get it for you with my store discount and bring it out on Friday night."

Then he asked her what she wanted for Christmas. By this time Esther was madly in love with Jack and knew he felt the same about her, but she wasn't about to jeopardize what they had by saying so…or telling him what she really wanted was an engagement ring. So, she smiled and told him she'd seen a blue cable-knit sweater in the window at Fi-Fi's Fashions on Main Street.

December was a busy month. Jack was tied up later than usual every day at the store and Esther took on two more houses so she could buy the leather jacket she wanted to give him for Christmas. Bobbye and Mark were in a Christmas pageant at school and Jack took Esther and Jed to see them perform. The kids closeted themselves in Esther's bedroom where they planned the gifts they would make for their mom and for Jack, whom they genuinely liked. Esther spent several hours each night making holiday cookies and candies, storing them in tins on the highest shelf of her closet.

Jack got off work at eight on Christmas Eve. He loaded his truck with the gifts he'd bought for Esther and the kids, a bag of groceries, and went straight out to the trailer park. To the delight of the kids, Esther had bought a big plastic inflatable Santa and put it beside her front door. Jack smiled as he drove in, remembering Christmases when he was a kid and how he'd longed to have one of those plastic Santas in his yard.

Jed, wearing his pajamas, greeted Jack at the door and gave him a hug while Bobbye and Mark jumped around like beans on a hot skillet. Then Bobbye took his hand and walked him over to the Christmas tree to point out the colorful packages that contained the presents they'd made for him.

Once they got the kids in bed, Esther and Jack sat down on the sofa together and began to talk. Jack asked if Esther had enough money to carry her through the week. "I'm fine," she replied. "The bills are paid, I've got a full tank of gas, and there's plenty of food in the house. I'm sure we'll have plenty of left-over ham, thanks to you. I don't know how I would have gotten through this fall without you, honey." She squeezed his arm. "You're so good to me."

Jack grabbed her and hugged her to his chest. "I've been crazy about you, Esther Barbee, since 9th grade," he whispered, his warm lips brushing her ear. "And I couldn't be happier. You probably don't know it, but you've changed my life. All I did before we started dating was leave work as fast as I could every night so I could run around with a bunch of drug store cowboys, drink liquor, and pick up women. Now, when I get off work I come out to your house and have a good home-cooked meal and watch TV with your kids." He held her away from him for a moment and said, "Just look at me, darlin.' You've turned me into an old homebody."

He stood up and pulled a little square box from the pocket of his jeans and handed it to her. Esther felt a surge of heat rise when Jack said, "Merry Christmas. Go on and open it." Her fingers shook as she tore the wrappings from the box to find a small diamond pendant on a gold chain. "Oh, Jack," she crooned, "It's gorgeous. Here, put it on me."

As Jack closed the clasp, he wrapped his arms around her, brushed his lips against her hair, and said, "One of these days, if you'll let me, Esther, I'll give you a ring to go with it."

Esther sank to the couch bringing Jack with her. "I love you," she said. "You're the sweetest man I've ever known and I'm dreaming of the day we'll be together." Then she closed her eyes and thought September...by September my divorce will be final, and I'll be free to marry you. "Come here, big boy," she whispered as she pulled Jack down on top of her. "Let mama show you what she thinks of your Christmas present."

* * * * *

No one looked forward to the future more than Esther Barbee Revels. On New Year's Day, she and Jack drank a champagne toast and, as Esther raised her glass, she smiled and thought—*just nine more months and I'll be free*. On Valentine's Day, they went to a party with friends and drank another champagne toast and, as Esther raised her glass, she smiled and thought, *just eight more months*. They drank green beer to celebrate St. Patrick's Day and Esther's only thought was *just seven months to go*.

For Esther, the spring that followed was the most beautiful of her young life. The rhododendrons and azaleas were at their peak on a warm April day when Esther and Jack took the kids for a picnic at Stern's Lake. Roses in vibrant reds, pinks, and yellows were in full bloom in June when they all went an outdoor concert at Hanging Rock. Later that month, Esther and Jack took the boys and Bobbye out for games and burgers to celebrate Bobbye's seventh birthday. That summer passed quickly as they talked more and more about what they would do when they lived together. Esther wanted to live in Roswell so she could be closer to her work. Jack told her he'd been thinking about renting both sides of his duplex and promised that they would start looking for a house soon. When he got a raise in August, he took Esther and the kids to Busch Gardens for the weekend. It was the first time the kids had ever seen a roller coaster, the first time they'd eaten cotton candy, the first time they'd spent the night in a motel.

On Labor Day, Jack invited Esther and the kids to his house. He grilled steaks for the two of them and hamburgers for the kids, who were playing Frisbee in his back yard. When Esther went into the house to use the bathroom, he dropped a diamond solitaire into her glass of tea. She returned and drank the tea down to the ice, but never saw it. In frustration, Jack turned the glass upside down into her open palm and the diamond tumbled out. Esther screamed when she saw it and burst into tears. Then she began sobbing and she sobbed and sobbed until Jack picked her up in his arms and carried her into the house, slipped the ring on her finger, and swore to love her forever.

When Tim showed up the next day and got out of his truck, Esther put her hands behind her back to keep the engagement ring out of sight. He handed her an envelope with money in it and when she took it from him, she used her right hand. Tim had been chewing on a toothpick when he'd arrived, but he spit it on the ground before he said, "Rick's gonna be sending you a set of divorce papers in about two weeks. You gotta sign them in front of a notary public and mail them right back to him."

On September 20, the divorce papers were delivered by special courier to the trailer park and Dora called Esther at work and told her they'd arrived. Esther left the house she'd been cleaning, flew home, got the papers, and took them to a bank in Roswell where she signed them before a notary. Then she rushed inside the post office, and when she dropped the envelope in the slot, it was all she could do not to kick up her heels. As she went up the street to her car, she felt as if she were walking on air.

That night, Esther put the kids to bed, and over a quiet dinner, she and Jack decided they would be married the Friday after Thanksgiving. As Esther poured champagne into Jack's glass, she told him she wanted them to be married by a preacher in Dora and Clem's living room with the kids as attendants. Jack nodded, and said, "You do all the planning and I'll foot the bill."

Later when Esther was washing dishes, she thought about the day she'd married Rick, about how hurried and impersonal it had been. They'd spent their honeymoon night in a cheap motel on the way home from Valdosta. This time will be different, she thought, as she took off her apron. This time I'll wear a real wedding dress and carry a bouquet. And we'll have punch and mints in Dora's dining room and a honeymoon in Savannah.

* * * * *

Two days before Halloween, Esther was out back hanging clothes on the line when Tim drove into the yard. He slammed the door on his truck and hurried down the driveway to where she was, sucking air by the time he got there. "Rick's had a accident," he gasped. "He was up on this high metal ladder and it swung away from the wall where he was working and took him all the way down with it and broke both his ankles…just crushed 'em. He's been in the hospital for the past two weeks. He wanted me to come tell you 'cause he ain't gonna be able to work for a while so there won't be no money comin' up here. Doctor said it would be five, maybe six months 'fore he's able to even walk again, much less work."

Esther's head began to swim as she sank to the ground beside the clothes basket. Oh. Lord, she thought, how could this happen? What am I gonna do? I can't pay the rent and pay what I owe Clem for the car on what I make. She looked up at Tim. "What am I supposed to do, Tim? You know I don't have the money to pay the rent and pay the bills and feed and clothe my children. What am I supposed to do?"

Tim shook his head and let loose a stream of tobacco juice. "Why don't you ask that rich boyfriend of yours? Why don't you ask him to help you? He's got money."

With that, he turned and walked back to his truck. He slammed the door again and stuck his head out the window.

"That's just like you, girl," he snarled out of the side of his mouth. "You don't give a flying fuck what's happened to Rick. Never did since the day you tricked him into marrying you." He gunned the engine, gouging a slash in the rough red clay that stung Esther's face as he sped away.

That night, as Esther and Jack sat on her couch, she poured her heart out telling him every detail of why she'd married Rick, and what Tim had told her about his accident, and the fact that she couldn't pay the rent on the trailer anymore, and what was she gonna do?

Jack said, "What about your parents? Won't they help you?"

Esther slumped against the back of the sofa. "My parents are divorced and have been for a couple of years now. One of the men who worked for daddy cut a sewage line under this old lady's house and it flooded, and she got sick and ended up in the hospital. Then she got a lawyer and sued my daddy and he lost the business. My mama left then and went to live with her sister in Memphis. She works part-time as a dispatcher. My daddy's out in California driving a dump truck making $3.50 an hour. They would help me if they could, but they can't."

Jack looked toward the front window, toward the road that led out of the trailer park. "What about the Williamsons?" he asked. "They have a good income from the rents in this park. They could help you."

But Esther shook her head. "I still owe them several payments for the car. And there's no need to even mention Rick's parents. They hate my guts for taking their boy away. They wouldn't give me air in a jug. Besides, Tim told me last week that his mama has lung cancer... it's pretty far along. There's nobody and I don't know what I'm gonna do."

Esther just knew that Jack would offer to help, that he'd give her enough money to get over the hump until they married. She was sure he'd offer to pay the rent. But that isn't what happened. No, what happened was nothing like she thought it would be.

Jack got up and walked over to the kitchen sink, took a glass from the drainer, and filled it with water. "I've got something I've been meaning to tell you, Esther," he said, his voice kind of quiet. "It's been on my mind for a while, and I know I shouldn't have waited this long."

He put the glass to his lips, slowly drank the water from it, and put it back in the drainer. But he didn't turn around. "I can't marry you as long as you have those children. There is no way in hell I'm gonna raise another man's bastards. Especially a son-of a bitch like Rick Revels. You probably don't know this, but Rick's daddy and my daddy hated each other's guts."

Jack continued to stand at the sink with his back to Esther while she tried to get her mind around his words, *I can't marry you as long as you have those children.*

Then Jack pulled a cigarette from the pack in his shirt pocket and turned around to face her. "It's like this," he said, sticking the end of the cigarette between his lips. "Old man Revels cut my daddy bad one night in a bar in downtown Atlanta and Daddy's never gotten over it." He lit the cigarette, sucking a long draw before he spoke again. "When I went to see Daddy last week and told him who I was gonna marry, I happened to mention the fact that you had three kids, he hit the ceiling. He was so upset that he told me I need not ever darken his door again if I took Rick Revel's trash to raise. Your kids are good kids, Esther. But I don't love them the way I love my daddy. And besides, they aren't my blood. Please try to understand, honey, I love *you* and I want to marry *you*. But I can't have Rick Revel's off-spring putting their knees under my table and eatin' my hard-earned food."

Esther's lips compressed into a thin quivering line as tears started down her cheeks. She couldn't understand how

Jack could treat her kids so nice one minute and not care a fig about them the next. She wanted to say something, wanted to ask him how that was possible. But all she did was sit there wringing her hands and crying. Several minutes passed before she got up and went down the hall to the bathroom and Jack went home.

* * * * *

On Thanksgiving Day, Esther began drinking before noon. She ruined the expensive pork roast she'd bought and forgot to put salt in the mashed potatoes, and the green beans she thought were cooked were still raw. The only thing that tasted good was the ready-made pumpkin pie. Once dinner was finally over, she sent the children out to play in the yard and retreated into her bedroom where she cried buckets over Jack Rollins. In between bouts of calling him a no-good, dirty, ass-hole-bastard and a sorry-ass, son-of-a-bitch, she sobbed her heart out over how much she missed him, how much she wanted to see him, how much she loved him. In between slobbery gulps, she said things like, "Buck up, girl, you'll get over him." But she knew she wouldn't.

Two weeks later she took the kids into Roswell for the Christmas parade. They stood in the crowd along the sidewalk and collected candies thrown by costumed revelers on the floats, waved to Santa, and saluted the flag as the high school band marched by. But her kids were unusually quiet the whole day just as they'd been since Jack disappeared. They missed him, missed his big laugh, missed his presents, missed playing with him.

After they got back into the Pinto and started down the highway, Esther made a quick right turn into the lot at Jack's grocery store. She pulled into an empty parking space and watched shoppers as they hurried in and out of the double front doors. Jack was not anywhere in sight. He was inside working. You're a damn fool, Esther thought, as she exited the parking lot. Just like some stupid teen-ager on the make. Buck up! It's over.

When she got home, she was surprised to find a letter from Rick. In it, he told her how sorry he was that he'd not been able to send her any money for a while and he was very sorry, but he wouldn't be able to send any more. The people at the rehab center had done everything possible to help him, but the doctors had told him that he'd have to go on disability and would never be able to work a regular job again. He went on to write that he was married to a fine woman and they were living in her apartment in Fort Myers. She was a nurse's aide at the rehab center. He wished Esther well and told her to please give the kids a hug for him.

After Esther tore the letter to shreds, she settled the kids on the couch in front of the TV, took a beer out of the fridge, and sat down at the table. She had to feed the kids, but she just kept chugging on that beer and staring across the room into a long dark tunnel where she saw herself down on her knees scrubbing another woman's floors, robbing Peter to pay Paul to pay the electric bill, stocking shelves at The Dollar Store on weekends so she could buy new shoes for her kids. The whole scene scared her so badly that she staggered to the counter and made a pot of strong coffee which she drank, black, while she made three sandwiches. As soon as the kids sat down at the table, she went down the hall to the bathroom where she scrubbed her face, put on fresh make-up, and brushed her hair. Then she picked up the phone and dialed Jack's number.

When he came on the line, she asked if he would please meet her at the Roll Bar Café that night, she had something to tell him. After she hung up, she put on a jeans skirt, her yellow boots, and that cute little vest embroidered with yellow and red flowers. The diamond pendant he'd given her hung just above her breasts like a beacon and the engagement ring danced in the light as she slipped it back on her finger.

At the Roll Bar Café, they sat in a back booth drinking Wild Turkey and eating shrimp while Esther made up stories about how much fun she'd had at the Christmas parade that day. She told Jack how good he looked and asked him to take her dancing. After dinner, they went to the Wild Bird Saloon to dance.

About two o'clock, they left Marietta and Jack took her back to Roswell to the café where she'd left her car. As they pulled into the parking area, she reached over and grabbed Jack around the neck. "I've never done it in a parking lot before," she said, her breath coming hard. Two minutes later, her bare feet were pressed against the dashboard of Jack's truck and he was down on his knees on the floorboard getting a taste of heaven.

When it was over, he offered her a cigarette and they smoked while they cooled off. Then Esther took a long draw and said, "I'll give up the children, Jack, if you still want to marry me."

* * * * *

At lunch time on December 14, Esther stood with her face in the wind outside a brick building while she removed her engagement ring and carefully slid it down inside her bra. Then she opened the doors to the offices of Social Services. There, she told the woman who had been her case worker, that Rick had been permanently disabled in an accident and wouldn't be able to work anymore, she couldn't pay the rent on the trailer, and she'd lost two of her house cleaning jobs because the owners had moved away. Esther's voice failed her and she began sucking air in short spurts. She tried to speak again, but her eyes filled with tears and her nose started running. The case worker handed her a tissue and Esther took a moment to dab at her nose and wipe smears of mascara from beneath her eyes. She put the tips of her fingers against her lips and held them there while she stared out the window trying to collect herself. Then she looked back at the woman behind the desk and said, "I want to put my children up for adoption."

The case worker urged Esther to be patient. "There are things we can do," she said. "We can put your children in foster care with a good family while we help you get back on your feet. We can help you get a loan to see you through the holidays. There are special funds available for families like yours. Please don't be hasty, Mrs. Revels," she urged. "Let us help you."

But Esther shook her head. "You can't help me," she replied. "No one can help me. My parents can't help. And Rick's parents can't help. I'm behind on my car payments and the kids need new shoes and I don't have a single thing to put under the tree for them from Santa. We won't even have a tree."

She squared her shoulders, sat up straight, and all the color drained from her face. "My mind is made up. I can't do this and there's no one to help me. You're my only hope. My children are good and they're smart. I want them to grow up in a decent home where they never have to worry about the electricity being cut off, where they never have to go to bed hungry, where they never have to wear second-hand clothes, where they can have a new pair of shoes just because they want them, not because they need them. I want them to have a better life than I can give them."

The case worker called in her supervisor, but it didn't do any good. Esther knew what she wanted, and she sat there, motionless, until the two employees gave in. As soon as she finished signing the papers, the supervisor gave Esther a steely look and told her that on the last day of the month her three children would be taken to a state-run facility near Atlanta.

Christmas was bleak in the Revels' household. Jack took pity on Esther and gave her a ham, a pie, and a box of candy canes for the kids. There was no tree. On Christmas morning, the kids awoke to find Santa had left each of them a cheap toy and a pair of new shoes.

After lunch on New Year's Eve, Esther sat her children down on the sofa and told them that she was going away for a while saying, "I've found a job making lots of money out of town. And you'll be staying in a nice place with other children until I can come back and get you."

She told them that they were to mind their manners and make good grades in school, so she'd be proud of them. Even though she cried the whole time, she never lost her resolve because she just knew that one day down the road Old Man Rollins would die and she and Jack would come back and get her children.

Mark jumped off the sofa, ran to the bathroom, and locked the door. Jed kept pulling at a thread on the sleeve of his sweater and asking questions like, "Why, Mama? Why?" Bobbye sat stone still, her eyes on the door, praying Daddy would show up and make everything right again.

At two o'clock, a case worker arrived with another Social Services employee to transport the children and their meager belongings to their new home. Esther stood in the yard waving, tears pouring down her face, as their car drove out of the trailer park. Then she went inside and packed her suitcase, lining the sides of it with pictures of her parents and children. She took the key to the Pinto from her purse and laid it on the kitchen table along with the key to the trailer. When she opened the door, she found Jack waiting in his truck.

Late on the afternoon of January 2, 1981 Esther stood with her groom before a magistrate in a dingy little office in the basement of the courthouse in Anniston, Alabama. The magistrate brought in her secretary and a file clerk to serve as witnesses. That evening, the newlyweds had dinner at a steak house and spent the night in the motel behind it. The next morning, Esther went to look for an apartment while Jack hurried off to his new job as manager of the Anniston Superette.

Dora and Clem fought like dogs to try to get custody of Bobbye, Mark, and Jed. But the courts concluded that, at ages 59 and 61, they were too old to raise them. That winter, Mark and Jed were adopted by a couple who owned pecan groves outside Macon and, two months later, Bobbye went to live with a couple in Monroe who would be her *first* set of foster parents.

From the moment he drew breath on a bright sunny day in April of 1973, James Edward MacAvoy III, was known as Tripp. At just over four pounds, he was small. But his was an auspicious beginning as he was the only child, and the only grandchild, born into two of the oldest and most prominent families in Atlanta. His mother, Caroline Cogdill MacAvoy, had been named Deb of the Year at the 1962 Atlanta Cotillion. A petite blonde with a lilting laugh, she was popular in high school and president of her freshman class in college. On a hot September day in 1966, she'd married Ed MacAvoy and, as they danced at their reception, she'd promised him a son before the year was out.

Over the next two years, Caroline miscarried three times. Just before Christmas in 1970, she was devastated by the birth, and immediate death, of a full-term baby boy. In September of 1972, the family doctor confirmed that she was pregnant once again and insisted that she stay in bed for the next seven months with a staff of trained nurses in attendance. Caroline always believed that this was the secret to her success in carrying and birthing her golden boy, Tripp.

Caroline and her twin, Catherine, were the only children of the Southeast Regional Vice-President of the Coca-Cola Corporation, Rand Cogdill, and his wife, Patricia. Rand and Patricia, who'd grown up in Atlanta, married in 1943 and moved into the stately Virginia Highlands home that had been built by Patricia's parents in 1920. The house, a sprawling three-story, had originally been red brick laid down with squash mortar. Decades later, it had been painted white and that shiny mortar oozing from between those painted bricks reminded me of icing oozing from the layers of a birthday cake.

A long circular drive, bordered in spring by flaming pink azaleas and purple rhododendrons, led to a flagstone porch. The oversized front door opened to a foyer with a floor laid in black and white marble. From it, a sweeping mahogany staircase rose to dizzying heights where oil portraits of family ancestors lined the walls leading up to the second floor.

Off to the left was an elegant living room with a sixteen-foot ceiling. A Steinway grand filled one corner and a set of matching sofas sat opposite each other in front of the fireplace on the far end of the room. Nearby, a small table held the most cherished possessions in the Cogdill home—a silver framed photograph of Rand Cogdill shaking hands with President John F. Kennedy on the morning of November 22, 1963. Beside the photo was a clear glass ashtray, its bottom a painted replica of the dark blue seal of the President of the United States. Beside the ash tray, a brown match book cover from the Texas Hotel rested on a white linen napkin embossed with the Seal of the President of the United States.

Early in November of 1963, Rand had received a call from the secretary to the CEO of Coca-Cola Corporation asking if he would please attend a breakfast for President Kennedy in Fort Worth on the morning of November 22. Rand's big boss would be in the Caribbean with his family the week of Thanksgiving and wouldn't be able to attend. The secretary went on to say that Mr. Cogdill was welcome to take the company plane. Rand replied that he'd be delighted to stand in for his boss. The secretary told him a driver would be waiting when he landed at the Fort Worth airport to take him to the Texas Hotel for the 8:00 AM breakfast. Rand hung up, let out a long whistle, and called Patricia.

When he'd arrived at the Texas Hotel that morning, Rand was shown to a seat at the head table beside Lady Bird Johnson and the Vice-President. He put his cigarette out immediately in the ashtray beside his place…the ashtray containing the Presidential seal. A band on the far side of the room struck up "Hail to the Chief" and the 300 specially invited guests sitting at long rows of tables across the ballroom rose and began cheering. The President entered, flashed a toothy grin at the audience, and slowly made his way to the podium where he stood while the Texas Boys Choir sang a moving rendition of "The Eyes of Texas Are Upon You."

Without warning, young Jacqueline Kennedy came in unannounced, and everyone burst into spontaneous applause. Mrs. Johnson turned to Rand and said, "Doesn't Jackie look wonderful in that pink suit and hat?" The President greeted his wife, and after she'd been seated, told his audience that no one cared about what he or Lyndon wore…which got a big laugh. Then he gave a short speech about narrowing freedoms around the world and how important it was that the United States help protect those freedoms wherever they existed, and the expanding role NATO would play in that effort during his administration. As soon as the President finished talking, Rand and the three other special guests at the head table, were invited to have their picture made with him before he left for that fateful trip to Dallas.

Like most Americans on that awful Thanksgiving weekend, Rand and Patricia Cogdill, along with their twin daughters, Caroline and Catherine, were glued to the television throughout, a box of tissues close at hand. The images of the assassination, jumbled with the joy of meeting the smiling, engaging young Jack Kennedy, would haunt Rand Cogdill and he would talk about the events of that day, and his impressions of them, with his son-in-law Ed, and grandson Tripp, for the rest of his life.

* * * * *

Even though Ed MacAvoy had known Caroline Cogdill through their families' business connections, they'd never attended the same schools mainly because he was four years older than she. Following graduation from The Citadel in June of 1960, Ed had returned home to Atlanta to spend the summer months working in his father's textile mill in the country south of Sandy Springs. On the Fourth of July that year, he attended a dance at Highlands Country Club and, when he walked into the party, he saw Caroline sitting at a table with several girls. One of them, a girl he knew from church, got up and asked him to dance. When their dance ended, she took him back to the table and introduced him to her friends. A few minutes later, the band began playing, "Sleep Walk," and Ed made his way around the table and offered his hand to the petite blonde with big brown eyes who smiled up at him as if she'd never before been asked to dance. As he slid his palm across the back of her beige silk dress, she moved closer to him. Neither of them said a word, they just looked directly into each other's eyes until the music came to an end. Then they walked back by the table to pick up Caroline's evening bag on their way out.

Ed's grandfather, Jim—the first James Edward MacAvoy—had moved to Georgia in 1912 when he was offered a job as floor supervisor in a cotton mill northwest of Atlanta. Over the next twenty years, Jim worked his way up to manager and eventually saved enough to buy a mill of his own where he produced millions of white cotton socks and underwear for the US government during World War II. After the war ended, Jim bought a second mill in Valdosta, and in 1948, a third in Birmingham. While hundreds of machines hummed in his mills, Jim concentrated on making them hum faster. It took him a couple of years of trial and error, but eventually he perfected a metal device that cut time on the threading machine in half. The patent for his device was approved almost immediately and every cotton mill in the South began buying it by the gross, which made Jim MacAvoy a very rich man.

In the fall of 1950, he and his wife, Lila, built a split level on forty rolling acres outside Sandy Springs. It was there that their son, James Edward MacAvoy II, whom they called Ed, and a daughter named Judith, grew up. When Ed finished high school in 1956, he went to college at The Citadel in Charleston and, from there, to the University of Georgia where he received his law degree in 1962. That fall, Caroline Cogdill went away to Queens College in Charlotte and Ed was named Associate Counsel for MacAvoy Enterprises. For the next two years, the two of them talked on the phone nearly every night. Every other weekend, they burned up the roads between Atlanta and Charlotte. When the time came for Caroline to return to Queens for her junior year, she begged her parents not to make her go back to Charlotte, telling them she'd commute to Agnes Scott to finish her degree. But she never did. She married Ed that fall in what was dubbed "Atlanta's society wedding of the year."

Following their honeymoon, the young couple moved into the spacious second floor of the Cogdill home on Virginia Circle where they raised their only child, Tripp. Caroline and Ed had a large bedroom suite and down the hall there was a sitting room they called *the TV room*. It had a small kitchen across the back wall complete with sink, refrigerator, and an apartment-size gas range where Caroline prepared breakfast each morning for Ed. When she was not having lunch with friends at the country club, she joined her mother, Patricia, downstairs on the sun porch for a delicious light meal prepared by Classie Dixon, their cook, who lived in two rooms on the third floor of the house.

Caroline read to her son every night before bed, a ritual that became their favorite time. After his first-grade teacher introduced Maurice Sendak's *Where the Wild Things Are* to his class at school, Tripp begged his mother for a copy. As soon as he got home from school each day, he'd open his new book and carefully study the images of Sendak's fearsome animals. Then he'd select a particular beast to imitate and fill his afternoon play time running up and down the stairs, and in and out of the kitchen, terrorizing Classie with grotesque faces, deep growls, and piercing shrieks of *Let the rumpus begin!*

Tripp was an active little boy with a big imagination and, while he behaved well at school, he always pushed the envelope at home. Patricia complained daily to her daughter about her grandson's annoying, rambunctious behavior, but Carolyn just ignored it. "He's a normal boy," she'd say, "and he's just having fun." Ed, who was much less tolerant, would occasionally threaten Tripp with a spanking, especially at dinner time when Tripp seemed to be at his worst.

One night while his parents and grandparents were enjoying their meal, Tripp brought a small green snake into the dining room and let it loose under the table. Ed managed to corner the snake and throw it out the kitchen door. When he returned to the dining room, he grabbed Tripp by the arm and told him to go up to his room. Tripp jerked away from him, ran around the table, and flung himself at Caroline. "Oh, no, you don't!" Ed roared, catching the boy by the scruff of his neck. "You're not going to hide behind your mother again." Ed hauled Tripp up the stairs and locked him in his room for the rest of the night.

But this was just one of many incidents that Tripp perpetrated over the next few years. Eventually, he evolved into what his Grandfather Rand called "a damn handful," and Ed found himself stuck between a rock and a hard place as he tried, over and over, to convince Caroline that their son was not in charge of the MacAvoy household.

* * * * *

One muggy morning in August of 1984, I started sixth grade at Inman Middle School and, during band class that day, made friends with Bobbye Revels and Tripp MacAvoy. I knew I wanted to play the clarinet because that's what my mom had played, and my dad had kept her instrument in its case on a shelf in a closet since she'd died. Over the years, he'd taken it out and shown it to me and told me he hoped I'd play it one day. So, that morning, I'd taken my mom's clarinet to school. When Tripp told the teacher, Mr. Curtiss, that he wanted to play the drums, Mr. Curtiss pointed to a set in the corner and told him to give it a try. Tripp sat down, took the sticks in hand, and it was immediately clear that he would never play the drums. But our teacher convinced him to play trombone. Bobbye had

had no idea what she wanted to play, but eventually settled on the French horn.

Not long after we got to know each other in band class, we discovered that we lived in the same neighborhood. Tripp and his parents and grandparents lived on Virginia Circle. My dad, Elliot Parks, and I lived on Kentucky Avenue in a small bungalow that had originally been the caretaker's cottage for a big mansion that had burned down in the 1930s. Bobbye and her adoptive parents, Janice and Russell Warren, lived on Clermont Drive along the back boundary of Inman Middle School. John Howell Park became the central location where the three of us met to ride bikes. After school, we sometimes hung out at the branch library on Highland Avenue and, on Saturday, spent hours horsing around and eating ice cream at a drug store down the street.

One Saturday morning that fall, after Bobbye and I watched Tripp and the Inman soccer team win a match, he invited us over to his house for pizza. After Bobbye and I rode our bikes up the hill to the birthday cake house, Tripp met us at the door. I left my backpack on a bench in the foyer thinking the sour-looking people in the gold frames hanging on the walls would keep an eye on it for me. From there we went back to the kitchen where the three of us sat at a round table and Classie served us gooey wedges of pizza right out of the oven. Tripp's mom, who asked us to call her "Miss Caroline," came in and talked with us for a while mostly about the match. Every few minutes, she put her hands on Tripp's shoulders, gave them a squeeze, and bragged about the fact it was her boy who'd made the winning goal. When we'd had our fill of pizza, she took our plates to the sink, brought out some bowls, and made hot fudge sundaes for us. She didn't eat anything and, as soon as we'd finished our sundaes, she disappeared.

Tripp took Bobbye and me into a big room with windows across the front he called *the library* to show us the elk's head mounted over the fireplace. Then we went into the living room to see a framed photograph of his Grandad Rand with President Kennedy. "You know who that guy is, don't you?" he asked. "Sure," I said. "He got shot. We read all about it in history class."

Tripp smiled, "Yeah, but my grandad was there when it happened."

We followed Tripp upstairs to what he called the *playroom* over the sun porch where we listened to Michael Jackson and took turns puffing on a cigarette he'd taken from his mom's purse. When it was time to go, Bobbye and I went back down the big staircase and out the front door. I remembered that I'd put my backpack on a bench in the foyer and left Bobby in the driveway while I went back to retrieve it. I didn't want to make a fuss, so I opened the door and went in. I could hear Tripp and his mother talking, their voices floating down from upstairs.

"I know who Stacey Parks is," Miss Caroline said. "Her daddy, Elliot, works for Brock Sanford at Georgia Power & Light. I met him last year at the Sanford's Christmas party. I think he writes technical manuals for the company. But I don't know that other girl...what's her name...Bobbye? Somebody told me that the janitor at Inman Middle and his wife had adopted a daughter. Isn't their name Warren?"

"Yes, Mama," I heard Tripp say. "Our janitor's name is Mr. Warren, but everybody calls him by his first name, Mr. Russell. And we call his wife Miss Janice. She makes the desserts in the cafeteria. Bobbye's parents are dead. Miss Janice and Mr. Russell adopted her."

Then Miss Caroline said, "Do you know when? Did they adopt her in the last couple of years?" Tripp must have nodded because Miss Caroline told him she hoped he'd be more careful in the future about whom he brought home, that no one knew where adopted children came from, that the real parents of adopted children might be mentally ill or something even worse. Evidently this upset Tripp because I heard him say, "I don't care if Bobbye is adopted, Mama! She's smart and she can really play ball and I like her. She's my friend."

Miss Caroline made a sound like *shush* before she said, "I know you like her. But you pal around with those two girls too much. Why don't you ask some boys over? You could invite some members of your soccer team. Or Phillip Sanford. Why don't you invite him?"

That's when I grabbed my backpack and hurried out the door being very careful not to make any noise. And I didn't tell Bobbye what I'd heard.

A couple weeks later, Tripp told us that his dad had season tickets to football games at the University of Georgia and he'd told Tripp to invite some friends to go to a game and sit with them in the box. I had no idea what *the box* was, but I was a huge Bulldog fan and couldn't wait until that Saturday in November for the big rival game with Georgia Tech. The box turned out to be a square enclosure that sat right on the 50-yard line. Inside, a dozen padded seats with black vinyl covers were screwed to the floor. Each had a bulldog painted on the back that looked like "Uga," the team's mascot. The boxes were outfitted with portable red tables where we ate hot dogs and drank Cokes. That morning, Miss Caroline, who wore a red suit trimmed with black fur, sat up front with Mr. Ed while Bobbye, Tripp, and I rode in the back seat of his big black Mercedes.

Tripp's granddad, Rand, followed with three friends in his new Coupe de Ville. They wore traditional red and black ball caps with an image of Uga embroidered over the bill. Every time our team held the Techies on the line, they jumped to their feet, yelling, *How 'bout them dawgs!* Throughout the game, they drank beer from red plastic cups, and I watched Tripp as he sneaked sips from one cup, then another, every chance he got.

My dad had given me enough money to buy a new black and red plaid skirt and matching red sweater. I'd let Bobbye borrow an old red jumper of mine that was too tight on me and her mom had made her a white blouse to wear under it. Bobbye, whose hair was as black as a raven's wing, always looked great in red and Mr. Rand and his friends commented on how pretty both of us looked. With my plain brown hair and gray blue eyes, I knew I wasn't pretty, but I smiled, showing them my straight white teeth, which were my best feature.

Miss Caroline was nice to us that day, too, bustling around like a mama duck making sure Bobbye and I had plenty to eat and introducing us to her friends in the boxes on either side. After lunch, she asked Tripp to pass around a Tupperware carton filled with Classie's delicious brownies and gave him a hug when he brought it back empty. Every time the dawgs scored, she grabbed Tripp and they clung to each other jumping up and down as one. Mr. Ed wasn't nearly as wrapped up in the game and, when the half-time show was over, he left the box and visited with people in the other boxes nearby. The old guys followed along behind him, but Miss Caroline stayed right there with Tripp and Bobbye and me.

* * * * *

That December, Tripp invited Bobbye and me to the big house on Virginia Circle for the annual holiday cocktail party hosted by the MacAvoys and Cogdills. Late that afternoon, Bobbye's dad, Mr. Russell, drove us over in his green station wagon, which he called "Green Bean." When we arrived, Classie took our coats and told us to go on up, that Mr. Tripp and his friend were up in the TV room.

I was happy that Tripp had invited Phil Sanford, a classmate who was on the soccer team and in our band class. Phil, who was taller than the rest of us, had coffee-colored eyes and dark brown hair that hung down around his chin like a page boy. Just below his left eye, high on his cheek, was a black mole that made him look like a pirate.

I looked at Phil and said, "Hi, I'm glad you came. I didn't know that you and Tripp were friends." He made a little noise, something between a giggle and a snort, and told me that he and Tripp had played together since they were in diapers. It seems that Phil's dad, Brock, and Ed McAvoy had been buddies since 1970 when they'd served together on the Steering Committee for the Atlanta Jaycees Annual "Miss Georgia Pageant." Caroline and Phil's mom, Phyllis, were involved in many of the same community organizations, so the two couples had become close friends. I knew Phil's parents a little because his dad, Brock, was my dad's boss at Georgia Power & Light. Phyllis Sanford was tall, very slender, and wore her short black hair cut like Peter Pan. Brock, who was balding, was even taller than Mr. Ed.

While the adults enjoyed a buffet in the dining room downstairs, us kids played Uno for a while, watched a John Denver Christmas special on TV, drank Coke, and helped ourselves to a plate filled with Classie's green cookies shaped like Christmas trees and red cookies shaped like bells. When I bit the top half off a green Christmas tree decorated with sprinkles, I blurted, "Gosh, these are so yummy!" Then I kept licking my lips to get all the sugar off. "Classie sure is a good cook."

Tripp cocked his head at me and frowned. "Well, I helped her make them," he said. "She rolled out the dough, but I cut them out and put all the decorations on. After Christmas, Classie's going to teach me how to make cheese grits."

"Oh, that's easy," I said, trying not to laugh. "Bobbye and I make cheese grits all the time. All you do is cook the grits and put some cheese in 'em."

Tripp shook his head. "I don't mean *that kind*," he smirked. "I mean real cheese grits with butter and eggs and lots of milk. I'm gonna make a cheese grits casserole."

Phil piped up then. "Why all this sudden interest in cooking, MacAvoy?" he asked, his deep voice making him sound older. "I'm surprised you even know where the stove is."

Tripp laughed. "Yeah, well... I don't know much, but I like cooking. And I like Classie. She's always nice to me and when I'm with her in the kitchen I have fun. Besides, my dad would never look for me there."

He reached out, picked up the cookie plate and as he offered it to Phil, said, "Some of the best cooks in the world are men. Ya'll want some popcorn? I'd like some, wouldn't you?" He looked directly at Bobbye, who nodded and smiled. Tripp went across the room to the kitchen area, opened the cupboard above the sink, and took out a carton of Jiffy Pop. He turned on the front burner of the gas stove with the kind of skill that let me know he'd done it before. The room filled with a mouth-watering smell and, minutes later, that bowl of popcorn was gone.

Then Tripp put a cassette in the tape player and held his hand out to Bobbye. They moved away from the sofa and started slow dancing to "Merry Christmas, Darling." Bobbye towered over Tripp like Big Bird on Sesame Street as her long straight hair swayed back and forth on each side of her head like black curtains. Every now and then, stray ends of it would brush the side of Tripp's face and he'd rise up on his tip toes and whisper something in her ear. Then she'd nod and beam down at him.

About nine, Tripp's dad, Ed, took Phil, Bobbye, and me home. When Phil ran up the steps to his house, we saw his mom open the front door for him. Bobbye leaned over and told me that Tripp had told her that Phyllis Sanford's dad was a state senator in South Carolina. "I'll bet they're rich, too," she whispered, "just like the MacAvoys."

* * * * *

One rainy Saturday in February, Bobbye, Tripp, and I were sitting in the Warrens' living room griping about the fact that we had nowhere to go and nothing to do. It wasn't fun riding our bikes in the rain and we'd seen all the movies playing at the local cinema. We put a pizza in the microwave, and while we ate it at the kitchen table, Tripp came up with a plan for our first joint venture into what adults call unacceptable behavior. Tripp told Bobbye he wanted her to get Mr. Russell's big key ring and give it to him so we could go on a treasure hunt. His eyes were dancing with mischief when he said, "We'll have fun roaming around inside the school and we might find something we want." But Bobbye refused to give him her dad's keys.

Tripp left the table and went down on one knee in front of her. "Please, Bobbye," he begged. "Please do this so we won't have to stay in this stupid kitchen all afternoon with nothing to do. We aren't gonna hurt anybody. Why shouldn't we have a little fun at school for a change? You said your dad and mom went downtown to buy her some new uniforms. They won't be home for hours and I promise we won't be in the school but a few minutes." He put his right hand over his heart, looked her in the eye, and said, "I promise."

Bobbye got up and took her plate to the sink. I grabbed my plate and followed, giving her a scowl as we began washing up. The look on her face told me she was struggling with

Tripp's idea, but I could tell she didn't want to disappoint him. "Okay," she said, with her back to him. Then she turned from the sink. "Just for a minute," she warned. "They never stay away long. I'll be right back." And she disappeared down the hallway.

As soon as Bobbye returned with Mr. Russell's keys, Tripp took them, got on his bike, and pulled his jacket hood over his head. "Ya'll meet me at the back door to the cafeteria in fifteen minutes," he said. Then he rode off in the rain.

I could tell Bobbye was furious, but she didn't say a thing. Five minutes later, we put on our jackets, got on our bikes, and headed for the door at the back of the cafeteria. Tripp showed up, leaned his bike against the wall, and handed Bobbye Mr. Russell's black metal key ring. Then he pulled another set of keys from his jeans pocket, a set secured by a shiny brass ring. "I'll just keep these handy for another rainy day," he said, as he slid a heavy silver key into the lock. "It pays to have friends who work in a hardware store," he sniggered.

Bobbye and I followed Tripp through a huge kitchen that smelled of lemon floor cleaner, between the rows of long white tables and metal chairs, and out the double doors that led to a suite of offices on the front of the main building. Tripp took out his set of new keys and tried several before he found the one that opened the main office. Inside, the secretary's desk and a row of file cabinets, a table and several chairs filled the area up front...a space all three of us had visited for various reasons. Behind the secretary's desk were two open doors. One led to Principal Morrison's office and the other led to Assistant Principal Crenshaw's. Tripp started toward that door but Bobbye grabbed him on his forearm.

"Don't go in there," she said. "Just being here gives me the creeps, Tripp." She looked up scanning the ceiling. "They could have video cameras in here."

But Tripp just pushed her hand away. "You're a big baby, Bobbye Revels. You take the fun out of everything! Old man Crenshaw deserves this. Can't you just see his face when he finds out somebody broke into *his* closet and took *his* stuff? He'll blow up like a bullfrog and huff and puff around mad as hell. I can't wait to see his face when we get to school on Monday."

Tripp sauntered across a span of beige carpet and into Mr. Crenshaw's office as if he owned the place. When he got to the door that led to the supply closet, he had to figure out which key fit the lock. Bobbye and I stayed in the outer office while he kept trying keys. Finally, the door opened and he went in, and moments later, came out with an armload of composition notebooks, cartons of paper clips and rubber bands, rulers, packets of colored construction paper, and a handful of ball point pens.

"Here," he announced. "Come and get it." But neither Bobbye nor I moved. Tripp put the stash on top of the secretary's desk. "I can't take all this stuff with me," he said. "Ya'll have to take some of it."

"I'm not taking anything," Bobbye answered, stepping away from him. "That's stealing," she went on, "and you know it. Besides, you don't need any of this, Tripp. You get two dollars a week allowance. Why would you want to steal stuff?"

"This isn't stealing," he insisted. "Schools aren't banks. All us taxpayers paid for this stuff, you dope. That's what my daddy said. He's told me all about how taxes work and how we MacAvoys have to pay lots of taxes because we own a business. And some people don't even pay any taxes. Like those women with all their kids living in the projects over in Southside. They're living off food stamps and free lunches at school that we pay for."

I watched as Bobbye's frame stiffened. Her head went up, her shoulders back, and she drew her arms close in like a fighter stepping into the ring. "No," she said.

42

Tripp picked up a blue composition notebook and held it out to her. "One little notebook," he said, waving the notebook in front of her face, taunting her. "Just take one little notebook."

Bobbye grabbed the notebook, stuffed it down inside her jacket, and zipped it up. "That's all," she whispered, turning to me. "You gotta take something, too, Stacey." I walked over, searched the loot and took the smallest item I could find...a red ball point pen that had Inman Middle School printed in gold on the side. I slid it down into my jeans pocket and walked out.

When Bobbye and Tripp caught up with me at the end of the hall, Tripp was carrying a plastic trash bag filled with the stuff he'd taken from Mr. Crenshaw's supply closet. We went back through the cafeteria and left by the back door we'd come in. Tripp took out his set of keys, found the right one, and locked it. Then he got on his bike, waved to us, and rode off up the hill.

Bobbye frowned at me but said nothing. "Don't worry, Bobbye," I said, trying to reassure her. "Your dad won't find out. How could he?" She didn't answer and we stood there in the rain like a couple of lost dogs until she finally got on her bike and started across the back lot that led to her house.

I watched until she was almost home. Then I turned my bike in the opposite direction and took a shortcut through John Howell Park where I threw the red ball point pen into some bushes. I didn't want my dad to see that pen, didn't want to have to answer questions about where I'd gotten it. He probably wouldn't have seen it if I'd been careful, but I didn't want to take that chance. Besides, I felt bad about what we'd done. I liked Bobbye's parents and didn't want them to get in trouble over the stolen keys. Odds were good that Russell Warren could lose his job over such a prank, and

I was worried that someone might have seen the three of us unlock the back door and go into the cafeteria.

The wind began to blow and suddenly rain came down in sheets. By the time I reached my driveway at home, I was soaked to the skin and my hands were shaking. I quickly climbed the front steps, hauling my bike up under the covered porch, and went in knowing my dad would be angry because I'd gotten so wet.

I found him in the kitchen where the flour cannister was sitting on the worktable beside the electric mixer. Nearby was a box of brown sugar, several sticks of butter, and an open carton of eggs. The old tube pan, scratched and dented from years of use, was greased and floured and I knew my dad was making what we called the "death cake." "Who died?" I asked.

He was standing at the sink with his back to me. "My secretary's mother," he said. "Remember old Mrs. Harrington from church? I think she taught you Sunday School for a couple of years. The wake is tonight and I'm going over to take the cake. You'd better get cleaned up now and put on something else because you're going with me."

Thankfully, the wake wasn't too bad. The mourners seemed pleased to see my dad and me, and their faces had lit up when they saw the plastic box that held the well-loved cake he always made when someone died. His secretary, Alma, had met us at the door and taken the box to the dining room table where she'd opened it, filling the room with the rich smell of chocolate. She'd hurried off to the kitchen and, a moment later, returned with a pot of steaming coffee. As she began cutting the cake, several people who'd been sitting in the living room hurried into the dining room and formed a line.

When I arrived at school on Monday morning. I was relieved that there were no police cars parked in front of the main building. And no one said anything about a break-in. During home room, Mr. Crenshaw came on the squawk box to make announcements for the week. His high-pitched squeaky voice sounded normal to me as he praised the basketball team for their win on Friday night. A long sigh escaped my lips when I realized Tripp had been right. No one knew we'd entered the building and taken things that didn't belong to us. I made a silent vow to never do such a thing again.

Seventh grade at Inman Middle was a lot like sixth except we weren't green anymore. Bobbye, Tripp, and I were happy to be in the same home room that fall, but disappointed that we had no classes together. Bobbye and I eventually wound up in the same PE class, but that was it except for band. Bobbye continued to play French horn and our friend, Phil Sanford, who played sax, was in our class. I struggled on with my mom's clarinet hoping I'd be good enough to play in the marching band at Grady High School.

Tripp and Phil made Inman's soccer team again, and the moment she let go a ball to the coach, Bobbye was chosen for the girls' softball team. I wondered how the Warrens would ever be able to pay for her uniform and shoes. She'd grown a couple inches over the summer and was at least three inches taller than Tripp. He'd filled out some, had more muscle in his shoulders and chest, but was still shorter than most of the guys on the soccer team. The biggest physical change for me over the summer was boobs. They weren't big or anything like that, but they were noticeable, and a complete embarrassment. And having to talk to my dad about it was sheer torture. I stumbled around trying to find the right words and he just nodded and pulled a five out of his wallet and told me to go buy whatever I needed. I ran into two girls I knew from Inman in the underwear section, and they helped me find the right size. Afterwards, we went for an ice cream where they pumped me with questions about Tripp.

With his thick blonde hair and eyes like burnished bronze coins, Tripp was quite the looker and all the girls were crazy about him. Everyone knew who his parents were, and they knew about the big house where he lived, and the big Mercedes that delivered him to school each day. Boys didn't like him much and he was rarely invited to do guy things. But girls were another matter. Several of our classmates formed a Tripp MacAvoy Fan Club and made complete fools of themselves by running over to say hi when he walked into a room, or asking him to dance at parties, or inviting him to their houses for pizza. And a group of them always sat together at soccer matches to cheer him on.

Tripp just laughed about those girls. Occasionally, he would dance with one or two of them at parties and sometimes he would go to their houses for pizza after a soccer match, but only if Bobbye was invited. Bobbye wouldn't go unless I went, so the three of us always ended up at the same places. We continued to meet every Saturday morning at John Howell Park to ride our bikes to the library. Afterwards, we went to the drug store on Highland Avenue for grilled cheese sandwiches.

* * * * *

It was just after Christmas that same year when Tripp's parents told him they had a big surprise. They were going to turn the space over their three-car garage into a rec room where he could have his friends over for parties. You're a young man now, Miss Caroline had told him, and you need to build up your circle of friends. Mr. Ed told Tripp that he'd already hired a well-known contractor to build a set of stairs up the outside wall of the garage and install a door that would open to the 30' by 40' space above it. A new floor would be laid, windows would be added across the front, and a kitchen with an electric range, cupboards, and a refrigerator would be separated from the larger area up front by a Formica-topped counter. A small bath, complete with shower, was being installed in the back corner off the kitchen. Tripp wanted to know when the project would be finished and his mom had said, "Just in time for your 12th birthday!"

That party room was the talk of the school. No one had ever heard of anyone having their own party room and certainly not some kid our age. It was the subject of lunchtime chatter for months. Everyone was dying to go to Tripp's birthday party on the 16th of April, but Miss Caroline had told Tripp that he couldn't invite more than thirty friends and, early in April, Bobbye and I went over to Tripp's to help him decide who should be invited. It was then that we saw a list of a half-dozen couples Miss Caroline planned to invite to help her and Mr. Ed chaperone. My father and Bobbye's parents were not on it, of course.

On the day of the party, the hours dragged like molasses in January, and I thought it would never end. After I'd pushed the food around on my plate at dinner, my dad told me I was excused. I gathered my things and ran over to Bobbye's house so we could dress together and help each other with our hair. I had a new party dress that was a pale blue fabric with a dark blue stripe, and Miss Janice had made a dress for Bobbye that was deep aqua organza with a full skirt and cap sleeves. After Miss Janice took several pictures of us in our first party dresses, Mr. Russell drove us over to the MacAvoys in Green Bean.

No one but the contractor, his work crew, and Tripp's parents had seen the new room above the garage. Bobbye and I had asked Tripp if we could help decorate for the party, but he'd told us that his mom was doing that. When we finally arrived at the birthday cake house that evening, my heart was beating as fast as the rhythm of "Thriller" which was blaring when we got out of the car.

Our eyes widened as we stepped inside. Dozens of paper streamers in his favorite colors, green and gold, had been hung from beams in the ceiling. A long green banner proclaiming **Happy Birthday, Tripp** was hung above the windows on the front wall. The pool table in the back had bows made of green and gold crepe paper at each corner. A dozen round tables, covered in dark green cloths, surrounded the dance floor. Bunches of green and gold balloons were tied to the backs of chairs all over the room. It was big, bold, and beautiful.

Some girls we knew from school were sitting at the tables giggling with one another and drinking from red Coca-Cola cups while a bunch of boys were in the back corner around the pool table. Miss Caroline and Mr. Ed, and some of their friends including Phil Sanford's parents, Brock and Phyllis, were at the kitchen counter putting chips and cookies on clear plastic plates.

Tripp emerged from the group of boys at the pool table and came toward us. "Come on in you two," he urged, waving at Bobbye and me. "Come on over and try one of these macaroons I made." He grabbed a plate from under the counter and thrust it at us. Beautifully shaped mounds covered in pale pink and soft yellow coconut were clustered together atop a fancy doily. "Classie helped me grind the almonds in the blender to make these," Tripp said, beaming. "And she taught me how to beat the egg whites, too. That was pretty hard. Getting them stiff enough took a long time. Then I had to use an ice cream scoop to drop the dough onto the cookie sheets to bake 'em. Here…have one."

I'd never had a macaroon before, and even though they weren't very sweet, the flavor of blended coconut and ground almonds was different and exciting. "You did good, Tripp," I commented, as I ate the last bite of mine. Bobbye nodded, her mouth full, and Tripp said, "I thought you'd like them, so I kept them out of sight until you got here. What say we get this party going?"

We followed him to the front of the room where an old Wurlitzer juke box stood. "This was my mom's contribution to the rec room," he announced, his voice gushing with pride. "She loves to dance and always wanted a juke box. Let's play one of her favorites and I'll get her to dance with me." He pushed a number and a yellow-labeled 45 magically landed on the turntable.

Tripp went over and got his mom and they stepped onto the dance floor together as the Isley Brothers began to sing "Shout!" No one joined them because we were so amazed at how well the two of them danced together. All the girls who'd been sitting at the tables got up and formed a circle around them and Bobbye and I joined in clapping to the beat.

When the song ended, a half-dozen girls rushed Tripp and begged him to dance with them. In their shiny pastel dresses, they looked like butterflies hovering around a golden flower. Tripp smiled at each one before he said, "Maybe later." He went back to the Wurlitzer and pushed another button. When Lionel Richie began singing "My Love," he made his way over to Bobbye. "Come dance with me, pretty girl," he said, as he led her onto the floor.

Phil Sanford, who was wearing a nice tweed jacket over a deep blue sweater, appeared at my side and the two of us joined Tripp and Bobbye. So did Mr. Ed and Miss Caroline. The Wurlitzer had been filled with 45s of Miss Caroline's favorites…the Drifters, the Supremes, the Temptations.

Added to this were hits of the day by Michael Jackson, Madonna, and the Commodores. Every girl in the room ran screaming to the dance floor when they heard Prince singing, "Purple Rain." Some of the boys stood back and watched for a while, but eventually they began to stroll over in small groups to ask the girls to dance. And all of us bunched together on the dance floor to help Pink Floyd sing Tripp's favorite, "We Don't Need No Education." As soon as he heard it, Mr. Ed rolled his eyes and fled to the kitchen.

Miss Caroline told Tripp that he had to dance at least once with every girl he'd invited. He fussed, but finally got around to all of them. In between, he danced with Bobbye. While I danced with Phil a lot, I also danced with Mr. Ed and some of the other boys from my class. About half-way through the party, I saw Tripp and a couple of eighth graders, who were on the soccer team with him, with their heads together in the corner behind the pool table. They formed a tight little circle so I couldn't figure out what they were doing. At first, I thought they were smoking. But I knew they wouldn't do something so obvious with Tripp's parents there. Then I noticed that each of them was holding a red paper cup. And I saw Tripp pouring something into those cups from a bottle.

I went over to Bobbye and asked if she knew what was going on. "They're drinking," she said. "Tripp's got a bottle of bourbon."

"Oh, God," I moaned. "How could he be so stupid? My dad will never let me come here again if he finds out."

A couple of minutes later, Tripp showed up and said, "Come on, Stacey. Dance with me."

"No thanks," I snapped, moving away from him. "I don't want to dance with you."

As I turned to walk away, he grabbed my arm. "What do you mean you don't want to dance with me? Every girl in this room wants to dance with me."

I jerked my arm away and fled to the bathroom where I locked the door. I didn't want to dance with Tripp, didn't want to talk to him either, so I thought I'd better get away by myself before I said something I'd regret. I stayed in the bathroom until someone knocked on the door.

When I came out, Phil was waiting for me. "You'd better come on out here," he said. "The party's over."

I couldn't see Tripp, but I could hear him. He was standing alone in the middle of the dance floor yelling at his father who was standing about ten feet away near the juke box. Most of the kids were standing back, clustered around the tables. Some stood against the walls. Phil whispered to me that Mr. Ed had unplugged the Wurlitzer and that had made Tripp mad. We watched as Mr. Ed walked back to the pool table and returned with an empty bourbon bottle in his hand. He held it out to Tripp and asked, "Where'd you get this, son?"

Tripp grinned back at him. "Where do you think, old man? I got it from your liquor cabinet in the library." He lowered his head, made a little bow to his father, and said, "Like father, like son."

Ed held the bottle up to the light. "I can see it's empty. How many of your friends did you give this to?"

Tripp lunged, trying to grab the bottle out of his father's hand. "None of your damn business," he said, with a smirk.

In two seconds, Mr. Ed had set the bottle on top of the juke box, taken one long stride toward Tripp, and caught him by the shoulder. "Sneaky little thief," he growled, as he drew back his hand. Miss Caroline suddenly came out of nowhere and put herself between them.

"No, Ed," she said, her voice so loud everyone could hear. "Don't you dare hit him. It's not all his fault. He didn't bring that liquor in this house. You did. Now leave him alone."

Mr. Ed let go of Tripp. After what seemed a long time, he turned around to face us and as his face sagged under the weight of what my dad would have called *personal mortification*, he bowed his head and said, "I'm so sorry. Please go home now."

Bobbye and I caught a ride with Phil and his parents. None of us spoke a word as we headed down the long driveway in front of the big white house. Bobbye and I were back at her house before nine-thirty, and I was so glad I was spending the night there so I wouldn't have to face my dad until the next day. I knew he would find out what happened at the party and ask me about it, and I wanted to put that conversation off as long as possible.

On Monday morning, the school was buzzing. When I opened the door and started down the hall several groups of students were huddled near the walls whispering and giggling. In the center of each group was one of Tripp's friends who'd been at the party, who knew all the details, who was boasting about everything they'd seen and heard. As I turned the corner and headed to home room, I heard someone say *George Dickel* and I knew it wouldn't be long before my dad knew everything, too.

When I got home about 4:00, he was sitting at the kitchen table reading the afternoon paper. I went straight into my bedroom, changed clothes, and came back out. "You'd better sit down, Stacey," he said. "We need to talk. Why don't you get yourself a Little Debbie Cake and some milk? I know you're hungry."

I shook my head. "I'm not hungry, but I know I'm in trouble."

"Well, I wouldn't say that exactly," he began, eyeing me from over the rims of his glasses. "But we do need to talk. I heard about the party at work this morning. You know Phillip Sanford's dad, Brock, is my boss. Anyway, he came by my office and told me what he knew...which was a good account because he was there. I left work early and went by Inman to see Principal Morrison. He told me that Tripp, and the other three boys who were drinking, have been suspended from playing sports for the rest of the year. This won't affect Tripp directly because soccer season is over, but two of those boys were on the baseball team. Well, they're not on it anymore."

He took a moment to fold the section of the paper he'd been reading and put it on the table before he continued. "This really wasn't a school matter because the drinking occurred on private property. But Principal Morrison told me that he and the parents of those eighth-grade boys decided their sons would have to complete thirty hours of community service and attend substance abuse classes this summer. They're really upset with Ed MacAvoy...and so am I. We all know that Tripp took the bourbon from his dad's stash, but his parents must take responsibility in a situation like this."

In the end, my dad and I decided that I would decline any invitation to visit the MacAvoy house again and that I would not be meeting Bobbye and Tripp at John Howell Park on Saturday mornings anymore. "You may continue your friendship with Bobbye," my dad said. "But you are not to see Tripp MacAvoy outside of school for any reason. Principal Morrison has arranged for you to be moved to a new home room, so you won't have to see him at all. When you get to school tomorrow morning, report to the secretary and she'll tell you where to go."

My dad got up from the table and began gathering up the paper. "I'm really sorry that your first big party turned out like this, honey. Now, go to your room and do your homework. I'll call you when dinner's ready."

Tripp didn't return to Inman Middle School that spring and I heard that he was going to Atlanta Country Day. Phil Sanford told me that Mr. Ed and Miss Caroline had had a big fight because Mr. Ed wanted to send Tripp to a military academy in Tennessee—that he'd been begging Miss

Caroline to let him send Tripp away to school for a couple of years. But Miss Caroline said Tripp was too young to be so far away from home. So, they compromised. Tripp would finish middle school at Atlanta Country Day. Then, he would be sent away to his Grandad Rand's alma mater, Woodbury Forest, in Virginia.

I didn't see Tripp MacAvoy for the next four years. Neither did Bobbye. Once in a while we heard something about him from friends like Phil Sanford who saw him around town. We knew he played soccer for Atlanta Country Day because we regularly checked the sports section of *The Atlanta Journal-Constitution* (which Atlantans called *the Constitution*), where we sometimes saw his name mentioned as the highest scorer in a particular match. When this happened Bobbye would crawl into a corner and shut me out for an hour or two. Unlike Bobbye, I didn't miss Tripp at all. And his being gone meant I had her all to myself for the most part. The only other friends she had were a couple of members of the softball team, but the only time she saw them was at practice.

Every other Friday, I spent the night at Bobbye's. On alternate Fridays, she spent the night with me. Her mom, or my dad, cooked our favorite dishes on those nights, usually spaghetti or lasagna. Then we'd sit in the living room with our parents and watch TV for a couple of hours. About ten, Bobbye and I would head upstairs to her bedroom...or to my bedroom depending on where we were. On those nights, I always brushed Bobbye's long black hair, hair so thick it tangled in the brush, and we played that game where you draw something on your friend's back with the tip of your finger and they have to guess what it is. We played that game for hours during those years, mostly with me doing the drawing and Bobbye doing the guessing. And we kept the radio on until midnight while we talked about how we'd fix up our dorm room when we went off to college at The University of Georgia. I wanted to live with Bobbye Revels more than anything and it never occurred to me that we'd do anything else.

* * * * *

After Bobbye, Phil, and I finished Inman Middle, we went on to Grady High. Freshman year, I signed up for a course in creative writing, and one of the requirements was keeping a daily journal. On the first day of classes, the teacher told us how important it was to jot down the events of our day and write something about our reactions to them. She'd smiled when she said, "Who knows? One of these days, one of you may become a journalist…or a novelist." I'd smiled back, but her words were complete hooey as far as I was concerned because I had absolutely nothing I wanted to write in a journal.

But things change in the wink of an eye as my dad often said, and that day they did. After lunch, I went to band class where I found Bobbye and Phil helping our teacher, Mr. Pridgen, arrange music stands and chairs in a semi-circle. Mr. Pridgen kept smiling and smiling as he told us about our new visiting band instructor. "She's a recent graduate of the Cincinnati Conservatory," he beamed, "and she'll be playing first chair flute with the symphony this season. You kids are too young to realize it now, but you'll look back on this and, hopefully, remember what it was like to be in the presence of a musician of Lark Loflin's caliber."

As a fourteen-year-old, my first impression of Miss Loflin was one of pure glamour. With her cloud of golden hair, eyes like sparkling emeralds, and a smile made of perfectly aligned pearly white teeth, she could have been a contestant in the Miss America Pageant. That morning, my creative writing teacher had come to class dressed in gray slacks and low-heeled shoes, but Miss Loflin arrived in a skirt, form fitting top, and high heels. She was about my height...maybe 5'5." Unlike me, she had a figure. After Mr. Pridgen introduced her to the class, she stood in front of us slowly scanning the group, giving each of us a smile. When she got to me, her eyes seemed to soften, her smile seemed to widen, and I sat there thoroughly enchanted while a faint tingle ran up my spine. She began the lesson that day by playing an arpeggio on her flute, a charming series of runs that sounded like bird song. I watched as her long graceful fingers flew over the keys like bees seeking nectar and knew Mr. Pridgen was right. Lark Loflin was an exceptional musician. That night, after I'd finished doing my algebra and history assignments, I got out my new journal and filled three pages.

At the beginning of our sophomore year, Bobbye had to drop out of band because of softball. But I continued with my clarinet, and Phil with his saxophone, and both of us enjoyed being in class on the days when Miss Loflin came. Mr. Pridgen was a genius when it came to getting incredible sounds out of our drum line, but it was Lark Loflin who'd opened a whole new world of music for us and proved to be one of the best *teachers* we'd ever had.

That year, I was elected vice-president of our class and Phil was chosen moderator of the Debate Club...the perfect role for him. In late April, we were both present at the Athletic Banquet when Bobbye won the MVP Award for Women's softball—the first tenth-grader at Grady ever to attain that honor. There wasn't a single male on Grady's baseball team that year who could match her pitching record or batting average. And in May, all three of us were tapped for the National Honor Society.

Neither Bobbye nor I dated much. In a school filled with big busted, heavily made-up flirty girls, I was simply not in the running. Bobbye was certainly attractive, but she towered over the boys, and I'm sure many were intimidated by her athletic prowess. Some of our classmates called her stuck-up, but I knew that wasn't true. She was just terribly insecure when it came to social stuff and could never quite bring herself to join in. Bobbye preferred to stay in the background where she could retreat, if necessary, into her zone of safety. On weekends, we hung out with a small group of friends, which usually included Phil Sanford.

Phil, who was well over six feet, walked with a sort of loping stride that earned him the nickname Ichabod. He wasn't particularly good looking, but he had a great sense of humor laced with a dry wit that made him popular. He loved to watch people from a distance and make up stories about them. He was a good-natured, bright boy who won the district science fair two years in a row. And Phil was generous. We'd pile into his car and he would drive us anywhere we wanted to go. Often, we went to the movies and, occasionally, blew our savings on a rock concert at the Civic Center. Most Saturday evenings found us scarfing down pizza and watching MTV in the Sanfords' big den.

One night in June of 1989, the week after Bobbye's 16th birthday, she called after supper and asked me to come over. This was not unusual. Bobbye was working in the day care at her church, and I was a counselor at a camp for kids, but we talked on the phone almost every night and saw each other at least three times a week. When I got to her house that night, Mr. Russell and Miss Janice were in the living room watching TV.

"She's in her room," Miss Janice said, giving me a wave as I came in. "You can go on up." I raced up the stairs and found Bobbye lying on her bed reading a book. She sat up quickly and said, "Close the door."

"What's up?" I asked, my eyes searching the room for clues.

"This," she said, pulling an envelope from inside the book she'd been reading. She held the front of the envelope toward me, and I recognized the bold handwriting.

"Tripp," I murmured. Bobbye got up, tiptoed over, and whispered, "He's at home and wants to see us."

"Oh, no," I shook my head. "We aren't gonna see him! And you know what will happen to you if you do and your parents find out."

"Just read it, Stace," Bobbye pleaded. "Tripp's changed. I can tell by what he wrote. He's working on the loading dock at his dad's mill earning money for the first time in his life."

I took the envelope from her. There was no stamp and no address, just her name scrawled across it. "Where'd you get this?" I asked. Bobbye moved the dial on her radio until she heard Bruce Springsteen and turned up the volume. "My supervisor told me someone had left an envelope for me in the church office. I went by there this afternoon and got it on my way to the bus stop." She hesitated a moment. "Tripp wants us to meet him tomorrow night at that convenience store on De Leon Street."

I threw the letter on the bed and started toward the door. "Not me," I said. "You can meet Tripp MacAvoy tomorrow night if you want to, but I'm not having anything to do with this. My dad would ground me from now until the day I graduate. No way!"

Bobbye slid between me and the door. "Wait a minute," she said, quietly closing it. "What Tripp did when we were in middle school was a long time ago, Stace. He's paid his dues, don't you think? What's wrong with meeting him and talking about old times? I'd love to see him, love to know how he's doing. Please Stacey. You and Tripp and I were such good friends. Besides, I can't do this without you."

She turned toward me, and I watched as her brows knit as she began devising a plan. "If I tell Janice and Russell that you're picking me up to go to a movie," she ventured, "they won't suspect a thing. But if I try to leave the house alone, they'll ask a million questions. Please go with me," she begged. "I promise we won't stay but a little while. I promise, Stacey, if you'll just say yes."

I'd never understood Bobbye's attraction to Tripp MacAvoy, but I knew she'd never forgive me for causing her to miss a chance to see him. So, I gave in and told her I'd pick her up the following night at 8:30. That way she could tell her parents we were catching the nine o'clock movie. I also told her that I'd have to spend the night with her because I wasn't allowed to be out beyond 11:00 and I was afraid we wouldn't get back by then.

The next night, when we got to the store on De Leon Street, dusk had settled over the city and the evening was warm and unusually quiet for a Saturday. I spotted Phil Sanford's brand-new orange GEO Tracker parked on the far right of the almost empty lot. He was sitting alone in the front seat and had the motor running. "Come on over, you two," he called as we got out of the car. "You get in front with me, Stacey," he said. "Bobbye, you get in back."

As soon as I opened the front door, a light came on and we saw Tripp slouched in a corner of the back seat. I moved my seat up so Bobbye could crawl in behind it, and when I closed the door, Phil threw the Tracker into reverse and swung out into the street.

I turned around to look at Tripp. He was so grown up, so mature looking that I hardly recognized him. His gold hair was a shade darker than I'd remembered, but his sparkling bronze eyes were as beautiful as ever. His shoulders seemed broader, and he had the muscular neck of an athlete. I'd have bet he weighed at least twenty pounds more than Phil. And he looked more like Miss Caroline than ever. He cocked his head and said, "Well, Stacey, do I pass the test?"

I flushed and turned around. "You look great, Tripp. It's good to see you again." From the corner of my eye, I saw Tripp take Bobbye's hand. While neither of them spoke, I could tell by the smiles on their faces that the time they'd spent apart hadn't cooled their feelings.

Phil cruised down the street and pulled into a drive-through where we ordered burgers and shakes. As soon as he'd put the bag of burgers on my lap, he backed the Tracker into a dimly lit spot behind the building. For the next hour we sat in the car munching our food and listening to Tripp tell us about life at Woodbury Forest where he'd pulled in some decent grades, played sports, and made friends with a bunch of rich guys like him.

He asked what we were doing that summer and Bobbye and I told him about our respective jobs. Then Phil described his job working as a surveyor's assistant for the line crews at the power company...something his dad had arranged.

"Well, you guys have it made," Tripp said. "I have the goddam worst job you can imagine. My dad told me last spring I'd be working in one of our plants this summer. He says I have to learn the business from the bottom up so I can run it one day. I just couldn't believe it when he told me I'd be working on the loading dock starting at *rock* bottom with some of the roughest old farts you ever saw. I'd rather eat shit off a toothpick from now til Sunday than deal with those mother-fuckers. They take turns knocking me around with their elbows and do their best to fuck me up when I'm hauling a big load and there's not one of 'em who doesn't outweigh me by a hundred pounds. I told my dad how they treated me and that I didn't want to work on the dock anymore. And he said, Fine...just put the keys to the Bronco on my dresser."

Tripp swallowed the last bite of his cheeseburger, balled up the greasy paper, and threw it out the window. "But the good thing is I'm saving up to buy a dirt bike and I've almost got enough to buy the one I want. This guy out at the air base bought it but he couldn't keep up the payments, so a bank in Roswell owns it now. It's black with turquoise and silver stripes."

He looked at Bobbye. "I know turquoise is your favorite color. That's why I bought it. It has a big, padded seat that's plenty big for the two of us. But I'll have to buy a trailer so I can haul it around behind the Bronco. My Grandad Jim and Grandmother Alice, who live up in Sandy Springs, have this big-ass spread with acres and acres of woods and trails, and I can't wait to take that bike up there. Maybe you guys could come ride with me some time."

He glanced at Phil and me, and in a tone much more somber than his last said, "Did y'all know about my Grandpa Rand? That he dropped dead of a heart attack on Thanksgiving Day?"

I nodded and told him that we'd seen the obituary in the paper. "Mr. Cogdill had a very successful career," I commented. "What would Coca-Cola Corporation have been without him?"

Tripp thanked me before he sucked up the last of his milkshake and changed the subject. "The good news is I won't be going back to Woodbury Forest this fall. My mom has this rare blood disease... a kind of leukemia. We just found out a couple of weeks ago. Anyway, she wants me closer to home. So, I'm going to The Darlington School in September. It's only about an hour from here, so I'll be able to come home twice a month on weekends." He reached up and tapped Phil on the shoulder. "What say we take a spin over to John Howell Park?"

When we drove by Tripp's house on the way to the park only one light was on and I knew it was the one in his parents' bedroom. I glanced at my watch. It was almost ten-thirty. The Warrens would be expecting Bobbye and me home before long because the movie would be out at eleven. Phil drove through the park entrance and pulled into the parking lot. Tripp said, "Is the bandstand still here? Come on, Bobbye. Let's let Phil and Stacey have some privacy."

They got out and went hand in hand up the walk toward the bandstand and Phil's eyes followed. "Look at them," he said. "They're just as crazy about each other now as when we were kids. He's been after me to call her for him for over a year. But I couldn't. My dad laid down the law and told me I couldn't hang out with Tripp anymore. The only reason I agreed to take him to that convenience store is because my parents are having a dinner party tonight."

While Phil and I waited in the car, we talked about our summer jobs. He told me all about the problems he had keeping up with the guys on the line crews and how they gave him a hard time. And I told him the only thing I liked about my job was the kids, who were so sweet. I kept looking at my watch because I was worried that Bobbye and I would be late getting back to her house. Finally, at quarter of eleven, I got out of the car and started up the walk. As I approached the bandstand, I could see the outline of their bodies pressed together and realized for the first time that they were now the same height. Tripp had Bobbye pressed against a post and the two of them were really getting it on. He kept running his hands up and down her bare arms. Then he grabbed the bottom of her tank top and began pushing it up over her breasts. She continued to kiss him, but she pushed his hands away and pulled her top back down. I could hear them breathing, could hear the scuffling sound the soles of Tripp's loafers made as he pushed his hips forward trying to gain purchase on the old wood floor. Then I heard him gasp and watched as he slowly pulled away from her. After a moment, he took her face in his hands and kissed the end of her nose. "Oh, Bobbye," I heard him say, "I've missed you so much."

I waited perhaps fifteen seconds before I coughed. "We gotta go, guys," I said. "It's late." I turned away and headed back to the car. A couple minutes later, they got in and we went back to the convenience store. It would become the designated spot for our Saturday night rendezvous for the rest of the summer. On those nights, Phil would come to my house at 7:30 and the two of us would pretend, for my dad's sake, that we were going out together. After we left my house, we picked up Bobbye. Tripp was always waiting at the store at eight. Bobbye would get into the Bronco and the two of them would drive off. At 11:15, the four of us met back at the store. Usually, Phil and I caught a movie. Neither of us had any idea where Bobbye and Tripp went. But I had a good idea of what they did and, eventually, I asked her about it.

One day while she and I were sitting at the counter in the drug store guzzling strawberry milk shakes, I asked her if she and Tripp were having sex. She looked over at me and took another pull on her shake. "Answer me," I said. "Are you and Tripp doing it?"

She glanced down at the countertop and whispered, "Yes."

Then she blabbed on and on about how she'd begged Tripp to wait. And when he kept insisting, she'd begged him to keep a supply of rubbers in the glove compartment of his car. But he was afraid his dad might find them. He had one with him sometimes, she said, but not always. The situation scared her so much that she'd told Janice she was spotting between periods and having awful cramps, so Janice had taken her to a gynecologist.

She turned and looked me in the eye. "I'm taking birth control pills, Stacey. But it's really none of *your* business, is it?"

The four of us continued to meet on Friday nights, but we varied the routine. Phil picked up Tripp at the post office and I picked up Bobbye at her house and the four of us met at The Chicken Shack, an old diner off the interstate that served crispy fried chicken and waffles. They heated the maple syrup and put the butter in it to melt, so the whole combination was scrumptious.

After we'd stuffed ourselves, we piled into one car and headed south to Hillcrest Park where we sat out under the stars on a big flat rock drinking bottles of beer Tripp always brought in a cooler from home. That was the summer I started smoking weed. Tripp always kept two joints, rolled and ready, in his shirt pocket and as soon as we got to our favorite rock, he brought those babies out, one by one, and slowly ran each of them under his nose. He'd give us a wink, smiling his approval, before he lit them. And soon the rest of us were smiling, too.

We saw each other only on Friday and Saturday nights, never during the week because Tripp thought it was just too risky. "Besides," he told us, "I need to be home at night with my parents some, especially my mom. My Grandmother Patricia is there with her all day and, as soon as I get home from work, I go up to her bedroom and sit with her so my grandma can have some time to herself. I stay with my mom for about an hour and tell her all about my day. My dad never gets home till about 7:00 and sometimes my mom doesn't feel well enough to eat dinner, so my dad eats whatever Classie left him in the kitchen. They go to bed fairly early these days and after they do, I put a pizza in the microwave and watch TV in my room."

Bobbye, Phil, and I didn't have much to say when Tripp talked about his mom. We felt for him, especially since we knew how close the two of them were. But there wasn't much we could say. Rumor had it that Miss Caroline was very sick and not likely to live more than a year or so. Tripp told us about the treatments she was having and how they'd made her hair fall out. Caroline MacAvoy had been a beautiful, vibrant woman and it was hard to believe things were that bad. But by the time summer came to an end, and all of us were getting ready to start school again, she'd lost twenty-two pounds. And, for the second time in her short life, she had nurses around the clock looking after her in the big bedroom upstairs. Tripp told us his dad had moved downstairs to make space for the special equipment they'd brought in for his mom.

Before he left for The Darlington School in late August, Tripp devised a plan so that he and Bobbye could write to each other and keep their correspondence secret. He rented a box for her at the post office on Highland Avenue and gave her a hundred-count book of stamps. They vowed to write to each other at least twice a week. Tripp was sure he'd be coming home every other weekend, so the four of us knew we'd continue to meet at the convenience store when he came home. The night before he left, he gave Bobbye a little gold heart on a chain. Russell and Janice asked where it came from and she told them I'd given it to her as a token of friendship.

* * * * *

Our last two years in high school were uneventful. We continued with our usual activities and both Bobbye and Tripp continued to excel in sports. Bobbye was captain of the Grady softball team not only junior year, but senior year as well. Tripp was captain of the soccer team at The Darlington School senior year.

I stuck with my clarinet, and Phil with his sax, and both of us marched in the Grady High band all four years. When I could afford it, I attended concerts performed by The Atlanta Symphony in Chastain Park and held fast to my dream of one day playing a duet with the amazing Lark Loflin.

A guy named Ryan Pilzer, who was in marching band, went to those concerts, too, and sometimes we sat together. One day at school, he asked me out. Ryan, who played cornet, was totally wrapped up in jazz, and I became the captive audience for his monologues on why jazz was more important than the Beatles. He always waited until late on a Saturday to call. Then he'd pick me up about 7:00 and take me out to a burger place for dinner where he droned on and on about Dizzy Gillespie and Charlie Byrd. Then we'd go back to his house and, for hours, listen to his collection of old jazz records. I knew that wasn't what other kids our age did on dates, but I didn't care one way or the other. It didn't last long and that was fine with me.

Lance was captain of the track team at Grady, popular and outgoing, and when he asked me out, I almost fainted. He played it cool the first time taking me to a basketball game at Georgia Tech. But the next time we went to a movie where he bought a big bucket of popcorn and two large drinks. And while I held that bucket of popcorn on my lap with one hand and my drink with the other, he ran his hand up my skirt and into my underwear. I sat there watching the movie and pretending nothing was happening because I sort of liked it. A few weeks later, he asked me out again. After we shared a pizza, he drove to a dark area in the park and tried to take my clothes off while he stuck his tongue down my throat. I bit a hunk out of his lip. It bled all over his new shirt, and he cussed up a storm and took me home.

I knew I wasn't like other girls who talked about boys incessantly and did stupid stuff like call them up and hang up when they answered. I watched those girls as they flirted and batted their eyelashes at different guys while they made dumb remarks like *don't mind little old me*. At sixteen, my interest in boys was limited to the "good buddy" category where Phil Sanford was top man. I liked hanging out with Phil, but I really wanted to be with Bobbye…just the two of us. And as long as Tripp was not around, she seemed to be happy with just me.

Senior year, I was elected president of the Journalism Club and got hooked on psychology when I took it as an elective that spring. In late April, we learned that Bobbye had won a full academic and athletic scholarship to The University of Georgia to play for the Lady Dawg's. On May 1st, our principal announced that I'd won the Edward R. Murrow Scholarship to study journalism. While I could use it to attend any college or university I wished, I knew I'd go to Athens with Bobbye.

After eighteen months of treatment, Caroline MacAvoy rallied and gained back a few pounds. When her hair came back, it was stark white. I saw her at a ball game and thought she looked very glamorous, like one of those film stars from the '50s, but skinny. In May of 1990, she felt well enough to go to The Darlington School to see her son graduate.

The summer following graduation, Bobbye and Tripp were thicker than ever, but still dependent on Phil and me as decoys. You might wonder why the two of us allowed ourselves to be used this way. And my only excuse would be it just made things easier because neither Phil nor I wanted conflict. If the four of us went to a movie, we went to the movie Tripp wanted to see. If we listened to music, Tripp was the one who chose the music. Bobbye, Phil, and I were more than family to Tripp—we were his refuge, the place where he was most comfortable when other things were stressful for him. But we never called him, never told him we wanted to get together. He not only called us, but also told us where we were going and what we were going to do when we got there. We fell into a habit, a habit called Tripp.

Bobbye and Tripp finally decided to come out about their relationship after Janice and Russell told Bobbye they wanted to host a graduation party for her in June. When they asked her if there was anything she wanted, she begged them to let her invite Tripp to the party. It wasn't a big affair, just hot dogs and hamburgers on the grill. About twelve of Bobbye's friends were there, most of them members of the softball team. I went over early that afternoon to help Miss Janice get things ready. Tripp showed up late with Phil at his side as if they were just casually dropping by. But they stayed later than anyone else and the four of us sat out on the front porch talking until midnight.

The next morning at breakfast, I told my dad about seeing Tripp at Bobbye's party, told him how Tripp was working at his dad's textile mill. I went on to say how much Tripp had changed and how nice he'd been. My dad looked up from his newspaper. "You're grown, Stacey, and I can't choose your friends for you. But I hope you'll always remember you're known by the company you keep," he said. "Bobbye Revels is your best friend and Tripp MacAvoy is her best friend. And, as long as you and Bobbye are friends, you'll be spending time with Tripp. Maybe he has changed. I hope so. But I wouldn't bet on it."

Phil and I continued to hang out with Tripp and Bobbye, but things were different once we finished high school. That summer, I saw Bobbye at least one night a week, but she spent almost all her free time with Tripp. The only time the four of us were together was when we went to Turner Field to see the Braves. Tripp's dad, Ed, had four season tickets and, when he was out of town on business, he always gave them to Tripp. Those games were lots of fun, but the real thrill for me was watching Bobbye. She sat on the edge of her seat throughout the game, punching her right fist into a make-believe glove on her left hand. The bleachers were one location where Bobbye lost all her inhibitions. She'd point at the first baseman and yell things like, *You're the one, bay-bee...you're the one!* while she slapped her right fist into the palm of her left hand. And every time a Brave stepped up to the plate with a bat, she'd yell, *All the way to Mars, bay-bee...all the way to Mars!* In between, she jumped up at the slightest provocation to scream at the umpires about how blind they were. Tripp egged her on, of course, and kissed her on the cheek every chance he got. Even though she couldn't afford tickets to their games, she was the most devoted Braves' fan I knew.

On August 26th, Tripp, Bobbye, and I helped Phil celebrate his eighteenth birthday at The Chicken Shack. After supper, we piled into Tripp's Bronco and drove out to Hillcrest Park where we sat on our favorite rock and drank beer. That's where I got a big surprise when I learned that Phil and Tripp had been making plans to room together in Mel Hall at the University of Georgia. I'd always thought they'd go off to private colleges out of state because they could easily afford to. Over the summer, Phil had mentioned Davidson and the University of Virginia. He was an excellent student and had been accepted at all six colleges to which he'd applied. Back in June, Tripp had told us he was thinking of going to Virginia Military Institute, but Bobbye told me later that he hadn't been accepted. Evidently UGA had accepted him, and I guess they had to, given the fact that his dad was a graduate of the law school to which he made generous donations every year.

When Phil started talking about how neat he thought it was that all of us would be moving in right across the quad from each other, I managed a thin smile. My expression may have conveyed jealousy, but what I really felt was a sense of abandonment. I'd been looking forward to rooming with Bobbye at UGA for years, looking forward to fixing up our room together, to late night girl talk, to sharing secrets, to making special plans like best friends make. Now I had to face the fact that Bobbye wouldn't be around much because she'd be with Tripp. That thought put a sour taste in my mouth that stayed with me all the way to Athens.

Part Two

If the pan is too full,
the batter may overflow.

Cakes, Cobblers & Confections
Maurice Lamont, Editor

Bobbye and I worked hard to make our dorm room as pretty and comfortable as possible. Lipscomb, like the other three dorms on the quad, had been built in the '60s and retained much of that era. The floors were beige linoleum, the windows were the kind that rolled out, and the walls were concrete block. We had to get written permission and pay an extra fifty-dollar deposit to paint the walls aqua, and that job took more money than we'd budgeted because those old block walls sucked up so much paint. We were happy with the outcome and glad we'd taken the time to brighten up our new home.

It was hotter than Hades the August morning in 1991 when we moved in. My dad took me, of course. I'd begged for a car, but he didn't think it was a good idea. "If you do well your freshman year," he'd said, "I'll help you buy a car next summer. Then you can drive it to Athens by yourself next fall if you can earn enough to afford to keep it there."

Bobbye didn't have a car, either. But Phil had his bright orange Geo Tracker parked in the student lot and Tripp's Grand Wagoneer, which his parents had given him when he turned sixteen, was beside it. I felt better knowing we could borrow one of those cars if we had to.

Bobbye's scholarship covered almost everything—tuition, room and board, books. But it didn't cover spending money, and Janice and Russell had told her that if their electric bill was not too high, they'd send her a check for forty dollars every other week. That was the best they could do. So, Bobbye got a job working Saturdays in the ticket booth at the stadium. My scholarship covered tuition, but not room and board, which my dad paid. He gave me a small allowance each month, but it wasn't enough. So, I got a job working in the library three afternoons a week. Both Tripp and Phil got generous allowances and neither had to work.

Like most first-year students, we had the usual adjustments to life on campus. I tried desperately to avoid eight o'clock classes but ended up with one MWF. Bobbye slept in those days as she had nothing until ten. But her biology lab was at eight on Tuesdays and Thursdays and I didn't envy her that. The thought of working on dead frogs at eight in the morning turned my stomach. Three meals a day were included in our dorm fees, but neither of us ever went to breakfast. At noon, we met Tripp and Phil at the dining hall where the four of us made pigs of ourselves. By Thanksgiving, I'd gained five pounds.

I know it sounds corny, but I really liked my classes, especially a course called "Researching and Reporting," required for my journalism major. The man who taught it was about sixty, had bushy gray hair and a pencil thin mustache. He wore baggy pants every day with one, or the other, of his two tweed sport coats. Thomas Henninger had worked for TIME for decades before retiring to teach. He taught me that the most important thing I would ever write would be my headline, and he gave me the skills to write a good one.

I liked Dr. Rankin, my psychology professor, from the moment I walked into his class and watched as he conducted an experiment on a fellow student. Because he was right out of graduate school, he was just a few years older than we were and would often start class by asking if we'd been to a certain football game or if we'd seen a certain basketball game on TV. He was a big sports fan and used sports events to teach the fundamentals of psychology, explaining how the alpha dog managed to hold onto the lead position and why the pack remained subservient to him or her. While he was in graduate school, he'd directed case studies and I never tired of hearing about those that dealt with various types of neuroses like schizophrenia, paranoia—and the most intriguing of all, narcissism. I left his class each day more curious than ever about the vagaries of human behavior and took to hanging around the campus bookstore after class observing students, professors, and staff in their interactions with one another.

Bobbye liked most of her professors and her courses, as well, but her load was greater than mine because so much was expected of her. In addition to regular classes each day, she had practice every afternoon from three to five. Even if it rained, her softball coach held practice in one of the gyms. Most nights, I turned out my bedside lamp by eleven, but she was up into the wee hours at least three nights a week.

That fall, Bobbye, Tripp, Phil and I made a pact vowing that, unless Bobbye had a game, we'd meet every Friday evening at seven and go downtown for pizza. From there we went to one of the local hangouts where we danced until about one because Bobbye had to be in the ticket booth at Sanford Stadium at nine every Saturday morning. (It wasn't until years later that I learned that the stadium was named for Phil's grandmother and grandfather. He never told us anything about that.) Phil and Tripp went to all the home football games that fall, and sometimes went to the away games, too. I rarely went with them because I had the dorm room all to myself on Saturdays when Bobbye worked at the stadium. And after I'd taken our laundry down to the basement and started the washer, I worked on papers and caught up on readings for my courses. No one was ever around much on Saturdays and I relished that time alone.

One of Bobbye's few luxuries was the perfume she wore...a floral and citrus mix that took a big bite of her little budget. If we sat on the sofa together watching TV, I'd sit as close as possible to her, breathing in the scent of that perfume. And like a child who adores her mother, I was always on the look-out for any excuse to touch her hair. One reason I volunteered to do our laundry was so I could be with Bobbye even when she wasn't there. Even after they'd come out of the dryer, Bobbye's clothes smelled of her perfume and nothing was more delicious than burying my face in her clean bras and panties before I put them away in her underwear drawer.

* * * * *

By mid-October, we had a steady group of friends who joined us in the dining hall and partied with us every chance they got. Several were from Atlanta and some had even been in school with us at Inman Middle and Grady High. Meredith Reynolds was one of the best, a classmate who'd gone out of her way to be nice to Bobbye. She had the kind of warm personality and good looks that had propelled her to the coveted position of Homecoming Queen our senior year. Meredith, and her ever-present best bud, Hampton "Hamp" Walker, lived down the hall from Bobbye and me. Although our room assignments had been integrated by floors with men on one, and women on another, Hamp had traded rooms with a girl he knew who wanted to be in the same room with her boyfriend who happened to be Hamp's roommate. This kind of thing happened a lot and I suppose personnel in student housing simply turned a blind eye.

Hamp was a nice looking, quiet guy who'd been a member of our championship track team at Grady. He and Meredith joined our foursome on Saturday nights regardless of what we had planned. Laura Beam and her steady guy, Jay Dubose, from Columbia, South Carolina also came along.

Laura, who'd never met a stranger, had thick wheat-colored hair and pretty hazel eyes while Jay's coloring was just the opposite…dark hair and black eyes. Laura had switched rooms with Jay's roommate early in September and she and Jay lived in Mel Dorm across the hall from Tripp and Phil. And then there was Keisha Kivett from Savannah. At 5" 1", size 2, with nutmeg-colored skin, big brown eyes, and a bubbling personality, Keisha was our pixie. Her boyfriend, Jason McNair, was an easy-going blue-eyed blonde from Macon.

Within that group only Jay Dubose was on scholarship (tennis) like Bobbye and me. The rest of the gang came from well-heeled families. I knew Meredith's parents well—as did Tripp, Phil, and Bobbye—because her dad, Hank, was the manager of MacAvoy Enterprises in Sandy Springs. Hamp Walker's parents were in the middle of a bitter divorce. His dad, a neurologist, had left Hamp's mom and his three younger siblings, rented a condo on the other side of town, and filed for divorce stating incompatibility as grounds. Everyone had known for years that Dr. Walker was having an affair with his head nurse. It was the talk of the town. But that didn't make it any easier for Hamp. I felt sorry for him because once he left home, his parents simply forgot he existed while they fought over alimony and child custody.

Right after Hamp went away to college, the Walkers put their house on the market. He never went home, had no car, and rarely had money. Hamp was a nice guy but a really sad one, which was understandable. Often, he came down the hall to our room at night where he'd lie across the end of my bed and tell me that he felt completely adrift because he didn't have a home anymore and nowhere to go. I tried to cheer him up, but I knew deep down inside that when the holidays came, he would probably sink into an even more depressed state.

* * * * *

Georgia had a dismal football season our freshman year. Even homecoming was a bit of a disappointment, especially for someone like me who felt cheated when we lost because I couldn't afford to go to many games. When the Bulldogs started losing early in the season, Tripp lost interest and decided we needed to find a new way to celebrate because *the Dawgs ain't gonna give us a reason*. To that end, he came up with an idea for a party.

Over lunch on a dreary October day, he told Bobbye, Phil, and me about "Trailer Park." Everyone had to dress in the kind of clothes we thought people who lived in trailer parks wore and come to the party with a food or beverage we thought trailer park people liked. Tripp was sure that people who lived in trailer parks ate gooey sandwiches made with things like marshmallow cream and peanut butter. He went on to warn us that we would be hearing lots of "trailer park music" (whatever that was) and lots of trailer park jokes. The person who came up with the best costume would win a nice prize and the person who told the most trailer park jokes would receive a six pack of Michelob.

Phil nodded while Tripp explained how things would work. I must say that I was not impressed, but not surprised either given it was Tripp's idea. Bobbye said nothing. She simply looked down at her plate while Tripp laid out his plans. Finally, Tripp looked over at her and said, "Well, babe, what do you think? Won't that be fun?"

Bobbye shook her head. "No," she replied. "Making fun of people who live in trailer parks is not my idea of a party. You can come up with something better than that."

Tripp balled his fist and slammed it on the table. "I don't know why I waste my time with you, Miss Tight Ass. You're no fun at all! Fuck it. Just fuck it and all the trailer parks in Georgia!" He jumped up, threw his chair against the wall, and continued cursing under his breath as he walked away.

That whole scene, and the way it unfolded, completely baffled me because I knew Bobbye Revels ate, slept, and drank Tripp MacAvoy. He was the air she breathed, the music she heard, the light in her eyes, the very essence of her being. If Tripp didn't like the shoes Bobbye was wearing, he'd tell her to take them off and she would. And then he'd take her to a fancy store in town and buy her a new pair. Where Bobbye was concerned, Tripp cast a long shadow. But he'd somehow struck a nerve with trailer park and I wondered why.

That night when I got back from the library, I found Bobbye sitting on her bed studying. I took a quick shower, put on my pajamas, and grabbed my psychology book. She looked up as I sat down across from her. "Stacey," she said, "I have something to tell you, but I don't want you to tell anyone else...especially Tripp."

I nodded and crossed my heart. She closed the book she was holding, put it down on the bed, brushed a strand of hair back from her forehead, and said, "I spent the first seven years of my life in a trailer park. I'm sure it was the best my mom and dad could do. My dad worked construction and my mom cleaned the houses he built. But my dad lost his job. I've never known why. But he left. I don't remember much about it, but I'm sure I'll never make fun of anyone who lives in a trailer park."

In all the years I'd known Bobbye, she'd never said a word to me about her *real* parents and I'd never asked. But I decided that since she'd brought it up, it was okay to ask about them.

"I don't remember much," she said. "My mom had reddish hair and I remember her singing with the radio. My dad was tall and had black hair... and when I was little, he'd put me up on his shoulders and walk me around the yard. Sorry, Stace, I just don't remember much about them. But I do remember what it felt like living in a trailer park."

She got up from the bed, went to the sink and filled a glass with water, and turned back to me. "You're the best friend I've ever had, and you know better than anyone how much I love Tripp MacAvoy. But sometimes he can be so… so insensitive. I guess he can't help it because he's always been the apple of his mama's eye. And Miss Caroline and Mr. Ed have given him everything he's ever wanted. I can't go along with some stupid party that makes fun of people. Tripp has no idea that I lived in a trailer. He thinks my real parents are dead because that's what I told him. It's taken me years to accept the fact that my mother simply walked away one day…she *abandoned* me. I guess that sounds harsh, but there's no other word for it. Please don't say anything. Okay?"

She put her hands over her face and began to cry. "Oh, I hate this," she hissed through long fingers. "All this lying. I'm as bad as Tripp!" I handed her a tissue, and she blew her nose. "Thanks, Stacey, for not saying anything."

"No problem," I answered, and quickly changed the subject. "Saturday is Meredith's birthday. Wouldn't it be fun to have a party that night to help her celebrate?" Bobbye liked the idea and told me that when she left the stadium box office after the game on Saturday, she'd go to the grocery store and buy a cake and some chips and stuff. "When I see Tripp tomorrow, I'll apologize," she said, resignation obvious in her voice. "And I'll ask him to pick up the beverages."

You may wonder how we always managed to have beer and liquor when, as eighteen-year-olds, we were not allowed by law to drink or possess alcohol. Tripp had a friend in Atlanta who ran a fake I.D. business. This guy had a laminating machine and all the equipment needed to produce any kind of license or document…even a passport. And Tripp had taken Phil to see him. They'd gotten a second driver's license and social security card made for Phil because he looked old enough to pass for a guy in his early twenties. So, it was Phil who made a run to the liquor store every Thursday afternoon dressed in a sport coat and tie as if he were just getting off work. He would pick up several bottles of bourbon and vodka and he and Tripp would transfer the contents to empty dark brown root beer bottles, replace the caps, and put them in the dorm fridge in their room. They even kept the cardboard cartons the soft drinks had come in so the bottles they'd filled with liquor would look like they'd just come off the grocery store shelf.

As soon as he'd moved on campus, Tripp had found a source for weed and his source lived on the second floor of Mel Dorm. Tripp told Bobbye and me that the two of us were in charge of making a batch of funky brownies for all the football games and parties. Every week, he gave us a small bag of grass and one of us would put it in our underwear and take it to the apartment of a friend who worked in the ticket booth with Bobbye. We kept a supply of box brownie mixes in that same apartment, and we added the grass to the mix before we baked them. Then we'd cut them, wrap each in wax paper, and arrange them in a single layer in the bottom of a shoe box. Bobbye would put a pair of tissue-wrapped shoes on top and return the box to a shelf in her closet so our brownies could "season." We also made vodka laced jello shooters. Those were much harder to conceal so we added fruit cocktail to the cherry gelatin in our glass dish so it would look like a congealed salad sitting innocently in the fridge.

On nights when we went downtown to dance, Tripp rolled small tokes for Bobbye and me which we stuffed inside our bras. Bobbye and I also loaded our pocketbooks with our special brownies. Using his fake ID, Phil would order a couple of drinks and all of us would take turns drinking from them in a corner away from the bar. Tripp always had a good supply of liquor and grass and he used both frequently.

* * * * *

His scheme to keep all this under cover worked well for a while. But the week before Thanksgiving, all hell broke loose. Two guys from Campus Security showed up and raided Mel Dorm. At the same time, other security personnel were raiding Lipscomb, along with the other two dorms in our quad. Fortunately for Tripp and Phil, our group had drunk all the liquor from the root beer bottles the weekend before and Tripp had put the empties in the recycle bin in the john closet. He did, however, have a sandwich bag filled with grass hidden in an inch-deep square hole he'd cut out of the interior of an old Encyclopedia of Mechanical Arts that he kept on the bookshelf above his bed. Security never removed any of the books from that bookshelf, but when they sniffed the empty root beer bottles, they smelled the bourbon. Tripp lied like a rug and said he knew nothing.

Two days later, he and Phil were summoned to the office of the Director of Student Housing who gave them a serious warning and threatened them with expulsion. "If you break the law again," he'd told them, "you'll be taken downtown to the precinct and booked by the Athens police. And they'll be the ones who call your parents. You're underage and this kind of behavior will not be tolerated anywhere on university property."

Late that afternoon, Bobbye and I, and our buddies, gathered in Laura and Jay's room, which was across the hall from Tripp and Phil's, to wait for their return. We kept the door open a crack so we'd know when the two of them got back...which was totally unnecessary because Tripp started yelling as soon as he opened the door to his room. "Those dumb-fuck bastards," he screamed, while the four of us trooped in behind him and Phil like Dopey, Sleepy, Grumpy, and Sneezy. He slammed the door with a bang and stomped over to his chest of drawers. "Just who do they think they are coming in here putting their big fucking noses in our stuff? This is OUR fucking room! And we can keep whatever we want in OUR fucking room."

Phil said nothing. He slunk in and slithered to the floor beside the bed where I'd sat down. Putting his head in his hands, he moaned, "Oh, God...what if they call our parents? My dad will kill me! And he'll make me go home and go to school in Atlanta. Jesus! What if they find out about that fake driver's license?"

"Shut up, Phil!" Tripp barked, his eyes shining with a kind of fury that frightened me. "Just shut up before you say something you'll regret." With one clean swipe, he knocked everything from off the top of his chest—bottles of after-shave, a glass of water, two silver hairbrushes and a leather shaving kit crashed to the floor. Out of the corner of my eye I watched as Hamp slipped out of the room. Meredith followed him and quietly closed the door.

Tripp pulled the chair out from under his desk and sat down. "Fuck 'em," he said, "they're not gonna get away with this!" From the desk drawer, he removed a legal pad and a pen. "I'm going to write a goddam letter to that fucking shit-ball in student housing," he fumed. "At least that way I'll be on record with that ass-kissing dick-head about how our privacy was invaded. Then I'm gonna call my dad and tell him that I'm not living in this shit-hole dorm anymore. It's just as cheap to live in an apartment and that's what we're gonna fucking do, Phil. Get us an apartment." He grinned at Phil, who remained unresponsive on the floor.

There was no need to mention that all of us had been warned about the consequences of liquor, or any illegal substance, found in one's dorm room. We had been warned during Freshman Orientation both verbally and in writing. There were several pages about it in our student handbook. All of us, including Tripp, had known from the start that we were breaking the law. But temptation had gotten the best of us. After all, any group of friends who'd spike the punch and go skinny dipping on prom night in high school was bound to be more adventurous once we were away from home.

Tripp chickened out on writing a letter to the Director of Student Housing, but he did talk with his father about getting an apartment. Ed told him that until his grades improved, he would stay in Mel Hall. At mid-term Tripp got an A in Spanish, a C in math, and two Ds. When Tripp asked his dad again about getting an apartment, Ed told his son that he would not even consider letting him have his own place until he had a solid B average. This made Tripp even madder, but it also gave him a strong incentive.

I was so surprised that he'd made an A in Spanish that I asked him about it. "Oh, Spanish is easy for me," he'd answered. "I started taking it in 7th grade at Inman... remember? My mom helped me with it. She majored in Spanish in college and her roommate was from Brazil. My mom and dad went to Rio on their honeymoon to visit her roommate's family. Didn't I tell you about that?"

Two nights later, the Saturday before we were leaving for Thanksgiving break, the whole gang went down to The Parthenon to dance. Bobbye and I had convinced Tripp that we needed to lay off the alcohol for a while (Phil was still scared shitless and needed no convincing), so the four of us passed a toke around in the car on the way downtown and I'd brought along several of our special brownies. Our new rule about alcohol didn't last, though. We always had plenty of it and plenty of weed, too. And we were very popular.

* * * * *

I dreaded going home for the Christmas holidays that year because it meant I'd have all this time on my hands with nothing to do. Bobbye had told me that she and Tripp were spending their first day together at his Grandad Jim's spread in Sandy Springs riding Tripp's dirt bike. I'd forgotten all about that bike and she'd had to remind me that Tripp had gotten it from the bank when it had been repossessed for lack of payment. She'd invited me to go to Sandy Springs with them, but I just couldn't see myself hanging on to Tripp's ass while he did his best to throw me off. Besides I knew my dad expected me to spend some time with him buying presents for our relatives and putting up a tree.

The only break in my holiday routine happened when Phil came by and picked me up and we went with Bobbye and Tripp to eat at what we now called The Shack. We knew we couldn't hang out in bars in Atlanta smoking dope and drinking the way we did in Athens because too many people knew us. So, when Tripp suggested that all of us, the whole gang, go down to his beach house on Tybee Island for New Year's, I perked up considerably. The biggest problem was how to tell my dad. I knew he'd never let me go to a house party at the beach with a bunch of friends, and I doubted that Janice and Russell Warren would let Bobbye go either. So, Bobbye and I put our heads together and came up with a plan. We told our parents that we'd been invited to spend the weekend with our friend Keisha Kivett down in Savannah.

On the morning of December 29, Bobbye's dad drove us to the bus station in Green Bean and we boarded a Greyhound. Neither her parents, nor my dad, knew that Keisha would not be picking us up in Savannah, that she wasn't even there. Only Tripp and Phil knew, and it was Phil who met us at the station that afternoon. I don't know what they'd told their parents, but Meredith and Hamp had no trouble getting away and arrived together that afternoon. Laura and Jay were coming in separate cars.

The MacAvoys' beach house was like something out of Architectural Digest. Sweeping wall-sized windows looked out on the ocean, top of the line stainless-steel appliances filled the kitchen, and four big bedrooms opened onto a living room-dining room area that comprised the center of the house.

As soon as I made my way through the main room, I peeped into each of the bedrooms praying that one would have twin beds. I knew I would end up staying in a room with Phil and I knew I wasn't about to sleep in the same bed with him. I found a set of twins in the back bedroom near the kitchen and put my suitcase on the bed nearest the bathroom. I liked Phil Sanford a lot, considered him one of my closest friends, but that's as far as it went. I'd never known a guy I wanted to sleep in the same bed with, much less have sex with. And Phil knew it. But he and I had made a pact about staying in the same room whenever we needed to. Our friends thought we were lovers and we let them think that because it made everything easier.

As I came out of the bedroom, Tripp came in the back door carrying bags of groceries and I hurried over to help him unload them—steaks, potatoes, sandwich makings, eggs—it was enough to keep a family of four for a week. As I helped Tripp put the stuff in the fridge and cupboards, I wondered where the beer and liquor were. A few minutes later, Phil came in with a case of Budweiser. "We'll have to make another beer run tomorrow," he'd commented.

Meredith and Hamp showed up then and Tripp met them at the door and took them to the bedroom on the front of the house that was opposite the one where he and Bobbye would be sleeping. It had a four-poster bed with one of those scalloped canopy things over it. I heard Meredith laughing. "I'm going to sleep really well," she said, "just like a queen." And Tripp said, "That's why I put you in here, honey. As far as your friends are concerned, you *still* are Grady's homecoming queen. Once a queen, always a queen."

Phil grabbed several bottles of beer from the fridge, passed them around, and we gathered in the living room where everyone settled into a spot and began talking about what they'd done over Christmas. A bit later, Laura and Jay arrived and put their gear in the back bedroom opposite Phil's and mine. As soon as everyone had finished a beer, Tripp suggested we go into Savannah. "Let's eat at one of those fish houses on the river," he said. "Get some crab and fried shrimp. Then we'll go to The Pirate's Den to see the Fantastic Knobs."

Bobbye, Meredith, and Hamp got into Tripp's Wagoneer and Laura and Jay and I followed with Phil in his Tracker. Just before we crossed the bridge onto the mainland, Tripp pulled off to the right and headed into the parking lot of a strip mall. We followed him back to a corner where he rolled down the window and pointed to the marquee above a theatre. "Look!" he shouted. "They're showing "JFK". What say we go see it?"

Even though the movie had gotten lots of publicity, I couldn't imagine anyone in our group being interested. But we had nothing better to do and a long afternoon ahead of us. I looked at Phil who shrugged his shoulders and said, "Why not? I heard it was good." Laura piped up, reminding us about the JFK keepsakes that Tripp's Granddad Cogdill had left him. All of us had seen the photo and ashtray with the presidential seal in the MacAvoy living room. "Makes sense then, doesn't it?" I said, nodding at Phil.

We spent the next three hours sipping Cokes and munching popcorn while Kevin Costner strutted in front of a jury in a New Orleans' courtroom in his role as Jim Garrison, the famous prosecuting attorney who had this theory about how the CIA was involved in the assassination of the president. Costner did a good job, but Tommy Lee Jones really creeped me out as that underground sleaze, Clay Shaw. And I was totally mesmerized by Joe Pesci who played David Ferrie, a real-life fairy, nut, weasel, weirdo.

After the movie ended, we stood in the parking lot talking about it for a while and everyone agreed that it was good, and that it was possible that the CIA had been involved. Phil told us that his dad had always said that there'd been a conspiracy and that he was sure Oswald didn't act alone. Then Tripp said that his Grandad Rand had told him that Jack Ruby kept a band of crooks who worked for him and that they'd killed a number of people during the decade before the President was shot…that Ruby had Mafia connections and knew too much…and that he'd always lived on money from the bribes people paid him to keep quiet. It was obvious that Tripp knew some stuff and thought the movie was based on fact.

"I've got an idea," he said. And Phil let out a groan.

"No, no," Tripp countered, "this is a good one. Let's have a real New Year's Eve party tomorrow night. Let's pretend it's 1963 and we're in Dallas…or maybe New Orleans. We'll pretend we're the people in the movie and we'll go find a thrift store in town and buy some old clothes like they wore back then and dress up."

He looked over at Bobbye. "You can be Jackie," he said. "And Meredith can be Marilyn. We'll find you two some evening gowns. And Phil can be Jack Ruby and I'll be Jim Garrison. Stacey can be that reporter from *The Washington Post*—the one with the inside scoop on the love affair between JFK and Marilyn. And Jay and Laura and Hamp can be witnesses for the prosecution."

Laura rolled her eyes, Jay squirmed, and Hamp looked down at his feet. None of them wanted anything to do with Tripp's idea. But Tripp kept pushing. "What else have we got to do tomorrow? Come on, ya'll," he urged. "It'll be fun."

So, we went into Savannah to the Salvation Army thrift store where Tripp bought a pink taffeta evening gown for Bobbye and a skin-tight gold lame for Meredith. Plus, a gray striped suit, white shirt and tie for Phil, and a similar outfit for himself that included a brown Fedora like the one Keven Costner had worn in the movie. Laura, Jay, and Hamp joined in finally, saying they'd be a couple of prostitutes and their john. They spent nearly an hour choosing some sleazy looking duds for their respective roles. I settled on a two-piece dress, white with black dots, plus a black straw hat, white gloves, and some tacky white heels. Pretty mundane, but right for my role as a reporter.

We went from the thrift store to the party store where Tripp bought a blonde wig for Meredith, a feather boa for Bobbye, and shiny party hats and noisemakers for all of us. We threw our bags in the back of his car and headed to the riverfront for a seafood dinner and a late-night bash at The Pirate's Den.

* * * * *

The next morning, the house was as silent as a tomb. About noon, I awoke to bright sunlight and a splitting headache. I dragged out of bed, went to the bathroom to pee, and pulled on a pair of jeans and a sweatshirt before I crept into the kitchen to fill the coffee pot. Over the next hour or so, the others joined me around the counter where each of us sucked down several cups and moaned about how lousy we felt. Tripp was the only one who didn't complain. He sat across from Bobbye smiling and talking to her in low tones about how pretty she looked with her messy bed hair. Then he took her hand, and even though it was a gray blustery day, they went off for a walk on the beach. The rest of us moped around until mid-afternoon when we finally felt well enough to tackle a bowl of cereal. After we'd finished eating, Meredith and Hamp went into their room and closed the door. Phil rummaged around in drawers until he found a deck of cards and he and I, and Laura and Jay, played rummy.

About five-thirty, I heard the unmistakable pop of a beer can. Tripp and Bobbye were in the kitchen mixing a marinade for the steaks and scrubbing the potatoes. Meredith and Hamp stood nearby having a beer. Phil put the cards away and, when we went into the kitchen, Tripp said, "Let's make some of that purple stuff they drank back in the '60s. What'd they call it?"

Phil smiled. "My dad calls it Purple Jesus. PJ for short. Do we have the stuff to make it?"

Tripp pointed to the dining room. "Probably everything we need is in that cabinet under the hutch," he said. "And there's a big metal pot downstairs in the garage that my dad uses to steam oysters. It should be big enough to hold it. Just mix it up in that."

Phil found an unopened fifth of vodka and one of rum in the cabinet. There was also half a fifth of bourbon and a bottle of Grenadine. He brought the metal pot up from the garage, washed and dried it, and poured all the liquor in. Then he added a half-gallon of grape juice and a quart of orange juice. The pot was about a third full.

"That's not enough," Tripp said. "Go down to the liquor store and get more rum and vodka and stop by the Food Rite and pick up some more juice." He handed Phil a couple of twenties. "And get some of those little smoked sausages and cans of refrigerated biscuits so we can have some '60s snacks with our '60s punch."

Phil left, and Tripp went into the living room where he opened the cabinet that held the stereo system. "Gotta set the atmosphere for tonight," he said, his eyes dancing as he grinned at us. "I'll put my mom's cassette tapes in and we can practice doing the Twist and the Watusi. Or whatever the hell it was they did."

On his way back into the kitchen, he hit the start button and soon The Beach Boys were singing "Help Me, Rhonda." He reached up and grabbed a pitcher from a shelf overhead, dipped it into the punch, and poured each of us a cup. "Drink up, my friends," he said. "It's New Year's Eve, 1991. We're gonna have the best New Year's Eve party ever!"

We spent the next couple of hours dancing, drinking PJ, and passing around joints. Tripp thought it would be more fun if we put our JFK costumes on before dinner so that we could get into character. I helped Bobbye with her elegant floor-length sheath, and she helped herself to a pair of elaborate rhinestone earrings she'd found in a drawer in the bedroom where she and Tripp were sleeping. She took a lot of time with her make-up, spreading a thick swath of violet shadow over each eye, putting on several coats of mascara, and covering her mouth with bright pink lipstick. I felt like the proverbial church lady in my old-fashioned polka-dot dress with the black straw hat perched on my head.

Even though they were wearing outdated, shabby clothing, Phil and Tripp looked nice in their old-fashioned suits. Laura and Hamp, our courtroom prostitutes, outdid themselves with a garish array of red and purple outfits and tacky jewelry that screamed New Orleans. Laura was dressed in a black sequin skirt that barely covered her rear and her face was obscured by the peek-a-boo veil of an outrageous black hat, its crown rimmed with floppy pink flowers. Hamp wore a short red wig, a tiara, purple tights, and a pair of lavender fuck-me pumps. When Jay came strutting into the dining room, it was obvious he was their pimp. In his navy blue and silver striped suit, silver tie, and high-heeled patent leather boots, he certainly looked the part. He carried a flashy black walking cane in his right hand, and when he approached Laura and Hamp and snapped his fingers, they fell to their knees with their heads almost touching the floor. "Get up, you worthless dogs," he drawled, playfully tapping each of them on their rears with the tip of his cane, "and get on down to that bus station and make me some money. And don't come back 'til you do!"

We laughed and laughed at them while Tripp poured each of us another cup of PJ. He raised his cup and we joined him in a toast to our collective ingenuity. We were still laughing and toasting each other when Meredith came out of the bedroom. I heard a low audible gasp from someone in the group but wasn't sure who it was. Jay let out a wolf-whistle and Phil moved closer to Hamp and nudged him in the ribs. Every eye in the room was on Meredith as she walked through the living room toward us, hips swaying seductively, her pouty mouth slightly open, a knowing look in her deep green eyes. About three feet away from the dining room table, she stopped and began preening and gushing just like Marilyn had in old footage we'd seen on TV. With her fresh-scrubbed cheeks and burnished auburn hair, Meredith had been one of the prettiest homecoming queens we'd ever had at Grady High. But I knew the moment I saw her in that platinum-blonde wig and skin-tight lame gown that that young girl was gone. Here was a woman—a mature, confident woman, flaunting her wares with the provocative air of a siren. I glanced over at Bobbye to gage her reaction, but all I saw was Tripp. And the look on his face told me everything.

When she reached the dining room table, Meredith lifted her gloved right hand to brush a silvery curl from her bare shoulder. "Well, gentlemen," she whispered in a feathery voice reminiscent of Marilyn's, "shall we?" Hamp pulled out a chair and Meredith hiked her gown and slowly lowered her shapely bottom onto it.

We took our places at the table and for the next hour tried to do justice to Tripp's delicious steaks and the rest of the meal. It wasn't long before we were groaning and pushing ourselves away from the table. We'd had too many dogs in a blanket before dinner and way too much purple punch.

Tripp got up rather abruptly and went into his bedroom. When he came back, he threw a plastic bag filled with glistening white powder on the table. "Happy New Year, my friends," he said, looking at Jay. Then he took a crisp ten-dollar bill out of his wallet and rolled it up. "You do the honors, Jay, while I set the mood." He walked over to the sound system where he put in a CD. Seconds later, Metallica was blasting their hit, "Enter Sandman."

Bobbye stood up and began collecting and stacking the garbage-laden paper plates from the table and I helped her take them to the trash can. When we were alone in the kitchen, I asked her about the coke and if she'd ever seen Tripp use it. "No," she said. "I guess it's something he picked up while he was in school at Darlington."

By the time we'd rejoined the others in the living room, Jay had several white lines laid out on the glass coffee table and was on his knees beside it. He bent down, put the rolled-up bill up to his left nostril, closed his right nostril with the tip of his index finger, and a snowy line on the table in front of him disappeared. Tripp sank to his knees and snorted the next line. Then Laura and Jay took a turn.

I'd never done any coke but was curious about what would happen. I told Bobbye that I'd try it if she would. Both of us went down on our knees, took a snort, and I was temporarily paralyzed by the sudden rush to my brain. We looked at each other and began giggling as we fell back against the front of the sofa. Hamp followed, which meant that everyone had had a turn except Meredith. She tossed back the tendrils of the blonde wig, flashed a goo-goo smile at Tripp, and said, "I've never done this before. Will somebody please show me what to do?"

Tripp reached up from where he was sitting on the floor, took her hand, and told her to kneel down beside him. It seemed like Meredith took a long time getting down on the floor and an even longer time getting herself settled beside Tripp. He gave her a smile and said, "Just put the end of this rolled-up bill into one of your nostrils and use your finger, like I did, to close the other nostril. Then snort...you know, suck it up into your nose like this."

I heard the rush of his breath as he demonstrated. Then he handed Meredith the rolled-up bill and she followed suit. She remained on her knees for a moment as her eyes began to water. Then her nose began to run. Suddenly, her head went down—which scared the shit out of me—-and when it came back up, she was snickering. That's when Hamp got up from the floor and went over to help her to her feet. Soon the two of them were dancing to Mariah Carey's "Vision of Love," their bodies nestled together like a couple of spoons. Tripp and Bobbye joined them and the rest of us watched. I put a pillow under my head, stretched out on the sofa, and was soon in another world. All I remember is a constant boom, boom, boom from the Beastie Boys, Nirvana, Smashing Pumpkins.

The wind got up about midnight and the sound of thunder in the distance brought me back. Not much had changed in the last couple of hours. Everybody was still sipping purple punch between snorts of cocaine. While the wind howled and the rain beat down, Tripp and Bobbye slow danced to Lionel Ritchie's "My Love" which they'd always called *our* song.

Heart's "Magic Man" popped up next and Tripp fell into a nearby chair pulling Bobbye onto his lap. Meredith let out a squeal and started twirling around the floor. Soon she was clapping her hands and bouncing her breasts in time to the pulsating rhythm of the lead guitar. Her eyes were on Tripp and she kept smiling while she mouthed the words *try to understand, try to understand, he's a magic man*. I didn't have to try to understand Meredith's fascination with Tripp MacAvoy. He was handsome, he was fun, he was the best dancer on the planet, and he had more money than God. He *was* a magic man.

When the song ended, Meredith slumped to the floor in a heap of gold lame. She rolled over, and as she sat up the straps of her gown slid off her shoulders. She looked down, giggled, and shrugged. Then she bunched her shoulders together until her breasts rose up over the top of her bodice. She looked over at Tripp for a moment, raised her eyebrows, and pressed her index finger against her lower lip. That's when the end of Tripp's tongue slowly crept from between his lips. It glistened there for an instant before it disappeared. I glanced at Bobbye, who was staring wide-eyed at Meredith, and realized she had no idea what Tripp was doing. When I looked back at Meredith, the top half of her evening gown had fallen to her waist. My eyes, and everyone else's, were focused on her magnificent tits.

Hamp came from out of nowhere, fell to the floor, and grabbed the bodice of Meredith's dress. He struggled as he moved it back in place and jerked the straps up over her shoulders. Then he took her by the arm and pulled her to her feet. "Stop it, Meredith!" he shouted, his face inches from hers. "What the fuck do you think you're doing?"

Meredith tried to pull away from him. "Leave me alone!" she screeched, hitting him in the chest with her fists. "You don't own me, Hamp Walker. I can do whatever I like!"

Hamp let go, gave her the finger, and staggered off toward the kitchen. When he came back, he had a can of beer in each hand and a little while later, he passed out on the living room floor.

Jay and Laura went to bed then. Phil took his last hit of coke and lay back in a chair opposite me for a few minutes savoring the rush. Then he got up and went into the bedroom he and I were sharing. I waited until I heard him flush the john before I joined him.

Someone turned off the stereo. I guess it was Tripp. And except for the sound of the rain tapping the windows, the house was finally quiet. I slept for a couple of hours but awakened to the sound of someone talking in the living room. I glanced at the clock, saw that it was a little after four, and slid out of bed. Phil was snoring like a freight train and I knew he wouldn't wake up, so I opened the bedroom door a crack and peeped out.

Meredith, who was wearing nothing but a pair of bikini panties, was kneeling on the living room floor beside the still figure of Hamp. Her hair was pinned back in the flat coil she'd made so she could wear the Marilyn wig. I watched as she put a hand on Hamp's back. "Wake up," she whispered. "Wake up, Hamp, and come to bed." When he didn't respond, she moved closer to his side, crawling on her knees with her ass sticking up in the air.

Across from her a door opened and Tripp stepped out in his underwear. He tip-toed over to Meredith and knelt down beside her. "It's okay, Marilyn," he said, sliding his arm around her waist. "Hamp's fine. He's just asleep. Why don't you come with me?" he purred. He put out his hand and Meredith took it and followed him into the bedroom with the canopy bed.

* * * * *

Why was it so hard to get back into the swing of things after Christmas break? Maybe it was those gray January days that seemed to drag on forever even though they're the shortest days of the year. Maybe it was the dull realization that the holidays were over and there was work to be done whether you wanted to do it or not. Whatever the reason, I dragged around for about a week before I got back into life in the dorm and my new schedule, which was not quite as demanding as the fall one had been.

I'd signed up for another course with Thomas Henninger called, "All the News That's Fit to Print," and another psychology course with Dr. Rankin, this one on deviant behavior. I had to have a math course, so I chose Advanced Algebra, which proved to be a breeze for me since I'd had it in high school. The two courses that worked me the hardest were "Shakespeare: The Tragedy of Being the Bard," and Advanced Composition. The professor who taught the latter had us write a paper every week which took a lot of time. Plus, I still had my job at the library.

Bobbye was much busier than I because she, and the rest of the Lady Dawgs' softball team, were preparing for a tough season. While she continued to have practice every day from three to five, she had to give up her job at the stadium because of the game schedule. But she was hired in the Admissions Office, making data entries three nights a week which paid more than her job at the stadium.

Tripp managed to fluff his schedule with three easy courses, but I doubted that he'd be able to pull off the B average he needed so his dad would let him rent an apartment the following year.

Phil continued with his well-thought-out plan to become an engineer. He was a serious student who cared about his work and, unlike Tripp, he was disciplined...more disciplined than any only child I'd ever known. His parents came to see him often, usually on a Sunday. They'd go to church together at University Methodist and then Tripp, Bobbye, and I would be invited to join them for lunch.

Meredith and Hamp still shared a dorm room down the hall from Bobbye and me, and Jay and Laura lived in the same room right across the hall from Tripp and Phil. Laura was enrolled Pre-Dental and, like Phil, had her course work laid out for her; Jay, a math major, hoped to become a high school tennis coach. All of us loved basketball and, that winter, we went to all the home games on Friday nights. It was always exciting to be in the stands yelling our fool heads off for Dominque Wilkins and Willie "Chill" Anderson as they scored three-pointers or stole the ball from the other team. Afterward, we went downtown to dance and, later, gathered in one of our dorm rooms to party.

The Bulldogs had two away games in January and on those Fridays, Tripp and Bobbye went down to Tybee to spend the weekend at the MacAvoy beach house. They invited Phil and me, but I knew from conversations I'd had with Phil that neither of us wanted a repeat of the infamous New Year's weekend, so we stayed in Athens. But I remember that Meredith and Hamp went to the beach with Bobbye and Tripp both times.

On Friday night, February 14, the gang got together and went to a sports bar to celebrate Valentine's. Everyone was there except Hamp, who'd left early that morning with his dad to attend his grandmother's funeral in Tallahassee. Corey Chrisman, the guy who rented the apartment where Bobbye and I cooked our batches of brownies, came in about eleven, took a hit off our joint, and told us about a party going on in his apartment complex. Bobbye didn't want to go because she had to be up early to help with Visitation Day in the Admissions Office. I didn't want to go either because I didn't like Corey's friends. But Tripp promised that he'd have us back at the dorm by one, so we climbed in the Wagoneer and headed out.

When we drove up, dozens of cars were parked on the lawn and about a hundred people had crowded into the first floor of the apartment. It was so smoky in there you could hardly see. Corey took Bobbye, Tripp, Meredith, and me back to the kitchen where the double sinks were packed with ice and bottles of beer. "Take your pick," he said, pointing to the counter. A large bag of weed, a saucer of Blue Angels, two strips of paper containing a dozen hits of brown dot acid, and four bottles of chilled champagne were set out like a buffet. Fifths of bourbon, vodka, and rum stood nearby, and a plate held a dozen pink cookies I knew were ripe with weed.

Off by itself in the opposite corner, partially hidden, was a mirror lined with coke. A tightly rolled ten-dollar bill stood in the center patiently waiting for the next player. I'd never had a Blue Angel before, so I picked up one of those pretty little amphetamines and washed it down with champagne. Bobbye decided to have a beer while Tripp and Meredith went for the coke.

As soon as we'd had our goodies, we went back into the living room where Laura and Jay were huddled around a bong with our friends, Keisha and Jason, and another couple I didn't know. Ozzy Osbourne's "Crazy Train" reverberated off the walls and I felt as if I were crammed inside a tin can while the drummer practiced his fanciest moves on my head. I told Bobbye I was going out on the porch and she came with me and we sat on the steps and talked with a couple of girls from our dorm. After a while, I got up and went back to the kitchen to get a beer. Laura and Jay, and Keisha and

Jason, were right where they'd been when I last saw them, but Meredith and Tripp had disappeared. I had a sneaking suspicion they were up to something and decided to have a look around. I pushed my way through the crowd to Corey and asked if he'd seen them and he told me he thought they'd gone upstairs.

It wasn't easy getting over all the people sitting on the stairs, but I persisted until I reached the upstairs hallway where I found the two of them on the bed in the back bedroom. Meredith's red cable knit sweater was up around her neck, Tripp's face was buried in her crotch, and his jeans were down around his knees. Neither of them had any idea I was there, and I watched for a moment before I finally walked over to the bed and let them know. Tripp flew into a rage, yelling, "Get the fuck out, stupid bitch!"

I stepped away from the bed and said, "It's time to go. Bobbye and I need to get back to the dorm." Tripp turned around, jerked at his pants, and pulled them up around his hips. When he finally got up on his knees, he grabbed his stiff cock and pointed it at me. "Fuck you, Stacey! Get outta here before I ram this missile up your goddam ass!"

Suddenly my head began to spin. I put my palm against the wall to steady myself and felt my way out of the room. Hands came from somewhere and helped me get down the stairs. When I finally reached the last one, I slid to the floor in a heap. That's the last thing I remember.

When I awoke the next afternoon, Bobbye told me that it was Phil who'd brought the two of us back to the dorm the night before. She'd worked all morning helping the Admissions staff register visiting high school seniors and their parents. "I haven't seen Tripp," she said, "and I hope I never see him again."

I dragged myself out of bed and headed to the shower thinking, *That won't last long... they'll be back together before dinner time.* But a couple of days went by and I began to have second thoughts. Bobbye wouldn't take Tripp's calls and she refused to leave our room. She didn't go with me to dinner that night or to lunch the next day. On Sunday evening, we ordered a pizza and invited Jay and Laura over to share it.

By then, all our buddies knew that Tripp was *persona non grata.* No one mentioned his name, and no one said anything about Meredith either. But it was hard for me to imagine that, after all these years, Tripp and Bobbye would call it quits.

The following Monday afternoon I went to my job at the library. It was almost dark when I left there and started back to the dorm. I was walking across Scott Plaza when I saw Tripp's Wagoneer come around the corner. Just before I reached the crosswalk, he made a quick turn to the right and I saw Meredith in the passenger seat beside him. They were headed toward town.

The next day, Bobbye got up early because she had a meeting with her advisor. I assumed we'd see each other at lunch, and I'd made up my mind to tell her that Meredith and Tripp had been screwing around upstairs at the party on Valentine's and at the beach house on New Year's Eve… and I'd seen them in the car together the day before.

But when I got to the cafeteria at noon, Bobbye, Tripp, Meredith, and Phil were standing together in the lobby. As soon as I walked in, Bobbye came running. "Look, Stacey," she said, thrusting her left hand at me. "Look what Tripp gave me!" A large square ruby, surrounded by diamonds, formed the setting in what I knew was an expensive ring.

"Wow!" I exclaimed. "That's beautiful!" I glanced at Tripp, who had a smug, self-satisfied look on his face. After he led us into the dining hall, Bobbye and I headed off to the salad bar where she went on and on about that ring. As soon as we'd filled our plates, she leaned over and whispered, "Meredith helped him pick it out."

* * * * *

One night in early April just before Easter break, Bobbye and I were studying in our room when Tripp showed up. "Something's happened," he said as he sat down on the edge of Bobbye's bed. He paused for a moment and looked back at the door as if he thought someone might be on the other side of it listening. Then he turned back around and blurted, "Meredith's pregnant." Neither Bobbye nor I said anything for a moment. Then Bobbye closed the book she was reading, gave Tripp a puzzled look, and said, "How do you know?"

Tripp looked first at me, then back at Bobbye. "Hamp told me," he said, his tone as matter of fact as if he were reading from a script. He glanced at the closed door again and lowered his voice to a whisper. "Hamp's a wreck! Just a goddamn wreck. I don't know why she puts up with him… he's such a pussy. Anyway, we've gotta help Meredith. She can't have the baby. And she told me she doesn't want to marry Hamp. So, she's going to have an abortion. It's all planned and ya'll need to go with her to this clinic in South Carolina."

Bobbye cocked her head while her dark eyes bore into Tripp's. "Why do *we* have to go?" she asked. "Let Hamp take her."

But Tripp shook his head. "No. Hamp can't. You know what a fucking dweeb he is. Besides, he doesn't have a car and he's not driving mine. Phil and I have talked this over and he's agreed to drive my car and take Meredith and the two of you to a clinic in this town called Anderson. It's a couple of hours from here and ya'll need to be there at 1:30 on Friday."

"No way!" Bobbye shot back. "I've already told you I'm leaving Friday morning. It's the first Friday this spring that I don't have a game and I going home to see the Braves play. Hamp can go with Meredith. It's his baby and he needs to take responsibility for it." She started to get off the bed, but Tripp slid closer and grabbed her hand. He got right up in her face before he said, "Would you excuse us for a moment, Stacey?"

When I came back in the room a few minutes later, Tripp was gone and Bobbye was in the shower. As soon as she came back into the room, she put on her pjs, got into bed, and turned out her lamp. And she never told me anything about what Tripp had said to her.

On Friday morning, we found Meredith and Phil waiting in the dorm parking lot beside Tripp's Wagoneer. Bobbye and I had on jeans and t-shirts. Meredith was wearing a loose-fitting top, beige running pants, white ankle socks, and running shoes. A small leather purse hung over her right shoulder. Even though she wore sunglasses, I could see she'd been crying.

I got in the front seat with Phil, while Meredith and Bobbye shared the bench seat in the back. It was a beautiful spring day as we made our way north, made prettier by the bright array of azaleas and dogwoods blooming along the highway. No one attempted to carry on a conversation. We were all so quiet one would have thought we were on our way to a funeral. And in a way, we were. Phil had the radio on, but it was very low. Every now and then, I glanced back to sneak a peek at Meredith who was slumped in the corner behind him.

We crossed the South Carolina line about eleven and Phil said he had to stop for gas. I was famished and figured Bobbye was too, since neither of us had had any breakfast. I remember that I'd just told Phil I wanted to get something to eat when I heard, "I think I'm going to faint," and turned around just as Meredith's head went down.

"Stop! Stop!" I yelled. And Phil slammed on the brakes and pulled onto the shoulder of the road. By then Meredith was making this low mewling sound and rocking back and forth like somebody insane. It took a moment or two, but Bobbye managed to unbuckle her seat belt. Then she took Meredith by the hand and said, "Lie down and put your head in my lap, Meredith. We're going to get you something to drink." As she tried to make Meredith more comfortable, Bobbye kept looking at me mouthing, *Do something! Do something!*

Phil grabbed the steering wheel, and his knuckles went white as he jerked the Wagoneer back on the highway. A couple minutes passed before we saw a billboard advertising a Burger Boy. Meredith began moaning again and he laid his long foot on the accelerator.

As soon as we pulled into the parking lot of the restaurant, I hopped out of the car, and went around to open the door for Meredith. She didn't want to get out, but Bobbye told her she needed to walk around and get some air. And she needed to drink something. Bobbye and I got on either side of her and held onto her while she stumbled along between us mumbling something we couldn't understand. Once inside the restaurant, we went straight to the women's restroom. I kept an arm around Meredith while Bobbye went out to the counter to place our order. Phil stayed in the car.

The door to the handicapped stall opened and an old lady with a cane trundled out and headed over to a sink. I pushed Meredith into that stall thanking God that it was large enough for both of us. While I held her around the waist and forced her toward the back wall, I put her left hand on the stainless-steel rail mounted just to the right of the toilet, a difficult thing to do as she was crying furiously by then and kept pushing, pushing, trying to get away from me.

I butted the crown of my head into her shoulder and said, "Hold on, Meredith. Just hold onto that rail." A dark red stain bloomed at her crotch and began spreading down her pants. She must have felt it because she let go of the railing, and with both hands, began clawing at the stain, and she kept pulling at it until she'd torn a fist-sized hole. Then she ran her hands inside it, drew them out, and cried, "My baby, my poor baby." She slumped against me and blood dripped in bright red spots on her white shoes and puddled on the floor around them.

Meredith was shaking so badly I was afraid she'd fall. "Sit, Meredith" I commanded. "Sit down on the toilet." Strings of snot trailed from her nose and her eyes blazed like pools of fire as she began screaming, "Tripp! I want Tripp! Where's Tripp?" Finally, she let go of me, and like a freak in a horror movie, began raking blood-stained fingers through her russet hair.

Trying to calm her, I blurted, "Tripp's coming. He's on his way. But he can't see you like this, Meredith." She fell against me, and I quickly moved her back toward the toilet. "Hold onto me, Meredith," I whispered, "while you sit down."

With stilted movements like those of a mime, she grabbed the sides of her pants at the waist, dragged them down her blood-stained thighs to her knees, and slowly lowered herself onto the toilet. A moment later, I heard a plop, plop, plop like pebbles dropping into water. Just as Meredith clutched her belly and groaned, Bobbye came through the restroom door. I glanced over my shoulder to see her standing outside the stall, a soft drink in each hand. Behind her, a little girl about seven was trying to come in. "Get that kid outta here," I said, "and help me."

After Bobbye sent the little girl back into the hallway, she set the drinks on the side of the sink and turned back to us. She stood just outside the stall and craned her neck to gape at Meredith's pasty face, the bloody pants bunched around her knees, her blood-stained hands. "Stop gawking!" I hissed. "Grab some paper towels. A lot of paper towels.

We've got to do something to stop the blood." Bobbye jerked several sheets of paper from the disperser and handed them to me. "Get in here," I told her. "I can't do this by myself."

She eased her way into the stall and took Meredith's left arm, while I took her right, and we brought her to her feet. When I stepped behind her to flush the toilet, I saw a half dozen clots of blood the size of acorns floating in watermelon-colored water. Bobbye started handing me paper towels and I tried to wipe the blood from inside Meredith's thighs. I wiped and wiped, but the more I wiped, the more there was.

"Fold some paper towels together and stuff them between her legs," I said. Bobbye worked at it, trying to make the stiff paper as pliable as possible, but it was obvious it wouldn't be enough. "Wait a sec," I said. "We're wasting time. Is there anything in the Wagoneer we could use...an old t-shirt or a towel...something we could stuff between her legs?"

Bobbye's lips formed a thin line as she wracked her brain. "Tripp keeps his gym bag in the back. Maybe there's something in it."

"You stay here with Meredith," I said, jerking the stall door open. "I'll go see."

When I came out of the restaurant, Phil jumped out of the Wagoneer and ran to meet me. "How's Meredith? Is she okay?"

I didn't want to make things worse, so I said, "She's okay, but there's blood on her clothes. We need to find something else for her to wear. Bobbye said Tripp keeps his gym bag in the back." I opened the hatch at the rear and all but fell on my knees with relief when I saw Tripp's nylon gym bag up near the back. I crawled in and unzipped it. Inside was a jock strap, a small towel, a pair of flip flops, some underwear—and wonders upon wonders—a pair of black sweats.

Bobbye and I were not able to wash the blood stains from Meredith's legs, so I stripped off her ruined pants and

Bobbye knelt down to remove her blood-stained shoes and socks. She held Meredith upright while I folded Tripp's gym towel and put it between her legs. Tripp's underwear went on next, up Meredith's blood-streaked legs, to help keep that towel in place. Then we pulled Tripp's sweatpants on over his underwear and tightened the cord at her waist. Bobbye took the flip flops from me and bent down to put them on Meredith's blood-stained feet. You could tell where her tennis socks had been because a brown stain encircled both ankles.

Phil was waiting for us in the hallway outside the restroom door. He picked Meredith up, carried her across the parking lot, and gently put her down on the back seat of the car. Bobbye got in beside her and we sped along Hwy 16 following the directions that Tripp had given us. A few minutes later we saw a sign for The Hopewell Clinic and Phil made a sharp turn and drove right up to the front door. I rushed around to open the back door for Phil, who lifted Meredith out, leaving a pool of fresh blood the size of my hand on the back seat.

Bobbye and I hurried to the double doors of the clinic, opening them so Phil could pass through with Meredith in his arms. A nurse in a blue dotted smock was standing just behind the front desk. She looked up, and without a word, walked over to a door on her right, opened it, and motioned Phil through. Bobbye and I sat down in the waiting room, which was empty except for a woman holding a little boy on her lap.

About ten minutes passed before Phil came back. He stood in front of us red-faced and sweating. "She's in...in surgery," he stammered. "They had me take her into a big room in the back and told me to put her right down on a table that was covered with white paper. They didn't even try to wash the blood off her or anything. The nurse came in with a pair of scissors and started cutting Tripp's sweatpants, and the doctor—I guess she was the doctor—came in with one of those white paper mask things in her hand. She started toward the sink, but then she saw me and asked me to walk back out into the hall with her. She told me that Meredith was hemorrhaging badly… that she was in shock and they were going to try to stop the bleeding… and Meredith will have to spend the night in a hospital because they can't keep her here. They'll call an ambulance to take her up to Greenville. The doctor said the surgery might take about two hours depending on what they find and how many stitches Meredith needs. They let me go back in to see Meredith just before they put her under."

Phil sat down, put his head in his hands, and let out a great wet sob. "I went back there," he muttered through his hands, "and I froze. I wanted to say something to make her feel better. But I couldn't. Her face was so white I thought she was dead, but her eye lids kept fluttering, so I knew she wasn't. I felt like an idiot standing there watching while her blood ran all over that white table and dripped onto the floor. Then the nurse came in dragging this metal thing with bags hanging at the top…you know, IVs… and one of them was labeled blood plasma. Meredith had to have a transfusion. A transfusion, for God's sake!"

"Dammit!" he cried, getting up. "Why me? Why did I ever agree to do this? I'm gonna kill Tripp MacAvoy!"

"Be quiet, Phil," I warned. "There are other people here. You don't want to upset that woman and her little boy, do you?"

I reached up and put my hand on his shoulder. "You did the right thing. And there's nothing any of us can do now but wait."

"Yes, there is," he answered. "I'm going down to Augusta and find Tripp. And Hamp. And I'm going to bring them back here so they can take care of Tripp's latest shit!" He started toward the door but turned to look at Bobbye and me. "You two stay here with Meredith. And if they take her to the hospital in Greenville before I get back, you all stay right here, and I'll come back and get you. The doctor told me they close the clinic at six. But don't worry. I'll be back before then." And, with that, he hurried away.

* * * * *

A thin, pale, very subdued Meredith returned to campus the week after Easter break to finish the semester. The day before exams started, she came by to tell Bobbye and me that she and Hamp had decided they wanted to stay in Atlanta next fall to commute to school. She would go to Agnes Scott, he to Emory.

It poured the next day, a steady rain that soaked everyone out in it. That afternoon, I was shelving books in the library when I saw Hamp come in, jacket dripping water, and head back to the Resource Room. I left my cart of books in the aisle and decided to follow him and see how he was doing. Like Meredith, he'd been more than quiet over the last few weeks. I waited until he sat down at a desk and opened a notebook before I spoke. "How you doing, buddy?"

He looked up at me, but didn't smile. I got a chair from another carrel, brought it over, and sat down beside him. "Meredith told Bobbye and me that ya'll are going to live at home next year and go to school in Atlanta. I'm really sorry to hear that, Hamp. We'll miss you guys."

Hamp looked down at the floor for a moment and when he looked back at me, grief was plain in his eyes. And while he'd never been what I'd call jolly, he seemed sadder than ever that day. "Meredith has had such a rough spring," he said. "And she needs time to get over it. I just can't believe what happened. If only she'd told me, maybe I could have helped her."

I was stunned by what Hamp had said…that he'd known nothing about Meredith's predicament. How could that be? He and she lived together, for God's sake. But I slipped into reporter mode and let him talk. It wasn't the first time he'd confided in me and I felt sure he had something he wanted to get off his chest.

He reached for a pen and began scribbling on the notebook in front of him, keeping his eyes on the paper while he talked. "She had one of those things Mrs. Turner used in biology class at Grady. Remember that little metal pointer thing she used when she showed us how the organs in those dead animals lined up together… how they lay against one another inside those little bodies. She'd lift the liver inside a fetal pig with that metal thing to show us the spleen underneath it. Remember?" He cut his eyes at me and I nodded.

"The night before Tripp told me that you all were going to take Meredith to that clinic in South Carolina, I saw one of those metal things sticking out of the end of her purse. And when she went into the bathroom to take a shower, I pulled it out and thought *what in the hell is she doing with this?* She was taking a zoology course and I thought maybe she was going to use it for a class project. Then I heard the shower turn off and I put that little instrument back where she'd had it and got into bed. Meredith went to bed right after that, but she was up several times during the night. I thought nothing of it because she's such a light sleeper. And she gets up and does stuff. Moves her make-up around on the shelf and hunts in the dark for her nose spray. Things like that."

Hamp left his chair and went to stand in front of a rain-smudged window where he kept talking with his back to me. "When Tripp and I went to that big hospital in Greenville to see Meredith, the doctor said she'd had to have three transfusions. He told us she'd survived one of the

109

deepest shocks he'd ever had to deal with. And there was unmistakable evidence that she'd tried to harm herself... and the baby. The doctor asked Tripp and me if we knew anything about that. And both of us shook our heads. I could not have told him what I knew, even if he'd held a gun to my head because I was so shocked by what he'd told us. She could have died, Stacey. The doctor told us that Meredith would never be able to have children because of what she'd done."

He turned around to face me. "Why?" he asked. "Why'd she do it? Meredith knows I love her. I've always loved her. And I'd have married her in an instant even if the kid wasn't mine. And it wasn't."

He shook his head and walked back where he sat down across from me. "My life has gone down the drain, Stacey. For the past couple of years, I've been standing on the brink of an abyss watching my parents destroy each other. And the only thing that's kept me from falling over the edge is Meredith."

He picked up the pen and began drawing a big circle on the paper, going around and around until he'd all but torn a hole in it. "I have to look out for Meredith, Stacey. She needs to be in a place where people care about her, where they won't take advantage of her. I don't want to live at home with my mom, but I'll do that for Meredith."

I bent down to give Hamp a hug. "You're a good man, Hamp Walker," I said. "Now I gotta get back to work before I lose my job." I started walking back through the stacks, and as soon as I got to my cart, I began shelving books. A moment later Hamp came up the aisle and stopped beside me. "Thanks for listening, Stacey," he said, pulling on a Braves' cap. "It isn't you. Our decision to move back home had nothing to do with *you*."

* * * * *

Grade reports arrived in Atlanta the middle of May and Bobbye and I had made the Dean's List and Phil had a 4.00 GPA. Tripp somehow managed to finish the year with a B- average, and the day before he left campus to start his summer job at the MacAvoy plant in Sandy Springs, he told us he'd made a deposit on a two bed/two bath townhouse about a mile from campus. Bobbye, Phil, and I went home to the very same jobs we'd had the summer before. The four of us continued to meet every Friday night for chicken and waffles at The Shack, followed by weed-inspired talks on our rock at Hillcrest Park.

During June, I called Meredith three different times to invite her and Hamp to go out with the four of us, but it never happened. And while I spent most days doing routine mindless things with the kids at camp, my nights were not so easy. I had this recurring dream of dead babies, of faceless little creatures streaked with blood. I dreamed of falling, falling and not being able to save myself. Then I'd awaken suddenly covered in sweat.

My dad told me he was worried about me. That sometimes in the middle of the night, he heard me crying. He said I looked haggard and threatened to take me to the doctor. So, I bought some undereye concealer and used it every morning and he never knew the difference.

The first week in August, my dad and Russell Warren took Bobbye and me camping in Nantahala National Park in the Great Smokies, a vacation I relished because I had Bobbye all to myself. We went hiking and white water rafting and, while our dads fished from the rock-strewn shore, the two of us tubed down the cool Nantahala River. My dad had reserved two rooms at the lodge, twin beds in one, and a queen in the other. When we saw them, Bobbye and I had quickly called dibs on the queen knowing our dads wouldn't want to sleep in a bed together. After a fun-filled day, we'd retreat to our room where I brushed Bobbye's long black hair until my arm hurt. Then she used me as a model while she experimented with all kinds of daring make-up, including the most outrageous shades of eye shadow. I didn't care what she put on me and would have worn iridescent chartreuse night and day to please her.

In a shop in a little railroad town called Dillsboro, I blew the last of my paycheck on a wrist-hugging silver bracelet for Bobbye and had our initials and the date engraved on the inside. After she put it on, she gave me a hug and told me she loved it. My eyes misted when I thought of her wearing it for the rest of our lives.

The nights turned cool there in the high country and, as we huddled together under our blanket, we talked about the townhouse apartment we'd be sharing with Tripp and Phil in a couple of weeks. My dad had taken me shopping for a car and we'd bought a four-year-old Toyota Camry, silver with gray upholstery, and I couldn't wait to park it in front of our new digs.

Miss Janice fussed all summer about Bobbye moving into an apartment with Tripp. She kept telling Mr. Russell that, at nineteen, Bobbye was just too young. Like any normal mother, she thought Bobbye would be better off living in a dorm. Russell reminded Janice that she'd been only nineteen when she'd married him and argued that Bobbye was mature enough to handle herself. But Janice needed more assurance. So, when the morning came for us to head back to Athens, Bobbye rode with me in my new Camry while my dad and Russell followed in Green Bean, both cars packed to the hilt with our junk.

My dad had insisted on seeing where I'd be living, particularly the layout of the rooms. And Janice had sent Russell along to be sure everything would be the way we'd described it to them. The apartment was a townhouse with a bedroom and bath downstairs and a bedroom and bath, plus a loft area, upstairs. Bobbye and I had told our parents that we'd be living upstairs.

The place came furnished with a sofa and two matching chairs in the living room, a small dining table and four chairs, and a set of twin beds in each bedroom. The kitchen had the usual appliances, including a dish washer, and they were in good condition. We had to provide everything else, so Bobbye and I brought the bedspreads and the linens we'd used in Lipscomb and a set of drinking glasses. Tripp and Phil had been on a shopping spree and bought new bedspreads for their room, a set of dishes, and pots and pans. When Bobbye and I arrived that first day with our dads, the freezer was already stocked with steaks, pizzas, and ice cream.

After my dad and Russell left, Tripp unloaded a grill from the back of his car and set it up, with a canister of gas, in the center of the deck. Then he brought out a brisket he'd rubbed with exotic seasonings and seared it above a blue flame before he lowered the heat, pulled the lid down, and let it cook. Meanwhile, I chopped onion and celery for the potato salad...a fascinating mix made with the usual cooked potatoes, but without the usual mayo. Instead, Tripp used sour cream, chives, and cream cheese...an intriguing combination. He wasn't the best student, but he was a hell of a cook! At dusk, the four of us gathered around the table, toasted each other, and relished the first meal in our new home.

My routine changed very little that fall. I had a couple of new professors and adjusted to their style and expectations without any problems. My schedule included another course in psychology (I was hooked!), a course in American history and one in American poetry, and "Journalism for the Masses." My journalism professor, who'd worked decades for United Press International, began every class with this axiom: The most important thing in journalism is to be in the *wrong* place at the right time and keep your eyes and ears open. In addition to my heavy course load, I'd be working three afternoons a week at the library.

Bobbye was trying to decide on a major and was moving toward Sports Medicine. Practice every afternoon consumed a lot of her time and she continued to do data entry in the Admissions Office three evenings a week. Except for a few hours on weekends, she had very little time to call her own.

Phil had his whole curriculum practically laid out for him with only a few electives allowed along the way and was content to live it as it came. And Tripp played his usual game by filling his schedule with the least demanding courses: Spanish IV, Parks and Recreation, Children's Literature 102, a history course, and one in computers.

By the end of September, we knew the people who lived in the apartments nearby. Most were single students like us, but there were also two married couples. Tripp and Bobbye began to spend more and more time at the home of one of those couples and the two of them began to talk more and more about what they were going to do when they got married. Lots of our friends thought the ruby and diamond ring Tripp had given Bobbye the year before was an engagement ring. Rumors flew, and eventually they reached Atlanta.

One Sunday morning in mid-October, Janice and Russell Warren knocked on our door. Bobbye, who'd slept in the downstairs bedroom with Tripp the night before, came flying upstairs to wake me. I threw on a tee-shirt and some jeans and woke Phil. The three of us rushed around picking up various pieces of clothing and odd shoes scattered throughout the living room and kitchen. I grabbed the bong that was still sitting on the dining room table and hid it under the sink thanking God that Bobbye and I had taken the empty liquor and beer bottles out back before we'd gone to bed. Phil swooped around like a giant crane collecting loose cigarette papers and roach clips that dotted the living room carpet. He stuffed them in his pockets just before Bobbye opened the door.

I could tell by the looks on their faces that the Warrens were not happy with what they found. The one good thing was, except for some lingering smells, there was not much evidence of the blow-out that had ended just a few hours earlier. I gave each of Bobbye's parents a hug and went back to the kitchen to make a pot of coffee. A moment later, Tripp came out of the bedroom in his underwear and staggered down the hall to the bathroom. He never saw us, or our company. But all of us saw him.

I took mugs of coffee into the living room and we sat around with the Warrens making small talk about the weather and their drive from Atlanta. Russell asked about my dad and Janice wanted to know how Phil's parents were doing. Bobbye excused herself and went into the bedroom and told Tripp to get dressed.

As soon as he came into the living room, Russell stood up and said, "See here, Tripp MacAvoy. What's this we're hearing about you and Bobbye being engaged?"

Tripp's face went blank, and he stood there looking like he'd been hit with a brick. I handed him a mug of coffee which he quickly put it to his lips. Bobbye looked at her dad and said, "We're not engaged. What gave you that idea?"

Russell shrugged. "Your friends in Atlanta seem to think you are. I saw Hamp Walker's dad in the drug store on Highland Avenue last week and he said he'd heard that you two were making plans to elope at Christmas. Are you?"

Tripp left his mug on the dining room table and went over to sit down on the sofa beside Bobbye. He took her hand in his, looked back at Russell, and said, "I love your daughter, Russ, and maybe one day we'll get married. But I don't have a pot to pee in, if you'll excuse the expression. And no, we're not engaged."

Janice, who'd been quietly listening, turned to Tripp and said, "The world is your oyster, son. And it won't matter very much whether *you* finish college or not. You'll go right into your father's business and you'll never want for a thing. But our daughter's education is more important to us than anything on earth. You see, neither of us was able to finish high school and we want Bobbye to be able do things with her life that we couldn't. It's our job to see that nothing, and I mean *nothing*, interferes with her education. I pray every day that she'll have the good sense to wait until she's older and more mature to get married."

Tripp got up and began collecting coffee mugs. "We're not going to elope, Miss Janice, no matter what you heard. It'll be a while before Bobbye and I marry. And when we do, we'll have a big wedding with a nice reception and all our friends will be invited. And Russ and I will dress up in monkey suits and you'll wear a beautiful evening gown. Don't worry now. We won't do anything behind your back. I promise."

Russell nodded at Janice. "I told you it was just a rumor," he said. "Now, come on, all of you. We want to take you to your favorite burger joint. And we're buying."

We sat at a long table together munching burgers and fries and sucking down milkshakes. While Tripp, Phil, and Russell joked around about Bulldog football, I tried to make small talk with Janice. Bobbye picked at her food and stared off at some unknown something in the distance. I looked over at her, at the blank expression on her face, and wondered if Tripp asked her to marry him when he'd given her that ruby and diamond ring. If he had, she'd never said a word to me. I was constantly looking for a sign, a comment from her, to let me know that she knew about Tripp's relationship with Meredith. Like most of our friends, I was sure Bobbye thought Hamp was the father of the baby that had been flushed down the toilet at Burger Boy. And even though she'd been in the restroom stall with Meredith and me—and knew very well what had gone on in the Hopewell Clinic and at the hospital in Greenville—I'd have sworn that no one had ever had the guts to tell her that Hamp was not the father of that baby. And I would not have told her for all the tea in China because I figured that was Hamp's business. He'd shared so many confidences with me in the past, including strange revelations about his parents, that I knew he was totally incapable of lying, especially about something as serious as a pregnancy.

As conversation at the table ebbed, I picked up my used tray, along with Janice's, and asked Bobbye if I could take hers. She didn't even look up when I spoke to her, just continued to stare straight ahead at nothing. Perhaps she was dreaming of the day she'd walk down the aisle in a flowing white gown and become Mrs. James Edward MacAvoy III.

* * * * *

The week before Halloween, Tripp told Bobbye, Phil, and me that he needed some help with a project for his kiddie lit class. He had to select a children's book and act out a scene from it for a group of second graders at the University Lab School on campus. No one was surprised when he chose, *Where the Wild Things Are*, because we knew it was his favorite book. He decided to play a gorilla, so we were off on a jaunt to find a gorilla suit. Bobbye and I were told to purchase several big sheets of poster board and lots of magic markers because he wanted the two of us to make a colorful jungle backdrop for his presentation.

The night before he was to present his project at the lab school, Phil, Bobbye, and I sat on the living room floor in a semi-circle pretending we were second graders while Tripp jumped around in his gorilla suit having the time of his life. Then he read the book to us between bouts of screeching, howling, and beating his chest. Phil commented about how the kids were gonna love it and Tripp just beamed.

After he'd taken the gorilla suit off, he joined the three of us in the living room for a beer. "You know what?" he said, sitting down on the sofa beside Bobbye. "That should be the theme of our next party—where the wild things are!"

Bobbye frowned. "Oh, no. Not another costume. I don't want to be one of those ugly hairy things from that book!" Tripp laughed as he reached out to hug her. "You couldn't be ugly if you tried, honey. Why don't you be something beautiful like a panther ...or a tiger? It doesn't matter as long as it's a wild animal. I think our friends would have fun pretending they're animals. And it's the perfect theme for Halloween."

About sixty people showed up at the apartment to play Trick or Treat with the big gorilla who greeted them at the front door. Their costumes were a riot and I'd never seen so many monkey masks and garish parrot heads. Several people had gone all out buying yards of fake fur and paying someone to make them a cat costume. Tripp had found a beautiful tiger costume for Bobbye— a low-cut, form-fitting kind of thing that looked like a one-piece bathing suit with a long tail. With it, she wore fish-net panty hose, spike patent leather heels, and a dozen black whiskers which I helped glue to her face. She looked adorable...and sexy.

Phil and I decided to take the easy way out and borrowed a couple of khaki uniforms from some guys we knew who worked in Oconee National Forest. Over the official patches sewn to their uniforms, we pinned one that read, "Animal Control" in bold black letters. Each of us carried a fake whip we'd bought at the party store and a bag of Purina Cat Chow.

We put out the usual refreshments—a bag of weed, freshly rolled joints, several kinds of liquor and beer, funky brownies, and a mirror lined with coke. We played the usual tapes on the stereo and quite a few people danced. Every time a girl walked through the door, Tripp rushed to meet her, grabbing his crotch while he screeched, scratched his hairy butt, and every now and then, beat his chest to a chorus of, *Let the rumpus begin!*

But an hour or so into the party, he removed his gorilla head, and sat down on the sofa beside Bobbye. I soon joined them, sitting down on the other side where I played with her tail and imagined taking her clothes off. A searing flame rose in my gut, traveled to my breasts, and bloomed on my face. Suddenly the room was stifling, and I fled to the kitchen for a cold beer. I just knew any minute somebody was gonna ask why my face was so red. Thankfully, no one did. Even though quite a few ferocious animals were present, it was a tame party overall. No one threw up; no one passed out; no one stripped off their costume and raced around naked. And no one knew it would be the last party the four of us would ever host.

* * * * *

During the Christmas holidays that year, Phil went with his parents to visit his mom's brother in Michigan, and my dad and I went down to Macon to visit our Parks relatives. Bobbye and Tripp stayed in Atlanta the entire time because Caroline MacAvoy had deteriorated to the point that she had to have 'round the clock care from a team of nurses working in shifts. Her mother, Patricia, had moved upstairs so Caroline could have the large bedroom downstairs that Patricia and Rand had occupied for forty years. Ed, who'd moved into a room across the hall, had hired a crew to come in and equip his wife's room with a standard hospital bed, nightstand, and a set of cabinets on rollers that held the many medicines she had to have every day. In one corner, a twin bed and a comfortable chair were available for the night nurse.

Bobbye and I had dinner with Tripp only once during the holidays. He met us at The Shack the night before I had to go to Macon with my dad. He looked thinner, a bit drawn, and there were dark circles under his eyes. After we ordered, he told us that his mom was not going to live much longer, maybe a month, maybe six weeks. "I hope she doesn't," he said as he stabbed a piece of waffle with his fork. "She looks like a corpse and I bet she doesn't weigh eighty pounds. And she's got these big-ass bruises up and down her arms and legs. You won't believe it, but she's as bald as a billiard ball. She's on one of those morphine drip things and she pushes the little button a lot. And when she tries to speak, she spurts and wheezes like a rusty faucet and I can't understand a thing she says."

Bobbye interrupted to ask about Ed, and Tripp told us that his dad was a wreck. "I can't get any sleep because he cries all night. My grandmother never cries, but my dad cries all the time, even after I go to bed. This afternoon, I moved the bed from my bedroom upstairs into the rec room over the garage." He grinned as he looked over at Bobbye and asked, "Want to come for a sleep-over, little girl?"

After we finished eating, Tripp told us that Patricia and Classie had bought a Christmas tree and set it up in the living room because his mom wanted a Christmas tree. "It's strung with lights and covered with all our old ornaments," he said, "and it's real pretty. Somebody even put some presents under it. Every night before my mom goes to sleep, my dad lifts her up out of bed and takes her into the living room so she can look at it. It's the goddam saddest thing you ever saw...him picking her up in his arms like she was a baby. He takes her into the living room and sits down on the sofa with her on his lap and talks to her as if she were four years old. And her head lolls off to the side and her eyes won't stay focused and it's just so goddamn awful."

Bobbye and I told Tripp how sorry we were about his mom and asked if there was anything we could do to help, but he just shook his head. "There's nothing anyone can do," he said, as he held the door for us on our way out. Bobbye and I got into my car as Tripp got into his Wagoneer. Just before he pulled out, he rolled down the window and said, "I'll see ya'll back in Athens."

* * * * *

January was filled with cold rainy days as we hunkered down to our new course schedules and the usual routine. We planned one of our almost-famous parties for Valentine's and invited all our friends. It fell on a Saturday that year which gave us time to decorate. We made it clear to everyone that if they came, they had to wear something red or pink to get in the door. Tripp wanted to have a contest. The person who ate the most cupcakes in one minute would win a case of Michelob.

That Saturday morning, Tripp and Phil left the apartment about ten to pick up some extra beer. Bobbye and I were hanging red, white and pink crepe paper streamers in the living room when the phone rang. I picked it up and heard a small voice coming from what sounded like a great distance away asking to speak to Tripp. After a moment, I realized that that little voice belonged to Ed MacAvoy. I told him that Tripp wasn't home. Ed made a sniffling sound and sucked his breath like he was trying not to cry. I asked him if I could give Tripp a message and he told me to please tell him to come home right away…that his mom wanted to talk with him one more time before she was completely unable to speak. I assured Ed that I would deliver the message and asked if there was anything I could do to help. He thanked me and said there was nothing anyone could do.

Tripp packed a duffle and left about noon. Bobbye, Phil, and I decided to go ahead with the party because Tripp had said that his mom would want us to. But none of us had the heart for it…an especially sad circumstance on Valentine's Day. We iced the beer and opened the liquor bottles and put out all the grass-filled goodies we'd made. People didn't stay long when they found out what was going on with Tripp. Most smoked a joint, had something to eat and drink, and left before midnight. By two o'clock, Phil and Bobbye and I had taken down the decorations and cleaned up. We hoped Tripp would call that night and tell us what was happening with his mom, but he never did.

Early the next afternoon he came back. When we asked about Caroline, he told us that his mom had told him she wanted to be cremated and he didn't want to talk about it. Then, he and Bobbye closeted themselves in the downstairs bedroom and Phil and I watched a movie on TV.

* * * * *

Caroline MacAvoy died late on Thursday afternoon March 11, 1993. Tripp got a call from his dad about five-thirty and left immediately for Atlanta. He called us a couple of hours later to say that the funeral would be Saturday.

But the storm of the century blew in and nothing went as planned. That Friday evening, the wind got up and soon it was blowing 60 mph. Then snow started pouring down in buckets and soon blizzard conditions existed all over central and eastern Georgia. Just after midnight, the electricity went out in the townhouse and we were stranded with no heat while the temperatures plunged to a record low of 18. Bobbye and I put on winter coats, hats, gloves, and huddled in one bed together with blankets up to our noses.

Some neighbors came over the next morning to tell us that people were trapped in the snow and ice on the interstates, that grocery store shelves were empty, and gas stations had no gas. Like everyone else on the East Coast, we were stuck. The phone lines were down, so we had no way of communicating with Tripp. But we figured he was in the same fix.

By Sunday morning it had stopped snowing, and that afternoon, a pale sun came out and melted the top layer. But all of it froze again that night. On Monday, power crews showed up to work on the lines, and by dinner time the electricity was back on and so was the phone. Phil called Tripp and learned that he, his dad, and grandmother had been stuck in the birthday cake house for three days and, like everyone else in Atlanta, they had survived on sandwiches and canned soup heated on a camper stove. Caroline's funeral would be held on Wednesday at two o'clock. Phil told Tripp we'd be there.

By two o'clock on Wednesday the temperature had risen to 55 degrees, but low-lying clouds and constant drizzle made for a nasty day. For the Cogdill-MacAvoy family, it started in the cemetery at ten o'clock where Ed placed the urn that held Caroline's ashes on a pink marble plinth beside the grave of her father, Rand.

At two o'clock, the pews at The Sign of the Shepherd Episcopal Church were filled with hundreds of mourners. Governor Zell Miller sat beside Senator Sam Nunn in the pew right behind Ed, Tripp, and Patricia. Tripp asked Bobbye and Phil and me to sit with the family, so we were just two rows behind them. Caroline's twin, Catherine, and her husband had come from California. Tripp had no cousins, but two great aunts and a great uncle were there. About thirty current and past members of the Junior League of Atlanta were in the front pews on the right side opposite the family.

The family had requested no flowers, but a pair of tall white wicker baskets, over-flowing with blooms, stood on either side of the altar. Under the pulpit seated in a semi-circle were four members of the Atlanta Symphony. I didn't know the woman who played the oboe, but the man who played the cello was Mr. Pridgen, the band instructor at Grady High. The flautist was the lovely and talented Lark Loflin. And David Duckworth, who had partnered with Lark on many of the duets I'd heard at Chastain Park while in high school, played the violin.

Caroline Cogdill MacAvoy had loved music so I wasn't surprised that it was much in evidence at her funeral. After the priest opened the service with a prayer thanking God for Caroline's brief life, a handsome black woman rose in the choir loft behind him and sang "Calm as the Night." I learned later that it had been sung by another woman standing in that very same spot in that very same church the day Ed and Caroline had been married twenty-six years before.

The eulogy was delivered by Caroline's college roommate, Maria Justina Castillo, a native of Rio de Janeiro whose family had immigrated there centuries before from Castille,

Spain. During her sophomore year, Caroline had spent fall semester in Rio with Maria Justina and her family. Maria Justina talked about Caroline's passion for art, her love of music, and her generous nature. Ten years before, Caroline had endowed a chair in Spanish History and Culture at Queens…something Tripp had never mentioned.

Following the service, the family hosted a reception in the Parish Hall. Bobbye, Phil, and I went to the refreshment table, filled our plates, and retreated to a corner. Tripp stood in line beside his dad for the next couple of hours shaking hands with friends and a slew of Atlanta big shots. Our friends from college, Laura and Jay and Keisha and Jason, came through and I saw Hamp Walker stroll in with his dad. I wanted to ask Hamp about Meredith, but I didn't get the chance because Tripp came over and invited us to supper at his house at five o'clock. "Ya'll don't need to hang around here waiting for me," he said. "Just go on over and watch TV or something. Classie and her girls are setting up and they'll let you in."

When we arrived at the house, Classie was placing large silver platters of beautiful food on the elegant dining room table—the kind reserved for friends who were special enough to be invited back to the house. Off to the side, on a table filled with luscious desserts, my dad's death cake sat on a footed silver tray that I knew wasn't ours.

The priest, soloist, and members of the symphony quartet were the first to arrive and Bobbye, Phil, and I met them in the foyer and told them what a lovely service it had been. I was thrilled to be with Lark Loflin again and, even more so, when she remembered me. I'd never met David Duckworth, but he seemed very nice. I'd heard that he and Lark had been an item for a couple of years and friends in the symphony expected them to marry.

Tripp came in and began pointing out all the gorgeous flower arrangements sitting everywhere and telling us about the bigwigs in town, and from all over the state, who'd sent them. He was so proud of those lavish bouquets. Then he took us over to meet his Aunt Catherine and Uncle Bill from California and his great aunts. He got caught up in a conversation with the Director of the Atlanta Public Library and we excused ourselves so he could pay attention to his guests.

I watched as Ed walked over to Lark and I assumed he was thanking her for playing for his wife's funeral. Ed had been on the symphony board when I was in high school, so I suspected he and Lark had known each other for a while. He took her hand and led her across the dining room to the portrait of Caroline that hung above the hunt board. They stood beneath it conversing for about five minutes. I watched as he looked down at her, and she nodded up at him, and they smiled and smiled as they talked. In those few moments, it seemed as if some of the burden of the last few days began to lift from Ed's face, because it was obvious to me that he was much more at ease than he'd been earlier.

Then Ed walked Lark to the front door, and as they said good-bye to each other, he took her hand and I heard him say he hoped to see her again. After he'd closed the door, he paused in the foyer to look at his watch, and then he started down the hall.

I whispered to Bobbye and Phil that I needed to use the restroom and went off to find one. The half-bath off the foyer was in use so I went around the corner to one I'd used before that was off the hallway of the downstairs bedroom wing. Just as I started to close the door, I heard Ed MacAvoy say, "What are you doing in here?" Then Tripp answered, "I'm looking for something."

I opened the bathroom door a little and realized that the two of them were across the hall in Ed and Caroline's bedroom. I heard Ed say, "What exactly are you looking for?"

126

And Tripp said, "The ring she left me." Then Ed said, "What ring are you talking about?" And Tripp replied, "The ring Mama left me in her will...her engagement ring."

There was a pause and then Ed said, "Close that drawer, son. You won't find it in there. I put it in the vault in my office a couple of months ago when her fingers swelled and she couldn't wear it anymore."

Then Tripp said, "I want you to bring it to me because I'm going to give it to Bobbye for her birthday."

Ed must have stood up then because his voice was much louder. "You most certainly are not!" he hissed. "You're not giving your mother's ring to that... janitor's daughter!"

And Tripp shouted back at Ed, "Oh, yes, I am! Mama left me her diamond ring and told me before she died that she wanted me to give it to the girl I'm going to marry."

I looked down at my left hand and pictured the ring I'd seen on Caroline MacAvoy's finger dozens of times...a large oval solitaire in a four-pronged Tiffany-style setting.

Ed started talking again, his words coming at a slower pace. "I worked my ass off my last year in law school to pay for that ring and it's worth a fortune. And you're not going to give it to Bobbye Revels. I don't know why you want to worry me like this, Tripp. You know how hard things are right now with your Grandad Jim laid up in that nursing home in Sandy Springs and all the problems we're having with management at the Birmingham plant. I'm going to have to fire a couple of men there. I've told you about this, but you just ignore anything I say about the business. One day, you'll be the CEO of MacAvoy Enterprises and then you'll know how it feels to have all this responsibility. By the way, I've told personnel at the Sandy Springs operation that you'll be working in the spinning room this summer."

Tripp's reaction to this news was not good. I heard him say very emphatically that he would *not* be working in the

127

damn spinning room because all the noise would drive him crazy. But Ed had other ideas. "You'll do what the three hundred other people who work in there do," he said, "and get a pair of earplugs."

A couple of minutes passed. Then Tripp said, "Okay, okay. I'll work in your stupid spinning room this summer. You always get your way, don't you, Ed? But I'm not leaving here today without that ring."

Evidently Ed got up from the bed and started out of the room because he was much closer to me when he said, "I'll make you a deal, son. When you finish law school at UGA, I'll give you that ring for graduation. And you can give it to any damn body you please. Now, leave your mother's stuff alone. We need to get out of here and say goodbye to our guests."

I stepped back into the bathroom and pushed the door leaving it open just a crack. I peeped through and saw Ed as he started down the hall with Tripp behind him. I carefully closed the door, put the lid down on the toilet, and sat there feeling guilty about having heard so intimate a conversation. But I'd learned one important thing—Tripp probably did intend to marry Bobbye. And while Ed had made it clear that he did not approve of the match, he thought Tripp would go to law school and take over the helm of MacAvoy Enterprises.

* * * * *

We expected Tripp in Athens the next day, but he didn't show up until late Friday afternoon, and when he arrived, he was driving a new car—a black 1988 BMW 325i four-door sedan. Bobbye and I were sitting out on the front porch watching when he got out and said, "I'm back. Time to celebrate!"

After we'd taken quick showers and dressed, we headed downtown for gyros at The Forum. While we waited for our food, Tripp told us that his mom had left him $25,000 in cash and he'd badgered his dad into letting him sell the Wagoneer so he could buy something more in keeping with *who he was.*

"We got a good trade on the Wagoneer," he said, "and that Bimmer is only two years old. The guy wanted $24,000 for it, but I jewed him down to $22,000. So, I've still got three thousand in an account at Georgia State Bank down on Peachtree. My dad told me I could have the BMW if I put the rest of the money my mom left me in an interest-bearing account to help pay for law school. I didn't want to do that because I can't touch it for the next two years, but I wanted that Bimmer. So Ed got his way, as usual. But hey, I brought ya'll some really fine hash I picked up in a bar at home. It's pretty heady stuff. What say we go out to the The Bull Pen tonight? Roustabout's playing. Eat up, kiddies, it's party time!"

Tripp had a really big night. He smoked a lot of hash, drank a lot of beer, and danced with every girl in the place, plus a couple of women who were at least thirty. Bobbye took it all in stride. She and Phil and I danced a few times but mostly we just sat back and watched Tripp. He'd obviously forgotten about his mom's funeral and about upcoming midterms, which were re-scheduled because of the storm. Tripp had taken two exams the Thursday before he'd left to go home, so he had three to go. But it was Friday night, and no exam was going to interfere with his fun. His speech got so sloppy that he slurred every word and, in the end, passed out. Phil put him in the back seat of the bargain Bimmer and Bobbye drove us home.

* * * * *

Tripp made up his mid-terms and did okay on all of them except history where he made a D. Bobbye tried to work with him encouraging him to pull up his grade, but Tripp wouldn't settle down. That spring, he seemed to be riding an emotional roller-coaster. He'd soar to the highest of highs. Then he'd plummet to the lowest of lows...what Bobbye called his "dark moods." When they came on, he'd climb into bed and didn't emerge from the bedroom for days. Bobbye told Phil and me that Tripp was crying a lot, that he was having bad dreams, but he didn't want us to know. After Bobbye offered this excuse, Phil asked if there was anything he could do to help, but I was unable to muster even a small amount of sympathy for the boy who had everything. After all, I'd lost my mom, too, and at a much more vulnerable age.

The days quickly passed and soon the semester was winding down. On a muggy gray afternoon late in April, Bobbye pitched her first shut-out against the Georgia State Panthers. She'd finally decided to major in Sports Medicine. And while Tripp had still not declared a major, he was paying more attention to his course work, determined to maintain a B average so he could continue to live in an apartment with us.

Tripp wanted to do something special on his birthday, April 27, which fell on a Tuesday that year. But he didn't want to have the kind of party we were known for. And that was good because final exams began the next day. He asked Bobbye to choose the restaurant where he'd treat us to dinner and she suggested a new steak house located a couple miles out of town on Hwy 16, The Rib Room, which was said to have the best steaks in town. That evening, we smoked a couple of joints before we left. Phil insisted on driving the Geo Tracker because he was worried that Tripp might drink too much on his birthday and wreck his new BMW.

The restaurant had red leather booths and brass wall sconces and a man playing a baby grand. As soon as we were seated, Phil ordered a bottle of champagne to toast the birthday boy. The rib eyes were great and, for dessert, we had cheesecake with cherries on top. Tripp's piece came with a lighted birthday candle. I think Bobbye must have arranged that.

We left The Rib Room about ten and headed out to Main Line Lounge, a couple miles further out Hwy 16. There was no band on a Tuesday night, but a DJ was working the sound board. We smoked several joints and drank several beers while we danced to U2, Pearl Jam, and Def Leppard. It was a quiet night, and we had the dance floor to ourselves most of the time. A little while later, we went back to our table where Tripp pulled a plastic bag out of his pants pocket and poured a couple of little red pills into his palm. He held them out to us but neither Bobbye nor I took one. "What are they?" I asked.

"They're heaven," Tripp answered. "You've never had anything like 'em." He popped one in his mouth and tried to get Phil to take the other one, but Phil refused. "No way, man," he said. "I've got a calculus exam in the morning." Tripp told us he didn't have any exams the next day so he was gonna have some fun 'cause it was his birthday.

He gave Phil the finger and went to the bar to get another beer. Then he went over to the DJ and chatted with him for a few minutes. Soon Lionel Ritchie was singing "My Love" and he and Bobbye were back on the dance floor. They smiled at each other swaying together for a few minutes. Then Bobbye's head went up, and she shoved Tripp away. He grabbed her by the arm, jerked her back toward him, and everyone in the place heard him when he told her to *shut the fuck up!* She turned toward the table where Phil and I were sitting, and I could tell by the look in her eyes that this was not the kind of *give and take* confrontation they usually had. I got up, started toward her, and Phil followed.

By then, Tripp was standing in the middle of the dance floor pretending to be a flamenco dancer, stomping his heels, and hollering *ole!* at the top of his lungs. The bouncer showed up and told us to leave and that made Tripp mad. He swung at the guy, who ducked. Phil stepped between the two of them, and with help from Bobbye and me, managed to get Tripp out the door.

Tripp refused to get into the back seat of the Tracker with Bobbye. "Screw you," he said, sneering at her through the window on the driver's side. "Who gives a shit what you think, bitch!" Even from where I was sitting in the front seat, I could see that his pupils were as big as saucers. Phil came around the front of the Tracker and tried to talk to him, but that just made things worse. Soon Tripp was jumping up and down in the parking lot, flapping his arms like a gooney bird, and whirling around in circles chanting, "Wild things! Wild things!"

I got out and climbed into the back seat with Bobbye and Phil went over to Tripp and told him he wanted him to get in the car. Tripp took a step forward, raised his hand, and gave Phil a shove. "I don't give a fuck what you want, dickhead," he mumbled. "Leave me the fuck alone."

Then he slammed his fist into the Tracker's door, pulled it back, and let out a howl. That scared the shit out of me, and I looked at Bobbye and saw she was on the verge of tears. With a sudden jerk, Tripp opened the door on the driver's side. He was laughing, but it wasn't a fun kind of laugh. It was a sinister laugh like a cartoon character makes when he's about to nail somebody. "Get in the car, Sanford," he said to Phil. "And give me the keys. The birthday boy's gonna drive."

Tripp did pretty well as long as we were in the parking lot, but once we pulled onto the highway, he started weaving back and forth across the yellow line. I held onto the edge of my seat and said a little prayer that we'd make it back to the apartment in one piece. I felt better when Tripp slowed down and actually stopped for a stop sign. But when he pulled away, he gunned it and soon the speedometer was registering eighty. On our left, a corn field flew by and I caught a glimpse of little plants about a foot high. Evidently Tripp saw it, too, because he slammed on the brakes and turned around. He pointed the nose of the Tracker directly toward the field, revved the engine, and yelled, "Let the rumpus begin!"

Bobbye and I began screaming but he paid no attention to us... and none to Phil, who kept yelling, "STOP! STOP! STOP!" Tripp tore up and down those rows of new corn like a mad man, crisscrossing back and forth until he'd wrecked the whole field.

He pulled out onto the highway, slammed on the brakes, and burst out laughing. And he was still laughing when we reached the outskirts of town. He turned into a car wash and got out to feed the coin machine. "Roll the windows up tight," he said. He threw back his head and laughed again as he took the wand down from the holder, adjusted the nozzle, and began spraying down the sides of the Tracker.

Phil made no attempt to help him clean the car. I think, at that point, he was just too fed up and afraid of what he might say or do if he got out and confronted Tripp. Finally, Tripp put the wand back in the holder. As he got into the car, he looked over at Phil and said, "Good as new, my friend. Good as new."

* * * * *

Tripp was still asleep the next afternoon when Phil went off to his calculus exam. I had to be at the library by three and was coming down the stairs when the doorbell rang. Bobbye was sitting on the sofa in the living room and got up to answer it. As I came into the room, I saw two men wearing beige uniforms with brown leather gun holsters standing outside our front door. Parked nearby was a big car with the *Clarke County Sheriff's Department* logo on the side. The men identified themselves as sheriff's deputies and asked to see Phil. Bobbye told them that he had gone to take an exam.

One of the men said, "Does he have an orange Geo Tracker?"

When Bobbye nodded, the man said, "We'll wait, if you don't mind."

Bobbye invited the men into the living room and asked if she could get them something to drink, but they declined.

I was headed into the bathroom when Tripp came out of the downstairs bedroom dressed in a t-shirt and gym shorts. He went into the kitchen and opened the door to the refrigerator. One of the uniformed men must have heard him because he stood up, looked across the counter, and said, "Are you Phil Sanford?"

I knew Tripp hadn't seen the men in the living room, and he hesitated for a moment before he responded with, "Huh? What?"

The man went around the counter and said, "Are you Phil Sanford?" Tripp quickly stepped away from him and sputtered, "No. No, I'm not. I'm Tripp MacAvoy."

That's when the other deputy came from the living room and joined them in the kitchen. "He's the one," he said, looking at his partner. "He's the one we saw on the video… the one who was driving the orange Tracker. The guy with blonde hair at the car wash. That's him."

Then the guy looked at Tripp. "Where were you last night?"

Tripp took a carton of orange juice from the refrigerator and stepped over to the cupboard to get a glass. "Went out to dinner," he said, filling his glass. "I was at The Rib Room."

The man nodded. "And after that, what did you do?"

Tripp looked over at Bobbye. "We went dancing at the Main Line Lounge. Ask them. They'll vouch for me. Tell'em, Bobbye."

Bobbye walked toward the kitchen and motioned for me to join her. "He's telling the truth, officer," she said. "We had dinner at the Rib Room and went dancing at the Main Line Lounge."

The man nodded and looked back at Tripp. "Were you driving an orange Geo Tracker?"

Tripp cocked his head and said, "What's this about? Do I need a lawyer?"

"Yes, I'd say you do. We have footage from Wonder Wand Wash & Wax on Hwy 16 that shows you washing an orange Geo Tracker...about 2:15 this morning. Were you there then?"

"What if I was?" Tripp asked. "Just because you have a video of me washing a car doesn't mean I've done anything wrong."

"I'm afraid it does. You see someone in an orange Geo Tracker tore up a farmer's corn field last night. The man who owns that corn field lives just across the road from his field and he woke up because of the ruckus you were making and looked out his window. He saw an orange Tracker leave and pull back out on the road. And we have a video showing *you* getting out of that same orange Tracker at the car wash."

The man's partner reached over and took Tripp by the arm. "Better put on some clothes, son. We're taking you to the sheriff's office."

Tripp tried to pull away, and when he couldn't, he started pleading. "Just give me a second, will you? I'll call my dad and he'll come straighten this out." He slammed the deputy up against the counter and, in two quick strides, sprinted into the bedroom and locked the door.

The deputies went straight to the door and had it open in seconds. I looked in but didn't see Tripp anywhere and figured he'd gone into the closet to hide. One of the men threw back the bunched-up covers on the bed and there he was huddled up in the fetal position crying his fool head off. The deputies slapped a pair of those plastic hand restrainers on and dragged him out the front door wearing nothing but his gym shorts and a t-shirt.

When the Clarke County sheriff called Ed MacAvoy and told him that his son had been arrested and they were going to keep him overnight if someone didn't post his thousand-dollar bail, Ed told them to go right ahead. Let him stew in jail, he told them, it would do him good.

The following Friday morning, Tripp was arraigned in court. Phil had to appear before the judge as well, because the vehicle involved in the crime was his. And his dad had to appear, too, because it was registered in his name. Phil was not charged with anything, but they threw the book at Tripp. He was charged with resisting arrest and willful destruction of property. Ed paid the court costs and a fine of $3,000 to reimburse the farmer for the loss of his crop. Tripp was placed on probation, sentenced to a hundred hours of community service, and had his driver's license revoked for two years.

As soon as the judge dismissed the court, Ed took Tripp home and made him hand over the keys to the new Bimmer, which Ed then parked in the garage. The next morning, he drove Tripp to the Sandy Springs plant and put him to work in the spinning room. But Tripp wasn't there long. In the short time it took us to finish our exams and move back home for the summer, Tripp had skipped town. Phil said his dad told him that he'd heard that Tripp had taken the remainder of the money his mother had left him out of the bank, hitched a ride to Hartsfield, and bought a ticket to Miami. Airline records confirmed this, so Ed hired a P.I. to find his boy. But Tripp must have outfoxed that investigator, because when the man returned to Atlanta several days later to report to Ed, he had nothing to report.

Bobbye was so worried that she went over to the birthday cake house to see Ed and begged him to double his efforts to find Tripp. But Ed refused. He's grown, he'd told her, and he has to find his way in this world. I'm not wasting any more money trying to find him.

On the first Friday evening in June, Bobbye and I met Phil at the convenience store on De Leon Street and the three of us rode out to The Shack to eat chicken and waffles. In between bites, I commented about how much I'd missed The Chicken Shack, especially the waffles. Phil picked up a piece of fried chicken with his fingers, bit a big chunk out of it, and smiled, his lips and teeth shiny with grease.

Bobbye sat across from us, her plate untouched, nervously fingering the ruby and diamond ring. She'd not said one word while we were in the car together and it looked like she might continue to give Phil and me the silent treatment throughout the meal. She finally poured some syrup on her waffle and picked up her fork. Then she got that far away look in her eyes like she did sometimes when she was upset about something.

"You know," she said, turning from us to stare out the window toward the interstate, "Tripp was always talking about going to South America. He was always saying he wanted to climb Machu Picchu and make a trek up the Amazon. Maybe he's not in Miami at all. Maybe he went somewhere else."

She put her fork down and leaned back in her chair. "But I can't believe he'd leave without telling me where he was going," she whispered. She began sniffing and I could tell she was on the verge of tears *again*. "Can you believe he did that? That he left without telling me? Where do you think he is?"

Neither Phil nor I made any attempt to answer her questions because neither of us had any idea if the stories we'd heard about Tripp's disappearance were true. He was as flighty and unpredictable as dandelion fluff and anyone who was brave enough, or *stupid* enough, to try to figure him out was just wasting time.

Part Three

Before mixing, divide the ingredients
into three parts dry and two parts wet.

Cake Baking in the Old South
Alice Lane Mumford, Editor

The summer that followed Tripp's disappearance was incredibly boring. Bobbye worked at her church day care again, Phil had an internship with Georgia Power & Light, and I went back to the kids' camp where I'd worked before. Phil wanted to continue with our old habit of meeting every Friday night for dinner at The Shack, so that June, we did. But early in July he called to tell me he didn't want to do that anymore.

"It sucks, Stacey," he said. "All Bobbye does is bitch about the fact that she hasn't heard from Tripp. I'm sick of hearing her go on and on like a broken record. This weekend I'm going with my parents to my grandad's fish camp in South Carolina. I'm sorry I won't be with *you* at The Shack, Stacey, but I sure won't miss being with Bobbye."

That Friday night, I picked Bobbye up at her house and, after we had a quiet dinner at a sandwich shop, we went to a late showing of "Gorillas in the Mist," which was a big mistake because she began crying the minute the cameras began panning the canopy of a dark green jungle. Just as the actors' names began popping up on the screen, she reached out, grabbed my arm, and sank her nails into my flesh.

"That's where Tripp is," she sniveled. "He's lost in a jungle somewhere and I'm never going to see him again. Please Stacey, don't make me watch this," she begged as her eyes filled. "Please take me home." I dug a tissue out of my pocket and handed it to her, retrieved my drink, and we went home.

The one thing that didn't change for Bobbye was softball. She played in the city league that summer and Phil and I, along with my dad, and Janice and Russell, were there for all the games. Every now and then, Brock Sanford would join us. Bobbye had an arm that wouldn't stop, and all her fans were totally mesmerized watching as she smoked the batters from opposing teams. She'd sorta hunker down on the mound and pause for a second while she gathered strength from the muscles of her long lanky torso up into her powerful right shoulder. Seconds later, she'd let go of the ball, but it was moving so fast you couldn't see it. The only way you knew it had flown was the resounding *thwack* that reverberated through the air when it hit the pocket of the catcher's mitt. Photos of Bobbye appeared regularly in the sports section of *the Constitution* and, if she saw one, she'd brighten up for a while. But that euphoria didn't last. She was so lost without Tripp you could see it in her eyes.

In early August, Phil and I met for dinner one night at Tina's Tacos, a little place out Peachtree Extension. Over gooey enchiladas, he told me that he'd called our landlord in Athens to see if our townhouse apartment was available for fall semester and learned that Tripp had already paid the deposit. He went on to say that if Bobbye and I could pay our two-thirds of the rent, that he would pay not only his third, but also the entire utility bill each month.

"You and Bobbye are good housemates," he said. "Neat and quiet. And I don't want to have to break in someone new. If you'll have me, I'd rather live with you. I know Bobbye is really upset about Tripp being gone, but I think she'll be better off living with the two of us than someone else, don't you?" Genius Phil. What a prince of a guy!

Later that month, Bobbye and I drove down to Athens in my car packed to the gills with all our junk, and found Phil already moved in. He'd taken his stuff upstairs and told us that he thought we'd be much happier in the downstairs bedroom and bath since they were considerably bigger and besides, he liked the idea of having his own TV in the loft area so he could watch games when we wanted to watch something else on the big TV in the living room. He'd filled the fridge, stocked the cupboards, and couldn't wait to show us the new espresso maker he'd just unpacked.

That fall, Bobbye and I returned to our old jobs—she to the Admissions Office and me to the library. Phil, who didn't need a job, spent his extra time keeping the townhouse neat and tidy and making regular runs to the grocery store. Junior year found all of us concentrating on the courses required for our majors—Bobbye in Sports Medicine, Phil picking up more courses from the advanced levels of his engineering requirements, and me working toward a double major in Journalism and Psychology. I was taking a course called, "The Psychology of Deviant Behavior," which opened my eyes to a whole new world. Who could have imagined the kind of damage done to a young child by a parent suffering with *munchausen by proxy*? I'd never even heard of such a thing. And one day following a lively class discussion about *bulimia nervosa*, I realized that I knew several people who were wracked by that awful disease. For the first time in my life, I became aware of the fact that there were just as many mental disorders as there were physical.

I loved that class, but my favorite that fall was, "Up Front and Personal: Mastering the Art of the Interview," taught by Mr. Henninger, who continued to come to class in his scruffy sports jackets and worn-out loafers and regale us with the best reporter stories in the world. Much of the required reading for that course consisted of interviews with well-known people, past and present.

As the days passed, the nights cooled and suddenly the leaves were red and gold. Football dominated conversations with our friends who were sure UGA would have a winning season. Bobbye and I attended only one home game that fall because neither of us could afford to buy a student pass. But we did have a party on Halloween…no costumes, though, for our little group…just hot dogs, funky brownies, and lots of beer. It was as quiet and uneventful as the rest of the fall had been. But the day before Thanksgiving break, Mr. Henninger changed things for me. He began class by reminding us that "Mastering the Art of the Interview" was a six-hour course that covered two semesters and that, during Spring semester, we'd have to interview a well-known Georgia personality and write an article about that person suitable for publication. My stomach turned over as he went on to say that several large newspapers from various cities around the state would be featuring our work.

When I left class, my head was spinning as I tried to think of someone to interview. My first choice was President Carter, but I let that go because I'd read where he'd signed on to help build Habitat houses in Haiti. Then I thought about Coretta Scott King. But who did I know who would introduce me to her? No one. I was working that afternoon and decided that when I got to the library, I'd consult *Who's Who in the State of Georgia.*

* * * * *

Every year on the Sunday before Christmas, Phil's parents hosted a holiday open house. And while we were home over Thanksgiving break, he'd called to make sure Bobbye and I had received our invitation. Neither Bobbye nor I had ever missed one of those parties, but we always fretted about what to wear.

That particular Sunday dawned cool and gray, and at four o'clock when I picked Bobbye up, it was raining. Phil and his parents lived in a mid-century modern that sprawled across a ridge on the western edge of Druid Hills. The exterior was covered in beautiful cedar shakes which made it look more like a lodge than a house. At Christmas, the wooden railings across the porch were entwined with heavy garlands of fresh greenery and the wreath that hung on the big front door was the size of a tractor tire. Phil answered our knock and told us to meet him back in the den.

We made our way through the crowded living room where Phil's mom, Phyllis, was at the piano playing for a group of carolers having lots of fun with "Let it Snow." Dozens of other guests sat on twin sofas and in elegant chairs near the fire. Up near the windows, a stately spruce was decorated with hundreds of dazzling ornaments and brilliant lights.

The den was even more crowded than the living room with all manner of happy folks enjoying drinks from the bar. After Bobbye and I lifted flutes of champagne from a tray, I picked up a plate, and we started down the buffet table heaping it with yummy stuff. I pointed to a couple of empty chairs on the far side of the room, and we wended our way toward them. Phil appeared, a bottle of Brut in one hand and a Bud in the other. He didn't bother looking for a chair, just sat down on the floor between ours. "I'm taking a break from door duty," he said, as he grabbed a deviled egg from off our plate and stuffed it in his mouth. "Somebody else can do that for a while. I'd rather sit here with you guys."

In between bites, the three of us engaged in a bit of conversation about what we'd been doing since we got home from Athens (buying presents, wrapping presents, putting up a tree, etc.) and when and how we'd get together after we'd done our duty with the family stuff on December 25th. Phil wanted to have a party for our old Atlanta friends who were home for the holidays. We set the date for New Year's Eve and I told Phil I'd ask my dad if we could have it at my house.

About that time, the steady hum of lively chatter that had been buzzing throughout the room all but ceased and I wondered why. My curiosity got the best of me and I looked down at Phil and said, "I think I'll get some more deviled eggs." I stood up, plate in hand, and turned back toward the buffet. That's when I saw several people start moving toward the door we'd come in. I looked that way and saw Ed MacAvoy just as he crossed the threshold. Seeing him at the party didn't surprise me, because he'd always come. But I wondered why so many people in the den had begun walking toward him. Lark Loflin came in behind him wearing an emerald-green sheath that hugged every curve and set off the mass of golden hair around she shoulders. I forgot all about the deviled eggs I'd wanted, and like almost everyone else, made a beeline across the room to say hello. Ed took my hand, smiled, and asked about my dad. Then he cupped his palm under Lark's forearm, drew her forward, and began introducing us.

But Lark interrupted him, saying she and I had been friends since we met in band class at Grady High. She acted as if she was genuinely happy to see me and wanted to know all about life at the University, what I was majoring in, and if I was still playing the clarinet.

I stood there like a fool with my mouth hanging open, beaming and beaming, because I felt so special being singled out by Lark Loflin in a room full of movers and shakers. Finally, I had the sense to ask if I might get some champagne for her and Ed, and the three of us walked together back toward the bar. I excused myself, left them at the bar, and returned to the corner where Bobbye and Phil were waiting.

"Well, well," Phil said. "Ain't that a kick in the head? Old Ed has got himself a new girl...and what a *girl* she is. God, did I have a crush on Lark Loflin when we were in ninth grade! I lived for the days when she came to class to demonstrate all the different instruments she played."

I sat there remembering how I'd lived for those days, too. How I'd fallen in love with Miss Loflin the first day she'd stood in front of us and talked about the fun we were going to have making music together. It was heaven seeing her again.

Phil brought me back to the present. "How old do you think Miss Loflin is now, Stacey?" "She looks great!" I blurted. "Like you said, she hasn't changed a bit. I think she's in her late twenties. She might be thirty, but she was pretty young when she moved here to take that job with the symphony. Right out of grad school, I think."

Phil smirked. "Wonder what she's doing with Ed MacAvoy? He's got to be fifty-four, maybe fifty-five... same age as my dad."

I didn't care if Ed MacAvoy was a hundred. He'd brought Lark Loflin to the party and that was all that mattered to me. I settled into my chair and, out of the corner of my eye, glanced over at the two of them. They were surrounded by people asking them about their plans for the holidays, Ed's business, and Lark's music. All of which they tolerated for about ten minutes before they finally broke away and headed back toward the living room.

I excused myself and followed them into the living room where the three of us joined the caroling group at the piano for a rousing rendition of "Winter Wonderland." As I stood just behind Lark lending my alto to her clear crisp soprano, I was thrilled to hear our voices blending as if we'd been singing together all our lives. Phil's mom kept the song going an extra chorus and when she brought it to an end, everyone cheered. As she rose from the piano bench, she smiled at us and said, "What a talented group! Thank you for making this party so much fun! Won't you join me for a glass of bubbly?" She gave Ed and me a hug before she shook hands with Lark and left the room.

Then Ed turned to me and said, "Have you heard from my son?"

"No, Mr. Ed. I haven't. And I'm pretty sure Bobbye hasn't either. Sorry."

Ed nodded and cleared his throat. "Please give your dad my best regards. I hope the two of you have a Merry Christmas."

I thanked him and told him I was happy to see him looking so good. "Handsome as ever," I gushed before I turned to Lark. "Would you mind if I gave you a call next week?"

"I'd be delighted," she answered, smiling. "Maybe we could go for coffee or something."

"Sounds good. It's been wonderful seeing you, Miss Loflin. Have a good holiday."

I waited until the two of them had walked out the front door before I let out a sigh of relief. Since the day I'd gotten home, I'd been wracking my brain trying to come up with the right subject for my journalism assignment. Seeing Lark had been like a bolt out of the blue, but I'd known the moment I saw her that she was the perfect Georgia personality for my interview. "Yes!" I said out loud as I hurried back to the den to tell Bobbye and Phil.

* * * * *

That year, my dad and I carried on with our usual tradition of spending Christmas Day in Clayton with my Grandmother Roper. I loved Granny Edith, loved going to the house where my mom had grown up, loved sleeping in her old room. Granny Edith was a great cook. At Christmas, she always prepared a platter of thin-sliced country ham so sweet it would make your teeth hurt and surrounded those wafer-thin pink slices with her latest batch of pickled peaches. Granny was not a drinker, but she made the best bourbon pecan pie in Georgia and, after we had our pie and coffee, the three of us gathered by the Christmas Tree in the living room to open gifts.

I gave Granny Edith the same thing every year—a box of Fleur de Lis Dusting Powder. It was her favorite and, regardless of what else she'd been given, she always made me feel as if that box of sweet-smelling powder was the most wonderful present she'd ever gotten. I may not have had a mother, but I had the *best* grandmother in the world.

While my dad cleaned up the table and washed the dishes, Granny and I sat in the living room looking through old family photo albums and my mom's high school yearbooks. Granny would tell me all about the awards my mom had won and how she had been Valedictorian of her class of thirty-six graduates at Clayton High School. Then we'd look at my parents' wedding pictures and I'd tear up at the sight of my beautiful mother smiling up at my dad.

Later that night, I retreated to my mom's bedroom where I found her bed covered in the same flowery bedspread she'd had as a girl, one that smelled of laundry soap and her stale perfume. I snuggled down into her pillows and pretended that she and I were in bed together whispering about girl things and giggling like girls do when they think no one can hear. Lying there staring out the window at a cold blue moon, I told my mom about Lark—about how pretty she was and how nice she was. I couldn't get Lark out of my mind and, every time I found myself alone, my thoughts would turn to her. I was so excited about seeing her again that I couldn't wait to get home to give her a call.

But that year, Christmas Day fell on a Friday and my dad decided that, since he had the next two days off, we needed to spend some time with his side of the family in Macon. As soon as we got home from Granny Edith's, he dumped our dirty clothes in the hamper and rushed out to fill the car with gas. That afternoon, we headed south to visit our Parks kin.

On Monday morning after my dad left for work, I took out a legal pad and began making notes about what I was going to ask Lark when I interviewed her. I wanted terribly to call her that day but made myself wait until Tuesday morning. During our conversation, she suggested we meet the next day for coffee at Java Joint.

I was pretty nervous as I drove to the café. I'd not told Lark that I had a reason for asking to see her, and I was afraid she'd turn me down when she found out what I wanted. When I arrived, she was waiting just inside the front door and greeted me with her dazzling smile and a warm hello. After we picked up our orders at the counter, we found a table near a window and sat down across from one another. For the next twenty minutes or so, we talked about the Sanford Christmas party and Ed MacAvoy. Lark told me that he'd taken her out to dinner together a couple of times, and that the Atlanta grapevine was abuzz with rumors of his dating a widow from church as well as a recently divorced CPA who had worked for his ailing dad, Jim. Then she changed the subject rather abruptly and began talking about the trip she'd made to Savannah to spend Christmas with her grandmother.

"That's enough about me," she said, poking the last of a cranberry muffin in her mouth. "I want to know more about *you*, Stacey."

I told her that I had an assignment for my journalism class, that I had to interview a well-known Georgia personality and write an article about that person from the information I'd gleaned. She laughed when she heard that. "Me?" she asked. "Why would you want to interview me? My life certainly isn't interesting."

"Oh, but it is," I said, pausing to take a sip of hot chocolate. "You've inspired so many young musicians, Miss Loflin. You certainly inspired me. I don't think you realize the influence you have in this city. Everyone who knows anything about music, about the stage, about education admires and appreciates you."

She leaned back from the table. "You'd better tell me more, honey. Is this interview and article you're supposed to write very important? What I mean is, will it carry a lot of weight for your overall course grade?"

"Yes, I'm sure it will. You see, our professor, Mr. Henninger, and a small panel of judges, will decide which of the articles submitted have the most appeal for the general reading public. And those that are selected will be published in area newspapers. I don't know a whole lot about you, Miss Loflin," I went on, "but I know you've had an interesting career with the symphony. When you went to college, did you think you'd be playing with a symphony? Why did you decide to major in music?"

Lark shook her head. "I had no idea when I went off to school my first year that I'd ever play with a symphony. I hadn't thought about majoring in music either, because I wanted to major in drama. I'd been in several plays in high school and loved that whole scene. You know, dressing up and pretending to be someone else. But during spring semester of my freshman year, I was asked to fill in at the last minute for a flautist who'd become ill, and I ended up playing with a trio for a wedding. And that summer, I started playing with them for all kinds of events and I really enjoyed it. So, when I went back to school the next fall, I signed up for a course in music theory. In the spring, I took one in composition. My playing was pretty good because I'd had an excellent teacher, but I knew my education was lacking when it came to the more complex fundamentals."

I nodded and jumped in to ask, "Did your parents play? Were they musical?" Lark's bright face suddenly changed, and I knew I'd hit a nerve.

"Oh, no," I said. "I didn't mean to upset you."

"That's all right, Stacey." Lark shook her head. "There's no need to apologize. I simply wasn't expecting a question about my parents." She looked down and began twisting the ends of her napkin. "My dad was killed in an accident when I was five years old," she whispered. "He was a helicopter pilot and he'd just gotten home from a tour in Vietnam. It was right before Christmas and he hadn't been home more than a week when he went out to the base to see some of his old buddies. And he and another pilot walked out onto the tarmac. They were standing several yards away from a bird that was warming up."

Lark paused to look up at me. "One of the blades flew off that helicopter and decapitated my dad."

She looked back down, and I was afraid she might not go on. After a moment, her nostrils flared as she drew a long breath. "The next summer, my mom drowned in a lake. My grandmother raised me, and it was she who had the awful burden of telling me that my mom had drowned. The truth is, Stacey, my mom committed suicide. No one ever said it, but I knew."

She looked back at me then, her eyes wet with tears. "I hope you won't include any of what I've just told you in your article, Stacey. I've never told anyone but my closest friends about my parents and I'd rather not have to talk about it again. The fall after my mom died, I went to live with my grandmother, Rosemarie, in Savannah. That's where I started school at Margaret Cochran Elementary. My grandmother raised me and taught me to play the piano, oboe, and flute. I'd really appreciate it we could start there. Okay?"

I nodded. "I understand because my mom was killed in a car wreck when I was six and my dad raised me. So, I know a little about what you've been through. I just spent several days with some aunts and uncles and both my grandmothers. My memories of my mom's death are hazy… sort of like a dream. But when I'm with my relatives, I sometimes think about how hard my mom's death must have been for them. Your poor grandmother. What she must have had to deal with. Not to mention the suffering she endured. Plus, knowing she could never convey that suffering to you."

As I said these words, I noticed a change in Lark's countenance. Her features softened and she allowed herself a thin smile before she spoke again. "Yes, you may be right. And my grandmother, who had been widowed by that time, probably suffered more because my mom was an only child."

She downed the last of her coffee and asked if we could meet again the following day. "I'm so sorry to rush off," she apologized, "but I have a symphony rehearsal at one o'clock and need to get down to the coliseum. We're doing a big benefit concert on Dr. King's birthday for the Center for Non-Violent Social Change. I haven't had my flute out since before Christmas, so I really must get home and run a few scales and loosen up my lip before that rehearsal."

She picked up her purse and turned to me. "Might we meet right here again tomorrow at ten? Would that work for you?"

"That's perfect. And I promise I won't mention anything in the article about your parents. If it's okay with you, I'll start my interview with questions about your early years at Margaret Cochran Elementary."

I walked Lark down the street to her car. After opening the door, she turned around and gave me a hug. "I'm honored, Stacey," she said, smiling. "And so humbled by the fact that you've asked me to be the subject of your project."

I stepped away. "No, I'm the one who's honored, Miss Loflin. And I can't wait to get back to campus next week so I can tell Mr. Henninger all about you."

* * * * *

The first week back at UGA, it snowed off and on for three straight days. It didn't amount to much, just enough to make a slushy mess and keep us home at night when the roads got icy. I didn't mind, because it meant I could concentrate on the readings for my new courses and start drafting the article about Lark. The week before I'd returned to Athens, she and I had spent about ten hours together and I'd found her story wonderfully interesting. But only time, and Mr. Henninger's assessment, would tell. The first draft was due mid-February and the final copy had to be in his office just before Easter break. In the interim, Mr. H and I would be meeting each week to talk about how all of it was coming together...or not.

Thanks to Phil and his new Apple computer, I didn't have to trudge over to the library to work on it. I'd make myself a cup of hot chocolate, settle down at the desk up in the loft, and let the muse take over. About once a week, I turned out a new draft which incorporated Mr. H's latest suggestions. And he and I would work from that version when we met the following week.

Mr. Henninger had said nothing about including photos with our work, but Lark had shared several that I thought readers would enjoy. So, in the last days before my paper was due, I numbered the back of each photo and left a two-inch square space on the right-hand side of three pages of text to indicate their locations within the narrative. After I'd double-checked everything to be sure it was in correct order, I sealed it in a brown envelope. On the day before spring break began, I gave the envelope a kiss and left it propped against Mr. H's office door. This is what I wrote:

On the Wing With Atlanta's Lark Loflin

Anyone who has ever spread a blanket on the grass at Chastain Park and settled down under the stars to spend a Saturday evening with the Atlanta Symphony knows Lark Marie Loflin. She's the lovely blonde woman who's the symphony's first-chair flautist. And while she's usually seated on stage just behind the viola player, more often than not, she's front and center playing one of her sparkling solos. If you've ever heard Lark Loflin play Bach's "Sonata in A Minor," you know what I mean.

One thing you may not know is that prior to playing a concert in Chastain Park, Miss Loflin spends time at New Life Farm and Animal Hospital, a rescue and rehab center for injured animals or those abandoned by their owners. Saturday mornings, you'll find Miss Loflin in the hospital clinic playing soothing refrains for animals recovering from surgery.

Miss Loflin sings first soprano with the Atlanta Choral Society and is a member of the all-female pops group, "Atlanta Attitude." And three days a week she teaches middle and high school students band and orchestra classes in the Atlanta Public Schools. Last summer, when Miss Loflin and her symphony colleagues represented Atlanta in an international concert series performed in the capitals of twelve European countries, she charmed audiences with solos on the flute, the oboe, and the bassoon.

How does a person become an icon in the world of music? How does a person with unusual gifts develop the skills that transform those gifts into show-stopping moments on stage? For Lark Loflin, that adventure began in Savannah, when in first grade at Margaret Cochran Elementary School, she stepped onto the stage alone to play a complex two-handed version of "Twinkle, Twinkle Little Star" on a child-sized marimba. By the time Miss Loflin had finished junior high, she was not only a skilled flautist and pianist, but also conductor of the Sunday School choir at her church, St. Mark's United Methodist.

As the granddaughter of renowned operatic soprano, Rosemarie Fincher of Savannah, Miss Loflin learned at her grandmother's knee. Many readers may remember Rosemarie Fincher performing as guest soloist with the Atlanta Symphony in the 1940s and early 1950s. Miss Loflin told me that some of the happiest moments in her life were spent on the piano bench with her grandmother, who taught her granddaughter to play before she could talk!

While a student at Savannah Central High School, Miss Loflin played flute in the marching band, sang in the glee club, and performed leading roles in productions of "South Pacific," "Annie Get Your Gun," and "Oklahoma!" During her sophomore year, she began taking voice and piano lessons from Dr. Rhal Messinger, Director of the Messinger Conservatory of Music. When I phoned Dr. Messinger and asked him about his former pupil, he told me that the time he spent with her was always uplifting. "Not only was Lark Loflin extremely talented," he'd said, "but she took joy from everything she learned. Lark studied at our conservatory for three years, and every year, she rose to new heights. She just blossomed right before our eyes."

During high school, Miss Loflin was selected to participate in the Georgia All-State Band every year, and senior year, was awarded the coveted John Phillips Sousa Medal of Excellence.

When it came time for college, Lark Loflin chose Wesleyan in Macon, because it meant she would be nearer home and her grandmother, Rosemarie. While there, she excelled not only in music, but in all subjects, and was president of her Freshman class, secretary of The Music Guild for two years running, and a representative on the Student Council. During the summer following her sophomore year, she was selected to perform at the Brevard Music Festival in the Blue Ridge Mountains of North Carolina, where she sang the title role of Mabel in Gilbert &

Sullivan's "Pirates of Penzance." Fall semester of her senior year she traveled to Florence, Italy to study opera with Maestro Pietro Valenti. That spring, she was inducted into the prestigious Beethoven-Bach International Music Society.

In 1984, Miss Loflin was graduated magna cum laude from Wesleyan College with a BFA in Musical Performance. Dean of the School of Music, Jeanette Shackton, commented, "Lark Loflin was one of the most talented students we've ever had at Wesleyan. She has a remarkable aptitude for all things musical and an unusual understanding of the myriad ways music enhances people's lives. And Lark is especially gifted when it comes to mentoring younger musicians. They simply adore her."

At the urging of her grandmother, Lark continued her education at the University of Cincinnati College-Conservatory of Music where she completed in a MFA in Performance and Composition in 1987. Later that year, when I was a member of the Grady High School Marching Band, Miss Loflin and I met for the first time when she came to our class and demonstrated various types of instruments. Every other week, she taught us the fundamentals of composition and told us interesting stories about some of the world's most admired composers and the obstacles they'd had to overcome to succeed.

When I asked Miss Loflin about her future plans, she told me she was in the process of developing a music program for people who suffer from chronic pain. "When I was in high school, my grandmother was in a car accident that put her in traction for months," she said. "And every afternoon when I got home from school, I'd play something comforting for her like Liszt's "Consolation No 3." And as I began to play, the strain began to lift from her face. I think people who are living with pain every moment find succor in the soothing sounds of the violin, the cello, the flute. Studies have shown that as a person relaxes, the number of nerve vibrations in their body is reduced and their level of pain decreases. Several of my symphony colleagues have signed on for this project and dozens of area high school students have also volunteered. Our plan is to bring healing strains of music to patients in Atlanta's hospitals and rehab centers several mornings a week."

On Saturday, May 12, the Atlanta Symphony will present a concert for the benefit of St. Anthony's Hospital, featuring Lark Loflin on flute and violinist, David Duckworth, performing duets from works by Haydn and Bach. Tickets will go on sale at the Civic Center box office beginning May 1. Please come out and support this most worthy cause and enjoy an evening of spectacular music.

* * * * *

That year, Easter break was a drag because it rained every day. Phil, Bobbye, and I had talked about spending a couple of days down at Tybee Island, but the weather jinxed our plans. We tried to make the best of it by going to see a couple of movies together, and one night Janice and Russell had my dad and me, and Phil and his parents, over for dinner. When the three of us met that Friday at The Shack, I suggested we head back to Athens on Saturday morning and Bobbye and Phil agreed.

I'd been nervous all that rainy week wondering how I'd done with my interview project and, as soon as I'd stashed my stuff at the apartment, I went over to Mr. H's office to see if he'd posted grades on his door. But there was nothing there.

When I got back home, Phil and Bobbye were in the kitchen unpacking the bags of food we'd brought from home. "Hey, Stace," Bobbye called. "There was a letter in the mailbox for you. I put it on the dresser in our bedroom."

I almost tripped as I ran to find that letter and could have cried when I saw what Mr. Henninger had written:

Hi Stacey, The panel of judges thought your article about Miss Loflin was one of the very best in the class and I know you'll be pleased to know you got an A. But here's the big news— The Atlanta Journal-Constitution wants to feature it, along with The Savannah Morning News and The Macon Telegraph. Three of the biggest newspapers in the state are going to run your article. Photos, too. Brava! See you next week in class. D. Henninger

"I got an A!" I shouted, starting back to the kitchen. "Hey, you guys," I yelled. "Where are you? I got an A on my article about Lark."

Bobbye came running out of the bathroom and Phil lumbered down the stairs. "Way to go, girl!" he said as he rounded the corner into the living room. "Yeah, congratulations, Stacey," Bobbye chimed in. "Let's celebrate. Maybe we could invite the gang over for a cook-out."

"Great idea," I said, grinning ear to ear. "And I'll buy the chicken and the beer and everything. It will be my treat. Hard to believe, but three more weeks and this semester is over."

Phil, who'd been smiling, suddenly wasn't. He sat down on the sofa with a thump, crossed his arms over his chest, and said, "Well, all I can say is you two have been great house mates. I sort of hate to see it end, but a little over a year from now," he paused to look at me, "if the good Lord's willing and the creek don't rise, we'll be in a fancy restaurant downtown drinking champagne with our parents."

It's hard to believe that twenty-five years have passed since I morphed from a college student into a full-fledged working woman, the hardest transition I'd ever made. But it came with several rewards, not the least of which was graduating with honors from the University of Georgia. When I think back on Graduation Day, May of 1995, the one thing I'll always remember is how my dad yelled when the Chancellor handed me my degree and announced I'd graduated *cum laude*. A resounding *wha-hoo* came from out of nowhere and I stood red faced, wishing I could fall through the floor, while it rang to the rafters. I couldn't see my dad and had no idea where he was, but I heard him loud and clear and so did the other eight thousand people who were there.

I was not the only one in our little group wearing honor cords that morning. Our pixie, Keisha, who was going to law school, also finished *cum laude*. Bobbye, going to graduate school in physical therapy, and Laura, heading to dental school, finished *magna cum laude*. Phil, with a GPA of 4.0, took the ultimate prize finishing *summa cum laude*. Laura grinned from ear to ear as she reminded us that she'd be changing her name from Beam to Dubose in June and we'd soon be getting invitations to her and Jay's wedding. Then we grads, our parents, siblings, grandparents, and several aunts and uncles, went downtown for a champagne lunch at The Acropolis. It was a big day and a joyous one for us and our loved ones.

During the spring before, I'd begged Bobbye to share an apartment with me when we moved back to Atlanta. I'd spent a lot of time checking ads in the paper looking for a one-bedroom furnished and told her that I thought we could get one for about four hundred a month. But she'd said, over and over, she couldn't afford it because she was going back to school and that meant she'd have to live with Janice and Russell. I was disappointed because I knew that, without a roommate to share expenses, I'd have to move back in with my dad.

But the week before graduation, Bobbye surprised me one night when she said she thought she might be able to share an apartment with me after all. "I have more money in my savings account than I realized. Maybe when we go home next week, we can try to find a place that's not too far from campus so I can ride the bus to class every day."

This came as a big surprise as Bobbye never had any extra money *ever*. After she went into our bedroom to study for final exams, I whispered to Phil to follow me out to the back deck. "What gives?" I asked. "How come, all of a sudden, she has money?"

He gave me a knowing look. "Maybe she earned it."

"No way," I shot back. "She makes $2.75 an hour. She couldn't have saved up enough to rent an apartment."

A tentative smile crept across Phil's face. "I didn't say she earned it working in the Admissions Office."

I reached out and clamped down on his forearm. "You better tell me what you know, Phil Sanford."

"I'll be back in a second," he whispered, heading for the door.

He came back with a magazine, handed it to me, and said, "Page 46."

I looked down at the cover, and beneath the name **POINTS,** saw a strawberry blonde seductively posed on a heart-shaped bed wearing nothing but a smile. "Oh, my God," I screeched. "Bobbye would never do something like this."

But when I turned to page 46, there she was. Her smallish, but well-rounded breasts, were completely exposed. And her lips, slightly parted, looked pouty and inviting thanks to a heavy coating of blood red lipstick. She had a come-hither look that was in serious contrast to the red and white softball cap perched playfully on the back of her head. But it was her legs that drew the eye. Climbing from wicked stiletto heels, her muscular calves were crisscrossed in leather strips that wound like vines up to her knees. From there, her long shapely thighs came together in an inverted V, the apex of which was covered in a tiny triangle of red fabric.

I closed the magazine with a loud smack. "I don't believe it!"

Phil took the magazine from me. "Sometimes, you're a bit naïve, Stacey," he said, putting his hand on my shoulder. "And you always want to believe the best about people. Especially people you love. And there is no one on earth you love more than Bobbye Revels. A mutual friend—and you don't need to know who—told me they paid her a thousand dollars. A thousand dollars, Stacey. Just think about that. She'll need several hundred dollars to pay tuition for summer session at Georgia Tech. Plus, she'll have to buy books and stuff. So, that's a couple hundred more. She'll have about five hundred left for rent when the two of you get an apartment. Now, promise you'll never, ever reveal that know what she did so she could share an apartment with you in Atlanta. Promise."

"Oh, all right. I promise. But I don't understand why she'd do something so *stupid*. And what happens if Tripp sees it? He'll have her head!"

Phil opened the door. "That's not your problem, Stacey," he whispered. "Now go on in the bedroom and try to act like nothing's happened. Because it hasn't."

I started toward the door but turned to look back at Phil. "You act as if this is nothing...like you're really cool with it."

"Cool…? I'm not being cool. I don't like it any more than you do. But you gotta admit she's really hot. Bobbye's a rock star!"

When I think about that now, I try to keep in mind how young we were. In retrospect, I have to admit that, even in those years, Bobbye was more complex than I'd realized. And while I had trouble accepting the fact that she'd sold herself to a trashy magazine, I was overjoyed that the two of us would be living together.

* * * * *

The first Monday following graduation, I picked Bobbye up and we drove over to Myrtle Street. I'd seen an ad for a one bedroom furnished there, and since I was starting my new job at *the Constitution* that Wednesday morning, I was hoping Bobbye and I could find a place.

We located the house without any problem. It was a two-story turn-of-the-century thing with double wrap-around porches, upstairs and down, shaded by big leafy trees…and only two houses away from a corner with a MARTA stop where Bobbye could catch a bus to Georgia Tech. Summer session began the following Monday and she'd made a formal written appeal to the Admissions Office asking permission to take three courses instead of the usual two, which meant she'd attend three classes every day for the next six weeks. To meet the requirements for a licensed physical therapist within a single year, she'd have to maintain that kind of workload throughout.

A small birdlike woman with frizzy hair answered my knock and I told her we were interested in renting her apartment. She led us around to the back of the house and up a set of stairs. When we reached the upstairs porch, she said, "I'm Mrs. Ferguson. Who might you be?"

We told her our names and I said I was going to work for *the Constitution* and Bobbye would be in grad school at Georgia Tech. She nodded and turned to unlock an old-fashioned door that opened into a wide hallway.

"This is the living area," she said, gesturing to the left. We followed her into a large square room I suspected had been the biggest bedroom in the house many years before. It had a large Victorian style mantle on the front end with tall windows on either side. A green shag rug outlined the sitting area where an old sofa, two chairs, and a badly used coffee table were grouped. Off to one side was a rickety stand that held a small TV. On the opposite wall, the one nearest the hallway, was what Mrs. Ferguson called *the kitchen*. A small refrigerator sat on one end. Next to it was the stove. Then a two-foot span of yellow countertop held a microwave and an old-fashioned sink with a skirt. A maple table and two chairs sat between this simple, but functional, layout and the living area.

Mrs. Ferguson took us back into the hallway where she opened another door to show us the bathroom, which was roomy and had one of those little square showers where you have to turn around a lot to rinse all the soap off.

From there, we went into the bedroom with its double bed and blue tufted bedspread, matching curtains at tall windows, and a big dresser with lots of drawers. Mrs. Ferguson opened two doors on the far wall to reveal a set of shallow closets.

As we started out of the room, she said, "I suppose you saw the school over there on the corner. It's a Christian academy of some sort and the only time I'm aware of it is when all the cars come in the mornings to drop kids off, and in the afternoons, when they pick them up again. You might hear an occasional bell ringing. There's one in the morning when school starts, and one in the afternoon when it ends, and for some reason, one rings at noon. They're set on a timer, so you'll hear them ringing on Saturdays and Sundays, too. The school's never been a problem for me, but I want to be sure you all know it's there. What do you think about the apartment? Does it suit you?"

After I paid the deposit, Mrs. Ferguson handed me the key and I took Bobbye home to start packing. Then I went to my house, called Phil, and told him our address. His new condo was about two miles from our apartment, and he told me that he'd moved into it the day before.

* * * * *

On Wednesday morning, I left the apartment about nine and sped north to meet with my new boss, Gary Shuler, the Assistant City Editor at *The Atlanta Journal-Constitution*. He was waiting for me in the lobby of an imposing building in Dunwoody that was the company's official headquarters. I'd heard that Gary was a hard-nosed newsman, but I found him warm and approachable. He took me up to the newsroom where a long row of big clocks lined the wall, each displaying different time zones around the world. The newsroom was a noisy place filled with steel-framed desks, telephones, computers, and busy people.

Gary led me through a maze of clacking machines to the back wall where he pointed to a small desk and said, "This is yours, Stacey." On one corner of the desk was an old-fashioned cradle phone with lots of buttons. A cream-colored PC with an over-sized screen took up most of the remaining space. I told Gary I couldn't wait to sit down at that desk and get started.

"Oh, you won't be here much," he said. "You'll be out in the field most of the time. You know that's what general reporters do. They're out and about looking for stories, but you can work from home, too. And we'll give you a hundred-dollar stipend each month for related expenses." He paused for a moment to give me a chance to digest that information. Then he showed me into his office where we sat down opposite each other in front of his desk. After he took me through my job description and watched me sign my contract, he stood up rather abruptly, put out his hand, and said, "Welcome aboard! Nothing like a pretty girl to brighten up things around here. Now, get out there and do your stuff. Right before you got here, I got a call about a wreck out on I-85 south…a tractor-trailer with a load of flammable liquids is stuck in the median with its tail sticking out across two lanes of traffic. We'll need an update on that for the afternoon edition… so get on out there and see what you can find out."

I spent the next two hours on the tarmac in miserable heat talking to the police chief, a sheriff's deputy, and a half dozen firemen on the scene. But it was worth it because one of them introduced me to the driver of the truck and I asked him how he got his rig into such a jam. The story I wrote made the front page of the local section that day and I knew I was off and running!

* * * * *

On the first Friday in June, Phil picked Bobbye and me up and we headed east to Columbia, South Carolina to see Laura Beam become Mrs. Jay Dubose. The rehearsal was that evening at six and, since all of us were in the wedding, we needed to get settled in our rooms at the Marriott and get our wedding stuff in order. I'd never been a bridesmaid before, and neither had Bobbye, and we wanted to be sure we had everything just right.

The rehearsal went well, no major screw-ups, and the dinner dance that followed in a ballroom at the Marriott

165

was lots of fun. The band was good and so were the drinks. But the party broke up early because Laura's mom had insisted that the band play for only three hours, from nine to midnight, because she wanted all of us to get our beauty sleep. So, all the bridesmaids and groomsmen ended up in our room where we partied for a couple more hours. I admit that when I walked down the aisle the next day, I felt pretty damn awful.

We had to be at the church dressed in our wedding finery an hour and a half before the service began because the photographer wanted to take some pictures that didn't include the bride and groom. He lined us up in front of the altar according to height, which meant Meredith Reynolds and Bobbye were beside each other in the center of six bridesmaids while I was way down on the end. When the photographer said he'd finished with us, Bobbye went up the aisle to the back of the church and I walked over to Meredith.

"You look very pretty," I began. The organza gowns we were wearing were the color of lime sherbet and, while it washed me out, it was perfect for her. "That color is just wonderful on you, Meredith," I went on, "with your hair and eyes. I'm sorry I haven't seen you for so long. How're you doing?"

She turned toward me, disdain plain on her face, and said, "I'm fine."

"Are you working?" I asked, giving her a friendly smile. "We never see you."

Her eyes went from sparkling hazel to muddy gray. "And you're not going to see me as long as you and Bobbye Revels are friends. Do you have any idea how much I hated having to stand beside her just now... stand there with a stupid shit-eating grin on my face like I was enjoying it?"

I could hardly believe what I'd heard. An image of Bobbye, down on her knees in that restroom stall struggling to remove Meredith's blood-stained running shoes flashed through my mind. "Why, Meredith? Why would you say that? You and Bobbye used to be close."

Meredith took a moment to look toward the back of the church where Bobbye was standing with some other bridesmaids. "Yeah," she began, "but that was before I really knew her… before I knew how she lies…before I realized what a sleazy bitch…"

I lost my cool. "Don't, Meredith. Bobbye's not a sleazy bitch. And she's not a liar!"

"Oh, God, Stacey," she muttered, her mouth drooping at the corners. "Sometimes I feel sorry for you. For somebody who's really smart, you can be really dumb. When you're with Bobbye, she's on her best behavior. But when you're not…" Then she stopped talking and her face, which had been bunched up in anger, softened. "I'm sorry to have to say this, Stacey, but I don't think you'd know the *real* Bobbye Revels if she fell on you like a ton of bricks."

She paused to dab at the pool of perspiration that had collected on her top lip and, when she spoke again, her voice took on a singsong quality like she was reciting a Bible verse. "Remember when Tripp gave Bobbye that ruby and diamond ring…the one she thinks is an engagement ring? And she told you I helped him pick it out. You believed her, didn't you?"

I pictured the day in the cafeteria when I'd stood beside Bobbye at the salad bar, and she'd told me that Meredith had helped Tripp pick out the ring he'd given her. "Yes," I said. "I remember."

"Well, let me set you straight. I didn't help Tripp pick out that ring. That ring belonged to his grandmother, Patricia. And after he'd stolen it from her locked jewelry box, he tried to give it to *me*. But I turned him down, so he gave it to Bobbye. What she told you about that ring, and my part in it, was a complete fabrication."

Meredith leaned in, her face inches from mine. "She made it up, Stacey," she whispered. "I hope you'll find another friend."

I watched as tall, willowy, beautiful Meredith Reynolds walked sadly away, my head buzzing with what she'd just said. Phil sauntered over then and asked if I was okay.

I gave him a quick smile and said, "I'm okay. How're you doing?"

"Hot as hell," he complained, running his index finger inside the tight collar of the stiff white shirt he was wearing. "Let's go down to the basement and see if we can find a Coke machine. I could use something really cold that's loaded with caffeine. God, my head hurts."

* * * * *

That was the summer that Atlanta hosted the Olympics and on July 27, a bomb went off in Centennial Park killing one person and injuring 111 others...and all hell broke loose in the newsroom. For the next week, I did nothing during the day but interview survivors. My nights were spent composing articles, working with the photographer who'd been assigned to the job, and talking with Gary and the staff in lay-out. By mid-August, I was back on a regular schedule which meant I didn't stop working until after seven. When I got home, Bobbye was usually at the kitchen table studying. I'd kick my shoes off, lie down on the sofa and, in a few minutes, be sound asleep. She'd wake me an hour later and hand me the sandwich or salad she'd made for me earlier and I'd force myself to eat. I was so tired all the time that nothing mattered much, not even food. I'd lost five pounds since we'd left Athens.

Early in October, my boss called and asked me to meet him for lunch at a well-known watering hole in Dunwoody.

Gary was waiting in a booth when I arrived, a cigarette between his fingers, and told me he'd ordered a glass of tea for me. As soon as I settled in across from him, he raised his martini glass and said, "Congratulations, Stacey."

He paused to munch on the olives from his drink. "Your work on the Olympics was first-rate and from now on, I'm putting you in charge of reporting on special events for the paper. You know—meetings and awards banquets—that kind of thing. You'll need to get a weekly pocket calendar so you'll always know when the city council and the county commissioners are meeting. And you'll need to attend press briefings at police headquarters and the various fire departments. Your new job comes with a twenty-five dollar raise. Again, congratulations!"

I sat there across from him as if I hadn't understood a word he'd said. When a waitress appeared, he started laughing. "You'd better order now, Stacey," he said. "You've got a lot of work to do and so do I. The Salisbury steak is good."

I ordered the steak and took a moment to squeeze the juice from a lemon wedge into my tea. "I'm so surprised, Gary. I wasn't expecting anything like this. I thought you wanted to see me about that fire the other night in Marietta. I thought you'd be upset with me because I didn't get there in time to talk with the fire chief."

"No, no," Gary shot back. "Nothing like that. The brass is interested in you because of your writing. The articles you wrote about the Centennial Park bombing and the people you interviewed were excellent and the editorial staff thinks you have the stuff to become an editor. But first, you have to pay your dues, and this new job is the place to start."

He put his hand in his jacket pocket, brought out a black leather case, and set it on the table between us. "I've had this little tape recorder for years. It's old, but it works. I want you to use it to interview people at the meetings and events you're covering. People like superintendents, CEOs, the governor. And the police chief. All the mucky-mucks. You'll need to get some new cassette tapes and you can pick them up anywhere they sell electronics. Oh, I almost forgot. I left a pager on your desk because I'll want to touch base with you wherever you are. It's in a little cardboard box beside your phone."

The waitress brought our food and Gary stubbed out his smoke. The Salisbury steak was some of the best I'd ever had, and I thanked him for recommending it. As we finished up, he said, "I've got one last thing before we go. The Southeastern Textile Manufacturers' Association is holding their annual meeting at the Peachtree Marriott the weekend of October 12-14. I want you to be at their banquet on Saturday night so you can interview every CEO who'll talk to you…and if one seems hesitant, just thank him and walk away. This NAFTA thing is a damn mess, and everybody's afraid they're going to be forced to re-locate off-shore or close down. Regardless of the huge money those guys make, I wouldn't want to be in their shoes. But hey, Stacey, you don't need to know what I think. You go find out what *they* think."

I waved good-bye to Gary as he drove out of the parking lot and sat in my car for a couple of minutes trying to calm my racing heart. I was excited and scared at the same time and couldn't wait to get home to tell Bobbye about my new job. After work, she and I were leaving for Tybee Island to spend the weekend at a motel on the beach. What a beautiful place to celebrate.

I hurried off to a meeting at the Civic Center and, when I left there a couple hours later, I made a detour on my way to the apartment so I could tell my dad about my new job assignment and remind him that Bobbye and I were leaving for the beach. I found his car parked in the driveway, which was unusual, as he always put it in the garage. I went in through the back door to find him standing with his back to me at the kitchen counter. On the table was a box of brown sugar, the flour cannister, a carton of butter, and a half dozen eggs. "I see you're making the death cake," I said. "Who is it this time?"

"Oh, honey, I guess you haven't heard, have you?" he said, turning around. "Brock Sanford came by my office about three to tell me that Patricia Cogdill is dead. She went down to Tybee to stay at their beach house for a couple of days and, on her way back home this morning, blew a tire and went off the road straight into a tree."

My hand flew to my mouth and I made a little noise like a rabbit caught in a trap. My dad shook his head. "I'm so sorry, honey" he went on. "They rushed her to the hospital, but she had such serious injuries to her chest they couldn't save her. I thought we'd go over to Ed's tonight and take the cake and see if there's anything else we can do. I don't know anything about the funeral arrangements, and I doubt anyone has had time to think about that yet. But it looks like you and Bobbye will have to postpone your trip to the beach."

So, that night Bobbye and I went to the birthday cake house to be with Ed. On Saturday, we went to Patricia's funeral at The Sign of the Shepherd Episcopal Church and, afterward, back to the MacAvoy's to help Classie with lunch. I thought about Tripp several times, and while she didn't say anything, I knew Bobbye was thinking about him, too.

* * * * *

On October 14, I was late getting to the Peachtree Marriott for the banquet where I was supposed to interview the CEOs of textile companies. I ran to catch an elevator that took me up to the Conference Wing and ran down the hallway until I finally found a restroom. When I jerked the door open, I was surprised to see Lark Loflin standing in front of me.

"Oh, my goodness," she exclaimed. "I'm so happy to see you, Stacey." I told her that I really wanted to talk with her but had to pee first. "I'll wait for you out in the hall," she said, as I hurried into the nearest stall.

When I emerged from the rest room, I found Lark sitting on an upholstered bench in front of a big window. "I know you're working for *the Constitution*. How's that going?" she began.

"Right now, I feel like a rabbit in hunting season," I laughed. "Run, run, run! But I recently got a promotion and I'm now the person who reports on special events like this textile conference. Forgive me, but why are you here?"

"Ed invited me for the cocktail hour and banquet where they'll give out awards and pat each other on the back. He told me that most of the CEOs' wives would be here and asked me to come with him. He's going to get an award tonight, but he doesn't know."

"But you do. That sounds pretty serious. Are the two of you making plans?"

Lark cut her eyes at me. "I wouldn't say that exactly. But we're not seeing anyone else...just each other. You want to come along with me to the banquet room where they've set up the bar? Ed's there waiting for me."

As we started down the hallway, she said, "He's had a pretty rough time of it lately. He loved Patricia and her death was so hard for him happening like it did. I'm sure you know his dad, Jim, died a couple of months ago."

I nodded. "Yes, I saw the story on the front page of the paper. People always liked Jim MacAvoy. His employees respected him and believed in him. Now, everything's on his son's shoulders."

Lark stopped and reached out to take my hand. "Ed sold the Birmingham plant last week... sold it to a group of Japanese who are going to manufacture fabric for athletic shoes. When you see him, please don't mention it. He's so upset about this NAFTA business...so worried about the workers who've lost their jobs because of what he's having to do."

We found Ed standing with a group of men near the back of the ballroom. He gave me a hug and seemed genuinely happy to see me. "I understand you're making great headway with the fourth estate," he joked, pointing to my Press Pass. I wasn't sure how to respond, so I just smiled. "Let's get you girls something," he said, motioning to a nearby waiter with a tray of drinks. Then the three of us sat down at a table and began to talk.

Ed asked me about my work, and we talked about the paper for a few minutes. He wondered if I knew that his dad, Jim, had died and I told him I did and that he had some big shoes to fill. "Don't I know it," he sighed. "And I know I'll never be able to fill them." He took a sip of bourbon. "Any word of my son?"

"No, nothing. Bobbye's been really upset."

Lark touched Ed on his wrist and gave him a smile. "Don't worry about Tripp," she said, her voice like silk. "He'll be fine, and he'll come home when he's ready. Would you mind talking with Stacey for a few minutes? She told me she's doing an article about the effect NAFTA is having on the home front...and the home folks." Lark paused and looked over at me. "And she'd like to know how you, as a CEO, are dealing with it. Do you mind if she asks you a couple of questions?"

Later that night as I was getting ready for bed, I decided to give Phil a call and tell him that Ed had sold the MacAvoy plant in Birmingham. But when I mentioned it, he already knew. "My dad told me yesterday," he said. "He and Ed had lunch together and Ed told him he'd sold that plant for $33 million."

I gulped. "Are you sure? I had no idea textile plants were worth that kind of money." But Phil assured me they were. I told him about being at the conference and the CEOs I'd interviewed, and that none had been more forthcoming, nor as interesting, as Ed MacAvoy.

* * * * *

Late that month, Phil called and invited Bobbye and me to come over to his new place and wet our whistles on the last Saturday in October. "That's when everybody will be celebrating Halloween this year," he'd said. "Can you be here about seven? Remember a guy named Zack Lindley who lived down the hall from us in Mel Dorm? He's working for this bio-med firm downtown and bought a condo in my complex. I asked him to come over, too, because I thought you and Bobbye would enjoy seeing him again."

Zack Lindley was just as cute as ever and I hoped Bobbye might take an interest in him. We ordered a couple of pizzas and sat around eating and drinking for a couple of hours talking about people we'd known at UGA. About nine, we headed to The Pit. I hadn't heard Crazy Dogs in a couple of years, but they were really rockin' that night. A talented group of musicians, they could cover just about anybody and did a great job with Eminem, Snoop Dog, Justin Timberlake, you name it. So, we spent a lot of time on the floor. Bobbye smiled more than usual and seemed to be having a good time dancing with Zack.

About midnight, the band broke into Queen's "Another One Bites the Dust" and the four of us formed a circle in the middle of the floor and morphed into a thoroughly obnoxious bunch of fools. Just as the song came to an end, I looked up to see Meredith Reynolds standing behind Phil. Before I could say hello, she reached out and grabbed Bobbye's wrist.

"Well, look who's here. And who's that?" she sneered, pointing at Zack. "Is that your latest conquest? Did you finally wise up about that fucking ass-hole Tripp MacAvoy? Well, it's a good thing you did 'cause I heard he's engaged to some Portuguese girl down in Rio. Never could trust that bastard Tripp, could you?"

Hamp Walker showed up and began apologizing. "Sorry, Bobbye, she's drunk," he said. "I'm gonna take her home now." He put his arm around Meredith and led her away.

I turned back to Bobbye and watched as she brought her fists up. She bounded away, jumped on Meredith's back, and began pummeling her on the side of the head. "Fucking jealous bitch," she wailed, throwing a punch that caught Meredith just above her left eye, "always making up shit about Tripp."

Phil grabbed Bobbye and pulled her off Meredith. He cupped her chin in his palm, forcing her to look at him. "Stop it," he said, as if he were speaking to an errant child. "Stop it, Bobbye. Meredith's leaving now and so are we."

After Zack and I followed them out to the car, I got in the back because Phil put Bobbye up front with him. He kept patting her on the arm, saying things like, *Don't pay any attention to Meredith. She's just jealous. It'll be okay, sweetheart.*

Bobbye started sniffing. "I hate Meredith Reynolds. I hate her!" she hissed, while snot collected under her nose. "She says things that aren't true." And I couldn't help thinking that, even from thousands of miles away, Tripp MacAvoy, had way too much influence.

* * * * *

That year, Janice and Russell invited my dad and me for Thanksgiving, so I made my Grandmother Edith's Bourbon Pecan Pie, and my dad cooked a casserole of corn bread dressing. When he, and Bobbye and I, arrived at their house at two o'clock, Janice was in the dining room filling glasses with tea. She gave each of us a hug, put a hot mat on the table for my dad's casserole, and took my pie with her back to the kitchen. "Won't be long before we eat," she said as she went. "There's a post card on the sideboard for you, Bobbye. It doesn't have a return address, but I think it's from Rio."

Bobbye's eyes widened. "Tripp," she whispered. "It must be from Tripp." After she'd spotted the card leaning against a vase of fall flowers, I went into the kitchen to help Janice and deliberately gave Bobbye a good five minutes before I went back into the dining room.

As soon she saw me, she sputtered, "He's okay, he's okay," handing me the card. On the front was a beautiful picture of sunset over the water. On the back Tripp had written: *Bobbye, my love, I spent the last 9 months in Rio cooking in a restaurant on the beach. You wouldn't believe how big the waves are here. I went surfing and got my butt kicked! Hey babe, never forget I love you and miss you very much. OXOX Tripp*

I handed the card back to Bobbye. "He didn't say anything about being engaged. Wonder where Meredith got that idea?"

Bobbye's nose twitched like she smelled something bad. "Meredith is an idiot. Tripp and I are engaged, and she knows it." She pressed the little card to her chest. "Thank God he's okay. If only he'd come home."

Janice came into the dining room bringing the turkey on a platter, and my dad and Russell followed with steaming bowls of veggies. "Run get the butter and butter knife off the kitchen counter," she said to Bobbye. As soon as Bobbye was out of ear shot, she looked at me and asked, "Is Tripp okay?"

I nodded. "Thank God. Now if she can just get through Christmas without another melt down. Why would Meredith Reynolds say such things to Bobbye?"

* * * * *

The following Sunday, Phil called and asked me to meet him for lunch on Monday at the drug store on Highland Avenue. When I walked in, he was sitting at the counter, and told me he'd already ordered for us. After our sandwiches and drinks arrived, we chatted about the upcoming Atlanta Christmas parade and our plans for the holidays.

After a waitress collected Phil's empty plate, he took a moment to dab at his mouth with a napkin before he said, "I have something to tell you, Stacey." Then he lowered his voice to a whisper. "Actually, I have something to *show* you, but we need to go out to my car."

I ate the last bite of my sandwich, washing it down with the last of my Coke. "You look awfully serious, Phil Sanford," I commented, climbing off my stool. He held the door open for me on our way out and we walked down to where his new Toyota 4Runner was parked on a side street. He unlocked it, took out a bag, and handed to me.

I slid my fingers down inside and drew out the Christmas edition of **POINTS** Magazine. On the cover, Bobbye stood in front of a holly-draped mantle holding an elegant package just above the gaping top of a red stocking. Her back was to the camera and she was gazing at the reader from over her right shoulder, her eyes big as if someone had caught her in the act of playing Santa. Down her naked back hung a shimmering strand of pearls, the end of which was buried in the crack of her beautiful pear-shaped ass. From there, her long shapely legs descended with the graceful symmetry of a Greek statue to wicked red stilettos. The caption beneath the photo read: ***Get in the season with Santa's Sexiest Elf.***

"Not again," I murmured, my eyes glued to Bobbye's derriere. "Why?"

Phil took the magazine and put it back in the bag. "For the money," he said. "She needed money for tuition spring semester. The guy who gave me the magazine told me they paid her $2,500 this time because she made the cover."

"But why?" I protested. "Why did she do it *again*?"

My car was parked further down the street and Phil started toward it. "I have to go, Stace," he said, and I hurried to match his long strides while he tried to explain. "You and I have always had pretty much everything we needed, and Tripp is the proverbial privileged white male. But Bobbye is different. My mom was on the board of Georgia Homes for many years. You know... the state agency that oversees the fostering and adoption of orphans. Just before all of us started at UGA together, my mom told me that when Bobbye was a kid in foster care, the agency had an awful time placing her with a family because all she did was cry. And it took months for the adoption agency to convince Janice and Russell Warren that Bobbye could be happy with them. You may not know, but the Warrens fostered Bobbye for over a year before they agreed to adopt her. So, I know it wasn't an easy decision for them—or for her. Your mom died when you were little, Stacey, and while that's pretty awful, just think how you might feel if she'd *abandoned* you instead."

I could not have imagined how I would have felt in such circumstances, so I kept my mouth shut while Phil went on. "God knows what would have happened if she hadn't gotten that softball scholarship," he mused. "That's the only thing she's ever had to call her own. She thought she had Tripp. Now he's gone."

As he opened the door of my car, he said, "Try to put yourself in her shoes, Stacey. She just wants the things you have. And I have. And other people have. And she wants to be loved."

* * * * *

For the first time ever, Bobbye and I got new outfits for the Sanford's holiday open house. I hadn't even thought about buying anything new, but Bobbye insisted, saying we'd be with lots of dressed up people and we needed to dress up, too. I expect she had some money left over from the check she'd gotten from **POINTS** and wanted to spend it. So, off we went to the mall where we searched the sales racks until she found a dress and I found a pants suit.

The day of the party was sunny and cold. When we got to the Sanford's, Phil answered our knock, and I was surprised to see Hamp Walker standing behind him. I'd not seen Hamp since the night Bobbye had attacked Meredith at The Pit. But I stepped right in and gave him a hug. Phil and Bobbye started down the hall together and, as Hamp and I followed, he leaned toward me and whispered, "I see you're still friends with Atlanta's newest porn queen."

That stopped me in my tracks, and I grabbed him by the arm. "What are you talking about?" He carefully removed my hand from around his arm. "Haven't you seen the latest issue of **POINTS** *Magazine*? Your pal Bobbye is on the cover as Santa's sexiest elf." He began snickering as he walked away.

I caught up with him. "That doesn't make her a porn queen, Hamp."

He turned to me, his face as devoid of guile as I knew his heart to be. "You and I have been friends a long time, Stacey. So, let's not split hairs over this. Bobbye Revels' bare ass is glowing like a Christmas ornament on the cover of a slut magazine."

I swallowed my frustration and re-arranged the expression on my face as Hamp and I caught up with Phil and Bobbye outside the entrance to the den. I peeked inside and it looked as if all the guests had gathered in that one room. "What gives?" I asked. "Why is everyone in here?"

Phil pointed toward the far wall where Ed MacAvoy and Lark Loflin were standing. "My dad just announced their engagement," he said, "and people have been making toasts."

As soon as she saw Bobbye and me, Lark excused herself from the group and walked over. "Merry Christmas, darlings," she said, giving both of us a hug. We returned her greeting and when I asked how she was doing, her face lit up. "What do you think?" she asked, thrusting her left hand toward us. A large oval diamond was centered in a gold mounting with two triangular-shaped diamonds mounted on either side of it.

"Oh, my goodness!" Bobbye exclaimed. "How gorgeous! Did Ed pick that out for you?"

Lark giggled. "I think he had it made. He has wonderful taste, doesn't he?"

She shifted her hand so that it was directly in front of me and, as I looked more closely, it was clear that Ed had had the stone from Caroline's old ring re-set for the woman who would be his new wife. I smiled at Lark again, wondering what Tripp would have thought at that moment knowing he'd never get that ring.

Then Lark inserted herself between Bobbye and me and propelled us forward. "Come on over. I know Ed wants to see the two of you. What are your plans for Christmas?"

The three of us started walking toward the group, and when Bobbye went ahead of us to say hello to Ed, Lark asked, "Has she heard from Tripp?"

I nodded. "She got a post card from Rio at Thanksgiving, so he must be okay."

"Good, good. I was hoping he'd write before Christmas. Ed has so many things on his mind and he'll feel better knowing that Tripp's okay. He had to sell the plant in Valdosta last week… to some people from Indonesia. So, now he only has the plant in Sandy Springs keeping him awake nights. He's just so worried about his workers…worried they won't be able to find jobs. He can sell the machines and equipment, the trucks, even the buildings…but what will happen to all those people?"

I nodded. "When I wrote that newspaper article about NAFTA, I talked with several former employees who've decided to move away to try to find new jobs. A lot of people can't afford to move. But this is your engagement party. Let's not talk about the business anymore. Have you and Ed set a date?"

As Lark shook her head, her hair rippled like waves on a golden sea. "I've made a verbal commitment to the people at the music festival in Brevard and I'll be away most of next summer performing up there, so we won't do it any time soon. Did I tell you that Ed and I are going down to Ft. Lauderdale next week? He wants to buy a yacht, and he found one advertised in a magazine that he thinks we might like. It was built in 1963, the year I was born, and it's 144 feet long. He's called and made an appointment for us to see it while we're there."

"Wow," I blurted. "When are you leaving?"

"December 26th. The plant is closed the week after Christmas, so we're staying at a resort in Miami for three days and, hopefully, we'll take that boat out one day. When we get back, I'm taking Ed to Savannah to meet my grandmother, Rosemarie. When I called her last night to tell her Ed had given me a ring, she said she hoped we'd be married in our church there in Savannah. Ed wants to ask a friend of his who's a judge to marry us in the garden behind his house. But my grandmother has been saving her wedding gown for me since the day I was born, and over the years, she's taken it out and shown it to me several times. It has a scooped neckline and a big swishy skirt like they wore back then. She'd be heartbroken if I didn't wear it and even more upset if I weren't married in our church. I think once Ed meets Rosemarie, he'll understand. Besides, the location of the wedding is the bride's choice, isn't it?"

I'd never known Lark Loflin to be haughty, but she'd tossed off that last remark in a way that surprised me. Then she'd turned, given me a big smile, and said, "No matter where we get married, Ed and I hope you and Bobbye will be there."

Part Four

Pay close attention when you are stirring,
creaming, and folding.

How to Bake the Perfect Cake
Ruth Heisman, Editor

My memory of the Christmas holidays that year is a bit of a blur because I had only four days off and they flew. On Christmas Eve, I went with my dad to Clayton to be with Granny Edith, but we didn't have a chance to visit our Parks relatives because I had to return to work. Since she was in grad school, Bobbye had almost three weeks off. She made the most of it, getting a part time job at Rich's so she could buy a new microwave for her parents.

I spent the next winter and spring rushing around the city reporting on various meetings and attending conferences and local political rallies. The highlight of the year occurred when, in May, my dad and I joined Janice and Russell at Alexander Memorial Coliseum on the Georgia Tech campus to cheer Bobbye, who graduated at the top of her class. Less than a week later, she started her new job working a four-day, twelve-hour shift in the Physical Therapy Unit at Piedmont Regional. That summer was hot and miserably wet, but neither of us noticed much because all we did was work. We saw the Braves play a couple of times and continued to meet Phil on Fridays for chicken and waffles at The Shack.

On Sunday evening September 7, 1997, Bobbye and I got gussied up for a party at the birthday cake house to celebrate Lark and Ed MacAvoy's first anniversary. When she called to invite us, Lark had explained that when she and Ed had married a year before, they'd hired a videographer to make a tape of their wedding but had decided to wait until they celebrated their first anniversary to see it.

Because he'd spent the previous weekend attending a seminar on solar electronic circuitry at The Greenbrier in West Virginia, we'd not seen Phil for a while. He offered to pick us up the evening of the party and, after Bobbye and I'd gotten into his car, she told him that we'd missed having our usual date with him on Friday night at The Shack.

As he pulled out of our driveway, he said, "I'm not sure I'll ever be able to eat there again after the meals I had at The Greenbrier. What an awesome place! So, how are you guys doing?" He glanced in the rear-view mirror at Bobbye. "How's your job going?"

"Patient in, patient out," Bobbye chirped.

I laughed at that cryptic description of Bobbye's demanding job. "We're fine," I said. "She's busting her chops, Phil, and I hardly ever see her. I don't leave for work until I hear the 8:25 bell ringing at the school across the street. But she's long gone by then. My job is the usual meetings with the old boys at city hall. Nothing new."

"Yes, there is," Bobbye piped up. "Aren't you going to tell him about the farm?"

Phil glanced at me. "What farm?"

"You don't know?" I asked. "Ed and Lark bought a farm in North Carolina."

As he steered around the corner onto Highland Avenue, he frowned. "Why in the world would Ed MacAvoy buy a *farm?*"

"Because Lark wanted one," Bobbye said, her tone dripping disapproval. "You know she spends every summer up in the mountains performing at that music festival in Brevard."

Phil nodded. "Yeah, yeah. I think I remember something about that."

Bobbye went on. "Well, in the past, she's always stayed in housing provided by the festival. But after she and Ed were married, she couldn't stay there anymore if he was with her—which he was several times. So, they stayed in this old inn downtown, but he wasn't happy. Lark told him they ought to rent something like a condo or an apartment for the whole summer. That way, Ed could be there with her as much as he wanted. So, the next time he went up to see her, they started looking at condos. And one day their realtor mentioned that she'd listed this farm a few miles out of town and they fell in love with it. Evidently, it's a working farm because Lark told Stacey and me that it's forty acres and has a herd of black angus. They hired a manager to take care of it."

As soon as Phil turned into the driveway at the birthday cake house, he pulled off to the right, put the 4Runner in neutral, and turned around to look at Bobbye. "Are you telling me that Ed MacAvoy bought a farm in the mountains of North Carolina so he could spend weekends there with his wife?"

"That's it," Bobbye assured him. "Lark told us she was tired of driving back and forth from Atlanta to Brevard. And Ed was concerned about her making that trip so often. So, buying the farm solved the problem." Phil turned around, put the car in gear, and started up the hill.

"Wait till you see it, Phil," I said. "While you were at The Greenbrier last weekend, Ed invited Bobbye and me up to see Lark perform. Boy, was she something! Brought the house down! And that night we stayed with them at the farm. It's called Balsam Peak Farm and there's mountains all around it and these beautiful meadows everywhere for their cows. And there's an orchard and woods with hiking trails. You're gonna love it."

Phil nodded. "I'll bet my parents will be up there with Ed and Lark before long," he said. "This will be the first time I've seen them since I got home, but I bet my mom is just bustin' to tell me all about the MacAvoys' new place."

Classie answered our knock and took us down the hall and out the back door to the flag-stone terrace where Phyllis Sanford was sitting on a rattan sofa talking with Lark's grandmother, Rosemarie. Brock and my dad were in chairs across from them, and nearby, Bobbye's parents were chatting with Lark and Ed. After we'd given everybody a hug, Bobbye and I settled onto the sofa with Rosemarie and Phyllis and soon we were hearing all about that new farm.

A little later, Ed tapped the side of his glass to get our attention. "One year ago today," he said, his face split by a wide grin, "I married the most wonderful, most beautiful woman in the world. And I cannot tell you how much it meant to us that all of you were there when that happened. Nor how happy we are that you're all here this evening to help us celebrate our first year together." He raised his glass. "To the most amazing woman I've ever known."

Brock jumped in with a quick, "Here! Here!" and we got to our feet as he said, "To Lark and Ed on their first anniversary, with many happy returns." Then Ed stepped over to Rosemarie, took her by the hand, and the two of them led us back into the house and up the hallway to the dining room.

Classie's duck was fabulous and so was dessert. The top layer of Lark and Ed's wedding cake had been carefully preserved in the freezer for a year and, as Classie brought in a tray filled with coffee cups, the anniversary couple rose as one and joined right hands around the handle of the same silver knife they'd used at their wedding reception to cut it. I don't know what Lark, or maybe Classie, had done to preserve that top layer, but whatever it was worked. It was still as yummy and rich as it had been the year before.

After dinner we were invited into the library where Ed took the floor again. "You may not have been aware of it at the time—and I hope you weren't—but I hired someone to make a video of our wedding day. Lark and I've not seen it yet, because we've deliberately waited until all of you could be with us for the premiere."

He turned to the TV system, pushed a button, and the opening script appeared:

The Wedding of Lark Marie Loflin
and James Edward MacAvoy II
September 6, 1996

I'd forgotten what a beautiful day September 6 had been and smiled when I saw myself on screen bathed in a stream of late afternoon sunlight wearing my new blue dress. Bobbye, who'd worn a turquoise watered silk pants suit, was standing beside me. Phil had ridden down to Savannah with the two of us and was in the picture, too.

The wedding had taken place at Lark's home church, St. Mark's United Methodist, in a little chapel attached to the main building. She'd wanted to keep things small and intimate and only a hundred guests had been invited. A few minutes after the three of us were seated, Rosemarie was escorted to her seat looking like a queen in sweeping apricot chiffon.

The organist, accompanied by David Duckworth on violin, brought Lark down the aisle in her grandmother's magnificent lace gown to the strains of Johann Bach's lullaby, "Sheep May Safely Graze." She was a vision of loveliness, as they say, with her gold hair piled high in an elaborate chignon trailing pink satin streamers knotted with pearls. Brock Sanford stood with Ed as best man and Lark's childhood friend, Cameron Alston, was her only attendant.

When we came out of the church, buses were waiting to take us to the Tybee Island Marina to board Ed's new yacht, "Mac the Knife." And when we arrived at the marina, the graceful outline of that huge boat could be seen in the distance because her decks had been strung with tiny clear lights that twinkled like magic against the evening sky. Garlands of smilax and white gardenias were wound around the tops of her rails and wreaths of greenery, tied with white satin bows, hung on either side of the gang plank. As soon as all the guests were aboard, the lines were freed from their moorings, a jazz trio began playing Bobby Darin's hit, "Mac the Knife," and soon we were moving into the big open waters of South Channel.

Heading around the point toward Old Tybee Lighthouse, Phil, Bobbye, and I stood on deck gazing at a blood-red sun that sat like an Early Girl tomato just above the shimmering waters of the Intracoastal Waterway. A waiter appeared with flutes of champagne and, after we'd helped ourselves, we went inside where the party was in full swing aboard the most incredible boat one could imagine. Phil told Bobbye and me that his dad said that Ed's "hotel on the water" had cost more than three million... and that Lark had named it "Mac the Knife" when she'd learned that Ed was known by that nickname because he was such a sharp businessman.

On the main level was a beautifully appointed open space with a large table laid out with all kinds of seafood canapes, prissy little sandwiches, and pyramids of fresh strawberries beneath a silver fountain flowing with chocolate sauce, all of it quite a feast. Above the entrance was a sign that read "The Shark Salon," a hint of things to come.

On the floor above the salon was a covered deck where dozens of chairs and several sofas, upholstered in white duck, sat before of a span of large isinglass windows. Centered above them was a carved wooden sign, "The Bobby Darin Lounge." The jazz trio was playing up near the front, while a dance floor took up half the remaining space. One of the most fun things about the video was seeing people dancing.

There'd been no shrinking violets in the group, and they'd gone to it as soon as Lark and Ed had led things off with a graceful waltz. About an hour into the evening, Lark had picked up a microphone and entertained us with "Someday My Prince Will Come," her eyes focused the entire time on Ed's adoring face.

The camera had followed us as we made our way back down the stairs to join Lark and Ed when they cut their wedding cake, a three-tiered beauty decorated with elegant streamers of pink satin ribbons knotted with pearls. Resting on the top tier was a nosegay of pink rosebuds, a miniature of the larger one Lark had carried down the aisle. The video ended as we consumed the last crumbs of that velvety cake and a lovely Hispanic woman named Rosa passed among us with cups of coffee while her husband, Enrique, came behind her with snifters of brandy.

One of the best things about that evening was having a personal tour of "Mac the Knife." The previous summer, Brock and Phyllis had been out on the boat with Lark and Ed a couple of times, and they took Bobbye and Phil and me down to see the cabins below the main deck. There, two sumptuously decorated staterooms opened opposite each other. The door to the left had a sign that read "Mac the Knife Suite;" the one on the right was called "Mac Heath Suite." Behind them, along each side of a passageway, were four roomy cabins fitted out with twin beds and private baths.

After we left the lower area, Brock and Phyllis led us back up through The Shark Salon and into the galley with its modern appliances and stainless counter tops. From there we went directly to the helm or, as Brock called it, the pilot's house. There we met Josh Ennis, who'd grown up on the Outer Banks of North Carolina and, according to Brock, knew the Intracoastal Waterway from Maine to Florida like the back of his hand.

Things were beginning to wind down and after we returned to the salon, I broke away from the group and made my way around the buffet table to a window to have one last look toward the west where a swath of purple lay just above the molten sea. I stood there for a moment watching as the last evening light disappeared beyond the horizon and thought about Tripp. What would he have done if he'd been with us? Would he have been his dad's best man?

* * * * *

In July of that year, I'd been promoted to a bigger job that including covering events at the State House and Governor's Mansion. I'd had to buy a whole new wardrobe of dressier stuff like long black skirts, silky blouses, and dressy pumps.

Bobbye and I continued to live in our apartment on Myrtle Street because I'd told her my dream was to own a little house with a yard where I could have a dog. And if she'd stick with me for a couple more years, I could afford to buy one and she could have the second bedroom. Bobbye had no resources other than her paycheck. She had to make a car payment each month, plus buy insurance and gas, and had little money to spare, so she stayed.

On October 19, Lark and Ed invited Phil and Bobbye and me over for a light Sunday supper. When we arrived, Lark met us at the front door and said, "Come on in. Everyone's on the terrace out back." We were surprised to find my dad and Bobbye's parents there as none of them had said anything about being invited to the MacAvoys. Lark offered us something to drink, and we took our glasses of wine and sat down on the rattan sofa with Janice and Russell.

A few minutes later, a man I'd never met came out the back door and gave Lark a hug. He shook hands with Ed, and with Brock and Phyllis. Ed introduced him to the rest of us as his attorney and close friend, Haynes Baxter Dobson. I recognized him because I'd seen his picture in the paper where the caption had identified him as Haynes Dobson, but I'd also heard him referred to as Bax. Mr. Dobson had kind gray eyes, and when he came over to say hello to Bobbye and me, he was friendly and seemed interested in what we had to say.

Ed cooked hamburgers on the grill, and we sat around a big table on the terrace enjoying ourselves while the sun went down. Phil helped Lark bring cups and a pot of coffee from the house and Phyllis brought out the trifle she'd made especially for the occasion. I hadn't thought of a light Sunday supper as an occasion, but that's what it turned out to be. After we'd finished our dessert and coffee, Ed stood up and said, "Would you join me in the library? I have a bit of news I want to share."

Dead dark was upon us as we traipsed single file through the kitchen and down the hall to the library. Ed, who went to stand under the mounted elk head above the fireplace, opened with, "I've invited Haynes Dobson here this evening for two reasons. He was not able to come when Lark and I were married because he was in Egypt. He's an amateur archeologist and had signed on for a dig long before Lark and I set the date. So, reason number one is I wanted all of you to meet him. Now, the second reason. Bax has been spending considerable time with me working on a project and we hope all of you will want to be a part of it. With Bax's help," he paused to smile at Mr. Dobson, "I'm completing the necessary paperwork to establish a foundation that will be known as the Lark and Edward MacAvoy Foundation for Young Musicians. Its purpose is to provide talented young musicians from all over the world with the funds they need to attend the college or university of their choice. The initial corpus for the foundation will be just over four million dollars. Lark and I invited you here tonight because we hope you'll help us make this happen."

A murmur went through the group and Phyllis stood up and began clapping. I started to clap, too, but turned to look at Lark and saw that she was smiling through tears. Bobbye, sitting on my left, leaned in and whispered, "Oh, God. Ed's giving away all his money."

Ed smiled and put up his right hand. "Thank you, my friends. In my heart I knew you'd want to be a part of this exciting venture. The beautiful and capable Lark Loflin MacAvoy will serve as chair of the foundation board and we've asked Brock and Phyllis to co-chair the new steering committee for membership. They've kindly agreed to take on that responsibility."

"If you're willing, Bobbye," he continued, "Lark and I invite you to serve on that committee, too. And Stacey, we're in dire need of a good writer with marketing skills. And we want Elliot to help oversee the completion of the necessary documents. When the time comes, Phil, we hope you'll serve on the student selection committee because we'll need a young person, or two, there. Janice and Russell, would you consider serving on the committee to develop the packet of information for prospective recipients and their parents?"

As far as I was concerned, asking Bobbye's parents to become involved in this project was one of the nicest things Ed MacAvoy had ever done. At that moment, I could have kissed him, even though I would have bet that it had been Lark who'd suggested that Bobbye and I, and our parents, be involved. I silently thanked her before I turned to Bobbye and said, "Isn't that great! I know your parents will enjoy helping with the scholarship stuff."

But Bobbye didn't think so. "Why would he ask them when he could have asked any number of well-educated people in this town to help him?" she snipped. "Neither one of them even finished high school. Why would he want them?"

I tried to reassure her. "Ed and Lark understand how hard it was financially for you to finish college and go to grad school. And how much Janice and Russell sacrificed to make that happen. Your parents know first-hand how important scholarships are for some people."

Bobbye sniffed. "You mean *poor* people, don't you? Isn't that what you mean, Stacey?" Her eyes darkened to pinpoints as she laid into me. "If it weren't for scholarships, people like me wouldn't amount to anything. Right?"

"Hush, Bobbye," I whispered. "Somebody's gonna hear you. This isn't the time to discuss the national economy. And regardless of what you think, this is a great idea."

Ed thanked all of us again and reminded us that putting together a foundation would take lots of work and it would be a while before it was up and running, perhaps within the next eighteen months if all went well. He and Lark would keep us posted.

Bobbye waited until the two of us were in my car before she started griping again. "I think Ed MacAvoy has lost his damn mind! Four million dollars! Four million!" she fumed. "I can't even imagine what a half a million dollars looks like, much less four million! You may not realize it, but he's giving away Tripp's inheritance."

She turned from me to look out the window. "When Tripp comes home, there'll be nothing left because Lark Loflin's spending it. She's got old Ed wrapped around her little finger. Three million for a yacht! Four million for a foundation! There's gonna be nothing left because whatever Lark Loflin wants, Lark Loflin gets."

* * * * *

Bobbye went to Janice and Russell's for Thanksgiving that year and my dad and I went to Macon to spend the day with our Parks relatives. It was a cool, blustery morning with low hanging clouds, but we were warm and cozy in my aunt's house where we enjoyed a traditional feast, the usual football games on TV, and arranging our schedules to see each other at Christmas. I got back to the apartment that night to find a message from Phil asking me to meet him for lunch the next day at the drug store.

That Monday, he and I arrived at the drug store at the same time but had to wait a couple of minutes for a booth. I ordered a sandwich and Phil got a burger and, as soon as the waitress left us, he said, "I've got something to show you, but you can't tell Bobbye."

He handed me an envelope that had no return address. "This came yesterday to my mom and dad's. My mom called and I went over and got it. It's from Tripp, but I didn't tell them that. I'm not telling anyone about it but you. Read it."

I pulled a sheet of paper from the dirty envelope and registered the date written at the top: *November 12, 1997.*

Dear Phil, I hope you're doing okay. I'm in trouble so send me a money order for $1700. I've got to get out of this fucking crazy country before they put me in jail. Send it to the address below. Tripp

James Edward MacAvoy III
c/o Western Union
432 Las Alameda Avenue
Manaus, Brazil 69050

I folded the letter and handed it to Phil. "What are you gonna do?"

He was busy with the last bite of his burger, chewing and chewing. Finally, he gulped it down and said, "I went to the

Western Union office yesterday and sent him a money order for seventeen hundred. Blew my whole savings account."

I leaned forward. "And you know that you'll never see that money again."

"Yeah, yeah. I know, Stacey. But I couldn't leave him hanging, could I? He's in trouble."

"Tripp is always in trouble, isn't he? Somehow, he always manages to come out smelling like a rose, doesn't he? Because somebody is always hauling him back from the brink."

I turned from Phil to check the bill the waitress had left and laid a five on the table. "I'll see you later," I said, getting up. "And don't worry. I won't say a word to Bobbye. She's on the brink herself, and this kind of thing might send her over the edge. Then I'd have to answer to Janice and Russell."

* * * * *

Two days before Christmas, on the day people call Christmas Eve *eve*, I awoke to the sound of sleet tapping the windows. I got up, pulled back the curtains, and groaned at the thin blanket of ice that covered our backyard. Oh, lord, I thought, climbing back in bed, there'll be a thousand car accidents on the interstates this morning. I was so relieved that I didn't have to cover them, didn't have to put chains on my tires and take my chances with a bunch of fool drivers wending their way through that treacherous mess. But I remembered that I had a luncheon at noon at The Radisson, so I pulled on my robe, and went into the kitchen.

Bobbye was sitting at the table eating a bowl of oatmeal. I grabbed a mug, poured myself some coffee, and sat down across from her. "You'll take the bus, won't you? You're not planning to drive, I hope."

Bobbye got up and took her dishes to the sink. "No need to mother me, Stace," she said. "I'll be all right."

Heavy footsteps sounded on the stairs. Then we heard a loud knock on the door. "God, I hate for anyone to see me like this," I mumbled, as I trudged across the living room to open it.

A man I didn't recognize stood just beyond the threshold, his damp hair bunched up in a scraggly knot on top of his head. He wore camo shorts that ended at his knees, scuffed boots, and a weather-beaten jacket. A trail of coppery freckles bloomed across the bridge of his nose and faded into honey-hued cheeks.

"Aren't you going to invite me in, Stacey?" he asked. And I fell back against the door and yelled, "Bobbye, Bobbye!"

He stepped into the hallway and Bobbye flung herself into his arms and they stood there clinging to each other while he laughed, and she cried. Finally, I said, "Come on in, you two. It's freezing out here."

Bobbye led Tripp to the kitchen table where she poured the last of the coffee into a mug and handed it to him. Tears streamed down her face, but she never stopped smiling. She took Tripp's hands in hers and said, "I was afraid I'd never see you again. That you'd never come home!"

Tripp smiled back at her. "What about my letters? I sent you three letters from Brazil. Didn't you get them?"

"No, I haven't gotten anything from you for over a year." Bobbye pulled out a chair to sit down across from Tripp, but he moved his own chair away from the table and motioned for her to sit on his lap. "I can't believe it," he said, as she settled against him. "I paid a guy to mail those letters for me. I wonder what happened?"

Bobbye shook her head. "Mail gets lost sometimes," she said, "and I'd much rather have *you* than a letter. We've been so worried about you, Tripp, wondering where you were and how you were doing…and if you were okay. Are you hungry? We have some eggs. Want me to fix some for you?"

Tripp shook his head. "My plane landed about five this morning and I had a sandwich at the airport before I caught the bus to town. But I'd love some more coffee." He handed his empty mug to Bobbye and looked up at me. "Well, Stacey, how's tricks? Are you working in your dream job at the paper? I'm sure you're the editor by now."

"Hardly. I'm just someone working a beat trying to pay the rent. But Bobbye has a great job." I looked over at Bobbye who was standing at the counter filling the coffee maker. "She's doing a fantastic job at Piedmont Hospital in the physical therapy unit. She was just leaving for work right when you got here. You almost missed her!"

Tripp shook his bushy head. "I would have been mad as hell if I had because I've missed her so much. I've missed *all of you* so much."

Bobbye came back and sat on his lap and he gave her a kiss on the cheek and lifted her left hand. "Still wearing my ring, I see," he said. "Well, that little ruby is going to be replaced just as soon as I can get home and get the replacement."

Bobbye beamed down at him. "Oh, Tripp, I've waited and waited all these years for you, and I just knew you'd come home to me."

I made my apologies then, saying I had to get a shower and dress for a luncheon. I left them snuggled together and, on my way to the bathroom, took a detour into the living room where I plugged in the lights of the Christmas tree. Just before I turned on the shower, I heard Bobbye on the phone telling her supervisor that she had a scratchy throat and low-grade fever and wouldn't be coming in.

A half hour later, I put on my warmest coat and went into the kitchen to say good-bye. Bobbye rose from Tripp's lap and followed me to the door. "What time will you be back?" she asked. "Is it okay if I invite Tripp to have supper with us?"

"Sure," I said, loud enough for him to hear. Then I leaned in and whispered, "You're gonna tell him about his dad and Lark...right?"

She stepped back and gave me a pleading look like *Do I have to?* I cocked my head and frowned, and after a couple of seconds, she nodded.

The sound of water dripping from the trees put a smile on my face as I hopped through puddles on the way to my car happy to know it was warming up. I was glad I'd left a little early as I had to be at the hotel by 11:00 to interview the president of the Greater Atlanta Christian Coalition for an article I was writing about the important work done by non-profits at Christmas time. Each year, the Christian Coalition sponsored a holiday luncheon for members of their sister organizations like women's shelters, soup kitchens, and thrift shops throughout the city—a pleasant change from my usual meetings of the old heads. I had a good time that day and came away with more information than I needed for my article.

On my way back home, I picked up a few things so I could fix a nice dinner for Tripp on his first night home. When I got back to the apartment, he and Bobbye were still sitting at the kitchen table, and I wondered if they'd been there all day. I told Tripp that Bobbye and I were going to make dinner, and he looked at his watch, and asked if he'd have time to run home and see his dad before it was ready. Bobbye told him to go on. As he threw on his jacket, he said, "Can I borrow your car? He's probably not home yet, but I'll go see."

"He's there," I said. "I saw him today at The Radisson. He's on the board of the Christian Coalition and we talked at the luncheon. He said he'd given his employees the week off and he was going straight home as soon as the luncheon was over."

I didn't mention that I'd seen Lark, too. That she, and three of her friends from the symphony, had played carols while the guests enjoyed their meal. I wasn't about to say one word to Tripp about Lark Loflin. And neither did Bobbye. She gave Tripp her car keys, walked him to the door, and held onto him for a moment. As soon as she closed the door, I said, "You didn't tell him, did you?"

"Oh, God, Stacey. I couldn't. All he's talked about is how he's going to open a restaurant and he's going over there now to ask Ed to bankroll him. When he told me that, I lost my nerve."

I put my coat down on the back of the sofa and went to the fridge to put the groceries away. "He's gonna be mad as hell when he comes back," I warned as I tossed a head of lettuce into a drawer. "You know that, don't you? And you're gonna have to buck up and admit you were afraid to tell him."

Tripp was back within the hour, red faced and fuming. He didn't bother to knock on the door, just busted in yelling, "He's married! Married to that music teacher…she's wearing a ring with my mom's big-ass diamond in it. Fuck me and the plane I flew in on!" He beat a path across the living room floor to the kitchen, stopping in front of the table. "You knew about this, didn't you?" he shouted. "And you could have told me, but you didn't!" He stood there, blown up like the Michelin man waiting for an answer.

Bobbye was standing on the other side of the table making a salad. "Yes," she whispered, "we knew. We were at their wedding. Your dad is very happy. They both are."

The legs on the old maple table shuddered as Tripp slammed his fist down on it. "Son of a bitch! That lying dog. He told me I could have my mom's ring when I finished school. He knew I was going to give it to you. Now, he's gone and given it to someone I don't even know. And she's living in my mother's house. And sleeping in my mother's bed. Son of a bitch!"

Bobbye went to the fridge, got a beer, and handed it to Tripp. "Just sit down and try to relax," she said. "Dinner's almost ready and Stacey's gone to a lot of trouble for you."

Tripp slumped into a chair where he continued to fuss. "I don't get it," he groused. "Why would he get married? I didn't know he even knew that woman. Wasn't she one of those symphony people who played at my mom's funeral?" He stopped as if he expected Bobbye to respond. When she didn't, he said, "I don't understand why my dad would marry somebody young enough to be his daughter."

I'd had enough and turned from the stove to say, "Because he loves her. That's why. And she loves him. You've been gone a long time, Tripp MacAvoy, and lots of stuff has happened. And nobody had an address for you. So, how were we supposed to let you know?"

He didn't like what I'd said and got up and stomped over to the living room where he plopped down on the sofa and continued to gripe. "I guess ya'll know they're leaving the day after Christmas to visit her grandmother in Savannah. I've been gone three and a half years, and as soon as I get home, he leaves. Some home coming! He asked me if I needed any money and tried to give me some, but I didn't take it. And she came over and handed it to me, and said, 'Merry Christmas, Tripp. I'm sorry we're not going to be here for a while. After we leave Savannah, we'll be cruising to Saint Croix.' Did you all know they were going to Saint Croix?"

Bobbye put the salad in the middle of the table. "Supper's ready," she said. "Come on, honey, and try to calm down. Yes, we knew your dad and Lark were going on a cruise. Before they married, he bought a yacht."

Tripp frowned at Bobbye as if he hadn't understood what she'd said. "A... yacht?" he stammered. "My tight-ass dad bought a goddam yacht? What the fuck?"

I held a plate of hot food in front of him, but he didn't even see it. "I'll be goddammed," he sputtered through clenched teeth. "A yacht? What the fuck will he do next?"

Bobbye begged Tripp to sit down and eat but he ignored her. "He's spending my inheritance, isn't he?" he ventured. "Blowing my Grandad Jim's hard-earned money."

Neither Bobbye nor I responded. Tripp would find out soon enough about what his dad was doing. "Please sit down and eat your dinner," I told him. "Phil's coming over tomorrow, and I know he'll be happy to see you."

* * * * *

Before I made a bed for myself on the sofa, I dragged the phone into the bathroom and called Phil to let him know that Tripp was home and staying with Bobbye and me for the time being. "I just didn't want you to be way-laid when you get here tomorrow," I said. "He looks really good. He's got a great tan and he's beefed up. His shoulders seem heavier or something. Anyway, can you come about three?"

Phil arrived at three on Christmas Eve and made a lot of noise about how good Tripp looked and how he couldn't wait to hear all about Tripp's time in South America, and skillfully kept the conversation going on that topic to avoid the issue of Ed and Lark. I'd made a pitcher of cranberry vodka coolers and the four of us sat around drinking and talking, with Tripp doing most of the talking telling us all about a man named Dutch and what it was like to go up the Amazon through the jungle on an old river barge.

Phil had brought in a shopping bag and, about four o'clock, he opened it and took out three beautifully wrapped packages. "My grandparents are coming today," he said, "and two of my cousins are here from New York, so I've got to leave soon and spend some time with them."

He handed a gift box to Bobbye and one to me. Then he gave the largest one to Tripp. Inside mine, wrapped in white tissue, was a pair of pajamas, soft blue cotton with our bulldog mascot, Uga, embroidered in red and black. Bobbye got the same pjs, but hers were pink.

Tripp removed the top from his box, pushed back a layer of tissue, and said, "Oh, man. That's really nice. Really nice." He lifted out a teal green cashmere sweater and held it up to his chest. Subtle threads of burgundy and gold were interwoven in the design and the colors were just right for him. He seemed a bit overwhelmed for a moment but reached over and grabbed Phil by the neck and hugged him. "I've missed you guys so much," he said, his voice a bit unsteady. "You'll never know how much I've missed you."

He went into the bathroom and we could hear him blowing his nose. Then he came back with a badly wrinkled paper bag. "I'll bet you think I never gave you a thought while I was gone. Well, you'd be wrong. There wasn't a day, not one single day, when I didn't think of *all* of you."

He fished three packages wrapped in brown paper from the bag. "This one's for my girl," he said, handing the smallest to Bobbye. Inside the wrapping was a lovely strand of salt-water pearls. Bobbye shrieked when she saw them and gave Tripp a hug. She held them up at her neck while he gathered the ends and closed the clasp.

He handed me a larger package that contained a beautiful tan leather notebook...the kind you put a legal pad in. And when I saw my name engraved down near the right-hand corner, I was just as surprised, and pleased, as Bobbye had been.

Tripp gave the last package to Phil, who took it with what seemed a bit of reluctance and said, "Man, you shouldn't have." He pulled the paper from around a dark green leather box with a sea turtle engraved on top. Phil looked at Tripp and said, "It's beautiful."

I complimented Tripp on his taste in gifts, but I couldn't help wondering if the money order Phil had sent him had paid for them.

Bobbye crawled under our tree and brought out a big square box and gave it to Phil. "This is from Stacey and me," she said, "and we can't wait to use them!"

She and I had scoured thrift shops for weeks looking for a set of crystal wine glasses we could afford because they were the only things missing from Phil's bar. He reached down inside the box, unwrapped one, and twirled it between his fingers. "Perfect," he exclaimed. "They couldn't be more perfect if I'd chosen them myself."

He retrieved his shopping bag from the floor and carefully placed the box of wine glasses and leather jewelry box down inside it. "I won't see you guys for the next couple of days," he said, getting into his coat. "But if you need me after that, just holler."

Tripp laughed as he grabbed Phil by his arm. "I need you, man! I'm going with Bobbye to Janice and Russell's tomorrow for Christmas. But on Friday I'm moving into the old rec room over my dad's garage. He said I could. But no one's been in it for years and it's filthy. So, I'm gonna clean it up and move my old bedroom furniture out there and Bobbye's gonna help me. Stacey's gotta go with her dad to see her granny in Clayton. So, can you come help me haul the chest of drawers and dresser over from the house?"

Phil nodded. "Let me know if I need to bring anything. I'll see you Friday morning."

Tripp and Phil shook hands. Bobbye gave Phil a hug and I did, too. Tripp stood just inside the door as Phil started down the stairs. "I hope you guys don't have any plans for New Year's Eve," he said. "I'm gonna fix the best feast you've ever had in my new apartment over the garage. Don't forget, Sanford, the four of us have a date on New Year's Eve."

1998 was right around the corner and now that Tripp was home, I couldn't help thinking that the coming year would be vastly different from the last one. I stood on the porch and waved good-bye to Phil as he climbed into his Toyota. Then I went inside and told Bobbye and Tripp that I'd called my dad earlier that day to let him know I'd be spending the night with him. For some reason, I wanted to be with my dad, wanted to hear him tell stories about Christmases when my mom was alive, wanted to open the pretty stocking she'd made for me when I was little—the one he'd secretly fill that night with gifts so I'd have a surprise on Christmas morning.

* * * * *

Our new year didn't start with a bang and we didn't bother watching Dick Clark drop the ball at midnight and no one mentioned going to a party or club. Instead, we had a very quiet New Year's Eve in Tripp's refurbished apartment over the garage. While I'd been in Clayton visiting my Granny Edith, Phil had helped Tripp move stuff from the rooms upstairs in the big house into his new digs over the garage including the sofa, chairs, and coffee table from Caroline and Ed's old TV room, along with the drop-leaf table and chairs, plus the furniture from Tripp's old bedroom. Bobbye and Tripp had picked up a rug in a thrift shop that became the focal point on which the new living area was arranged with the old furniture. As she gave me the tour, Bobbye told me it was she who'd bought and hung a set of burgundy print drapes to define the bedroom area and give it some privacy. All in all, the effect was good and who wouldn't want to live rent-free in that space with its kitchen and bath, not to mention a classic Wurlitzer juke box?

The floor was crowded with boxes I'd assumed were filled with things from the big house. But Phil told me they contained souvenirs from Tripp's time in Central and South America, and that he'd had to grease quite a few palms to get them across the Mexican border. I saw a stuffed armadillo sitting on a stack of boxes back near the bedroom and a huge blue feathered parrot perched atop a lamp shade at the far end of the sofa. When Phil pointed to the massive anaconda that he and Tripp had mounted on brackets above the front windows, I had to cover my mouth to keep from shrieking. That monster, which was at least twenty feet long, was covered with green iridescent scales the size of my hand and brownish spots as big as bicycle tires. The head, at least a foot and a half in length, was shaped like a turkey platter. Because it had been preserved with its mouth open, a double row of curved fangs glistened in the light from the lamps below. When I saw them, a shudder raced through me like a chill and I stepped back and said, "Oh, God..."

Tripp nudged me with his elbow. "Don't be so hard on her, Stacey. She put up a good fight and died a valiant death. And the villagers who killed her chanted her spirit up to animal heaven. I watched when some boys cornered her in a stream off the river and shot her with their poison blow darts. Then they threw ropes around her and hauled her up on shore. It took about an hour for her to die. They did a fine job of removing her skin, keeping the head intact. And they gave her to me, and I had her stuffed in Manaus. Anaconda meat is very tender and sweet. She was big with babies— more than a hundred—and the women fried them in hot hog fat, and we ate them like candy." He looked over at Phil and smiled. "They were quite tasty."

After that I didn't have much of an appetite, but Tripp had prepared a fabulous meal which he served on elegant gold-rimmed plates. I commented about how beautiful the china was and he told us it had belonged to his Grandmother Patricia. "Remember Christmas Eve when you went over to

206

spend the night with your dad?" he asked. I nodded, my mouth full. "Well," he went on, "after you left, my dad called me at the apartment and apologized…and asked me to come over. That's when he told me about my grandmother and how she'd hit a goddam tree and died. Then he gave me a letter she'd written to me, and in the envelope with it was a list of things she wanted me to have…like this china."

Patricia had also left her only grandchild crystal bowls and stemware, a set of sterling flatware, lots of stuff that had belonged to her mother and father, the people who'd built the birthday cake house. "I'm gonna miss her," Tripp said, his voice so quiet we could hardly hear him. "I never dreamed she wouldn't be right here when I got home."

After we finished dinner, Tripp made a pot of coffee and put four liqueur glasses and a bottle of cognac on a small silver tray…something I never dreamed I'd see *him* do. We made ourselves comfortable in the living area and, as he poured cups of coffee for us, he said, "I haven't told Phil and Bobbye much about my time in the Amazon, Stacey, because we decided we'd wait to do that after you got back."

I took a sip of coffee while I tried to summon up a bit of sincerity. "Thanks. I want to hear all about it."

"Well," he began, "the most important thing is I made it home safe and sound thanks to my friends Dutch and Malcolm. I was sick…*really* sick… for a while."

Tripp sat down on the end of the sofa next to Bobbye and put his arm around her. "I'd never made it back if Dutch and Malcolm hadn't taken care of me. The Amazon is a dangerous place and if you get sick, you're fucked. But Dutch and Malcom made sure I got what I needed to get well. Did I tell you how I met them? I was working as a cook in this little café on the river in Manuas, and one day these two dudes showed up…they came right off a river barge they'd been living on for a couple of months. And the older one told me they'd eaten nothing but fried monkey meat for days and were craving paella. I'd just made a big pot of it that morning...which was just a stroke of luck. When they finished eating my paella, the older guy, Dutch, told me if I ever needed a job, he had one. They were leaving in a couple of days to go back up the river, but their cook had run off. So that's how I got a job cooking on a river barge."

He opened a large brown envelope, upended the contents, and hundreds of photos scattered across the coffee table in front of us. "I just want to show you a few things," he said, grabbing several of them. "This is The Yellow Tulip... my home away from home on the Amazon with Dutch and Malcolm. And here's the crew." He handed the pictures to Bobbye who passed them on to Phil, who passed them to me.

I frowned at the picture of The Yellow Tulip, wondering how such a piece of junk could have such an elegant name? The photo of the crew was fascinating though. With faces that looked as if they'd been carved from stone, all eight were small and skinny. The tops of their heads were flat, and some had distinct scars on their arms and legs.

"This is Dutch," Tripp said, holding a photo of an old guy with salt and pepper hair and a scraggly beard. There was something around his neck made of rope with a pendant that looked like the tooth of a big animal.

"And here's Malcolm," Tripp went on, giving Bobbye a smile as he handed the picture to her. Malcolm's skin was even more wrinkled than Dutch's and his eyes were small like a weasel's, and you could tell he hadn't been keen about having his picture taken. Just below his waist, his thick belt held a leather holster where the hilt of a pistol stuck out.

There were lots of pictures of parrots, monkeys and armadillos. And several of deer the size of lambs. And pink dolphins that looked as if they were laughing up at the camera as they hovered in the water off the side of the boat.

One picture was of a group of boys standing over the body of the dead Anaconda.

Tripp took a sip of coffee and said, "I don't know if I've told you all or not, but I'd made plans to join a group of people who were going to Quito, Ecuador. Well, that didn't happen because while I was waiting for them to arrive, I stayed in a boarding house in this town called Tabatinga and somebody stole all my money. Dutch had just paid me, so they got a haul." Tripp went on and on about his money being stolen and I wondered if that was just another lie.

Bobbye coughed bringing me back to the moment and I heard Tripp say, "After my money was stolen, I hitched a ride on a boat going back down the Amazon to the village where Dutch had told me he'd be stopping to pick up some armadillo hides. I was damned lucky that I found him. And he hired me again to cook on The Yellow Tulip for the trip back home to Manaus. The journey home was not nearly as long as the one up-river because we didn't need to make stops at villages along the way. But the day before we got to Manaus, I got this goddam headache you wouldn't believe. Then I started shaking and couldn't stop. Dutch piled blankets on me, but I was freezing.

I looked over at Bobbye and watched as all the color drained from her face. But Tripp didn't notice, he just took a sip from his coffee and went on. "The next morning when we got to the docks in Manaus, Dutch called an ambulance, and they took me to the hospital. The doctors put me in quarantine and said I had a virulent strain of malaria. That was the word the doctor used...virulent. I had a fever of 104 and kept puking all over myself. They gave me some medicine for the infection, and something for the vomiting, plus a sedative, so I slept the rest of the day. When I woke up the next morning, I had an IV in both arms. I slept most of the time for the next three or four days, but whenever I woke up, Dutch was always sitting in the chair beside my bed. My fever finally broke and he helped me sit up and fed me some kind of fish stew. And every day, he got me into a wheelchair and pushed me up and down the hallways to get some air. But I'd get tired, and he'd have to take me back to bed. Most of the time, I was so weak I couldn't even stand up. And I couldn't walk as far as the other side of this room.

Tripp stopped talking for a moment. "I couldn't believe it, but I was in that hospital for ten days. Then Dutch came and got me in his pickup truck and took me to his house where I stayed with him and his wife for a week. While I was there, Malcolm brought us some fresh deer meat and Dutch's wife made a delicious stew. By that time, I had this huge damn appetite and was eating like a pig. Dutch and Malcolm decided that as soon as I was strong enough, I'd go home with Malcolm to Bogota, Columbia.

Tripp paused to stare up at the ceiling like he was trying to remember something. "I think it was the eighth of October when Malcolm and I boarded a launcha—that's a big three-tiered boat—and started back up the Amazon. When we arrived at Tabatinga, we spent the night in the same fucking boardinghouse where my money had been stolen. The next morning, we took a bus into the mountains. It was hotter than fucking hell and raining off and on, and the wheels on the bus got mired in mud and we had to get out and push. But we finally made it to Bogota.

He looked over at Phil and grinned. "You guys would love Bogota! It's 8,000 feet above sea level, one of the highest cities in the world. It's beautiful, man, beautiful! Anyway, I told Malcolm I needed to find a job so I could earn enough money to fly back home. He took me to this neat place called Atlantis Plaza where there are lots of restaurants and big-ass hotels and, just like that—Tripp snapped his fingers—I got a job as a prep cook at the Ines Regency Hotel. All I had to do was make a frittata for the chef and he hired me. The hotel gave me a uniform and toque, plus two meals a day, and a small room I had to share with one of the waiters.

"The food in Bogota is amazing. While I was working as a cook, my buddy Malcolm was gone for a couple of months working as a guard on river boats. He's a scary mother and really in demand because the banditos that live in the jungle and rob the boats know his reputation and stay away from him.

Tripp paused and stumbled around saying things like 'bad-ass dude' to describe what a terror the villagers thought Malcolm was. Finally, he said, "He's like those guys dictators hire to get rid of their enemies—you know, a mercenary.

"Now, where was I? Oh, yeah. I was telling you about what Malcolm did for me. When he got back to Bogota, he took me to buy a plane ticket. But I had only enough to cover the cost of my flight from Bogota to Miami, so Malcom gave me the money to fly stand-by from Miami to Atlanta. I didn't think I'd make it home in time for Christmas."

He ran his arm around Bobbye's waist and gave her a squeeze. "But I did! I made it back to my girl just in time for Santa. And Dutch and Malcom made that happen. I don't know why those old guys took me under their wing. I guess they felt sorry for a dumb-ass gringo like me. They taught me a lot and I'll never forget them."

Tripp glanced at his watch. "Just one minute to go," he announced, pouring each of us a cognac. He got to his feet, raised his glass, and said, "To friends and happy times together in 1998!"

After we'd polished off our cognacs, we came together in a group hug, one that lasted longer than those of the past. It seemed that Tripp was genuinely happy to be home again, to be with his friends, to be living in a nice house with all the amenities his upscale life could provide.

I started back to the bedroom area where I'd left my coat. "I gotta get," I said. "My dad and I are leaving early in the morning to go to Macon to see my aunt and uncle. But before I go, I want to ask you something. Of all the places you went, Tripp, which was your favorite?"

"Gosh, Stace," he began, pressing his index finger into his chin while he considered. "I've been to so many wonderful places and met so many interesting people over the last few years it's hard to say. But I was in Costa Rico for several months before I went to Brazil and, if I had to choose my favorite *place*, it would be the eco lodge where I worked high in the mountains above San Jose. It was magical." He looked over at Bobbye. "I'm taking you there for our honeymoon."

* * * * *

Tripp was not happy working in the spinning room at the plant, but he told us he was trying to learn as much as he could about the various looms and how they converted miles and miles of thread into fabric. The Sandy Springs plant, which specialized in upholstery for automobiles and furniture, had a reputation as one of the best. And while it was obvious that Tripp thought all of it was beneath him, he was up and out before seven every morning, determined to earn enough to support the kind of lifestyle he'd always had in Atlanta. He paid no rent and his dad let him use an old pick-up truck that belonged to MacAvoy Enterprises to drive back and forth to work so he didn't have to make that daily trip in his Bimmer.

I never saw Tripp in his work gear, but Bobbye told me he had to wear a hair net to keep the lint out of his hair and ear plugs because the noise in the spinning room was deafening. She said that Ed had had Tripp sign a one-year provisional contract and that when his year in the spinning room was finished, he'd go to work in the office learning the business side of the operation. I kept hoping that one day he'd pay Phil back, but I was afraid it would never happen.

Bobbye and I met Tripp and Phil every Friday evening at The Shack. Then the four of us went downtown to a movie or to a club to dance. Every now and then, our old friends Laura and Jay Dubose, who'd bought a high-rise condo in mid-town, would join us. Laura was in her last year of dental school at Georgia Tech and Jay was teaching math and coaching tennis at Grady High. Whenever we got together, I always asked them if they'd seen Meredith Reynolds or Hamp Walker, but they hadn't.

Throughout that winter, Tripp begged Bobbye to move in with him, but she'd told him she'd promised to live with me another year so I could save enough money to buy a little house. Tripp laughed when he heard that and told Bobbye I didn't have a prayer of saving that kind of money. But Bobbye kept her promise and stayed with me, at least most of the time. Bobbye also mentioned that Tripp had asked his dad to loan him the money to open a restaurant. But Ed had reminded him that he had a one-year contract at the plant and an obligation to honor it.

Bobbye spent every Saturday night with Tripp in his apartment above the garage. And on Sunday mornings the two of them joined Ed and Lark for breakfast in the big house. Bobbye described Lark's yummy stuffed French toast and told me how she could poach eggs to perfection for her benedict. Bobbye said that Lark and Tripp often cooked together, he at the grill, and she behind the counter doing the prep work for some of the dishes he'd learned to make in Costa Rica and Brazil. Classie had Wednesday afternoons off, and when he got home on those days, Tripp cooked dinner for the four of them.

One thing that did change that winter was the growing relationship between Tripp and Lark. After a couple of months, they began to warm up to each other and he even mentioned to Bobbye and me that he thought Lark was good for his dad.

"He's different when they're together," Tripp admitted. "When he's with her, my dad forgets about whatever's bothering him at the plant and gives her his full attention. And she has lots of good ideas. She tells him things about how to deal with the workers and what to say to them to help them do a better job."

Because of his time in South America, Bobbye thought Tripp had turned a corner. "He's changed," she'd said to me one day. "He's not the selfish boy we used to know. He's more mature now, Stace. And he can even be thoughtful at times." I listened and kept an open mind about her observations, but I wasn't convinced. Bobbye loved Tripp and love is blind.

On the last night in March, temperatures plummeted, and a mix of freezing rain and sleet fell for several hours. The next morning everything was covered in a beautiful, but dangerous, glaze. Just before eight-thirty, I was putting on my coat about to walk out the door when the phone rang. I answered and heard Classie's trembling voice say, "Please, Miss Stacey... please bring Miss Bobbye and come over here. Mr. Ed and Mr. Tripp had a fight and Mr. Tripp run out the front door and left in that old truck and when Mr. Ed run after him, he slipped and fell and he's not moving!"

"Oh, no! Have you called an ambulance, Classie?"

"Yessum. Did that first thing. But I'm here by myself 'cause Miss Lark had a rehearsal this morning for a funeral at that Rougemont church and she ain't here. Can you and Miss Bobbye come over and help me with Mr. Ed? I can't move him."

"Don't try to move him, Classie. Just cover him with blankets and try to keep him warm. Bobbye's already left for work, but I'll be right over."

When I got to the birthday cake house, EMS was just pulling in and I followed them up the driveway. I saw Classie kneeling on the walk, saw that she'd covered Ed with a blanket and put a pillow under his head. Even from a distance, I could see it was soaked with blood.

The EMS crew, a woman and two men, rushed from the ambulance hauling their gear, knelt down beside Ed, and began examining him. Classie got up then, and when she saw me, hurried over and fell in my arms. "Oh, Miss Stacey," she wailed, "what a awful morning."

"Let's not talk about it in front of these people...wait until Bobbye gets here," I cautioned her. "She's on her way."

One of the men who'd been kneeling beside Ed stood up and looked over at me. "Do you live here, miss?"

I left Classie and joined the EMS crew. "I'm just a friend," I said. "Classie called me because Mr. MacAvoy's wife's not here. Maybe I can help you though, so you can get him to a hospital." I remembered that Ed had served on the Board of Visitors at Piedmont Regional and told them to take him there.

As the ambulance went down the right side of the drive, Bobbye's car came up the left. As soon as she got out, I said, "Ed's had a bad accident, cracked his head open. Tripp left the house right before it happened. Please take Classie into the kitchen and make her some coffee or something and try to keep her calm. She tried to tell me what happened between Tripp and Ed—evidently, they had an argument. I told her not to talk about it until the EMS people were gone. I'm going to Rougemont Congregational where Lark is rehearsing and tell her what's happened."

By the time I reached the church, it was after nine and the rehearsal was in full swing, but that didn't stop me from going straight up the aisle to where Lark and three other musicians were seated. She stopped playing the moment she saw me, and I pulled her aside and told her what had happened and, not to worry, I'd pack up her flute and sheet music and take it with me. She ran out of the sanctuary as if her heels were on fire.

When I got back to the house, Bobbye met me at the front door and told me that Classie had started crying when she'd tried to tell her about the fight Ed and Tripp had had, so she'd insisted Classie lie down in the library. We went in to find her stretched out on the big leather sofa. She started to get up when she saw us, but Bobbye put a hand on her shoulder and told her to lie back down. "Just relax, Classie," she said. "Stacey found Miss Lark and she's on her way to the hospital now, so there's nothing any of us can do until we hear from her. We're going to stay here with you until Lark calls to let us know how Mr. Ed is doing."

Classie rested her head on a sofa pillow, let out a deep sigh, and sniffed a couple of times. Bobbye and I sat down across from her and she began telling us what had happened. "I'm sure glad Miss Patricia won't here today to see what went on. She always said Mr. Tripp would come to no good…that he was a spoilt boy. I sure do hate to have to say it, but she could be right. I been working for this family a long time. Come here in 1953 when Miss Caroline and Miss Catherine was eight years old, and I won't but eighteen. But Mr. Rand wanted a cook more than he wanted a baby-sitter. He didn't know it when he hired me, but I started cooking before I started school. I got lucky, got myself a good steady job here and a couple of nice warm rooms with a coffee pot and a little hot plate so I could heat up a can of soup on my day off. Cookin' is a lot of work and I been cookin' here nigh on to fifty years. Anyway, after Mr. Rand died, Mr. Ed give me time off in the summers when he shut the mills and his workers had the week off for the Fourth of July. He'd give me a twenty-dollar bill and drive me to the bus station and buy me a ticket to La Grange so I could go see my brother, Raeford.

She looked at me and smiled. "That was nice. But most of the time I was right here cooking and cleaning. And over the years, I seen some troubling things in this house, and I heard some things maybe I shouldn't. But I never thought it'd come to this. Mr. Tripp always was a active little boy. Rambunctious, always running and jumping. Miss Caroline had such a hard time with her babies. And Mr. Ed, he wanted a boy so bad. And when they finally had Mr. Tripp, it was like the second coming. Nothing was too good for that boy."

I leaned toward the sofa and said, "Tell us about what happened this morning, Classie."

Classie raised up on one elbow. "It really started last night. Mr. Tripp come home from the plant and went up to his apartment. A little while later he come over here to the kitchen all cleaned up and ready to go out." She paused and smiled at Bobbye. "Got hisself cleaned up to go over to see you, I 'spect. Anyway, Miss Lark come in then and they set down together at the table and I poured each of 'em a glass a tea and they set there talking kinda quiet like until Mr. Ed come in through the back door. Then Miss Lark, she jump up and goes over and gives Mr. Ed a kiss and tells him to wash-up 'cause supper's ready. Mr. Ed goes off to wash and Mr. Tripp gets up to leave. But Miss Lark, she say, Don't go just yet, Tripp. Sit down here for a minute and talk with your daddy and me. So, Mr. Tripp set back down and then Mr. Ed come in and set down and I started serving the salad. And Mr. Tripp say he don't want any...that he's going out with friends. And Mr. Ed say he hope Mr. Tripp won't be gone long 'cause they say freezing rain and sleet coming during the night. Mr. Tripp got up and he say, Don't worry about me, old man. I can take care of myself. Don't you know that? Then Mr. Ed say, Well, don't do nothing stupid in that fast car of yours. Looks like Cobb County and places north and west gonna get the worst. Then Mr. Ed tells us he done delayed the first shift until 8:30 and he's 'fraid he might have to delay it again for the sake of the workers that was drivin' in. Then he say to Mr. Tripp, You come on home at a reasonable hour, so I won't have to worry about you, too.

"Mr. Tripp just laugh. He looked down at his daddy and say, When in the world did you ever worry about *me?* All you ever worry about is your business and your employees. Nobody's worried about me since my mother died. He stomped 'cross the room, opened the door and when he left, all but slammed it offen the hinges.

"Things went kinda quiet and I got busy slicing the coconut pie I'd made. As I turned around to put on the coffee, Miss Lark say, You shouldn't talk to him like that, Ed. He's not a child. He's a grown man twenty-six years old. And Mr. Ed said, Humph! I don't care if he is twenty-six. When I think about what I was doing when I was his age it makes me wonder if he'll ever be a man. Then he got up and told me he'd have his pie and coffee at the table in the library. Miss Lark went on upstairs and I brought Mr. Ed his dessert in here."

Bobbye frowned. "But what happened this morning, Classie?"

Classie sat up, straightened the skirt of her uniform, and turned to face us. "Well," she began, "things got worse. Mr. Tripp got up but not as early as his usual time. And he didn't come down for his breakfast 'til 'bout seven-thirty. Miss Lark come through right after that on her way to the garage. And she stopped beside Mr. Tripp's chair and put her hand on his shoulder, and he looked up at her and smiled. You know they been getting along really good lately...Miss Lark and Mr. Tripp. Then she went on outten the door. Mr. Tripp got up and took his plate to the sink and I come on in here to the library to get Mr. Ed's dirty dishes. Mr. Ed musta gone into the kitchen right after I come in here 'cause I heard Mr. Tripp say, You ain't got no idea what that spinning room is like, Ed. You wouldn't believe how them people cheats you. Then I hear Mr. Ed say it weren't none of Mr. Tripp's business, that he oughta keep his mouth shut and do his job. And Mr. Tripp tell his daddy, You're too old for this, you know? You need to get out of the way so I can take over."

Classie pointed toward the end of the sofa, to the table Ed used as a desk when he worked at home. "I was standing over yonder by that table under them windows when I heard Mr. Ed call Mr. Tripp a shave tail boy. You ain't got no experience and no work ethic, he say. You need to show them workers respect. He told Mr. Tripp that the boss man in the spinning room had told him that his son was always findin' ways to get around what he was supposed to be doin' and half the time, he didn't know what he was doin'.

"Then Mr. Tripp start yelling at his daddy saying things like, That's not true! They just tell you that stuff 'cause they don't like me. They laugh and call me rich boy lint head under their breath. They think I don't hear 'em, but I do. Then Mr. Tripp say, They gets away with murder, and you don't do nothin' bout it!

"I could hear what sounded like chair legs scraping 'cross the floor and I reckon Mr. Ed had got up from the table. He was talking real low and I hear him say, Just get on outten here and leave me alone. But I could tell he was really mad 'cause it come from back in his throat sorta like a old bear a growlin.' Then he start yellin', Go to work, boy! Get on outta here!

"And Mr. Tripp fire right back, You gonna make me!

"Mr. Ed musta come after him 'cause I heard somebody running in shoes with soft bottoms. That woulda been Mr. Tripp in his tennis shoes. A moment or two later, I heard somebody running in shoes got hard soles on 'em like them wing tip things Mr. Ed wears. And I put the dishes back down on that table over yonder and run out into the foyer. The front door was open, and I seen Mr. Ed crumpled on the brick walk with his head busted. And Mr. Tripp, he already gone down the driveway in that old truck."

Bobbye frowned. "But why didn't Tripp come back and help his daddy?"

Classie shook her head. "Not sure, Miss Bobbye. I don't think he knew Mr. Ed had fell. I heard him when he started that old truck a few minutes earlier than usual this morning because it was so cold and then he back it down and parked it right outside the front door. By the time I got out to the porch, Mr. Tripp and that truck was down at the bottom of the drive. I don't think he had any idea that his daddy had fell. I didn't give it much thought 'cause I was so worried 'bout Mr. Ed and trying to think of somebody to come over here and help me.

Classie sat on the sofa a moment longer, muttered 'um, 'um, tried to get up, but went back down. "Oh, law, my back," she cried, slumping against the cushions.

Bobbye sprinted over and dropped in front of her, "Are you sure you're all right, Classie?"

Classie gave Bobbye a vigorous nod. "It ain't nothin' but this misery in my back that come on sometime. I'll be fine." Bobbye took Classie by the arm and, as soon as she had her on her feet, Classie said she was going in the kitchen to see about lunch. She left Bobbye and me in the library and a moment later I heard the phone in the kitchen ring. "Yessum, yessum," I heard her say, "they still here." Then she came to the door of the library, looked at me, and said, "Miss Lark want to speak to you."

I went into the kitchen and picked up the phone and Lark proceeded to tell me everything she knew. When he'd fallen, Ed's scalp had been cracked open and required eight stitches. He'd suffered a subdural hematoma—a bleed in his brain. They'd done a CT scan and it looked as if it had already begun clotting because the internal bleeding had stopped. That was a good sign. But Ed would need lots of rest and medical supervision. They'd just admitted him to the hospital, and he was now undergoing another test, an MRI, to determine if there'd been any further damage. When that was over, he'd be taken to a private room.

I asked if there was anything Bobbye, Classie, or I could do. Lark asked me to call Hank Reynolds, manager of the Sandy Springs plant, and tell him what had happened. But he was not to tell anyone else. Then she asked if Tripp knew, and I told her that Classie had told Bobbye and me that Tripp was in the truck and down the driveway before Ed fell. There was a long pause and she said, "I think you'd better ask Mr. Reynolds to call Tripp in and tell him. I wouldn't want Tripp to think we'd deliberately kept anything from him." I asked if she needed for Classie to pack her a bag, and she told me she'd come home later after Ed went to sleep and get some things so she could stay overnight with him.

* * * * *

Ed's recovery was slow. They kept him in the hospital for a week before they sent him to the physical therapy unit on the 3rd floor where Bobbye worked. On his first morning there, she became his therapist and, following that, he would have no other. Perhaps her supervisor had known about their connection.

On the sixteenth of April, Lark brought Ed home. She and Classie had set up the whole bedroom wing on the first floor as a kind of treatment center for him, putting exercise equipment into one of the extra bedrooms and installing a portable whirlpool in the other. They'd moved Lark's clothes and toiletries up to the second floor bedroom suite.

That afternoon, Bobbye, Tripp, and I were there at the big house waiting in the kitchen with Classie when Lark pulled into the back drive. Tripp took off like a light, sprinting across the terrace to help Lark get his dad get out of the car. Over the past few weeks, Tripp had spent most nights in the hospital room with his dad so Lark could go home and get some sleep. Because he worked the 7:30-4:30 shift at the plant, he was usually there in the evenings by five. Bobbye dropped by Ed's room each afternoon before she left the hospital and told me that Tripp had been a Godsend as far as Ed's nurses and doctors were concerned.

Every day, Tripp got Ed out of his hospital bed and held onto him while they walked up and down the halls together. Ed's hands were unsteady, and he couldn't hold onto anything, so Tripp fed him his dinner every night. And once Ed fell asleep, Tripp took a shower and curled up in a recliner beside him. Classie kept a stack of clean clothes for Tripp in Ed's bedside table. This went on the whole time Ed was in the rehab center, too, and by the time Ed arrived home on that warm April day, the relationship between him and his son had improved considerably.

That evening, Classie served some of Ed's favorites for dinner. After dessert, we went into the library where Tripp poured each of us a little brandy. The doctors had told Ed he could not have alcohol in any but the smallest quantity and not more than once a week. He sat in one of the wing chairs near the fireplace, sipped his drink, and told stories about the nurses who'd been good to him and the ones who hadn't. And how he'd gotten to know some of the staff, whom he called *the real people*, who'd emptied his bed pans and scraped up his vomit. He knew them by name and told Lark that, as soon as he was able, he was going back to the hospital and take those people something nice.

Then Ed got quiet and, when his eyelids began to flutter, Tripp helped him out of his chair and supported him as they started on what must have seemed to Ed a long trek to the bedroom. Lark's eyes had followed them out of the room. "Lord only knows what I'd have done without Tripp," she murmured. "I could not have weathered this storm without him. Just having him here at night in this big rambling house is such a comfort to me."

Tripp as a *comfort* was a tough concept for me, but I gave her a reassuring nod just as Bobbye said, "I hate to mention this, but it's gonna be a while before Ed can go back to work, Lark. He's just not very steady, you know."

Lark sighed. "I know. The doctors told him he can go to the plant for a few hours each day starting next week. Tripp and I have decided that he'll take Ed with him in the mornings, and I'll go get him at ten. They were adamant with Ed about his need to take his time and rest, rest, rest for the next few months. You know how impatient he is, so it won't be easy. You two have been wonderful through all of this. I can't thank you enough. And Classie. What a saint!"

I stood up and said something about having to work tomorrow, while Bobbye retrieved our purses. "You'd better go on in there and see if he needs you to do anything for him," I said to Lark before giving her a hug. She clung to me for a moment. Then she stepped away from me and put her arms around Bobbye. "I hope one day soon you'll be a member of this family," she whispered, as tears filled her eyes.

* * * * *

On the Saturday during Memorial Day weekend Bobbye and Tripp, and Phil and I, went to The Varsity for lunch.

Over dessert, Tripp said, "I have a big surprise for you bums. My dad is doing really well now, and he and I think it would be fun to get the whole gang together for a cruise on "Mac the Knife."

He looked over at Bobbye. "So, we decided that since Bobbye's birthday is coming up, we'd leave on the June 18th for a cruise to Bimini and back." Bobbye shrieked and everyone in the restaurant turned to look at us. "Oh, Tripp," she cried, throwing her arms around his neck. "That's so cool!"

Tripp beamed as he said, "We want everybody to come. My dad and I want you to invite Janice and Russell. And Stacey, you bring Elliot. Phil's parents already know because Ed told them yesterday. So, get your work schedules fixed so you can have that Friday off because we're going cruisin'. Don't forget your bathing suits!"

When we arrived at Tybee Island Marina that Friday, it was clear and sunny, and as we made our way up the gang plank a warm breeze was blowing from the south. Lark and Ed, and Phyllis and Brock Sanford, had arrived the day before to make sure all was in order before the rest of us came aboard. Lark greeted Bobbye's parents as if they'd all been friends forever and took them down to the Mac Heath Suite. Then she invited my dad into the first cabin on the right, and Bobbye and Tripp went into the one next to it.

"You and Phil can have separate rooms," she said, smiling at me, "if you want. But that would mean Phyllis and Brock will have to sleep on the sofas up in the lounge." Phil broke in then. "No, no," he said. "Stacey and I will sleep on the sofas up there and we'll use that little head off the galley. Please give my parents the cabin and don't worry about Stacey and me. If we need a bath, we'll go for a swim!"

As the sun went red and disappeared behind a bank of golden clouds, we gathered on the upper deck for drinks.

Frank Sinatra crooned love songs in the background while Ed made a pitcher of margaritas, and another of martinis, and Rosa and Enrique passed among us with trays of savory bites.

About an hour into the festivities, Tripp turned Frank off. He held up a half empty glass and began tapping it with the edge of a spoon. "Ladies and gentlemen," he said, "may I have your attention? I have something to say."

Suddenly, it was so quiet I could hear the soft patter of waves slapping the hull. Tripp took a step toward his dad. "First, I'd like to thank my dad and Lark for inviting us to join them for this special week-end." He raised his glass in Ed and Lark's direction and we joined him.

"And second, I'd like to thank everyone here for all the nice things they did for my dad last spring when he was not well." He raised his glass and drank to all of us.

Then he walked over to Bobbye, who was sitting on the sofa between Phil and me. "And I'd like to especially thank Bobbye Revels for all her hard work and care on behalf of my dad. He simply would not be doing as well as he is now if Bobbye hadn't been so diligent… and so patient with him." We joined him in a toast to Bobbye.

Then he surprised us by getting down on one knee in front of her. When he drew a small box from the pocket of his shorts, Bobbye's mouth dropped. He removed a ring from it and said, "I have loved you all my life, Roberta Ann Revels. Will you marry me?"

Bobbye burst into tears and fell back against the sofa laughing as hard as she was crying. "Yes, yes," she shrieked, grabbing him. "Oh, Tripp," she sobbed, "I thought you'd never ask."

* * * * *

After a quiet Fourth of July at home, Ed went back to work five days a week. His doctors insisted that he work only half a day for the first two weeks, so Tripp took him in the mornings and Lark went to get him at noon. Ed could have hired a driver, but I think he enjoyed his time in the old truck with Tripp. Occasionally on Saturday afternoons, they drove it out to Lake Lanier to do some fishing.

When I was not working, I spent hours with Bobbye and Janice planning the wedding. Bobbye had always wanted to be a June bride and wear a fancy white gown and one of those puffy tulle veils like the models she'd seen in *Bride Magazine*. We spent so much time pouring over wedding magazines and photos of beautiful women in white gowns I thought I'd throw up.

But Bobbye's dream of a June wedding went down the drain when she and Janice met with the rector at their church, Hillcrest Methodist, and were told that all the Saturdays the following June were taken. And so were all of the Saturdays in May except the first one, May 6, which became *the* day. As soon as they'd set the date, Janice began calling friends and family. Her sister, Joyce, who lived in Knoxville, jumped right in to say she, and her daughter, Camilla, would be hosting the bridesmaids' luncheon the Friday before. That put Bobbye in a bind as she knew she had to do her duty and invite "Cousin Cammie" to be a bridesmaid. She and I had known for years that when she married, I'd be her Maid of Honor. The only other friend she'd asked to attend her was our college buddy, Laura Dubose.

For several weeks, Bobbye and I spent Saturday afternoons in the bridal salons of stores like Nordstrom's trying the find just the right gown for Cammie, Laura, and me. Bobbye knew she wanted us to wear either turquoise or aqua, but the problem was the style. Since I was the only person around in that role who was always available, I became the model for all the gowns she thought she might like and, consequently, spent hours changing into, and out of, awful dresses knowing that no matter what Bobbye chose, I'd wear it only once. She finally settled on a clingy thing with a shirred bodice, and I knew the moment the saleslady struggled to zip me into it, I needed to lose ten pounds. Afterward, I dragged Bobbye down to the basement where electronics were sold and bought a Walkman that became my companion five mornings a week while I did laps around our neighborhood.

* * * * *

It was around that time that Tripp told Bobbye the two of them would be living in his garage apartment for a few years while they saved enough money to buy something of their own. But in August when Bobbye saw an ad for a condo in a real estate magazine, she talked me into going with her to see it. I loved it as much as she did and, as we wended our way through its spacious rooms, I couldn't help wondering if Tripp had repaid Phil the money he'd borrowed to get back home. In the upscale kitchen, Bobbye ran the tips of her fingers along the granite countertop and said, "Tripp will love this, and I think Ed will lend us the down payment."

I shrugged. "Why should he? Tripp has a nice apartment that's plenty big for the two of you. Plus, there's the whole upstairs where he and his parents lived for years...with *another* kitchen. I don't think a sharp businessman like Ed MacAvoy is going to be chomping at the bit to lend his son, who's working in the spinning room, thousands of dollars."

Bobbye gave me a hard look. "You'll see," she said. "He and Tripp are really thick now and I think Ed will want to give his son a nice wedding present. And Tripp won't be working in that damn spinning room much longer. Come

January, he'll be moving up to the business office and he's already told me the kind of money he'll be making."

* * * * *

In late July, Lark had returned to North Carolina to sing the female lead in Puccini's, "Tosca," at the music festival in Brevard and she hadn't been home since. But she and Bobbye and I were planning a surprise birthday party for Ed and Phil, whose August birthdays were only two days apart in the last week of August—Phil's on the 26th and Ed's on the 28th. Behind Ed's back, Lark had conspired with his Captain, Josh Ennis, to plan another weekend cruise aboard "Mac the Knife." And she'd hired the baker in Savannah who'd made their wedding cake to make a birthday cake for the occasion.

One Wednesday afternoon in mid-August, Lark called from Brevard to say she'd be coming home that weekend and wondered if Bobbye and I could come over for lunch on Saturday so the three of us could talk about final preparations for the surprise party.

But when I woke up that Saturday morning, I heard Bobbye in the bathroom and got up to see what was going on. I found her down on the floor, her face as white as a sheet, her eyes red-rimmed. "I feel just awful," she mumbled. "That tummy bug that's been going around must have caught up with me. I've been in here all night. Do we have any Imodium?"

I rummaged through the shelves in the medicine cabinet but found nothing that would help. "I have to go over to Inman Middle, and I'll swing by the drug store and get some on my way home. I won't be gone long. Do you think you could eat something?"

Bobbye frowned and I could tell she wasn't sure, so I said, "Why don't I make you some hot tea and dry toast? Now, go back to bed and I'll bring it in to you."

I left the apartment before eight and, as I approached Highland Avenue, I decided I'd run up to the birthday cake house to tell Lark that Bobbye wouldn't be coming for lunch that day. A few minutes later, I turned onto Virginia Circle, went up the driveway, and parked just below the front door. Classie answered my knock and told me Miss Lark was still in her bedroom upstairs and hadn't come down yet. "But she's awake," she said. "I heard her moving around up there. Why don't you go on up, Miss Stacey. And tell her breakfast is almost ready."

I hurried up the curved staircase, taking two steps at a time. Just as I reached the landing, I heard Tripp say, "Don't go. Not yet. He's not even awake. Stay just a few more minutes."

I took a couple of steps and pressed myself against the back of the door that led into the bedroom. It was open just a crack, just enough for me to see them together in the bed that, years before, had belonged to Caroline and Ed. Lark, who was completely naked, was on her knees with her rear end in the air. Tripp, who was lying beneath her, had his hands on her breasts. He kept squeezing them while he begged her to stay.

She sat up and pushed his hands away. "I can't, darling," she whispered. "I need to help him get dressed. You and he are going fishing this morning. Or have you forgotten?"

Tripp laughed. "No, I haven't forgotten, but you can bet he has. He forgets just about everything and sometimes when I'm talking to him, he falls asleep. He just nods off right in the middle of what I'm saying." Tripp threw his arms around Lark, drew her down to him, and said, "Fishing it is! And as soon as that old man and I get back here this afternoon, you and I are going downtown to buy him a birthday present and one for Phil, too. And on our way home, we're going to make a detour into John Howell Park."

Lark giggled. "What if there are musicians playing in that bandstand? We won't be able to hide there, will we? We'll have to come up here and do it lying down instead of standing up."

As Tripp buried his face in her breasts, he murmured, "God, I love you. You're the best thing that ever happened to me."

I watched as Lark put her hands on either side of his head and held it. "I don't know about that," she demurred. And as she bent down to kiss him on the forehead, condensation from my breath morphed into a ghostly little figure on the door frame and I stepped back.

Lark sprang off the side of the bed like a young antelope and, when she turned to blow kisses at Tripp, I felt a rush like the one I'd had when I'd snorted cocaine at the beach years before. She looked so lovely, so innocent, standing there like Botticelli's Venus rising from the shell. I waited until she'd turned toward the bathroom before I slipped across the hall into the old TV room. I stayed behind the door, my heart pounding in my ears, while Tripp came out of Lark's room twirling his underwear on the end of his finger whistling his way to his apartment. As soon as he closed the door, I bounded down the stairs and out the front door.

After I'd stopped by Inman Middle, I started driving up and down the streets of my old neighborhood trying to kill time because I couldn't bear the thought of going home. I could never tell Bobbye what I'd just witnessed, could never tell anyone, not even Phil. Somehow, I had to find a way to deal with the rest of the day, the rest of the month, the rest of the year. Oh, God, I thought, how could Lark have done such a thing? She's married to the nicest, best-looking man in town...and what does she do? She screws his son!

I turned onto the street that led up to John Howell Park, pulled off, and cut the engine. While I sat there for about ten minutes, images of Lark and Tripp doing it in the bandstand clouded my brain. I kept trying to figure out how a woman I'd loved for so many years, a woman who was respected and admired by so many people, could be the same woman I'd just seen in bed with her stepson. It was obvious that their little trysts had been going on for some time and, while the two of them were much closer in age than Lark and Ed were, I couldn't get my head around the fact that the Lark Loflin I knew was the same Lark Loflin I'd heard making plans for another rendezvous.

An hour later, when I finally *made* myself go home, I found Bobbye sitting on the sofa in the living room watching an old cowboy movie on TV. She turned around, looked at me, and asked, "Well, were you able to get it?"

I'm sure my face turned red because I felt heat rising on my cheeks. "What?"

"The Imodium. You said you'd go to the drug store and get some. Didn't you get it?"

I felt a fool as I'd forgotten all about it. "Oh, golly," I sputtered backing toward the door. "There was a wreck on De Leon and the cops were there and they made everybody take a detour and I completely forgot. I'll go back right now and get it for you."

Bobbye stood up. "That accident must have upset you," she said, giving me a puzzled look. "Your face is red. Are you getting sick? You don't have to go back, Stacey. I feel a lot better now."

"No, no," I began. "I don't mind. We should have some anyway. I'll just run to that new store on Lenox Parkway. That's closer." I opened the door, but stuck my head back in. "I'll be back in a little while," I assured her. "You rest."

I was so glad to have an excuse to be away from Bobbye that I took the steps two at a time. But when I reached the landing, my knees buckled, and I had to sit down. I grabbed hold of a post as my head began spinning and a moment later, my heart was racing so hard I couldn't catch my breath. *What am I gonna do... what am I gonna do?* kept running through my brain.

Nothing came to me, so I sat there while sweat gathered along my hair line and ran down inside my collar. A glance at my watch told me it was almost eleven. "Oh, God," I mumbled. Then the door to our apartment opened and I went as rigid as stone. Bobbye called, "Stacey, Stacey... are you still here? Where are you?" And I stood up.

She put a hand to her forehead to shield her eyes from the sun, and said, "Why are you sitting out here? Are you sure you feel like going to the store? You don't look so good."

And suddenly I knew I had my excuse. I started back up the steps and when I reached the porch, Bobbye said, "You're so flushed I'd swear you have a fever."

I nodded. "I have this God-awful headache," I said, as I went inside.

Bobbye nodded. "That's how mine started. Why don't you put on your pjs and go to bed? I'll call Lark and tell her both of us are down with a bug and won't be able to come for lunch. Then I'm going back in the living room and finish watching my movie. I promise to be as quiet as a mouse." As she leaned in to give me a gentle pat on the arm, the sun struck the diamond in her ring all but blinding me and I fled into our bedroom.

* * * * *

On the last Friday morning in August, I got up thirty minutes earlier than usual so I could get in a walk before I had to clean up and dress for a breakfast meeting of the city council. As I made my way downtown, a lump kept forming in my throat and I kept trying to swallow it as I wrestled with the fact that before the day was over, I would be with Lark Loflin again.

By lunch time, dark clouds were rolling in and the weather wizards were warning that a tropical storm was brewing in the Gulf. It would move northeast over the Florida panhandle in the late afternoon and across the southern coast of Georgia during the night. Lark had called Bobbye the day before to be sure we were still coming down to Tybee for the double birthday celebration, and Bobbye had assured her we were. So, at three o'clock that afternoon, Tripp and Phil arrived in Tripp's Bimmer to take Bobbye and me to Tybee.

As we headed south, Bobbye began throwing out little tidbits of news, some of which were ridiculous rumors, to keep Phil from thinking we were doing anything but what we'd told him we'd planned to do—spend his birthday weekend in Savannah. She kept turning around from her seat up front and looking back at me as if to say, *Come on, Stacey, help me out here*. But I had nothing to say. I just wanted it to be over.

Since Phil was his usual quiet self, and I was in a miserable mood, Bobbye and Tripp did most of the talking. Bobbye went on and on about the wedding and how beautiful she thought it would be, with all her attendants in turquoise taffeta and the guys in their black tuxedos. A friend of her mom from church had offered to make the wedding cake and was giving it as a gift. It would be four tiers and have those plastic columns in between and lots of rose buds and baby's breath and be sort of like the bouquets the bridesmaids would carry. After a while, Phil looked over at me and rolled his eyes and the two of us began to giggle.

About thirty minutes out of the city we stopped at a store where Tripp bought a six pack of beer. As soon as he was behind the wheel again, he opened one and started chugging. Then he began to talk. He went on and on about how stupid his dad had been about the NAFTA stuff and, since it began with the old George Bush, his dad had had almost a decade to deal with it and make the changes he needed to, but he hadn't. "Ed could have diversified," Tripp said, between gulps of beer. "He could have converted the plants to new technology and bought some robotic equipment. But no, he was just too goddam stubborn. I overheard Hank Reynolds say that MacAvoy Enterprises has been stuck in the red for the past five years. They think I'm so stupid that I'm gonna stand by with my fucking thumb stuck up my ass while everything goes to shit. I'm telling you right now, when I take over, things are gonna be different." He rolled down the window and slung the empty beer can into the median. Then he told Bobbye to pop the top on another one.

He went on and on about how many times he'd told "Old Ed" he needed to catch up with the times and get rid of some workers. "Those thugs on the loading dock," he said, "are stealing my dad blind. I've told him about it, but he won't listen. They lift at least one roll of fabric from an order every single day and send it to their hidey hole. Then it gets shipped up to their buddy in Detroit and they divide up the money. We're talking thousands of dollars a week."

When we reached the marina on Tybee Island, Tripp pulled into a parking spot not far from "Mac the Knife" and through the car window I could see Ed standing on the upper deck talking with his captain, Josh Ennis.

When I got out of the car, the air felt as thick and heavy as a wet blanket. There was no wind, and the bay was as still as a bathtub. Phil handed me my suitcase and I walked alongside him as we followed Bobbye and Tripp to the dock. As we made our way to the berth where the boat was moored, flocks of seas birds—gulls, pelicans, sandpipers—rose into an ever-darkening sky and headed east.

The four of us went straight down to our quarters and for once, I didn't have to share a cabin or sofas with Phil. I had a cabin all to myself. I took a few minutes to sort out the shoes and outfit I'd planned to wear that evening. On the way to the upper deck, I heard Phyllis and Janice talking. We exchanged hellos and hugs and I told them I'd see them upstairs in The Bobby Darin Lounge when we gathered for drinks.

Phyllis frowned. "We may not, Stacey," she said. "Captain Ennis says there's a big storm coming this way and he may not be able to take the boat out. But I expect you're right about meeting up there because that's where Ed will gather everybody to tell us one way or another."

I went on up to the lounge anyway thinking that Bobbye and Phil would be there, but Bobbye wasn't, and I had no idea where Tripp was. I walked up to the front to the big white sofas and overstuffed chairs near the windows and saw him standing out on the deck talking with his dad. Phil came over, handed me a beer, and said, "They've been out there since Tripp came on board and it ain't pretty. They're arguing about something, but I don't know what. Come over here and sit down and see if you can figure it out."

The two of us went to the sofa nearest the windows and sat down opposite each other. Phil sat with his back to Tripp and Ed, and I sat down on the other end facing him. Every now and then I moved my mouth like I was saying something to Phil while I watched father and son as they sparred like two boxers in a ring.

Ed said, "I've told you before that I can't loan you fifty thousand dollars to open a restaurant. Even if I could, I wouldn't, because you don't know anything about running a business. And my hands are tied anyway." I watched as his shoulders went back and his chest rose as if he were about to lower the boom.

Then he pointed a finger at Tripp and said, "You need to be looking for another job because the one you have in the spinning room won't exist after October first."

Tripp took a step back. "Why?" he asked. "What the hell is going on?"

And Ed said, "On the first of October, all current one-year contracts at the plant will be rendered null and void. The company has the right to cancel them at any time, as you may know, as long as we give personnel involved a thirty-day notice. Hank Reynolds told the other contract workers about this last week, but I decided to tell you myself. We don't have any choice because the Sandy Springs plant has been losing money hand-over-fist for the past five years." He paused and took a deep breath. "You knew I was forced to file for Chapter 11."

Tripp's mouth formed an O and his face went white, and, for a moment, I thought he might pass out. But he roared back with, "What the fuck are you talking about? You had no right to file for anything because that plant doesn't belong to you. That plant is *mine!* Grandad Jim told me that Sandy Springs would be *mine!*"

"Well, it isn't going to be yours, son. It isn't even mine...not now it isn't. I had to file for Chapter 11 back in April when the creditors forced my hand. So, all employees, including you, will have to find another job. All the assets at the plant, the buildings and the land they sit on, plus the equipment and trucks, are in the hands of the bank. And I have no say in what happens. We're at the mercy of the creditors—the vendors and suppliers to whom we owe several million—not to mention The Bank of Sandy Springs. If I were to withdraw fifty thousand dollars they'd be on my ass in a second."

Just then dozens of screeching gulls careened across the dark sky and Ed took a step toward the rail to watch as they swept, as one, out to sea. After a moment, he looked back at Tripp and said, "When your job in the spinning room ends in October, why don't you come down here and stay in the beach house and look for work in Savannah? I think your chances of finding a job might be better here."

Tripp didn't respond. He just stood there as if he'd not heard a word his dad had said. Then Ed resumed an all-business attitude to deliver his coup de grace. "Don't ask me again to loan you fifty thousand dollars. I could give it to you, but they'd make you give it back to the court and I can't take that kind of risk."

Tripp's face flushed as he raised his fist, shaking it at Ed. "You can't take a risk on your own son? What kind of a father are you?" He paused a moment as if he thought his dad might say something, then started up again. "Never mind. You don't have to answer because I already know the answer. You're one hard ass mother-fucker, Ed MacAvoy. Mac the knife is right," he spat. Then he stomped his way down the deck.

I watched as Ed reached for the rail, but his hands never made contact. He staggered toward it, swayed like a wounded deer, and fell. Phil shot out the door, knelt down beside him, and yelled, "Call 911!" I grabbed the phone from the wall and began punching. I didn't know the number of the berth we were in but told the dispatcher that the EMS people wouldn't need it because the man in trouble was on the deck of "Mac the Knife," the biggest boat in the marina, they couldn't miss it.

When I hung up, I heard Lark say, "Don't move him! Get some blankets." And Phil came in and took an afghan off the back of a chair and went out with it. I ran down the stairs to my cabin, grabbed two blankets, and took them back up. When I got to the deck, Lark was on one side of Ed and Bobbye was on the other with her hand on his wrist. She turned, looked at me, and whispered, "His pulse is just racing."

I bent down and tucked a blanket around him. "What does that mean?"

Bobbye turned toward me, mouthed the word *stroke*, and I looked at Lark. While she wasn't crying, her hands were shaking and the fear in her face gave her a look of the aged. Phyllis came to stand behind her while Brock ran down the gang plank to the dock to see if the ambulance was anywhere in sight. Janice and Russell must have been napping because they never showed up. And neither did Tripp.

We heard the siren as the ambulance approached and, fortunately, they were able to back it right down the dock and park beside the boat. By the time they'd arrived, Captain Ennis and a crowd of onlookers had gathered. Bobbye went right over to the woman who appeared to be the head of the EMS crew and talked with her while the other two workers put a still unconscious Ed into the back of the ambulance. One of the men held his hand out to Lark.

She turned to me and said, "Stacey, will you please call my grandmother? You'll find her number in the book on my bedside table." She climbed in beside her husband and the man who'd helped her looked at me and said, "We're taking him straight to the ER at University Medical on Waters Avenue." Brock took Phyllis by the hand and they ran together to their car and followed the ambulance.

As it pulled away, Tripp leaned over the rail on the upper deck and asked, "Did I hear a siren? What's going on?"

Phil took a couple of steps toward him. "Your dad," he said, "your dad collapsed. And Stacey called an ambulance. They've taken him to the hospital in Savannah. Stay up there and we'll come tell you what happened."

Phil turned to Bobbye and me and said, "You guys better come help me. I have a feeling he has no idea the role he may have played in this. And you can bet he's gonna be upset when he finds out."

It took a little longer to get to Savannah than usual because it began raining really hard and the wind kept

238

buffeting the car. When we got to the hospital, we found Lark sitting with Brock and Phyllis in the ER waiting room. She told us that Ed was still unconscious and had been taken to another floor to have a scan. The room was crowded and only a few chairs were available, so Phil and I went out to stand in the hallway. A moment later, Rosemarie Fincher walked in and came straight to us.

"Where is she?" she questioned. "Where's my girl?"

As soon as Lark heard her grandmother's voice she came running into the hall and, after the two of them embraced, she said, "Oh, Mama, we think Ed's had a stroke. He looks just awful." Then she burst into tears.

Rosemarie led Lark back to her chair and Brock vacated his so Rosemarie could sit down beside her. I couldn't hear what Rosemarie said to Lark, but whatever it was soothed her. After a moment, she blew her nose, wiped her eyes, and turned to give her grandmother a weak smile.

A tall dark-skinned man dressed in green scrubs appeared and told us that Ed had suffered a cerebral hemorrhage and there was considerable bleeding involved... that they were taking him to the OR so the surgeon could open his skull and relieve the pressure. It would take some time, so everyone might as well go home and come back later.

Lark explained that we were from Atlanta and home was too far away. "And besides," she added, "I have no intention of leaving my husband." Just then a monstrous clap of thunder rattled the windows, lightening flashed across the dark sky, and rain began falling in torrents as the brunt of the storm rolled in.

A couple of hours later, Tripp told Lark that he would stay with her at the hospital, as did Brock and Phyllis. Rosemarie went home and Bobbye, Phil, and I took Tripp's car back to the boat so we could get some clothes and toiletries for Lark. It was still raining when we left, but by the time we got to the marina, the storm was almost over.

After breakfast the next morning, we headed back to the hospital where we learned that Ed was in ICU on the fourth floor. We went up the elevator and found everyone in the waiting room except Tripp who was having his allotted five-minute visit with his dad. The hours of that Saturday are forever etched in my mind in five-minute increments… only two per hour…when either Lark or Tripp went back to the inner sanctum to be with Ed. At lunch time, Tripp urged Bobbye, Phil, and me to go to lunch, so we went downtown to one of our favorite places on the river. While we were gone, Rosemarie brought lunch in for everyone else.

The doctor finally showed up about four-thirty and told us that Ed was stable. "I'm sorry I have nothing to report beyond that," he said. "Only time will tell. If all goes well, he'll be out of here in a day or two and into a regular room. This will be a long recovery and it may be some time before he's able to leave the hospital. He's getting the best care possible, and it might be best if all of you went home."

He looked at Lark. "I'm going to stay," she said. "In fact, Tripp and I are both going to stay. My grandmother has two extra bedrooms, and we can stay with her." She looked at Phil and Bobbye and me. "I called Hank Reynolds today to give him an update on Ed's surgery."

Then Tripp interrupted and said, "And I told him I wouldn't be coming in for a few days. Phil, why don't you drive my car and take Bobbye and Stacey home. You guys have to go to work. My dad's car is here, and Lark and I can use it."

Brock got up, walked over to Lark, and took her hand. "Phyllis and I are going to stay on the boat again tonight," he said, "if that's okay. And we'll come by the hospital tomorrow morning before we leave for Atlanta."

* * * * *

240

Tripp took his dad's advice about getting a job, but he didn't wait until October. As soon as Ed was moved from the hospital ICU to a private room, Tripp went down to the Savannah River Walk and found a job as assistant cook in a well-known pricey restaurant called Vera Cruz, working lunch and dinner six days a week. Over the next few weeks, he came home to Atlanta only once, to get some clothes and shoes. Whatever free time he had he spent with Lark and Rosemarie. Bobbye went down to see him early in September, but he told her not to come again because he'd had to work both nights she'd been there, and it wasn't worth it.

Bobbye cried when that happened and told me she was worried about Tripp. That he wasn't his old self anymore... that he'd changed. I reminded her of what Tripp had just been through with his dad and how hard that must have been for him and she seemed to accept that. But she was miserable without him, and I continued to put up with her complaining and the dark moods that took her to another world. Thank God we both had jobs to go to every day. That left only the nights, and I got into the habit of turning on the TV as soon as I got home so I wouldn't have to hear her moon about Tripp.

Ed stayed in the hospital in Savannah three weeks. He was able to use his right hand but not his left, and while his speech was slurred, he could be understood if one paid close attention. He begged his doctors to let him go to Piedmont in Atlanta, and finally on September 18, he was taken there by ambulance. Lark called Bobbye's supervisor at the hospital and asked if Bobbye might take care of Ed's physical therapy needs, so Bobbye began working with Ed almost from the day he arrived in her unit. She devoted a lot of time to returning movement to his left hand and restoring his speech. And she insisted he get up for a walk every morning. She'd position herself on one side of Ed, while Lark took the other, and they'd sort of drag him up and down the hallway while he hobbled along between them like he had both feet in one shoe.

Back at the birthday cake house, Lark had a double-railed walking exerciser brought into the bedroom where the equipment from Ed's last round of therapy still stood, and by the time he finally left Piedmont and came home, he was able to walk down it without Bobbye's assistance.

* * * * *

On Friday evening, November 5, Phil and I, and Janice and Russell, waited in a hallway out of sight until Bobbye, and a couple hundred of her hospital colleagues, gathered in the ball room at the Peach Tree Hyatt Hotel for their annual awards' banquet. Two weeks before, Bobbye's supervisor had called to tell me that Bobbye would receive an award for Piedmont's Physical Therapy Unit and she hoped I'd come and bring Bobbye's parents, but to keep everything under our hats as Bobbye didn't know. She said I could bring up to four guests, so I invited Phil.

I think Bobbye was genuinely surprised when her name was announced as the winner of The Rookie Award because she just sat there in her chair with her hand covering her mouth for what seemed forever. As she got up, she hesitated. And on her way to the podium, she began crying. Our little foursome, sitting at a table in the back, clapped and whistled to let her know we were there for her.

Later than night, as Bobbye and I lay in the bed we shared, she turned to me and said, "I wish Tripp could have been there tonight to see me get that award. He would have been so proud, wouldn't he?"

I responded with a little *umm* and she went on. "Stace, have you noticed anything between him and Lark?" I froze, thanking God she couldn't see my face. Then she said, "Do you think they have an unusual relationship for a son and stepmother?"

I gave myself a moment before I spoke. "I think they're really close now because Ed has been so sick. I think that's what's drawn them together."

"Well, that may be true, but I want to tell you what happened the last time I spent the night with Tripp at Rosemarie's house. For some reason, I woke up about three o'clock and Tripp wasn't in the bed. So, I decided to get up and see if maybe he'd gone down the hall to the bathroom. But when I opened our door, I saw him across the hall in Lark's bedroom. She was sitting in a chair, this pink plaid chair, and he was down on his knees in front of her. There wasn't much light…just this low beam from a little lamp on her dresser. But I could see she was crying. She kept saying, 'I can't keep doing this. I can't.' And Tripp kept rubbing her arm and saying, 'It's okay. Everything's gonna be okay. Don't worry. Stop crying now and go to bed.' When he started to get up, I closed the door. I heard him go down the hall and, in a few minutes, the shower came on. Then he came back to bed and I pretended to be asleep."

Oh, I wish I could pretend to be asleep, I thought, so I wouldn't have to say anything. I decided to use the old trick of throwing the ball back into the opponent's court. "What did you think when you saw them?"

Bobbye sighed. "I don't know. Maybe I'm over-reacting. Tripp must have heard Lark crying in her room and went in there to try to check on her."

"Well, we both know he's been paying a lot of attention to her lately and he should. Ed is so sick, and Lark told us what a comfort Tripp is."

Bobbye rolled over and, with her back to me, said, "You're probably right, Stace."

I lay there as still as a statue wishing she'd go to sleep because I knew I wouldn't. Visions of Tripp and Lark together played in my head like scenes from a movie and I wondered if she'd seen them naked as I had. I decided she must not have because if she had, she'd have come screaming home in the middle of the night to tell me all about it. When her breath slowed and I knew she was asleep, I got up. I went into the living room, turned on a lamp, and took the new book I'd bought that day, a murder mystery, from my purse. Then I settled down on the sofa for what I hoped would be such an interesting read that it would take my mind off things.

* * * * *

Ed made wonderful progress that month. Bobbye put him through a strict routine every day and before long he'd regained his speech and his equilibrium. The two of them began taking little walks together going out the front door, down the steps, and around the house. Ed's appetite returned and Classie put the soup pot away and made his favorite dishes because he could chew again. Tripp called about once a week to talk with Ed about his job at the restaurant. Because he was the newest employee, he had little time off, but promised to come home for Thanksgiving. Lark had invited Phil and his parents, Janice and Russell, my dad, and Bobbye and me to join them for dinner that day to celebrate Ed's recovery.

On the Monday evening before that Thursday, Bobbye came home, sat down at the table, and over dinner, told me that when she'd arrived at the big house that morning, Ed was already dressed and waiting for her in the library. When she'd gone in, Ed's attorney, Bax Dobson, and his personal physician, Dr. Clark Wells, and several other men were there with him. They'd all stood up when she'd walked in and she'd said hello to Bax, and to Dr. Wells, whom she knew, and then Ed introduced her to Judge Randall Whitlow, Judge Charles Normand, and to his son, Frank, whom she learned, was a partner in Bax Dobson's law firm. Nancy Boles, the day nurse, had smiled and waved at Bobbye from one of the wing chairs near the fireplace. Opposite her, sitting in the other chair, was Meredith's father, Hank Reynolds.

Ed had taken Bobbye's hand and said, "Would you do me a favor, Miss Revels, and sign a paper attesting to the fact that I am of sound mind and body on this day, Monday, November 22, 1999? I need to sign a number of documents this morning and these gentlemen are here to oversee the process. But first, I need for you and Nurse Boles to put your signatures on a document that affirms my health. Would you do that for me?"

Then he'd turned and addressed the group, "You all know that Bobbye is my future daughter-in-law, don't you?" And the men had nodded and smiled.

Then she and Nurse Boles had followed Bax over to the big table under the windows where four sets of papers had been organized in rows. Bax had picked up the first one—the one that attested to Ed's physical and mental state—and pointed to the places where she and Nancy were to sign. Then he'd handed Nurse Boles a pen. While Nancy was busy signing and dating her signature, Bobbye said she'd taken a quick look at the other documents on the table. Headings on the next two were **The Dissolution of MacAvoy Enterprises** and **The Disbursement of Assets for MacAvoy Enterprises**. The last document, which was down on the far end of the table, was labeled **Last Will and Testament of James Edward MacAvoy II.**

As soon as Bobbye had signed the statement attesting to Ed's health, he'd asked her to tell Classie that they'd be ready for lunch in about fifteen minutes. Then he'd given her a hug, pressing his lips to her forehead.

* * * * *

Thanksgiving Day dawned bright and sunny, but bitterly cold. I got up at seven and put on my warmest walking gear, grabbed my Walkman, and headed out. When I got home about an hour later, Bobbye served me a bowl of steaming hot oatmeal, a welcome treat, and we talked about the day ahead and how we were looking forward to it.

When we arrived at the birthday cake house, Classie answered our knock and invited us into the library for hot chocolate or mulled cider, whatever we preferred. Lark had told us that we'd be dining earlier than usual as Ed would need an afternoon nap. I could hear someone running down the stairs and a moment later Tripp burst into the room and came over to give Bobbye a kiss. As he made his way around the group hugging all the women and shaking hands with the men, I commented to Bobbye about how good he looked. "It's the job," she said. "It's been really good for him and I think he's found his calling at Vera Cruz."

"What if he decides to stay there?" I asked. "Will you move to Savannah?"

But Phyllis interrupted us. "Come on over here, Bobbye," she said, "and tell me all about your honeymoon plans. Phil said you and Tripp are thinking about cruising to Barbados on "Mac the Knife." Can Brock and I come along?"

For me, the day passed as if it were a dream. I sat at a beautifully decorated dining table eating the most luscious food imaginable watching everyone around me as they bantered back and forth filling that big room with laughter. I kept an eye on Tripp, and on Lark, to see if anything passed between them, but nothing did. Ed, who seemed to relish every moment, constantly reached out to take Lark's hand. He kept smiling down the table at Bobbye telling her how much he was looking forward to having another wonderful woman in the family.

At one point, he'd looked over at Janice and said, "I don't know what I would have done without Bobbye. She's given me a new lease on life. And it hasn't been easy. She's a hard task master, your daughter, but a gentle one. I wish there was something I could do to repay her for all she's done for me." Janice beamed back at him and said, "Oh, Ed, you don't owe her a thing. She loves you just as much as you love her."

After dessert, we adjourned to the library where Lark served coffee and brandy. Bobbye and Tripp sat down together in one of the big wing chairs near the fire and Lark and I moved several chairs to form a circle around them. Soon, the talk turned to their wedding. Janice and Russell told everyone that, after the rehearsal on Friday night, they would be hosting a dinner at Justine's, a French restaurant at Lennox Square. Lark and Ed asked everyone to hold the weekend before the wedding for a big party aboard "Mac the Knife." And my dad announced that he and I would be hosting a cook-out to welcome Bobbye and Tripp home when they returned from their honeymoon.

As the clock on the mantle chimed three, Ed stood up. "I don't want to," he began, "but my caregivers will beat me with a stick if I don't take a little nap." A murmur of soft laughter rippled among us before he went on to say, "Please stay here with Lark and enjoy the rest of the afternoon. It's been grand having all of us here together on this special day and I hope we'll do this kind of thing more often in the future."

I'd never thought of Ed as sentimental, but in that moment his eyes filled with tears. "Life is full of surprises, isn't it?" he mused. "And I never dreamed that I'd be the one who...who..." His head dropped and, in a voice trembling with emotion, he said, "You'll never know how much I cherish all of you."

* * * * *

On the first of December, Bobbye went back to her regular job in the physical therapy unit, but she didn't remain there long. Two weeks later, Ed tripped on his way into the bathroom and fell headlong hitting his head on the edge of the sink. Lark was teaching a band class at Grady and Classie was left once again to deal with poor Ed. She dialed 911 first. Then she called Bobbye, who rushed to the big house and rode with Ed in the ambulance to the hospital.

Ed spent a couple of days in intensive care where Bobbye was allowed to visit him five minutes each day during her lunch break. She told Phil and me that he was making a valiant effort to recover, that he kept trying to reach out to her with his good right hand while he called her name in a garbled whisper, the only thing he could manage. After a few days, he'd regained strength and they moved him to Recovery where, eventually, he was strong enough to sit up in a wheelchair. His speech had suffered, the left side of his body was worthless, but he had the use of his right hand. One day at lunch, he wrote *Bobbye* on a napkin and when Lark went to see him that afternoon, the nurses showed it to her. Lark called Bobbye the next morning and Bobbye began spending every afternoon with Ed. By the end of the next week, the doctors decided he could go home...but only if Bobbye would continue to work with him there.

So, every morning Bobbye was up at six so she'd be at the birthday cake house early enough to get Ed up and feed him. She told me that Lark was teaching in the schools, that she had rehearsals for the symphony two afternoons a week, and most days she didn't get home until after five. "So Classie and I take care of Ed," she said. "I shave him while he's still in bed. Then Classie comes in and helps me get him dressed.

And while I massage Ed's leg muscles, Classie changes the bed and cleans up. After that, the three of us have breakfast together in the kitchen...we're very casual when Lark isn't there... and then I take him out in the wheelchair and we sit on the terrace and talk. He's making progress and can say a few things now like *door* and *bed* and *hot*...but he can't form the letters for something like *breakfast* yet. But I think he'll get there."

But he didn't. The weekend before Christmas, Ed suffered another fall and had to be rushed back to Piedmont. Two days later, the doctors told Lark and Bobbye that Ed's blood vessels were just too weak to recover, that his protoplasm was dissipating at such an alarming rate they feared he wouldn't live much longer. Lark begged them to let him go home for Christmas and they'd agreed because there was nothing left for them to do.

So, on Christmas Eve, Ed went home in an ambulance. He was taken into the house in a wheelchair, which he never got out of again except when he was put to bed. He'd lost all use of his left hand, he couldn't speak, and his hearing was gone. But when people spoke to him, he'd cock his head, so we knew he was trying to understand. It was a pathetic sight.

On Christmas Day, Lark and Bobbye bathed Ed and dressed him in clean pajamas and a red plaid robe before Tripp wheeled him into the library. Lark had invited our little group over for brunch that morning in an effort, I'm sure, to try to brighten Ed's day. I was stunned to see that most of his hair was gone and his eyes, which had been such a bright blue, were now a lifeless dish-water gray. He knew me, though. When I bent down to kiss his cool, dry cheek he gave me a crooked smile because only the right side of his mouth worked. That was the last time all of us were together because Ed died on New Year's Day.

Part Five

If the temperature in your oven is not properly controlled, your cake may develop what is commonly known as a "sad streak."

Pound Cake and Other Staples
of the Colonial Hearth
Muriel Danesmore, Editor

On the morning of January 5, 1999, Bobbye sat with Tripp and Lark in the front pew of The Sign of the Shepherd Episcopal Church for Ed's service. With them was Ed's sister, Judith MacAvoy, who'd come from Sante Fe. My dad and I, Phil, Brock and Phyllis, and Janice and Russell, sat in the pew behind them. Lark wanted Tripp to deliver the eulogy, but he refused, telling her he was just too upset. So, Brock did the eulogy for his old friend. He talked about Ed's business acumen, his love of family and his God, the respect he'd always shown his employees, and his generous gifts to the community…in other words, all the things a person would mention if they were doing a eulogy for a well-liked successful businessman.

The Atlanta Symphony Chorale brought me to tears with a stunning rendition of "Be Still My Soul." For the benediction, Rosemarie Fincher took us to another place and time with the most beautiful arrangement of "The Lord Is My Shepherd" I'd ever heard. The chancel was filled with magnificent flowers and the blanket that covered the copper-colored casket was a sea of golden Star Gazer lilies. Workers from the Sandy Springs plant were there in great numbers, as were members of several civic groups in town. Ed would have been pleased.

The burial afterwards at Oaklawn Cemetery was private. Tripp's Aunt Judith rode in the limousine with Lark, Tripp, and Bobbye. My dad, Rosemarie, and I followed along leading the rest of our small group. As the funeral cortege moved off, I was reminded of the cold gray day when my mom had been buried. While my memories of it were muddled, several vague images had been stored like scepters in the dark recesses of my young mind... tears flowing like water from my dad's eyes as he walked behind the casket; my Grandmother Edith's face, stoic and resolute, as she'd held my little hand at the muddy graveside; the quartet of gray-haired men who'd sung "Abide With Me" as we'd stood there whipped by a wind that lashed the gloomy lyrics of that old hymn across my heart, making me hate it for the rest of my life.

After Lark, Tripp, Bobbye, and Judith were escorted to seats beside Ed's casket, the rest of us went to stand behind them and I was surprised that there were so few of us. But that was what Lark had wanted. Just family and our little group, she'd said, when Tripp had asked about who'd been invited to the cemetery. Standing off to one side was Meredith Reynolds' father, Hank, and Bax Dobson. Two other men I'd never met stood with them. After the service, Bobbye told me they were Judge Whitlow and Judge Normand, the men who'd overseen the writing of Ed's will.

The family plot sat on the side of a gently rolling knoll surrounded by a low stone wall. In the center was a large marker engraved with *Cogdill-MacAvoy* that had been erected by Caroline and Ed after Rand Cogdill died. Patricia had been buried beside her husband. Ed's casket sat over a raw opening, surrounded by bright green astro-turf, beside the pink marble plinth that held Caroline's ashes. As the minister droned on about the promises of the afterlife, I couldn't help thinking about the four dead people inside that stone enclosure and their years together in a beautiful house on a hill in Virginia Highlands. Now, all that was over.

The service was brief, thank goodness, as a cold rain swept in. Lark invited everyone back to the house for a late lunch. When we walked into the foyer, Classie called my dad and me from the dining room where she was pouring cups of hot coffee and invited us to the large buffet she'd set out on the sideboard, and to the dessert table where my dad's death cake was surrounded by pies and puddings. My dad thanked her, and he and I and Rosemarie filled our plates and sat down at the table which had been set for fourteen.

It wasn't long before Bobbye came in with Tripp accompanied by his Aunt Judith. Bobbye sat down at the place beside me, Tripp took the chair at the end of the table, and Aunt Judith sat across from us. I knew she was older than Ed, but she sure didn't look it with her shoulder length silver hair and slender figure. I asked about the turquoise and silver necklace she was wearing, and she told me it had been made by the Anasazi who'd built ancient cities in New Mexico and Arizona. Then she asked me what I did, and I told her about my job at *the Constitution.*

While she and I continued to talk, Bobbye and Tripp carried on a private conversation of their own, most of which I could hear. Tripp had leaned toward Bobbye and said, "In just a few minutes, you and I will be set for life, my love. Any time now, those guys are gonna call me in for the reading of my dad's will and I'm gonna buy you a new car so you won't have to drive that old thing of yours anymore."

Out of the corner of my eye, I saw Bobbye reach for Tripp's hand under the table. "I don't mind driving that car a little longer," she said, "what I really want is a condo. I know you said that after we got married, we'd have to live in your apartment over the garage for a while, but maybe now we won't have to."

Tripp nodded to her just as Judge Whitlow, who'd been sitting at the other end of the table, got up and made a little bow toward Lark. "If you'll join me in the library when you're ready, Mrs. MacAvoy," he said, "we'll have the reading of Mr. MacAvoy's will."

He looked down the table at Tripp and then at Judith. "Would both of you please excuse yourselves and join Judge

Normand, Mr. Dobson, and me in the library? And Miss Parks, would you please ask Miss Dixon to come in, too?"

Oh, my, I thought, Classie's going to get something from Ed. I jumped up and hurried into the kitchen where I suggested Classie remove her apron before she went into the library. But she stood there with a funny expression on her face and said, "They don't mean me. That judge don't mean me, Miss Stacey."

"Yes, he does," I assured her. "Judge Whitlow asked me to tell you to go into the library for the reading of Mr. Ed's will." I urged her to take off her apron and get going. But she remained rooted to a spot in front of the sink. It took some doing, but I finally got that apron off. As she walked away, Phil came from the dining room carrying a stack of dirty dishes.

"I thought we'd help Classie," he said, "by getting these dishes in the washer." I looked down at the expensive plates he was holding. "No, not those," I said. "Better not put those in the dish washer." I turned around, closed the drain in the left side of the double sink, and turned on the tap. "Just put them in this sink and I'll wash while you dry." Bobbye and Janice came in, too, bringing trays of dirty glasses, which they took to the bar sink to wash.

None of us said a single word while we worked. An eerie hush fell over the house as our minds, eyes, and ears focused on the library. I'd just handed Phil the last of the washed plates when someone screamed, "You're a goddam liar!" It was Tripp, and soon he sounded even louder. "That's a fucking lie! He did no such thing!" Now his voice was closer, and I knew he'd come out of the library and was in the hall outside the kitchen. "I'll get my own attorney," he yelled, "and we'll see about that. Half that money is *mine!*"

He burst into the kitchen like a whirlwind, grabbed Bobbye by the hand, and said, "Come on, we're leaving this fucking shit hole!"

She jerked away from him. "Wait a minute, Tripp. I need to get my pocketbook and coat." While she ran into the dining room, Tripp stood at the back door, his hand clutching the knob. "They're crazy!" he fumed. "Fucking crazy! Fifty thousand lousy dollars! They think that's my share, but those bastards have got another *think* coming because my Grandad Jim left me millions."

When Bobbye returned, he pushed her out the door, slamming it behind him without a word about where they were going or when they'd be back. Janice looked over at me and said, "Here we go again."

Two nights later, Bobbye showed up at the apartment. She had dark circles under her eyes and her hair was stringy and she told me she hadn't eaten a meal since she'd left with Tripp. I hurried over to the fridge and pulled out some stuff to make her a sandwich and she sat down at the table and began to cry.

"What a nightmare," she wailed. "For the past two days and nights, I've been living in the most god-awful nightmare. You wouldn't believe it, Stacey. Tripp has lost his fucking mind." She glanced at me as if she expected a response. So, while I spread mayo on bread, I asked her to tell me about it.

"Well," she began. "What you know about Ed's will? Did anyone talk to you after we left?"

"Only Classie," I answered. "She told me Ed had left her fifty thousand dollars. I just about fainted, but I'm so happy for her. She said the will stipulated that, if she wanted to retire, she had to stay with Lark in the big house for at least a year so Lark would have time to find her replacement." I cut a ham sandwich in half and put it on a plate in front of her. "Is that right?"

"Yes, that's one of the things Tripp told me. He was so furious that Classie got the same thing he did. Ed left Tripp the fifty thousand that Tripp had asked him for over and over so he could open a restaurant. I think I told you about that, didn't I?"

I nodded. "Yes, you did. But I remember you said that you thought Ed would never give Tripp money for that."

"Evidently Ed changed his mind. But Tripp just went crazy when he found out fifty thousand was all he was getting. Judith got a million from Ed and he left the church a hundred thousand and the law school at UGA got a quarter million for scholarships. But Lark got everything else...the house and the beach cottage and "Mac the Knife" and the farm in North Carolina. *And* the rest of the money. Those attorneys wouldn't tell Tripp how much money she got, just that she got the bulk of Ed's estate. It's been put into a trust and she gets a pre-arranged amount quarterly. Evidently, it's enough to run the houses and pay Classie and the boat crew and travel and do all the things she's used to doing."

I sat quietly thinking about what I'd just heard and had to admit I was surprised that Tripp hadn't gotten more money. But Ed had always been brutally honest in his feelings about his son's lack of interest in the business. I think he always thought that if he left the business to Tripp, Tripp would sell it before you could say "jack rabbit." Now the business was gone, and the only thing left was Ed's personal fortune.

I looked over at Bobbye. "I can understand why Tripp might be upset, but I think Ed had the right to give his money to whomever he pleased. Just look at Classie. She's worked for the Cogdills and MacAvoys almost her entire life. And she's been there every minute, except for two hours on Sunday mornings when she went to church, and on her afternoon off. I think she's earned every penny of the money Ed left her."

Bobbye sniffed. "You're probably right about Classie. Oh...did you know Ed left Tripp his gold signet ring with the M engraved on it? Lark has it now, but she's going to give it to

Tripp. I'm glad Ed left that beautiful ring to Tripp, but I wish he'd gotten more money."

It took some doing but I finally summoned up the guts to ask about something I knew I shouldn't. "Hum," I began, "do you have any idea how much money was involved?"

"Not exactly. But Tripp told me his dad had millions. After his Grandad Jim died a couple of years ago, both Ed and Aunt Judith inherited several million from their dad's estate. And then there's the millions Ed got when he sold the MacAvoy plants in Birmingham and Valdosta."

Using the tip of my finger, I drew the outline of a dollar sign on the place mat in front of me. "So, what's Tripp going to do?"

"I don't give a damn what he does and I'm staying as far away from him as possible. He's drinking, drinking, and doing some really fucked-up stuff. We went into Savannah yesterday to Vera Cruz to see if he could get his old job back and the manager told him he had a nerve coming there again after what he'd done. I don't know what he'd done to make that man talk to him like that and I don't want to know. Last night, he had his usual liquid dinner, so I drove his car to the grocery store to buy a frozen pizza because he wouldn't take me out to eat. He wouldn't go anywhere. When I left the beach house this morning, he was passed out on the floor in the living room, and I couldn't wake him up. I kept shaking him, but he never moved."

I took a deep breath. "What do you think he's using?"

"I checked his duffle bag and found nothing. But you know how good he is at hiding stuff."

I nodded. "There's a new drug on the streets called PCP. Maybe he's doing that."

"Maybe he is, but I don't give a shit what he does, Stace. He dragged me off to the beach and then he left me in the lurch. This morning, I walked from the beach house to that convenience store on the corner, you know the one, and they called a taxi for me and the driver took me to the bus station in Savannah. That cost twenty-four dollars. Thank God I had some cash. I bought a ticket for Atlanta and it took all day to get here. The bus stopped in Dublin and Barnesville and all these little towns before we got to the central bus station downtown. Then I took a MARTA bus to the stop down on the corner."

Bobbye ate the last of her sandwich and got up to put her empty plate in the sink. "Do you mind if I take a bath now, Stacey? I'm so grungy. I think I'll get a bath and go to bed."

* * * * *

Early Friday morning, Tripp came to the apartment. He was red-eyed, unshaven, and still wearing the pants and shirt he'd worn to Ed's funeral. As soon as I opened the door, he began apologizing. Then he asked to see Bobbye, and I knocked on the bedroom door and told her he'd come. I left Tripp in the living room and went to the kitchen to make a pot of coffee. Bobbye came out in her robe and sat down in a chair and Tripp sat down across from her on the sofa. "I'm such a fool," he said. "I wouldn't blame you if you never spoke to me again."

Bobbye said nothing, so he tried again. "I'm sorry, Bobbye, for ignoring you at the beach, for not taking you out to dinner, and for all the drinking I did. But you've got to understand how hard this is for me. I have nothing. No parents. No grandparents. No job. Nowhere to live. And nothing to live on! When I was little, my Grandad Jim put me on his knee and told me I didn't have to work if I didn't want to...that I could hire people to run the businesses and do whatever I wanted. He told me that I'd never have to worry about money because he was gonna leave me well fixed. And I believed him!"

I poured three mugs of coffee, added cream and sugar, and took one over to Bobbye and one to Tripp. Then I picked up the one I'd prepared for myself, went into the bedroom, and closed the door. I didn't want to hear another sob story from him. You'll have to get a job and make a living like the rest of us, I thought, as I sipped my coffee and stripped off my robe and pjs. I heard the 8:25 bell begin to ring at the school and quickly dressed because I wanted to be out of the apartment now that Tripp had come.

But when I got home that night at six, the two of them were together in the kitchen cooking dinner. They greeted me with friendly hellos making me wonder what they had up their sleeves. Bobbye was still in her hospital scrubs, so I knew she'd been to work. And Tripp had shaved and put on clean clothes.

I hung my coat in the hall closet and went into the bedroom to change. It was obvious that Tripp had been over to his apartment and gotten some clothes and his shaving gear because all of it was lying on the bed. Bobbye came in behind me and closed the door.

"Oh, Stacey," she began, "please say you don't mind if Tripp stays with us for a few days…just 'til he can get a job and get on his feet. He doesn't want to live in the garage apartment anymore and I told him I didn't think you'd care if he stayed with us until he can find somewhere else to live. He called an attorney today and made an appointment. He's going to contest the will, Stacey, and he won't be here long." With my back to her, I sighed a little sigh as I pulled a sweatshirt over my head. "It's okay," I said, "but it can't be for long. This place is not big enough for three people, Bobbye. I'll sleep on the sofa tonight, but I'll go over to my dad's tomorrow. I wouldn't want to cramp Tripp's style."

On Monday morning, Tripp dressed up a bit for his appointment with his new attorney, Sneed Langston, but his appearance counted for nothing. That night at dinner he told Bobbye and me that, as soon as Sneed learned that Ed's will had been administered by Judge Whitlow and Judge Normand, he'd told Tripp he couldn't do anything for him except offer some advice. "You won't have a prayer in the state of Georgia," he'd said, "and if I were you, I'd forget about contesting anything those guys have done. No one knows estate law like them. Your only hope is your dad's widow… your stepmother. She's the one with the money. So, you'd better make nice and buy some flowers and go see her right away. Prey on her mercy and maybe she'll feel sorry for you and give you an allowance."

Bobbye served dessert and the three of us were quiet for a few minutes while we consumed it. Tripp got up, filled three mugs with coffee, and put them on the table. "I'm going over to the house tomorrow," he said, "and do what Sneed Langston suggested and ask Lark to help me get back on my feet."

We didn't see Tripp for a couple of days. He finally showed up on Wednesday evening and told us he was going back home to live in the apartment over the garage. Lark had told him he could stay there for as long as he wanted, and she had a job for him…she wanted him to help her run the MacAvoy Foundation for Young Musicians. She was the chair and she wanted him to be the vice chair, a position that would pay forty thousand a year and include an expense account. They could set up an office for him in the old TV room upstairs. And he'd be traveling with her attending recitals given by prospective scholarship recipients and accompanying her to well-known musical events all over the country and visiting schools in Europe.

Bobbye's reaction surprised me. She hugged Tripp and congratulated him on his new position using words like *exciting* and *fun*. Then she went into the bedroom to help him pack. The words she'd just used had come to my mind, too. But not in the same way. Oh, lord, I thought, now he and Lark will be traveling together, staying in hotels, screwing from Salzburg to Shanghai!

I held the door for Tripp as he hurried out with his bags. "Good luck," I said as he started down the steps. "Let us know how you're doing." Bobbye said nothing until we were both back inside. She went straight to the table and began scraping plates. "Thank God for Lark," she said, as she headed to the sink. "At least Tripp has something to keep him occupied and out of my hair."

Tripp called Bobbye on Thursday night and told her that he and Phil would pick the two of us up on Friday after work and we'd go to The Shack for dinner and maybe later to a club, which proved to be very much like the old days. While we ate our chicken and waffles, we laughed a lot. And we giggled a lot while we smoked a couple of joints in the car before we went into The Black Cat Club downtown. The band was good, and we danced and drank with the kind of abandon we'd known in the old days. About two o'clock, we headed back home, stopping to drop Phil at his condo on the way. It was obvious that Tripp planned to stay all night, so I went into the bathroom to change and grabbed a blanket off a shelf before I hit the sofa. Then I lay there fuming at myself for not saying anything. I knew I'd have to be the one to broach the subject of Tripp staying in our apartment even when he had his own place.

I'd had a fair amount to drink that night, but I didn't go to sleep right away because I kept hearing Tripp and Bobbye. They talked and talked, bantering back and forth like they were arguing. I couldn't hear exactly what they were saying, but every now and then I heard Bobbye clearly say *No, I'm not...*or *No, I won't*. Tripp's voice sounded as if he were giving someone directions when he said things like *then you do this, then you do that.*

The next morning, I got up about eight, pulled on some jeans and a sweater thinking I'd go over to my dad's. I made quick work of my toothbrush and wash cloth and, just as I heard the 8:25 bell ring at the school, I opened the door and headed down the stairs. When I reached the landing, I stopped. I hadn't heard Tripp leave, but his Bimmer was gone. So, I went back up to the apartment to see if Bobbye wanted to go with me to my dad's.

As soon as I opened the bedroom door, she buried her head under the covers. "What's up?" I asked, watching her burrow deeper. I sat down on the side of the bed and said, "Hey, are you okay? What's going on? Why did Tripp leave so early?"

From beneath the covers came something that sounded like a snort. Bobbye stuck her head out and I knew right away she'd been crying. "He can go straight to hell!" she blurted. "When he left this morning, I told him he'd better keep his fucking ass away from here!"

"Whoa!" I said, surprised. "When you and Tripp went to bed last night you two were all lovey-dovey. What happened?"

Bobbye threw back the covers and swung her legs over the side of the bed. "He's just plain crazy," she shouted. "He's leaving Saturday with Lark. They're going to Puerto Rico to interview students for the scholarship foundation, and they'll be gone for two weeks. Two weeks! They're taking "Mac the Knife.""

She stomped across the room, snatched her hairbrush from the top of the dresser, and threw it against the wall. It landed with a thwack and I hurried to pick it up. "Stop!" I warned. "Mrs. Ferguson will be up here any second to find out what's going on."

Bobbye scowled at me. "Fuck her! And fuck Tripp MacAvoy! He can rot in hell for all I care." She jerked the diamond ring from her finger and, a second later, I heard *ping*. After I'd retrieved it from behind a chair, I said, "Bobbye, you've got to get a hold of yourself. This ring cost a lot of money, and even if you're mad at Tripp, you can't just throw it away."

"I tried to give it back to him last night," she sniffed. "But he wouldn't take it because he said nothing had changed between us. But I don't believe him, Stacey. If he's goes to Puerto Rico with Lark, it's over."

Bobbye dragged over to the dresser, opened her jewelry box, and tossed the ring inside. "I guess I'd better not throw it away, huh? I might need some money one day and I can sell it."

At that point, I gave up. "Bobbye Revels, you're such a piss-ant pain-in-the-ass. Do whatever you want. I don't care." I began walking toward the door but turned back. "I came in here to ask you if you wanted to go with me to my dad's for breakfast."

"No, thanks," she said, rather curtly. "I think I'll take our dirty laundry over to my folks. I'll see you later this afternoon."

Instead of going to my dad's as planned, I changed my mind and went to Phil's. He answered my knock in his robe and I apologized for waking him up. "Not a problem," he said. "Come on in. Have you had breakfast? Why don't I get dressed and we'll go down to The Fireside. I'll be back in just a sec."

Over coffee and pancakes, I told him what had happened when we'd gotten back to the apartment the night before, how mad I was about having to sleep on the sofa, and how hard it had been to go to sleep because Tripp and Bobbye kept arguing. I told him about Tripp leaving early that morning and what Bobbye had told me about the two-week cruise he and Lark were making to Puerto Rico on "Mac the Knife."

Phil put his fork on the side of his plate, let out a long whistle, and shook his head. "That bastard never lets any grass grow under his feet, does he? Moved right in on her, didn't he?"

I looked at Phil from the corner of my eye. "Do you know something I don't?"

"I doubt it. But I know Tripp MacAvoy. And he'd jump his grandmother if she had money and he thought he could get it. And from what I've heard, we're talking about a lot of money."

I settled back against the padded booth. "Well?"

Phil pushed his empty plate away. "Remember when we were leaving the cemetery after Ed's funeral and I got in the car with my parents to go back to the MacAvoy house?" I nodded and he went on. "Well, just before we left, Hank Reynolds came over to shake hands with my dad and the two of them were standing near the back of our car talking. I cracked the window and that's when I heard Hank say Ed's estate was worth about fifty-five million."

"Oh, my god," I gasped. "You've got to be kidding! I thought Ed filed for bankruptcy. How can somebody file for bankruptcy if they have that kind of money?"

"Evidently, that was just the Sandy Springs operation, but he must have known what to do to protect his personal fortune. I'm not an attorney, so I don't know how it works. I just know that it does." He began counting on his fingers, "Number one, we know that Judith MacAvoy got a million. Two, Classie and Tripp each got fifty thousand. Three, UGA got two hundred and fifty thousand, and four, the church got a hundred thousand. A quick calculation tells me that Lark must have gotten about fifty million. That's a lot of clams."

I nodded. "And it looks like those little clams are safe in their shells, too. The attorney Tripp went to see, that guy

Sneed Langston, told him he didn't have a prayer of changing anything in Ed's will." I looked down at my hands, hesitating before I said, "I shouldn't tell you this. I promised myself that I wouldn't ever tell anyone. But things have changed, so I'm going to tell you. Tripp and Lark have been having an affair."

"Yeah, I know. It's been going on since last summer when Ed bought that farm up in North Carolina."

"You little shit! You knew and you didn't tell me. Why?"

"I was afraid you'd tell Bobbye. I've been wrestling with it for a while, and I thought I'd wait and see how things played out. But it looks like neither one of us will have to tell her because she might figure it out herself."

"How did you find out Tripp and Lark were screwing around?"

"I'm not going to tell you anything beyond the fact that Tripp made a mistake when his dad was in the hospital in Savannah, and he was staying with Lark at Rosemarie's house."

All I said in response was *hum*, but my head was more engaged than my mouth. I couldn't help thinking that Bobbye had had a reason to be suspicious when she saw Lark and Tripp together in Lark's bedroom at Rosemarie's. I was sure there was more to that story.

* * * * *

On Saturday morning, Bobbye and I were sitting in the living room talking when Tripp showed up. I opened the door for him, but he ignored me and went straight over to Bobbye and asked her to go into the bedroom with him so they could have a private conversation. She told him to leave her the fuck alone. Then he bent down, got right in her face, and said, "If you don't come into the bedroom with me, I'm going to do what I told you I'd do the other night and go see

Janice and Russell and tell them about some of their star athlete's extracurricular activities."

Bobbye stood up, turned to look him full in the face, and spit the words, "You're a lying no good asshole, Tripp MacAvoy!"

He grabbed her by the arm and replied, "You can call me anything you want to Miss Shit Bitch. But you're coming into the bedroom where we can have some privacy, because I have something important to say to you."

They went in and closed the door, and nothing in their conversation was audible except Bobbye's voice when she said *no… no.* I could hear Tripp talking in low steady tones, but I couldn't understand what he was saying. They were in there about three minutes before he came out and went out the front door. He was halfway down the stairs when she ran out behind him. "And you can cram your fucking ring up your sorry fucking ass, you lying turd!"

I managed to get to the door in time to see the ring arc through the air. Tripp was in his car by then, and as I hurried down the stairs, he pulled onto the street. While he went his merry way, Bobbye stood on the landing giving him the finger.

It was very cold, and I was wearing nothing but jeans and a sweater, but I stayed out in the yard searching through the frozen grass for an hour. The wind got the best of me and I gave up long enough to go back upstairs to drink a cup of coffee. Bobbye refused to help me search saying, "I hope the goddam thing is buried in some rabbit hole where it'll never be found!"

But I put on a coat, went back out, and a short while later, found it under the front fender of my car. I tried to give it to Bobbye, but she wouldn't even look at it. So, I put it in my wallet and later that day, took it over to my dad and asked him to put it in his safe deposit box.

* * * * *

The following week, Old Man Winter descended bringing fierce winds, freezing rain, and sleet. The storm brought down two oak trees in our back yard, and a half-dozen on the school property across the street, along with the electric lines in our neighborhood, leaving us in the dark with no heat or hot water. After we'd shared a can of soup heated on our camper stove, Bobbye and I snuggled into our sleeping bags trying to stay warm. The public schools closed, as did the city and county offices, and Georgia Power was all over the map trying to restore electricity.

Phil called to tell us he was working 'round the clock doing dispatch in addition to his regular job. A couple days later the streets were declared safe, and he came over and brought us a carton of milk and a loaf of bread, along with a box of doughnuts and cups of hot coffee. We sat at the kitchen table and talked about the storm. He was careful not to bring up Tripp's name, and I wasn't about to mention him either, so we steered the conversation to safe topics and made plans to go out to eat together Friday night.

Bobbye stayed busy at work as usual and, when she got home in the evenings, she put on her pjs and robe. After dinner, we retreated to the sofa to watch TV. She had not said one word about her parents or what she'd told them about Tripp...or if she'd told them anything at all. So, I was in the dark on that score. One night she went to a movie with some women from work, and another night, she and I went to an art opening at The High Museum.

On the first Thursday in February, Phil called me at work to ask if I could meet him for a pizza that night at a local place near his condo; he had something to tell me. When I walked in, he waved to me from the booth near the back. I began taking off my coat in anticipation of sitting down across from him, but soon discovered that Brock and Phyllis were already there. "Gosh," I exclaimed. "What a nice surprise!"

Phyllis gave me a big smile. "Sit over there with Phil, honey. I hope you don't mind that we came along. It just seemed like a good idea at the time. They have really good calzones here. Are you up for one?"

"Sure," I answered, "whatever you guys are having is fine with me."

We ordered a variety of calzones and kept the conversation going between bites. Brock asked me about work. Then Phyllis asked about my dad. And while this seemed normal under the circumstances, it felt as if we were in a play with the director was feeding us our lines. Phil had not said one word and it was obvious his thoughts were elsewhere.

My calzone was quite good, and I was about halfway through it when Phyllis said, "We have something to tell you, Stacey." She looked at Brock. "Do you want to tell her or should I?"

Brock glanced at Phil and quickly back at me. "Lark and Tripp are married," he said. "Captain Ennis called me yesterday from "Mac the Knife" to tell me because he thought someone here ought to know. I think he's hoping that some of us will go down to Tybee tomorrow to meet them when they return from their...adventure... and give them a little welcome home. But it won't be any of the Sanford clan. We asked you to join us tonight, Stacey, so we can decide the best way to approach Bobbye. I'm sorry for the strange way we contrived to tell you, but I just couldn't bring myself to call and tell you on the phone."

Phil turned to me and his look said, *I told you so*. I pushed my plate away and murmured, "Oh, God." I'd always thought Lark was just having fun with Tripp, that he was just her boy toy. I'd never dreamed the two of them would marry. But

Brock and Phyllis didn't need to know what I thought, so I fell back on what I *knew*. "Bobbye is really mad at Tripp. She told him off and threw his engagement ring out in the yard. But I don't think she had any idea…"

Phyllis jumped in. "That's why we're here, honey. I wouldn't want you to be alone with Bobbye when she finds out. She's so fragile, emotionally, there's no telling what she'll do. Brock and I decided earlier that he'll be the one who breaks the news to her because he's the one who got the call from Captain Ennis."

Brock said, "I don't mind telling Bobbye. In my business, I've had to deliver lots of bad news. And I'm not sure it's such bad news anyway. If Bobbye were my daughter, I'd be damn glad she wasn't going to marry Tripp MacAvoy." Phyllis nudged him with her elbow, and he cleared his throat and said, "I'm leaving in the morning, Stacey, for a week-end conference at The Homestead up in Hot Springs, Virginia. Phyllis and Phil have arranged their schedules so they can go with me and I'd like for you and Bobbye to come, too. It will help take her mind off what's happened. Better pack your ski togs as the slopes are perfect right now. Don't worry about skis. We'll rent them. We're taking the company plane and we'll pick you and Bobbye up in our van about nine. Okay?"

I was dumbfounded by what Brock had just said, by how nice a guy he was to invite Bobbye and me to spend time at a resort with him and his family. I suspected that Phil had had a role in the decision to invite Bobbye and me, but either way it was a nice gesture. I smiled and said, "You're a saint, Brock Sanford." And he laughed and said, "Boy, have I got *you* fooled!"

Brock paid the tab. Phil helped me with my coat and when we got to my car, he got in behind the wheel and Brock and Phyllis followed us in their car down Memorial Drive to the apartment. My feet were as heavy as concrete blocks as I climbed the stairs going up, up to a hard place I'd managed to avoid for months.

* * * * *

That was a difficult winter. Not difficult because of bad weather, or an epidemic of flu, but because Bobbye was trapped in a maze of emotional turmoil. She didn't know what to say when people asked her about Tripp. She didn't know what to do when they looked at her ring finger and saw no ring. She didn't know how to deal with the minister at her church, and the florist, and the caterer with whom she'd been planning the wedding. The turquoise gowns she'd chosen for her attendants had never been ordered, thank goodness. But Janice had five yards of white French taffeta and nine yards of white silk illusion sitting on a shelf in a closet at home. Eventually she sold it to a friend to make a canopy and bedspread for her daughter's new princess bedroom.

Bobbye buried herself in her work. I left each morning when I heard the 8:25 bell ring at the school. But Bobbye was gone long before that and on the hospital floor by 7:45. And she never came home in time for dinner anymore. If someone in her unit needed time off, Bobbye took their shift. If someone in her unit got sick, Bobbye took their place. Bobbye worked her regular twelve-hour, four-day shift and then picked up as many other twelve-hour shifts as she could. When I complained that she was never home, she shrugged and said, "I've got to stay busy, Stace. It keeps my mind off things."

Often, after she'd had a long day, she'd do paperwork in her office, which meant she didn't get home until nine. When that happened, she'd put on her pjs and, without saying a word to me, she went to bed. I'd turn off the TV, or put down the book I'd been reading, and go to bed, too.

On those nights, when she was really beat, I'd put my arm around her, and she'd let me hold her until she fell asleep… just enough to make me long for more.

Valentine's Day was especially hard for her, but Phil came through like a champ and sent a bouquet of red roses to her office. She refused to go to church on Easter with Janice and Russell and told them that she'd never attend Hillcrest Methodist again. That spring, someone offered her two tickets to see the Braves' opening game, but she turned them down.

As Saturday, May 6 loomed, Phil and I began making plans thinking the three of us needed to do something on that ill-fated weekend. Phil booked us into one of those big resort hotels at Disney World, one of Bobbye's favorite places, and told her to be ready to take a little drive that Thursday at noon. Be sure to pack your swimsuit and some shorts, he'd told her. We got to Orlando in time to have dinner in one of those swanky seafood places that sits out over the water. We were up early on Friday, had a big breakfast, and went to Universal Studios. Every moment was jam-packed, just as we'd intended. And for the first time in months, Bobbye laughed. She laughed when Mickey Mouse hugged her, and she laughed when Pluto threw her a kiss during the parade on Friday afternoon. And the next morning when we went to The Country Bear Jamboree, she laughed so hard she cried.

The best thing that came out of that trip, though, was Bobbye's letting go of what I saw as her need to be everything-to-everybody-every moment. After Orlando, she got back to her old routine of regular shifts, of coming home in time for dinner when her shift ended at seven, of going to an occasional movie, or having dinner with Phil and me at The Shack—a place I thought she'd never go to again.

Late in June, my dad suggested that he and I host a cook-out at our house for the whole gang on the Fourth of July. So,

Janice and Russell, Phyllis and Brock, and Phil, Bobbye and I joined him in our back yard for beer and brats.

We enjoyed the usual topics of conversation which included the Braves, the upcoming football season at UGA, my work at the paper, Bobbye's work at the hospital, and way more than anybody wanted to hear from Phil, Brock, and my dad about Georgia Power & Light. We were all careful not to say the words *trip* or *lark*. The sunset was stunning, and I couldn't help thinking about the one I'd seen from the deck of "Mac the Knife" on the evening of Ed and Lark's wedding. My dad had an expression he used a lot about how everything can change in the wink of an eye, and I kept thinking about how quickly things *had* changed, and how helpless we humans are when it comes to determining our fate.

About nine, we heard the first boom of fireworks as they began to go off all over the city. We watched in awe as bright reds, brilliant blues and greens, and cool, starry whites burst across a black velvet sky. It wasn't long before my dad started cleaning up the picnic table and I got up to help him. The Fourth had fallen in the middle of the week that year and he had to work the next day. So did I.

Bobbye and I left soon after and, when we pulled into the driveway at the apartment, a new black BMW was sitting there. I knew the moment I saw it that it was Tripp. And so did Bobbye. While I got out of the car, she turned to lock the door on her side. But it didn't matter. Tripp was standing there in seconds begging her to listen to him, just give him five minutes, please let him explain. I ran up the stairs and into the apartment leaving Bobbye to deal with the person who had, for years, been the man of her dreams.

I went about my usual routine, brushing my teeth, washing my face, and finding something to wear to work the next day. About ten thirty, I looked out the bedroom window and saw that Tripp's car was still there and, when I realized that he and Bobbye were sitting in it, I went to bed knowing it would be a long night.

Bobbye came in about seven the next morning and the first thing she said was, "Don't start on me, Stacey. I did the only thing I could under the circumstances. He got all upset and I thought he was going to cry. He kept begging me to listen to him and I couldn't help myself... he's just so pitiful. We rode over to John Howell Park and listened to the band and watched the fireworks 'til they ended. Then we rode out to The Shack for waffles. After that, he took me to see the waterfall at Piedmont Park. And he kept telling me what a fool he'd been and what an idiot he was to marry a woman old enough to be his mother. She really isn't—and you and I know it—but he said it felt that way because all she wanted to do was hang out with these old dudes from the symphony, play long-hair music, and talk about concertos and stuff like that. He just hates it, Stacey. And he told me he misses you and Phil as much as he does me and hopes the four of us can do some things together while Lark is staying at the farm in North Carolina and performing at that music festival."

I poured a mug of coffee for her. "Sit down, Bobbye," I said, "and try to get a hold of yourself. Last week you told me you'd never speak to Tripp MacAvoy again. So, I'm a little puzzled by this latest... and curious about the saga of Lark and Tripp. But I've got to go to work and so do you. There's some porkchops in the fridge for dinner *if* you're going to be here."

Bobbye took a sip of coffee. "I'll be here. And I'm going to get cleaned up and go to work. Tripp isn't coming over here, I promise. But I did tell him he could call me if he needed to. I feel so sorry for him, Stacey. He has no friends now and nowhere to go and nothing to do beyond that silly job Lark made up for him. He's managing the music foundation, but he told me he could do that with one hand tied behind his back."

I didn't mean to, but after what she'd just said, I couldn't help myself. "Be careful," I warned, "or you'll be right back where you were when Tripp ran away to South America—mooning around and wondering where he is and what he's doing."

* * * * *

I thought Bobbye was handling herself well where Tripp was concerned, until a couple weeks later when I had to go home early because my period had puddled on the back of my skirt. I knew the minute I pulled into the drive and saw Tripp's Bimmer that he was in the apartment with her. The door wasn't locked so I walked in expecting to see them in the living room, but they weren't there. I heard Bobbye's voice coming from the bedroom, heard her say *I will not...* followed by *no, no I won't*. Then Tripp said *just listen to me, will ya?*

I decided to let them know I was home and went back to the front door, gave it a good slam, and trotted off down the hall to the bathroom to tackle the stain on my skirt. When I came out, the two of them were sitting on the sofa holding hands.

Tripp got up quickly. "Don't be mad at Bobbye, Stacey. I came over here because I wanted to tell you what's going on."

He eased himself back down on the sofa and I sat down in one of the chairs across from them. "Well," I said, "you could have called. What's so important that you had to come over here?"

"I'm getting a divorce, Stacey. I made a big mistake marrying Lark, and she and I both know it. She's up in Brevard, but she'll come home in September and we've

275

agreed to see other people until she can get back here and sign the separation papers. She told me she knows I've always loved Bobbye and that I'll never love *her*, and she doesn't want to be married to someone who doesn't love her. I know I screwed up, but I'll never love anyone but Bobbye."

"You'd better watch yourself, Tripp MacAvoy. Adultery is a serious offense and Bobbye has a clean slate. You wouldn't be planning to screw that up, too, would you?"

Tripp grinned back at me. "Oh, Stacey...ever the mother hen, aren't you?" He laughed, slapped his palms on his thighs, and said, "What say we go out to dinner? My treat. I heard that Chinese place at New Towne Square is good. Want to try it?"

Bobbye and I grabbed our pocketbooks and the three of us headed out the door. As we went down the stairs, Tripp said, "Hey, Stacey, I heard you interviewed the mayor last week. How'd that go?" When I didn't respond, he started laying it on thick. "You're sure getting around town with all the big shots these days, aren't you? You've gotten to be quite the celebrity reporter. Over dinner, I want to hear all about it."

* * * * *

On the first Friday in August, my boss, Gary, called about eight to tell me that the Board of Directors at Piedmont Hospital were meeting at 9:30 that morning to deal with an unexpected request for emergency funds to cover a problem in one of their clinics. He wasn't sure what the request was for and wanted me to find out.

When I got to the meeting room, I sat down in one of the chairs designated for members of the press and opened my purse to take out my tape recorder. But it wasn't there. I took everything out of my bag and stacked it on the seat of

276

the chair beside me, but the tape recorder wasn't there. It *lived* in my purse, and every time I used it, I slipped it right back down inside a pocket in the center of my bag. No piece of equipment is more important to a reporter than a tape recorder and I couldn't believe I'd misplaced mine. Left it on the dresser, I thought, as I took out a pen and my faithful notebook.

The meeting ended at eleven and I went to the hospital's lobby where I called Gary and told him what was going on at the drug clinic. He asked me to draft an article and FAX it to him so we could run it in next morning's edition. I told him I'd misplaced my tape recorder, the one he'd given me, the one I'd decorated with a little triangle of pink plastic tape to distinguish it from dozens of others in the newsroom. I asked him to ask around and see if anyone there had seen it. When I hung up, I decided to go up to the third floor to the Physical Therapy Unit and invite Bobbye to lunch. I hadn't seen her for several days and assumed she'd been staying nights at the big house with Tripp.

I went straight to the therapy day room where she usually worked, but she wasn't there. I went down the hall to her office, which was empty. On my way back to the elevator, I ran into her supervisor, who told me Bobbye had taken a couple of days off. "She didn't come in yesterday either," she said. "She has loads of vacation days and I've urged her to take some. Sorry, Stacey, but I have no idea where she is."

When I left the hospital, I drove over to the big house on Virginia Circle, where no one was home but Classie. After she invited me in, I went back to the kitchen and sat down with her at the table. I asked about Tripp and Bobbye and she said, "They left here real early yesterday morning. Went down to Tybee thinking they was gonna take that big boat out. But the captain told Mr. Tripp he couldn't take the boat without Mrs. MacAvoy's permission. That he had it in

277

writing from Mr. Ed's lawyer as part of the settlement. I guess that means the Will, right?"

I nodded and Classie went on. "Mr. Tripp and Miss Bobbye come on back from Tybee yesterday 'round lunch time and he was 'bout as mad as I ever seen. He went upstairs to that new office of his and I could hear him on the phone carrying on with somebody. Then he come back down here with a face like thunder and say they was leaving. I ask if they'd be back in time for dinner and he say not if he could help it.

"About three o'clock I heard this commotion sounded like a big engine grindin' and look out yonder toward the garage and here he come on a big new Ford truck, or maybe it was a Dodge, pulling this trailer had a black and red boat on it... long and shiny. And Miss Bobbye come in behind him driving his car. They put the car in the garage and then they come in here and packed some clothes, and before they left, he told me they was going to a lake up in North Carolina with a funny sounding name that started with a T."

Oh, God, I thought, Janice was right. Here we go again. If it isn't one thing with Tripp MacAvoy, it's another. But I was curious and went into the library to get an atlas. I sat down and began looking for lakes in the southwestern part of North Carolina and found one called Lake Toxaway. "Is that it?" I asked Classie.

"Sound right to me," she answered. "Yessum, I'm pretty sure that's it. Anyway, Mr. Tripp told me to take care everything 'round here and they come on back Sunday."

I left there happy knowing I'd have the apartment all to myself and spent an hour turning everything upside down looking for my tape recorder. It wasn't in any of my drawers, or Bobbye's, or in any of my coat pockets. I had only two other purses, and after I'd checked them, I unearthed everything in the kitchen. But I never found it. So, early Saturday morning, after a quick trip to The Grocery Bag, I bought a new one that was a bit larger than the one I'd lost.

On Sunday night about ten, Bobbye came home. I was watching some stupid show on TV and turned it off when she sat down on the sofa and began telling me all about her weekend, and all the fun she'd had with Tripp. "He took me to this beautiful place called Lake Toxaway," she began, "and the first night we stayed in a nice motel. But the next morning, we went to a real estate office and Tripp leased this neat cottage for the months of August and September. It's right on the water and has a big dock where we can keep Tripp's new boat."

I interrupted her. "Tripp bought a boat?"

Bobbye smiled, "Oh, he's always wanted a ski boat. You know he loves to ski and so do I. Anyway, the cottage has hardwood floors and big windows and a deck and lots of trees. And it's down in this cove near the end of the lake, so it's really private. The best thing is it has two bedrooms and two baths so you and Phil can come."

"That must have cost a pretty penny," I said. "But I guess Tripp can afford it with his new job and all." I wanted to say *his rich wife* but held my tongue.

Bobbye nodded. "Yeah, I guess. But I think he wanted to be up in that area close to the farm so he can see Lark if he needs to. I have thirteen vacation days and I'm going to take every Friday off for the next two months so I can spend weekends up at the lake with Tripp. He told me that Lark is usually at the farm during the early part of the week. Monday through Wednesday, I think he said. She performs on the weekends. They're doing *Hello, Dolly!* and she's playing the lead, of course. So, Tripp and I can be at the lake house while she's in rehearsals and on stage."

"Oh, Bobbye," I said, leaning toward her. "Do you think that's wise? I mean, they aren't divorced. They aren't even separated. Tripp is married."

"Lark told him she didn't care if he spent time with his friends. She told him he should enjoy himself while she was working. Tripp went back to see that attorney, Sneed Langston, last week, and he told Tripp that because Ed's death had occurred so soon after he and Lark were married, that she could apply for a special dispensation from a judge that would cut the necessary time required for a divorce in Georgia by half. So, Tripp and Lark could be divorced by January."

"That's what *Tripp* told you...right?"

"Yeah, that's what he said. And I'm sure he was telling the truth because he sorta teared up when he told me that Lark had agreed to give him a divorce. He's so relieved that he won't have to go to those concerts anymore and hang out with her friends."

I left Bobbye sitting on the sofa and went into the bathroom to brush my teeth. When I went into the bedroom she was already in bed. She raised up on one elbow and said, "Please don't be mad at me, Stace. This is what I want. It's what I've always wanted. And I hope you and Phil will be happy for Tripp and me. I couldn't bear it if you shut me out."

I slid into my spot on the other side of the bed. "I'd never shut you out, Bobbye. You know that. But you've got to be careful. This is the kind of thing that ruins people's lives, their careers, their families. You know as well as I do that Lark Loflin's greatly admired in this city. You and Tripp need to remember that and take your time. When all of this comes out—and it will—some people aren't gonna like it. You and Tripp have the rest of your lives to be together and if I were you, I'd coast."

* * * * *

Early the following Friday, Bobbye went back up to Lake Toxaway to be with Tripp. She asked me to go with her but spending a weekend with the two of them was the last thing I wanted to do. I called Phil, and when he and I went out that night for dinner, I told him all the stuff Tripp had told Bobbye about his separation and upcoming divorce. "I've never heard of any kind of dispensation being allowed in a divorce," he said, dragging a French fry through a plop of ketchup on the side of his plate. "What the hell does that mean?"

"Beats me," I answered. "But I'll do some sniffing around to see if anyone I know has ever heard of such a thing. By the way, have you stumbled across a tape recorder anywhere... like in the back seat of your car?"

Phil shook his head. "The black one you keep in your purse? Have you lost it?"

"Yeah, I guess so. I've searched my car and my desk at the office and turned everything in the apartment upside-down looking for it. I went out last week and bought a new one, but I need the old one because it has interviews on it that have to be transcribed for the paper's archives."

Phil took a sip of Coke. "I'll check my car tomorrow morning when the light's good and let you know if I find it. It's black... right? About the size of a deck of cards...right?"

"That's the one... and it has a little piece of pink masking tape on it." I shook my head. "I can't believe I've lost it. I mean that tape recorder is like my wallet. I'm never without it. But, hey, thanks for looking."

Phil finished his burger, pushed his plate away, and said, "Tripp called me yesterday. He wants you and me to come up to Lake Toxaway for my birthday. Wants us to take next Friday off so the four of us will have a long weekend together. But, honestly, Stace, I don't think I want to be stuck with him and Bobbye for three days. Did you tell Bobbye you'd go?"

"She hasn't said anything to me. But they may have decided that Tripp would call you first and feel you out. I'm like you, though. I don't want to spend that kind of time with them at some lake. Why don't we come up with an excuse about why both of us have to work Friday? That way, we could go up there on Saturday, *that's your birthday*, and come back home Sunday."

Phil stood up and threw his napkin down on the table. "Sounds like a plan to me." He took a five from his wallet and stuck it under the rim of his plate. "Why don't I pick you up Saturday morning about eight and we can grab breakfast at this little mom and pop place I know that's just north of Roswell. A few years back, I went up to Toxaway with some friends and I think it's about three hours. I'll call Tripp and tell him to expect us in time for lunch on Saturday."

There was no rain in the forecast for Saturday which made our drive north easy. But Phil and I had trouble finding the cottage and had to stop at a convenience store to get directions because it was so far off the beaten path. As soon as we pulled into the drive, Bobbye came out and told us that Tripp had gone to get some gas for the boat...that he was really pumped about spending the day on the water skiing.

"I've packed us a basket for lunch," she said, taking us into the cottage, which was just as cute as she'd described it. We walked right into the living area which was separated from the bedrooms by a galley kitchen. From there, Phil and I followed Bobbye down a hallway that had two doors on the same side. When she reached the first one, she said, "This one's yours. We're in the next one down."

Our room had twin beds, a dresser, and a chair. There were pictures of raccoons and bears on the walls and the bedspreads were yellow and red plaid. Mountain stuff. A big window filled the front wall. On the back wall, a set of doors opened to a bathroom and a closet.

About the time I got my swimsuit on, I heard the chug-chug of a powerful engine and looked out the window to see Tripp maneuvering his ski boat alongside the dock. Phil was standing in the yard and ran to help him tie it off. I found Bobbye in the kitchen closing the top on a big picnic basket. "Grab the cooler, Stacey" she said. And I hauled that heavy mother across the porch and down the dock. Tripp smiled and said hello as he took it from me.

We started up the narrow channel beside the cottage, then cruised out into a wider section of the lake and kept going until Tripp saw several shady oaks clustered along the bank. He slid the boat beneath them and cut the engine so we could enjoy our picnic lunch out of the sun.

Our afternoon passed quickly as each of us took a turn on the skis. Then Tripp attached an over-sized tube to the back of the boat. What fun that was! I gulped down more water than a guppy and laughed and laughed while the waves lifted and lowered me up and down like a cork. The sun was hot, the water refreshing, and every now and then, we stopped to have a beer being very careful to keep our cans out of sight as alcoholic beverages were not allowed on Lake Toxaway.

About five, Tripp said he thought we'd better call it a day. "I bought some steaks to grill tonight. How does that sound?"

Bobbye and Phil and I agreed that grilled steaks would be perfect, so we headed back to the cottage. While the guys took turns at the shower outside, Bobbye and I went inside. A couple minutes later, I heard the water come on in her bath, and stepped into my shower with my suit on to make quick work of rinsing it out.

A few minutes later, I found Bobbye and Phil in the kitchen arranging little crackers around a bowl of dip. Tripp came in smelling like minty soap, removed four glasses from a shelf, and set them on the counter. From the fridge he brought out a pitcher of a pinkish concoction he told us he'd made that morning. "This is called diablo," he said, filling the glasses. "It's a very popular drink in Brazil made with tequila, rum, guava juice, and grenadine. No ice needed."

Phil picked up a glass, and said, "Bottoms up!" And we were off. We headed out back to the deck where we sipped our diablos and puffed on weed.

Tripp did his usual masterful job with the steaks and Bobbye's salad and baked potatoes were great, as always. It wasn't long before we had the CD player going full blast and were dancing up a storm. "Just like the old days," I shouted to Phil as he bobbed around me doing his stupid chicken walk. He just grinned his goofy grin and kept going. ZZ Top, Pink, and Cyndi Lauper kept us moving for the next hour or so.

When a song by the Beastie Boys ended, Tripp put another CD in the player. Then he went over to Bobbye sitting on the sofa, bowed at the waist, and asked her to dance. "You two look like you're in sixth grade at Inman Middle," I commented, as they moved to the center of the floor and Lionel Ritchie began singing "My Love."

Tripp smiled back at me. "That's the way it's always been for my girl and me. Isn't that right, my love?" Bobbye nodded, giving him the look of a love-struck teen.

God, they're disgusting, I thought, as I headed out to refill my glass, and Phil's, with diablo. When I came back from the kitchen, Beyonce was singing "Naughty Girl." I handed Phil his drink and the two of us began slithering around like a couple of lizards in heat. I tried to do one of those deep hip rolls I'd seen Beyonce do on a video and ended up on the floor. Phil fell on top of me, and we lay there giggling for a couple of minutes before he got up and pulled me to my feet. "That's enough," I said. "Time to call it a night."

"Ah, come on, Stace," Tripp groused. "It's not even midnight yet... too early to go to bed."

But Phil said he thought he'd turn in, too, and headed off. As I followed him into our room, I said, "At least we got a room with two beds." The words were hardly out of my mouth before he fell like a rock face down on one of them, and moments later, began breathing deeply. I didn't need to count any sheep either and drifted off pretty quickly.

But it didn't last because something woke me. I turned to look at the clock on the bedside table. Two thirteen. A moment later, I heard Tripp say, *Wild things! What you need, girl, is a wild thing!* Oh, lord, I thought he's off on one of his drunken rages. Poor Bobbye, I don't know why she puts up with him. A few moments passed before Tripp said, *I'm crazy all right, Bobbye. Crazy about you.*

Then he exploded into a deep rumbling gorilla growl that reverberated against the wall and Phil jerked awake. "What the hell?" he mumbled from under his pillow.

"It's Tripp," I answered. "He's in there yelling about wild things." A couple moments later, we heard Tripp say, *Let's show 'em how to do it, baby. You know what do to!* Then he shouted, *Wha-hoo! Ride 'em, cowgirl!*

Phil got up, walked over to the wall, and said, "Shut the fuck up, MacAvoy." Things got quiet. But just after I'd snuggled down, I would have sworn I heard Bobbye laughing.

I fell into a fitful sleep filled with strange visions of naked tree limbs scraping against one another, making an awful sound like someone moaning. Somebody kept calling my name, and when I woke up, I felt clammy all over. I looked at the clock on the table and saw that it was a little after four. I got up and groped my way through the dark to the bathroom. As I lowered myself onto the john, I heard voices coming from the other bedroom and moved way up to the front edge of the toilet seat so I wouldn't make any noise when I peed. As I wiped myself, I heard Bobbye say, *Stop it, Tripp MacAvoy.* When she started crying, I lost interest and went back to bed.

Phil had set the alarm for nine that morning. It blasted us awake, but neither of us got up. "My head," I mumbled. "I feel like I've got a bag of wet cement on my head."

"Me, too," Phil began. "I wish I'd never seen that damn diablo shit."

I padded out into the kitchen in my bare feet, found some Alka-Seltzer tablets in a cabinet, and fixed a fizzy glass for each of us. When I got back to the room, Phil was dressed and had his gear packed. He looked at me and said, "What say we get out of here?"

"You mean leave before they get up?"

"Why not? We're the ones who need to go home. They don't."

"Okay. Just give me a few minutes to brush my teeth and dress." I grabbed some clothes and when I took them into our bathroom, I could hear someone moving around in the other bathroom and knew that either Bobbye or Tripp was awake, too. As soon as I was decent, I went into the kitchen where Bobbye was spooning coffee into the pot. She asked me how I'd slept, and I said fine except for all that racket you and Tripp made about two o'clock. She murmured a little apology before she set out some mugs. "Coffee's ready," she called loud enough for Tripp and Phil to hear.

The four of us sat down at the table and Tripp offered to make scrambled eggs and bacon. But Phil told him we had to get on the road, that we'd grab something on the way.

Tripp said, "Okay. Well, do you mind if Bobbye and I ride back to Atlanta with you? We left her car at my house and drove the truck. But I want to leave it here at the lake to haul the boat if I need to. I'm gonna drive my Bimmer up next time. Do you guys have room for us?"

Phil nodded. "Sure. But we need to go before long."

As soon as we'd finished our coffee, Bobbye gathered the mugs and washed them while I made the beds, and the guys covered the boat with a tarp. Tripp parked his truck on the far side of the cottage where it would be out of sight and went around checking all the windows inside to be sure they were locked. "I think that's it," he called from the kitchen. We threw our bags into the back of Phil's 4Runner and climbed in.

On the way home, we had a leisurely lunch at a restaurant outside Gainesville and took our time getting back on the road. About three-thirty, we turned onto Virginia Circle and went up the hill to the birthday cake house where a blue and white Atlanta police car was parked outside the front door. Behind it was a car with the logo "Transylvania County Sheriff." Up near the garage was an unadorned black SUV. Four men in various uniforms stood together with a guy dressed in a gray suit and, as soon as Phil parked the Toyota, they started toward us.

The man in the gray suit came to the driver's side and Phil rolled down the window. "Are you Mr. MacAvoy?" he asked.

Phil shook his head. "No, sir. I'm Phil Sanford. Mr. MacAvoy's in the back."

Tripp hopped out and asked, "What's this about? Who are you?"

The man pulled out a badge and showed it to Tripp. "I'm Agent Clay Rafferty, North Carolina SBI. Are you James Edward MacAvoy III?"

Tripp nodded and the man took a moment to return the badge to his coat pocket. "I'm sorry, Mr. MacAvoy, but it's my duty to inform you that your wife is dead."

When Tripp didn't respond, Agent Rafferty took a step toward him. "I'm sorry, sir. Your wife's body was found this morning at Balsam Peak Farm near Brevard and you'll need to come downtown with me to answer a few questions."

"What the hell are you talking about?" Tripp snarled. "My wife isn't dead... she performed last night at the Brevard

Music Center." As he stepped back, his fists came up. "Why should I go with *you*?" he spat. "You got a warrant for my arrest?"

Agent Rafferty lowered his voice. "No, sir… but I can get one if I need to, Mr. MacAvoy." And there was no mistaking his intent.

That's when I heard Bobbye crying. She kept repeating, "No…no…no" until Tripp stuck his head through the open window and told her to hush. "Go home and call Sneed Langston," he said. "And stop crying."

Agent Rafferty told Phil, Bobbye, and me to take out our driver's licenses. My stomach did back-flips while he snapped photos of each using a camera about the size of a match box. Then he put his hand under Tripp's elbow, walked him across the yard, and put him in the back of the SUV. On his way down the drive, he stopped to tell us he was taking Mr. MacAvoy to the main precinct downtown.

As they pulled away, I got out of the car and walked up the front steps of the house where two Atlanta police officers were tying off a strip of yellow plastic they'd strung from one side of the house, across the big windows, to the other. The words KEEP OUT BY ORDER OF POLICE were emblazoned at intervals in black letters along the bright background. Oh, God, I thought, as tears welled in my eyes. Poor Ed. I'm glad he isn't here to see this.

Phil walked up behind me. "May we go home now, officer?" he asked. One of the men said, "Yes, you can go home. But don't go far. Understand?" The officer turned, walked up the front steps, and knocked on the door. I waited until Classie opened it and waved to her just before I got back in Phil's car. I felt bad that she was all alone in that big house with no one to comfort her or tell her what was going on.

In his haste to get away, Phil swung onto the driveway too fast, all but throwing me against the door. When we reached the end of the drive, he pulled over and turned off the ignition. "God dammit," he said, banging his fists on the steering wheel. "Thanks to MacAvoy, we're in the middle of another fucking shit storm! Why didn't he just *stay* in South America!"

Without warning, Bobbye reached up and slapped Phil on the back of his head. "Shut up," she barked. "Just shut up, Phil, and drive."

None of us spoke again until we reached the apartment. As he pulled into the driveway, Phil took a moment to clear his throat before he said, "If y'all don't mind, I'd like to come in for a minute...okay?" I was relieved because I didn't want to be alone with Bobbye.

After the three of us plunked ourselves down in the living room, Phil looked over at Bobbye and said, "I'm sorry I lost it back there, Bobbye. I can't seem to wrap my head around what that SBI agent said. How can *Lark* be dead?"

He put his head down and was quiet for a few seconds before he spoke again. "It really isn't any of my business, Bobbye, but if I were you, I wouldn't call that guy, Sneed Langston. I'd call Baxter Dobson. Bax is a well-known attorney with a solid reputation and he's your best bet in my opinion."

I jumped in saying I agreed with Phil. "Bax is the one to call," I assured her. "And you'd better call him now."

When Bobbye got Bax on the line, she told him where we'd been and what had happened. Bax told her he'd come over that night to discuss the situation. But first he was going to the police station to get Tripp. "I'm taking him straight home," I heard him tell Bobbye, his words emerging in a strident cadence. "And the three of you are not to see him, or talk with him, under any circumstances. The last thing you all need is to be implicated in whatever has happened to Lark MacAvoy. Oh, God, what a damn shame." He'd signed off, saying he'd be at the apartment about six.

As soon as Bax arrived that evening, he told us that Tripp had not been charged with anything *yet*. But when he'd called the sheriff up in Transylvania County, Bax had learned that authorities there had some evidence they thought might incriminate Tripp. "That SBI agent, the one who took Tripp downtown, is in constant touch with the state medical examiner who's conducting an autopsy," he said. "Tripp went ballistic when he heard about the autopsy and begged me to stop it because he didn't want Lark *butchered like a side of beef*. But when I called Judge Ragsdale in Brevard, he told me under the circumstances, an autopsy would have to be done."

I shuddered at the thought of an autopsy being performed on Lark Loflin, at the thought of her delicate breastbone being ripped apart by a saw so slivers of her heart and lungs could be removed and put under a microscope, the thought of parts of her stomach and intestines being removed and tested for poisons, the thought of her beautiful golden hair being cut off in clumps to be treated with chemicals. Thanks to my job, I was aware of the gruesome procedures used during a criminal investigation and, when I heard the word *autopsy*, a lump formed in my throat and I had to excuse myself and to the kitchen and drink some water.

For the next hour, Bobbye, Phil, and I told Bax about our time with Tripp…about being out in the boat, what we'd had to drink, the foods we'd eaten, the music we'd danced to, and the fact that we'd gone to bed early for a Saturday night. I told Bax how I'd been awakened about two-thirty because Tripp was howling like a gorilla. And Phil had said, "Yeah, the damn fool."

Bobbye went into more detail telling Bax that Tripp had been on his wild thing kick, explaining how he acted like an animal when he drank, and sometimes he howled and growled.

Bax looked over at me. "You said you heard him doing that stuff, right Stacey? Is that the only time you heard him?"

"No," I shook my head. "I woke up again about four and heard him talking. I couldn't hear what he was saying, but I heard him."

Phil said, "I heard him, too. But I tuned him out. Tripp and I lived together when we were in college, and I learned to tune him out early on. He's a high-strung, belligerent kind of guy and when he doesn't get his way, he gets nasty and loud."

And Bax murmured, "Hmm...that's the kind of statement I hope you'll never make in front of a judge or jury, Phil." He looked at Bobbye, then at me, and we both nodded.

Then he leaned back in his chair and said, "If he's lucky, Tripp may have to appear at a hearing in front of a judge in Transylvania County. If the sheriff up there has evidence—if he has proof that Tripp was present when Lark died—then we'll likely go to trial. But that's something for a Grand Jury to decide. I'll know more tomorrow when I get the results of the medical examiner's report. In the meantime, you three are not to communicate with Tripp MacAvoy in any way. Do you understand? A young woman has been found dead and I cannot over-emphasize the seriousness of this situation— which has been made even more serious by the fact that all of you not only knew her but knew her well." He got up and let out a long sigh. "This is especially difficult because Lark and Tripp hadn't been married but just a few months. It's just a damn shame," he said, turning to leave.

We walked with him into the hallway and, before he opened the door, he told Phil that he could go home, but he was not to discuss the case with anyone, including his parents. "I hope all of you have some vacation days you can take because you need to stay out of sight for a few days. You can go to the grocery store—things like that. But otherwise, keep a low profile, at least until we know if that Transylvania

County sheriff has anything or not. And you're not to speak to any TV or newspaper person for *any* reason."

He looked at me from the corner of his eye. "I'm sure your boss is expecting you to tell him everything you know, Stacey, so the paper will have a good story to sell about the mysterious death of one of Atlanta's most talented and well-loved musicians. But you simply cannot reveal *anything*. You understand, don't you?"

"If Gary calls me," I began, "I'll tell him I can't discuss it. Before you leave, may I ask a favor? Would you please go by the MacAvoy house and talk with Classie? She's there all by herself and I know she must be out of her mind with worry. They wouldn't let me speak with her yesterday."

Bax gave me a nod. "Thanks for mentioning Miss Dixon, Stacey. I'll stop by there now on my way home. Good night, guys, and remember—be careful."

Phil had followed Bax down the stairs and, as soon as she heard the sound of their car doors slamming, Bobbye hurried off to the bedroom. That was the last place I wanted to be that night, so I stayed in the living room reading, hoping it would help me get to sleep. But it didn't and after a while, I found myself pacing the floor like a caged tiger, back and forth, back and forth, from one end of the hallway to the other. Then I began to cry. I was so mad and so sad, and none of it made any sense. I'd loved and admired Lark for so many years. And even when she'd disappointed me with Tripp MacAvoy, I'd known deep in my heart that I would always love her.

A heavy rain began to fall, and the sound of it hitting the metal roof of that old house soothed me. Eventually, I gave up and went to bed. That was another mistake, as I simply lay awake for hours while Bobbye thrashed around calling out in her sleep. I'd shake her awake and she'd be okay for a few minutes. Then she'd fall asleep and start mumbling and groaning again. I thought the night would never end and, about five, I gave up and left her in bed.

I made a big pot of coffee, knowing she and I would need it to get going. Then I called my dad and told him the news. "How awful," he'd moaned. "That beautiful young woman dead. I guess I'd better be sure I have all the stuff I need to make the death cake."

I told him to hold off on that because a coroner was conducting an investigation and it might be a couple of days before we knew anything. "Bax Dobson is going to let us know what's going on," I said, "and I'll let you know."

Phil came over about three to see if we'd heard anything and when he learned we hadn't, he decided to hang around. A little after four, we finally got a call from Bax, but the news wasn't good. Bobbye had taken the call and when she hung up, she told Phil and me that the coroner had not yet completed his report and, as soon as the sheriff in Transylvania County heard that, he'd called Bax to discuss a *waived extradition*, which meant they'd taken Tripp from Atlanta to their jail up in Transylvania County. Bax was leaving for Brevard within the hour and he'd spend the night up there because District Court Judge Hunter Ragsdale had graciously agreed to meet with him the next morning. Bax said he'd call and give us an update as soon as he got back.

After Bobbye reported this to Phil and me, I went to the fridge, got some beers, and the three of us sat down in the living room. Phil told us he'd been to see his parents and told them what little he could. Then he told us that Bax had called and asked Brock and Phyllis to drive down to Savannah and tell Rosemarie about the death of her precious granddaughter.

"God, I don't envy them...or her," he said. "That poor old woman losing the light of her life and her only living relative. I just hope she doesn't kill the messengers." Then he suggested we order a pizza and I got up to make the call.

Just as I put my hand on the phone, it rang. I picked it up and Bax said, "Stacey, you and Phil and Bobbye get your ducks in a row and get up here tomorrow. Judge Ragsdale has scheduled a hearing for one o'clock. I'll be seeing Tripp in the morning and, after that, I want you guys to meet me at noon at City Lunch on Main Street...okay? We need to talk about a few things before you're questioned at the hearing. See you then."

The food at City Lunch was good, but the only one who ate much was Phil. Bax had ordered a pastrami sandwich, but he talked the whole time and never got a chance to eat it. Bobbye sat at the table, a salad in front of her, staring into space. I gobbled a few bites of my grilled cheese while Bax prepped us for the hearing.

"You'll have to swear that what you're about to say is the truth," he'd said, "and whatever you do, do not say more than you need to. Do not elaborate. Simply answer the questions of the District Attorney, Brother Thaddeus Wilkinson. He's called Brother because he's a lay minister at Heart of the Rock Baptist. But don't let that minister stuff fool you. From what I've heard, he's a tough litigator. And Judge Ragsdale may ask a few questions, too."

"I'll do most of the asking though, to try to let them know who you three are, the fact that you're all old friends of Tripp... and of Lark... and how you were together in a cabin on Lake Toxaway the night she died. That's the hard part. If I were the prosecutor, the first thing I'd want to know is why the husband of a dead woman is out partying with friends of hers. Go slowly and let me guide each of you through. Okay? Don't offer up anything by way of explanation. Remember that detective on that old television show, the one who always said, *Just the facts, ma'am, just the facts?*" I nodded vigorously as I wolfed down the last of my sandwich.

Bax got up and went to the restroom and, when he came back, Phil had paid the bill and he and Bobbye and I were waiting just outside the door of the café. "We won't be in a courtroom today," he said, as we started up the street to the old red brick Transylvania County Courthouse. "This isn't a trial...and we hope it won't become one. This hearing will be held in a room set up with tables and chairs and you'll just sit quietly until you're called."

When we reached the front of the building, I paused to look up at the tower above the entry and wondered if there was a bell in it. Bax got my attention. "Not that door, Stacey," he cautioned before leading us around the side to a set of double doors that opened onto a long hallway. About half-way up, he stopped in front of one. "This is where we'll be," he said, opening it. "You might see some people in here that you know, but please don't speak to anyone. Just go on up to the front," he stopped and pointed, "and sit down in those three chairs grouped together on the right. Tripp is sitting on the left." He glanced at his watch. "It's twelve fifty-five. I need to speak to Brother Thaddeus before we start."

A couple dozen people were seated in folding chairs on either side of the aisle and, as Bobbye and Phil and I walked between them, I was surprised to see my Granny Edith sitting in one on the far left next to my dad.

After we sat down in our appointed places, Bax came in with a silver-haired man dressed in a stylish blue suit and whorled cowboy boots. They sat down in wooden chairs on either side of an executive style leather chair, all of which had been grouped together behind a long table that faced us and the others assembled. At precisely one o'clock, a man who was at least ten years younger than Bax, came in trailing a black robe and carrying a manila folder. A bailiff appeared and said, "All rise." We stood and watched as Judge Ragsdale sat down in the leather chair between Bax and the man known as Brother Thaddeus. The judge picked up a gavel, banged it couple of times, and said, "This hearing is called to order. Mr. District Attorney, you may begin."

Brother Thaddeus looked toward the back of the room. "Dale Mason," he called. "Please come sit up here in the chair across from Judge Ragsdale."

A thin rangy man dressed in jeans and a plaid shirt came up the aisle and took the proffered seat. He was sworn in by the bailiff and told the judge that he was the manager of Balsam Peak Farm, which was owned by Mrs. Lark Loflin MacAvoy. He began by saying that when he'd gone to the farm on Sunday morning about seven to feed the stock, he'd driven his truck up the driveway and right out to the barn, which was a couple of hundred feet behind the house. And after he'd taken care of the cattle, he'd walked up to the back door of the house and knocked. He said he always did that when Mrs. MacAvoy was at the farm to let her know he'd been there and seen to things, and that she always came to the door and thanked him. Sometimes she invited him in for coffee. But that morning, she didn't answer the door.

He paused then, coughed behind his hand, and Brother Thaddeus told him to go on and tell the judge what happened. "Well, the door weren't locked," Mr. Mason said. "So, I went on in the kitchen and started callin'. I knew she was there 'cause I seen her car parked under the shed. When she didn't answer, I walked up the hall to the living room and that's where I found her." He paused, and I saw his shoulders lift a bit as he took another breath. "She was lying on the floor over by the coffee table…lying on her stummick with her head turn't to one side. I knew she was dead soon as I seen her. But I got down and felt her wrist to be sure."

The room began to buzz, and I leaned forward to see Tripp squirm in his seat. Judge Ragsdale banged his gavel, nodded at Mr. Mason, and told him to please continue. And

Mr. Mason said, "That's when I went back to the kitchen and called the sheriff."

Then Brother Thaddeus asked Mr. Mason if he'd seen any blood on, or near, Mrs. MacAvoy's body, if he'd seen any bruises or marks of any kind? Mason said he hadn't. He went on to say he'd seen nothing out of place in the living room… and the only thing he'd noticed was a wine glass on the kitchen counter with some red wine in the bottom of it and a plate on the counter beside it that had some little pieces of green stuff that looked like lettuce on it. After he'd called the sheriff, he'd gone back out to wait in his truck.

The judge thanked Mr. Mason and told him to return to his seat. Then he turned to Bax and asked him to bring his client forward. And Tripp—a pale, visibly nervous Tripp— got up and went to sit at the table.

Bax said, "Mr. MacAvoy, please tell Judge Ragsdale where you were, and what you were doing, the night your wife died. Tripp told the judge all about buying a new truck and a new boat and renting a cottage at Lake Toxaway, and how Lark had wanted him to have fun with his friends while she was performing at the Brevard Music Festival.

Brother Thaddeus had interrupted to ask Tripp where he'd gotten the money to buy the truck and the boat and rent the cottage. And Tripp replied that his wife had given it to him.

The judge gave Tripp a puzzled look. "Why did you bring your boat up from Atlanta when there are so many nice lakes down there? You could have taken your boat somewhere more convenient like Lake Lanier or Sandy Springs. Why didn't you do that, Mr. MacAvoy?"

Tripp seemed to brighten a bit. "Because I wanted to be near my wife while she was up here in North Carolina. I wanted to take her out on the boat when she wasn't working at the music festival. And I thought it would be fun if we rented a cottage at Lake Toxaway, because I could keep the boat there. There's nowhere to take a boat out in Brevard."

He was wearing Ed's signet ring on his right hand and Bobbye had told me he'd never taken it off since the day Lark had given it to him. But what caught my eye was the gold band on the ring finger of his left hand. He hadn't been wearing it when he came to the apartment a month before, and I was sure he'd not worn it during our weekend at Lake Toxaway. Why was he wearing a wedding ring now?

Bax stepped up and asked Tripp to tell Judge Ragsdale about the last time he'd seen his wife. Tripp said he'd gone up to the farm in North Carolina the Monday before and he'd spent Tuesday and Wednesday there with his wife. On Wednesday night Lark had had a dress rehearsal for "Hello, Dolly!" So, he'd cooked an early dinner for them, and she'd left about six-thirty. He went on to explain that when Lark was playing a major role in a production at the festival, she always stayed in accommodations provided for performers in Brevard on those nights and usually returned to the farm after the final performance.

Judge Ragsdale interrupted. "So, the final performance of "Hello Dolly!" was on what night, Mr. MacAvoy?"

Tripp hesitated. "Saturday... Saturday night was the last performance."

Judge Ragsdale moved forward in his seat. "And did you see your wife that night, Mr. MacAvoy?"

And Tripp moved toward him and said, "No, Your Honor. I did not. I spent Saturday night with my friends in a cottage at Lake Toxaway."

Judge Ragsdale excused Tripp and told him to return to his seat. Then he motioned to Bax, who called Roberta Ann Revels. Bobbye took the seat Tripp had vacated and told the same story she'd told Bax earlier about what the four of us had done at Lake Toxaway.

When she finished, Judge Ragsdale said, "I understand that you and Mr. MacAvoy were engaged at one time, Miss Revels. Is that correct?" Bobbye nodded and Bax told her to respond verbally to the judge's questions for the sake of the court recorder. Bobbye said, "Yes." Then Judge Ragsdale said, "And where did you sleep on the night in question, Miss Revels?"

Bobbye looked down at her hands and said, "I slept on the sofa in the living room."

My heart jumped to my throat, but I never got to refute that lie because, when Bax questioned me, he skirted that issue entirely. Instead, he asked what I'd heard during the night at the cottage, and I told him I'd heard Tripp yelling. He asked me to replicate the kinds of sounds I'd heard. I felt like an idiot when I started howling, and even more so when several people started giggling. Then Bax asked me if I was absolutely sure it was Mr. MacAvoy who'd made those sounds. And I replied, "Yes sir, I'm sure it was him."

"And *why* are you so sure it was him?" he asked.

I shifted in my seat a little to look directly at Judge Ragsdale. "That's what he does when he's drinking. Tripp makes animal sounds and runs around doing his imitation of a gorilla. I heard him doing that, Your Honor, a little after two o'clock that night...er...that morning."

Bax said, "And did you hear anything else from Mr. MacAvoy that night?"

"Yes, sir. I woke up again about four o'clock and heard him talking."

Judge Ragsdale rubbed his index finger across his chin, looked at me, and said, "Are you sure it was Mr. MacAvoy you heard, Miss Parks?" I assured him it was.

I was excused and Bax called Phil and led him through the same series of questions that were the same ones Phil had answered at the apartment on Sunday night. Phil's part of the testimony was over in less than three minutes.

Then Brother Thaddeus stood up and called Tripp back to the chair again. "Mr. MacAvoy," he began, "your fingerprints were found on a wine bottle in the kitchen of your wife's farmhouse. The same bottle, according to Dr. Hazlitt's report, from which she drank on the night she died. Did you drink any wine while you were with her at the farm?"

Tripp nodded. "Yes, sir. I did. On Wednesday night, I cooked dinner for the two of us and each of us had a glass of wine from that bottle. I'm the one who took it to her. She'd called our house in Atlanta that morning before I left and asked Classie to go down to the wine cellar and get a certain bottle for her, a 1973 Montrachet. It was a Bouchard...that was the brand... her favorite. She told Classie to give that bottle of wine to me so I could take it when I went to the farm."

Judge Ragsdale looked around the room. "Classie Marlene Dixon, are you here?"

And Classie surprised me when she stood up from three rows back. I hadn't even seen her there. The judge said, "Miss Dixon, did Mrs. MacAvoy call you last Monday morning and ask you to send a particular bottle of wine to the farm with Mr. MacAvoy that day?"

Classie's voice was loud and clear when she answered, "Yes, Your Honor, she did. I went on down to the cellar and got it, put it in a paper bag, and give it to him."

The judge thanked Classie and called for the State Medical Examiner.

I'll not bore you with all of the technical details of his report, but Dr. Ben Hazlitt did a thorough job of explaining how he'd formed his conclusions about Lark's death. The bailiff brought in an easel and set it up at the end of the table near where Bax, Judge Ragsdale, and Brother Thaddeus were sitting. Then the doctor introduced several enlarged photographs showing Lark on the night she'd died. I had to lean forward a bit to see them, and in retrospect, I wish I hadn't. The first one showed her body sprawled on the hardwood floor in the living room, the fingers of her right hand clutching the leg of the coffee table. She was wearing a pink night gown and her legs were splayed in a way that suggested she'd fallen. The next photograph was a close-up of her head, which was turned to one side. I could see the end of her tongue, swelled so large it protruded from between her lips…lips that were a ghastly blue like the surface on a frozen lake. Seeing her like that almost did me in. I was so afraid I'd throw up that I snatched a tissue from my pocketbook and held it over my nose while I gulped air hoping to control my jumpy tummy.

The doctor explained that there were no bruises, nor visible marks of any kind, on Lark's body, except for a small scratch on her left thumb that had scabbed over days before. During the autopsy, he said he'd examined and tested the contents of her stomach and her intestinal tract. She'd eaten some leafy greens, raw vegetables, and shellfish. She'd washed her dinner down with red wine a few hours before she'd died, which he estimated to have been sometime between midnight and six o'clock on Sunday morning.

Dr. Hazlitt surprised us when he said, "I believe this beautiful young woman died of heart failure." I was not the only person who gasped at that. A ripple went through the room forcing Judge Ragsdale to rap his gavel again. Then Dr. Hazlitt put a poster on the easel showing a diagram of the interior chambers of the human heart. "Mrs. MacAvoy suffered from a heart defect…a septal ventricle defect that she'd probably had since birth. My examination revealed a small hole, approximately three tenths of a centimeter in diameter, in the wall that separates the two lower ventricles." He paused and pointed to the two lower chambers on the diagram. "The tissue around that little hole was unusually thin and so severely abraded that I knew she'd died very quickly, perhaps in a matter of seconds, of what is commonly known as a heart attack."

The breath all but went out of me. I couldn't believe I'd known someone thirty-seven years old who'd died of a heart attack. But what the doctor said next was even more surprising. Lark MacAvoy had been pregnant.

Dr. Hazlitt turned from the judge to look at Tripp. "Your wife was nine, perhaps ten weeks pregnant, Mr. MacAvoy."

Judge Ragsdale's dark eyes narrowed as he turned toward Tripp. "Did you know your wife was pregnant?"

Tripp put his hands over his face and, from behind them, murmured, "No, sir."

Dr. Hazlitt finished by saying, "The fact that Mrs. MacAvoy was pregnant had nothing to do with her death. It was just a tragic coincidence."

Judge Ragsdale thanked the court, gathered up his folder, and motioned to Bax and Brother Thaddeus and the three of them stepped away from the table where they engaged in a brief conversation. A moment later, Judge Ragsdale summoned Dr. Hazlitt and I watched closely as he addressed the examiner directly. The doctor nodded once, then twice, in response to whatever it was the judge had asked him. The judge went back to his place at the table, banged the gavel, and said, "I declare this hearing adjourned." The bailiff walked over to Tripp and told him he was free to go.

* * * * *

Bobbye rode back to Atlanta with Bax and Tripp. Phil and I followed. Classie, who'd been driven up to Brevard by her brother, Raeford, was already at home preparing dinner for us. When Bobbye and I went into the kitchen to see if we could help, she asked us to set the table in the dining room and pointed to a stack of plates, napkins, and flatware sitting on the counter.

As soon the swinging door closed behind us, Bobbye told me that on the way home Tripp had asked Bax about Lark's will. And Bax had told him that Lark didn't have one, that she'd signed a pre-nup before she and Ed were married that stipulated that, following her death, no funds would be disbursed from the original trust unless she and Ed had had a child.

"Tripp was really upset when he heard that," Bobbye confided. "Bax told Tripp that his father had been specific about what would happen to his hard-earned money once he was gone...and long after he was gone. And he told us that he wouldn't be able to reveal anything about Ed's wishes regarding his estate until after Lark's service."

Bobbye finished putting the plates around the table and then she helped me set out the flatware while she continued with her story. "The authorities from Transylvania County told Bax that they'd release Lark's remains tomorrow. Tripp's gone upstairs now to call the funeral home to arrange for them to be picked up. Tripp told Bax he wanted to have a private burial the following Thursday and the memorial service would be on Friday. I guess Tripp will tell everyone about that at dinner."

After Classie brought in the platter of ham and the bowls of vegetables she'd prepared, Tripp invited everyone to the dining room. Then he opened a bottle of Lark's favorite Montrachet and poured each of us a glass. "To Lark Loflin MacAvoy," he said, "may her beautiful soul rest in peace." I joined in the toast but had no enthusiasm for it because it seemed so absurd given what I knew about the two of them. I looked over at Phil, but he ignored me and began filling his plate. Classie appeared again with a pie and, soon after, brought in a tray filled with coffee cups. On her way back to the kitchen, she stopped just inside the door. "Will that be all for now, Mr. Tripp?" she asked. Tripp nodded and told her to go have her dinner.

After we'd finished our dessert and coffee, Bax told Tripp that he'd return the next morning to discuss the financial details of Lark's burial and arrange for the funeral home to be paid out of the trust. As soon as he'd left, Tripp closed the front door and came back in while Bobbye and Phil and I were stacking the dirty dishes. "You guys don't need to do that," he said. "Just leave that stuff for Classie and come on in the library."

Once we were in the library, he closed the door, and when he turned back to face us, I flinched because there were tears in his eyes. "Please don't leave me," he begged. "I don't think I can be alone in this house."

"But Classie will be here with you," I reminded him.

"She's not the same as you guys," Tripp whined. He sniffed a couple of times and wiped his nose on the sleeve of his shirt. "Just run home and get your pjs and toothbrushes and come back. We'll watch a movie or play cards or something. Please say you'll stay here with me …at least tonight." He looked over at me. "Bobbye and I will stay out in the apartment, Stacey, and you and Phil can sleep in the bedrooms down here. And maybe tomorrow we can go to The Varsity for lunch."

When no one responded, Tripp began to back away. "I don't think I can do this without you," he muttered. "I need you to help me and I need Phyllis and Brock and Janice and Russell. I need all of you because I don't know what the hell I'm supposed to do." So, Phil took Bobbye and me to our apartment. Then he went to his condo, came back and got us, and the three of us spent the next two nights with Tripp.

Sleeping in a room across the hall from the bedroom where Ed and Caroline had slept—*where Ed and Lark had slept*—was misery. I hardly slept at all but spent most of the night in the kitchen where I indulged in a couple of Classie's oatmeal cookies, made myself some peanut butter and crackers, and drank a big glass of milk. Then I went into the library, studied the magazines on the rack, and took some of them back to my bedroom. I tried hard to read but my mind kept churning with images like those in a kaleidoscope… Lark's pink night gown, Lark's blue lips, Lark's lifeless eyes in their sunken hollows, Lark's pale fingers grasping the leg of the coffee table.

On Thursday morning, no one outside our small group was invited to her burial. Tripp told the rector from The Sign of the Shepherd to keep his remarks brief. Rosemarie was in bed too ill to make the trip to Atlanta. God help her, why would she? Phyllis, Bobbye, and I held onto each other, tears streaming down our faces, while Lark's rose-covered coffin was lowered into a muddy hole to the right of Ed's grave. Tripp swayed back and forth, mumbling incoherently throughout, with Brock on his right and Phil on his left.

At two o'clock the following Friday, a record number of mourners crowded into the sanctuary at The Sign of the Shepherd for the memorial service. When the "family" came in—family being Tripp, Bobbye, Phil, his parents, Classie, and me—I noticed dozens of people, including Judge Whitlow, standing in the back because there were no more seats. Lark's fans, and hundreds of her former students, crowded into the pews along with a large contingent of the symphony. David Duckworth delivered a moving eulogy for his friend whom he called one of the most beautiful people he'd ever had the privilege of knowing. Tripp had asked that the rector deliver an up-lifting message, so the man had read several passages from the Bible about the soothing nature of music and praised Lark for her generous nature, her musical gifts, and the joy she'd brought to others.

Brock and Phyllis hosted a reception afterwards in the Parish Hall where cakes baked by the women of the church had been arranged, along with my dad's death cake, on a buffet table and served with coffee and tea. While Bobbye cut slices of cake, and Phil and I poured coffee, the three of us kept an eye on Tripp. Off to the side, on a separate table, were several bottles of wine and that's where Tripp stayed. He kept glancing at his watch and, after a while, came over and put his arm around Bobbye's waist. "Let's get this fucking shit over and get on with the important stuff," he said in a loud voice. He looked around, studied the group, and yelled, "Bax...where are you, Bax?" A hush fell over the room and Phil went to the rescue, somehow convincing Tripp that the two of them needed to go outside.

When we finally arrived back to the big house, Bax came with us. I was surprised that Janice and Russell had come, but Bobbye told me that Bax had invited them. I soon knew why. Once all of us were seated in the library, Bax, who was standing in front of the fireplace, said, "This won't take long. As the Executor of Ed MacAvoy's estate, it's my responsibility to continue to carry out his wishes and to act as custodian of the MacAvoy Trust." He withdrew an envelope from inside his jacket, walked over to Bobbye, and handed it to her. She looked up at him, frowned, and said, "For *me*?"

After he'd assured her that it was, she opened it and removed a sheet of paper. I watched as her eyes quickly scanned it. Then she threw it to the floor and ran out of the room. Bax retrieved the paper, and said, "I was afraid that would happen. I'm sure she won't mind if I read this to you." He looked at Tripp. "Your dad wrote this a few weeks before he died."

11-20-1999

Dearest Bobbye,

If you're reading this, then my beloved wife Lark is on her way to Heaven where she'll outshine the angels. Many years may have passed since her death and my best hope is that during that time you and my son, Tripp, have had a happy marriage. Perhaps by now I'm a grandfather. If my friend Bax Dobson is still living, then he'll have told you that Lark had no will because that was something we agreed upon before we married. I have stipulated in my will that following the death of Lark Loflin MacAvoy, that you, Roberta Marie Revels (hopefully MacAvoy by now), are sole heir to my estate.

You may be wondering why I chose to make you my heir—and one reason is that I've always admired you for your hard work and determination. No one did more for me than you, Bobbye, during my illness. Lark and Classie took good care of me, but it was you who provided me with the skills and stamina to maintain some quality of life right up to the end.

As you know, my son has never been a good manager of money. But I feel confident that you'll take as good care of it as you did of me and see that it isn't squandered on "pipe dreams." Please safeguard it and spend it wisely. Thank you for that.

Yours most sincerely,

Ed

Bax held the letter up for all of us to see and I watched Janice move to the edge of her seat to get a closer look. "This letter," Bax continued, "was an addendum to Ed's original will and testament, and it has been witnessed and signed by Judge Whitlow and Judge Normand. It's certified by a notary and is completely legal."

Tripp bounded out of his chair. "What the hell? You're fucking crazy, Dobson!"

But Bax let Tripp have it. "Sit down and be quiet. You have no say in this, Tripp. None at all. Ed MacAvoy has made his wishes known and his estate was *his*, not yours. And this house, the beach house, the farm in the mountains, the Mercedes in the garage, and "Mac the Knife" now belong to Bobbye Revels, along with a trust of over fifty-seven million dollars."

Janice staggered up from her chair. "Oh, God... oh, God," she muttered before Russell grabbed her arm and pulled her back down. Bax looked at him and said, "Go find your daughter."

Bobbye had gotten all the way down the drive and up Virginia Circle to Highland Avenue before Russell caught up with her. He put her in the car and came back to the house to get Janice. I didn't hear from Bobbye until the following Sunday night when she left a message on the machine telling me she wasn't coming home, she was taking the rest of her vacation days to stay with her folks.

* * * * *

There's no need to tell you where this story is headed because you read the prologue. But there were some interesting twists along the way. I didn't hear from Bobbye for quite a while, but one evening in late October she called to ask if I'd meet her at the drug store on Highland Avenue the next day. She had something to tell me.

That Wednesday was warm and muggy with a strong breeze from the south that felt like a hurricane was brewing. Bobbye arrived at the drug store in her scrubs. "As you can see, I haven't quit my job," she said, by way of greeting. I told her I found that admirable and pointed to an open booth where we sat down.

As soon as the waitress had taken our order, I said, "You must have had some scrubs at your parents."

"No...no, I didn't," she shook her head, "but I bought some because my old ones were beginning to fade. I'll come over to the apartment soon and pack up my stuff, Stacey. And I'll keep paying my half of the rent until you can find a new place."

"I can't afford a new place," I countered. "You know I've been saving up for the past two years to buy a little house, but I don't have enough to make a down payment. I guess I'll have to find a one-bedroom apartment to rent instead."

The waitress returned with glasses of tea and we paused in our conversation to take a sip. Then Bobbye said, "I could lend you the money to buy any kind of house you want."

I thanked her and told her I'd think about it, but I knew I wouldn't. The last thing I wanted was to be beholden to Bobbye now that she was a multi-millionaire. The waitress brought our sandwiches and, as she set the plates in front of us, Bobbye said, "I've been really busy lately, Stacey. There's been an awful lot to learn. Bax and I have been meeting every afternoon for the past couple of weeks going over all the information from Ed's estate. There's file after file of deposits...lots of money coming in... and withdrawals that have to be made...not to mention all the work that has to be done before the scholarships can be awarded from the music foundation. Tripp is still looking after that, but I can tell you right now he's gonna need help."

Tact vanished and I interrupted her. "Are you living with him at the big house?"

I thought she'd be offended, but she wasn't. Holding the uneaten remains of her sandwich, she said, "No. I'm living with my parents, Stacey."

"But you've seen Tripp, haven't you? I mean you two have seen each other since Lark's funeral, haven't you?"

"Of course, we've seen each other. As Bax keeps reminding me, Tripp's *my employee*." Bobbye got that far away look in her eyes and I knew she was going to say something I wouldn't like. "Tripp's so pitiful," she began. "I mean, he's so sad. He goes on and on about his mother and how much he misses her. He's lost somehow... he can't seem to find his way. And he rambles around in that big house with no one but Classie for company. I'm selling the farm up in North Carolina—the land, the buildings, and the cattle. I want to be rid of it as soon as possible because I don't need any reminders of what happened there." She turned to look at me. "And I'm giving some of that money to Tripp. Rand and Patricia left Tripp a lot of money...several million... plus a load of Coca-Cola stock. But he can't touch any of it until he's thirty."

"Thirty?"

"Yeah. Bax told him he can't get access to it until his thirtieth birthday. After that, he'll have plenty of money of his own and maybe he'll stop badgering me."

"Maybe in the interim he can get a job cooking in a restaurant," I ventured. "He's a great cook. Surely someone would hire him."

"I mentioned that to him, but he told me he's not ready. And I promised I wouldn't mention it again because he gets mad if I bring it up." She took a moment to down the last of her tea. "Tripp wants us to take his dirt bike to John's Mountain next Saturday to ride the trails, but I can't because I need to get over to the apartment and pack up my stuff." She pulled a pocket calendar from her purse. "Let me check that date. Hum... next Saturday is November 5. Will that be okay with you, Stacey? If you have plans, don't worry. My dad will bring me in Green Bean so we can get everything. My room at home and the garage are gonna be jam packed with all my junk until I can decide what to do."

"You liked those condos we saw …remember?"

"Yes, but I can't think about that now. I've got way too much to do with all this estate business." She opened her wallet, took out some bills, and laid them on the table. "I've got it, Stace. See you next Saturday morning about nine. Okay?"

She started to walk away but stopped and turned back. "My parents want you and Elliott to come to our house for Thanksgiving."

* * * * *

On Thanksgiving Day when my dad and I arrived at the Warren's blue Cape Cod, I reminded him that Tripp would probably be there and he'd better be on his best behavior no matter what. He'd frowned at me and groaned, "Oh God" just as Janice opened the door.

She'd taken us straight down the hallway into the kitchen so we could put my dad's pie on the counter and my congealed salad in the fridge. "Phil is in the living room with Tripp and Bobbye," she said, smiling at me. "Why don't you go on in and join them while Elliott and I check the bird."

As soon as I crossed the threshold into the living room, Phil got up and gave me a hug. "Long time, no see, Stacey. Where've you been lately?"

Tripp, who was sitting next to Bobbye on the sofa asked if I'd fallen off the edge of the earth. "It's been weeks and weeks since we've seen you. What's new?"

Phil poured a glass of wine for me and I sat down in the chair opposite him near the front window. "Not much," I said, "just working, working. How are you guys doing?"

Phil nodded at Tripp. "MacAvoy's the one with news. Tell her what you're doing, man."

Tripp reared back and squared his shoulders. "There's really not much to tell. I have a new office though. It's

311

downtown in that same tall building where Bax has his law firm. And I have this great assistant—he's Bax's nephew—helping me with the music foundation. On weekends he plays jazz piano around town, but three days a week he helps me with all the paperwork for the foundation."

Bobbye had not said one word, but she jumped in to tell me that the guy's name was Patrick Dobson and he'd gone to Juilliard. "He's a musical genius and he's really good with computer stuff, too. He's organized these spread sheets and takes care of all the financial stuff for my businesses and the foundation. There's just so much I can do, but Patrick knows everything about everything I own… dozens of high-rise apartments and condos and lots of shopping malls," she turned to look at me. "Did I tell you I have nine shopping malls in New Jersey? Anyway, back to Patrick and where we are with the foundation. Lark and Ed never got a chance to get it going, so we're gonna do that next spring. You'll help us, won't you, Stacey?"

Janice interrupted us to say dinner was on the table and we went into the dining room for a traditional feast. While we ate dessert, Russell kept us in stiches telling stories about the farm where he'd grown up. "We didn't have a turkey," he said, "just fried squirrel and peas and corn bread. I didn't know what a cranberry was. But my mama would make a peanut pie sometimes…and sometimes she'd make one from sweet potatoes. But hers wasn't nothing like yours, Elliot."

We weren't sure if he'd meant it wasn't as good as my dad's, or not, which made the story even funnier. As the laughter died down, Bobbye brought up Christmas and asked if Phil, and my dad and I, would like to join her and Tripp, and Russell and Janice, on a cruise aboard "Mac the Knife." She said Tripp wanted to take the yacht down to Cancun because he'd spent several months living and working there.

You can imagine the sense of relief I felt when I told her that my dad and I were going to visit our Parks relatives. "We'll spend Christmas Eve and Christmas morning up in Clayton at my Granny Edith's," I explained, looking across the table at my dad. "Then we're going down to Macon and we'll be there for a couple of days."

Phil thanked Bobbye and told her he was sorry to miss it, but he and his parents were going to South Carolina to visit his grandparents in Camden. "My grandmother's having hip surgery in a couple of weeks," he said, "and we're going as soon as they release her from rehab to help out at home and stay through Christmas."

I could tell Bobbye was disappointed, so I said, "We'll see you when you get back." And Tripp chimed in to say, "Well, it's gonna be a while. Janice and Russell are flying home from Cancun on New Year's Eve, but Bobbye and I won't get back until the middle of January."

I looked at Bobbye and said, "What about your job?"

She smiled at Tripp and said, "I've given my notice. December 15th is my last day."

* * * * *

On the first Friday morning in January of 2000, Classie called to ask if I could come by that day. I was up to my ears writing an article about Atlanta's new fire chief, Simon Delbridge, but told her I'd be there about two.

When I got to the big house, she met me at the front door and invited me back to the kitchen to have a cup of coffee with her. It was a cold rainy day, and nothing lifted my spirits like sitting there in that beautiful kitchen drinking coffee with Classie. We talked about the weather, the story I was working on, and my dad. Then she said, "I have something for you, Miss Stacey. Something Miss Lark wanted you to have."

A sensation like a little bolt of thunder raced across my chest. "Lark wanted you to give something... to *me*?"

I watched as Classie rose from her chair, all the while holding onto the back of it, and slowly shifted her way across the floor to the china hutch where she opened the door at the bottom. She came back with a small shopping bag. "You've got a birthday coming up, don't you?" she asked as she set it down on the table in front of me.

"Yes... January 12th. How did you know, Classie?"

"Miss Lark was planning a party for you. It wasn't gonna be a surprise 'cause she was gonna tell you. Anyway, last time she was home back in August, she made a list of people she was gonna invite to your party."

I sat there staring at that little bag for what seemed a long time. I was so overcome by the thought of Lark having a birthday party for me that I was afraid I might burst into tears. But why had she begun planning it so far ahead? Finally, I said, "Why was Miss Lark planning a party for me in August when she knew my birthday wasn't until now?"

"Well," Classie began, as she eased herself back into the chair across from me, "one reason was she and Mr. Tripp was going to Europe in September."

"*Europe?* Lark and Tripp were going to Europe?"

"Yessum. They was going to visit some them music colleges." Classie paused and looked away for a moment as if she were gathering her thoughts. "'Bout two weeks before she died, they come home here, the two of them, from the farm. I remember it was a Tuesday morning. They got here 'bout eleven and ask me to fix 'em some lunch. And that's when Miss Lark told me they'd be leaving the end of September to go to London. And after that, they was going to Paris and she was gonna buy her some new evening gowns there 'cause they was going to the opera in Italy. And she say they wouldn't be back home til the first of November. Then she had all these concerts with the symphony over the holidays. Plus, they was gonna have a big Christmas party here for the folks what give money for the symphony. Let's see...what did she call 'em?"

"The Board of Directors? Is that what she said?"

"That was it. Anyway, while Miss Lark and me was down here in the kitchen that day fixing lunch, Mr. Tripp was up in his office talking to somebody about plane tickets. After lunch, they went off to the bedroom so Miss Lark could get some clothes and shoes. Then they left. Weren't here more than a couple of hours. But that's when she told me about the party and showed me what she was gonna give you for your birthday."

I kept clutching my hands trying to comprehend what I'd just heard. Lark and Tripp were going to Europe. Lark and Tripp were hosting a Christmas party. Lark was planning a birthday party for me. I kept looking at that little bag, trying to make myself open it. I wanted to, wanted to know what was inside, and at the same time, I didn't.

Classie leaned toward me. "Are you okay, Miss Stacey? You look kinda peaked. Can I get you some water?"

When I shook my head, she said, "I know this must be a shock 'cause it's always a shock when the dead come back to life, ain't it? But Miss Lark was always thinking 'bout other people, always trying to do something nice for somebody."

She reached into the bag, took out a piece of paper, and handed it to me. On it was a list of names...my dad's, the Sanfords, Janice, Russell, Bobbye, Laura and Jay Dubose, Hamp Walker, Gary and his wife, and several friends from work. Seeing those names written in Lark's hand got to me and my eyes began to water.

Classie pulled a hankie from her apron pocket and pressed it into my palm. "Miss Lark loved you," she said, her voice as soft as down. "Stop crying now and reach in there and get that little box."

315

The box, made of burgundy leather, had a note taped to it that read, *For Stacey on her Bday.* I lifted the lid and took a breath. Lying on black velvet was an oval-shaped pendant on a delicate gold chain. The name *John Phillip Sousa* was engraved across the top; at the bottom were the words, *Award of Excellence.* In the center, an elegant baton, raised in bright silver relief, provided a nice contrast to the gold rim around it.

"Oh, no," I exclaimed. "Surely Lark didn't mean for me to have this, Classie."

"She said you'd say that, Miss Stacey. The last day she was here, she wrote that note and stuck it on the box and told me she was gonna give it to you on your birthday in January. Well, we know that ain't gonna happen. God rest her sweet soul."

Classie began pushing herself up out of her chair and I got up with her. "You go on now, child," she said. "You got better things to do than sit here all afternoon with me. And don't forget to take your medal."

She took our cups to the sink and, with her back to me, began washing them. "I'm leaving, Miss Stacey... going home to live with my brother, Raeford, in La Grange." She jerked down a dish towel and began drying the cups. "I'm just too old and too tired to do this anymore. Raeford is coming to get me tomorrow. I've already started packing."

I walked over, put my arms around her and, as she fell against me, I whispered, "Oh, Classie. This place won't be the same without you. I'm going to miss you so much."

She clung to me a moment longer before pulling away. "I'm going to miss you, too, Miss Stacey. But I know it's time for me to go."

She didn't look back as she sought refuge in the privacy of the pantry. On my way out, I picked up the burgundy box and put it in my jacket pocket. I'd planned to meet a friend after work for dinner, but I was just too upset…upset that Classie was leaving, upset about the news that Lark and Tripp had planned a trip to Europe, that Lark had wanted me to have her prized medal. I thought I was doing better when it came to Lark. But standing there in the MacAvoy kitchen—the kitchen where she and Tripp had cooked so many meals together, the kitchen where she'd begun planning a birthday party for me—I knew I wasn't.

I hurried home to my apartment where I called my friend and told her I couldn't meet her for dinner. Then I stuffed an old t-shirt and toothbrush in my purse and headed for the interstate. What I needed was a Granny Edith fix.

"I made a batch of coffee brownies this morning," she said, as I got out of the car, "because I knew I was going to have company today… felt it in my bones. And here you are." She hugged me with a kind of fierce possession that told me I belonged and, as she led me up the steps into her little white house, the burdens of the day began to lift.

While Granny prepared a meal for us, I set the table and rattled on about my job, my dad, and the article I was writing about the new fire chief. I dared not mention Classie, nor Lark, for fear I'd ruin our evening. After dinner, we took a plate of brownies and cups of coffee into the living room where we sat in front of a fire and Granny told me a story about her mother's mother—my great-great grandmother, Laura Ellen McNair (for whom my mother, Ellen, had been named), and how, as a youngster, she'd immigrated to Philadelphia in the 1880s, and later, to upcountry Georgia where she'd taught school before The Great War.

I tried to listen, tried to focus on what Granny was saying. I nodded, smiled, and even asked her questions, while my mind took me back to ninth grade band class at Grady High, to starry nights filled with glorious music at Chastain Park, to a beautiful wedding in a little chapel in Savannah, to the harsh reality of unadulterated Kodachrome in a courtroom in Brevard.

That night, as I lay in my mom's old bed while rain lashed the windows, I grasped Lark's Medal of Excellence in one hand, the corner of the bed sheet in the other, and sobbed my heart out. It wasn't long before Granny Edith came up the stairs and sat down on the side of the bed. "I knew something was bothering you the minute you got out of the car," she whispered. "It's Miss Loflin, isn't it?"

I nodded. "It's those pictures, Granny," I blubbered, "the pictures the medical examiner showed us at the hearing... the ones of her lying on the floor in that pink nightgown with her tongue...her tongue... I can't get those pictures out of my mind. When I close my eyes and try to go to sleep, it's like they're stuck on the insides of my eye lids. I start sweating and my heart starts jumping and..."

Granny got up, went into the half-bath, and came back with a glass of water and two aspirin. After I'd taken them, she sat down beside me. "That medical examiner is not in charge of your memories, sweetheart," she crooned. "And while Miss Loflin's death was an awful thing, you cannot allow it to consume you. If you do, it'll drag you down so far you'll never again see the light of day."

She reached up under the covers, sought my hand, and drew it out. "You must think of Lark Loflin as a gift, Stacey, a special gift from God. You must try to remember her not as she was in death, but as she was in life...in all her beauty and glory." She pressed her soft dry lips to the back of my hand, and in a voice reminiscent of my mother's, told me to go to sleep.

* * * * *

Phil called in early February to tell me that Tripp had asked if the four of us could get together for Valentine's and, if so, he and Bobbye would meet us that night at The Shack. Valentine's fell on a Tuesday that year, so I agreed, but said it would have to be an early night for me as I had an eight o'clock meeting the next morning.

Phil picked me up and when we got to the restaurant, Tripp and Bobbye were already seated in a booth. They got up and gave both of us a hug and, in unison, said, "Happy Valentine's." Then Bobbye thrust her left hand at us. I was not a bit surprised by the ring on her finger, but I tried my best to pretend I was. It was obvious that the stone in her new ring was the diamond solitaire from Caroline's old engagement ring, and I figured Tripp had had it reset after he'd removed it from Lark's dead finger.

Phil made a great deal over it, too, congratulating Bobbye and Tripp and saying how pleased her parents must be. When our favorite waitress came to take our order and Bobbye showed her the ring, she said, "Lord, honey. That's some rock you got there!"

For the next hour or so, we talked about my job, and Phil's job, the cruise Bobbye and Tripp had taken to Cancun, and what a God-send Patrick Dobson was. Bobbye mentioned that the first meeting of the charter members of the music foundation board would be held on February 20th and asked Phil and me to please try to be there. Then Phil asked if she and Tripp had set a date.

Bobbye preened a bit as she replied, "We're going to wait until April because we want to get married in the back yard at home when all the azaleas and dogwoods are in bloom. It'll be really simple with just a few people and we're praying that it won't rain. I'd like for you to be my Maid of Honor, Stacey. And you can wear anything you want."

Tripp looked over at Phil and said, "And if you're willing, old man, I'd like you to be my best man. Bax is a Justice of the Peace and we've asked him to marry us."

And that's the way it all unfolded. The wedding took place on a beautiful Saturday, not a cloud in the sky. Bobbye wore the strand of fresh-water pearls Tripp had brought her from Brazil with a lacey peasant blouse, ankle length skirt, and sandals. And a beaming Tripp was the most handsome groom I'd ever seen.

The same intimate group who'd been at Bobbye and Tripp's wedding in April made plans to be together again aboard "Mac the Knife" the weekend before Memorial Day. Phil, Brock, my dad, and I had arranged to have Friday off so we could cruise down to the Bahamas and back in time to be at work on Tuesday. Unfortunately, the weather wrecked our plans.

Friday afternoon when we arrived at Tybee Marina, the blue skies of Atlanta had been replaced by dark water-filled clouds. Captain Ennis told Bobbye that a tropical storm was headed east, and he wasn't comfortable taking the yacht outside the waters of the intracoastal. My dad said something like, "I knew it. I knew this would happen when I checked the weather last night. I think I'd rather go on back home and not waste a vacation day sitting here in the rain."

Brock had nodded. "I think you're right, Elliot." He'd thanked Bobbye and said he hoped he and Phyllis would be invited again. Then the two of them, and my dad, had gotten in the Sanford's car and left.

Phil and I stayed long enough to have a beer with Bobbye and Tripp before we decided not to sacrifice our precious vacation time on what would probably be a lousy outcome. I thought Bobbye was going to cry when we told her we were going home. She could have gone, too. But Tripp wanted to stay, so she stayed.

On Monday, I drove out to Piedmont Park to do a feature story on the restoration of the carousel there. I interviewed several people who were slaving away on that sunny, warm Memorial Day scraping, making repairs, and painting hoping to return all those magnificent horses, and the four old-world Venetian benches, to their original glory.

From there I went to a late afternoon picnic with my dad and was in bed by nine o'clock. At one-forty, I was startled awake by the ringing of the phone and even more startled when I picked it up and heard Bobbye speaking in a voice so garbled I could hardly understand her. She kept repeating something that sounded like *Come, come get me.*

"Where are you?" I asked.

"In…in…" she began, gulping air, "in the ditch by the road. Tripp's gonna kill me. He'll kill me, Stacey, if he finds me. I'm hiding in the ditch down by the road. Please, come get me!"

I sat up and turned on the bedside lamp. "What happened? No, never mind that. Just tell me exactly where you are, Bobbye, and I'll come. Are you at the beach house?"

"No… no," she stammered. "I'm down where that clump of bushes sits right beside the drive-way. You know…right where you turn onto Virginia Circle. I can't keep talking. He might hear me. I gotta hang up."

I didn't bother to dress, just ran to the car in my pjs. I broke the speed limit, and in about eight minutes, arrived at Virginia Circle where I slowed down. I didn't want Tripp to know I was there, so I turned off my lights. And that's when

Bobbye slithered out of the ditch and started crawling on her hands and knees toward the car. I jumped out, swooped down, and grabbed her by her arm. "No, no," she cried. "I think it's broken!" Even in that dim light I could see streaks of blood in her hair and dark smudges of something matted on the pink tank top she was wearing. She was shaking so badly she could hardly move, but I got her to her feet and held onto her while we stumbled to the car. She lunged toward the handle on the back door crying, "Go!" before she threw herself down behind the driver's seat.

I sped back up Virginia Circle and made a right onto Highland Avenue. "I'm taking you to the ER at Piedmont," I said, glancing in the rear-view mirror. "Not there, Stace," Bobbye muttered, "they know me. Take me to St Jerome's."

You read the opening of this book, so you know about the gash in her head, her broken arm, and all that. But what you don't know is what happened three nights later when I went back to the hospital, helped her dress, and got her in my car.

As I put it in reverse, I took a quick look at her. Her left eye, which was still swollen and a sickening shade of purple, was not nearly as bad as it had been two days earlier and the large bruise that was splayed across the right side of her face had faded to a ghastly yellow. As I'd pulled out into the street, she'd slumped against her pillow and said, "Will you please take me to the beach? Maybe we can spend the night in a motel somewhere and, first thing tomorrow morning, I'll call Captain Ennis to let him know I'm coming. I'm going to stay on the boat for a few days because I don't want my parents to see me like this. You'll call them, won't you, Stacey? Call and tell them I'm staying on "Mac the Knife" for a few days to get some sun."

"Don't worry, Bobbye," I'd said. "I'll call them. But first you've gotta get some sleep."

I managed to stay alert for the next three hours. Then my eyes began to blur. On the outskirts of Savannah, I pulled in at a chain motel and went into the office to get a room. Bobbye was still asleep when I got back to the car, but as I drove around to the back of the building, she sat up and said, "Thanks for getting a room on the back, Stacey. That way, if Tripp comes nosing around down here looking for me, he won't see your car and we'll be safe."

When we got into the room, she didn't bother to take off her clothes, she just fell onto one of the beds. And moments later, she was asleep again.

We slept in, and the next morning when I had to get up to pee, I wanted to go back to bed. But I didn't because I'd left my pager on the dresser and saw it flashing. Gary was trying to reach me.

I put on the same clothes I'd worn the night before, picked up my phone, and walked out to the center of the parking lot away from the buildings and trees. When Gary answered, I said, "Hi. I'm coming in today about noon…okay?"

"Stacey," he said, "your friend Phil Sanford has been trying to reach you. Tripp MacAvoy is in the hospital. I don't know the details, but evidently someone found him unconscious at the house in Virginia Highlands. You'd better give Phil a call."

I called Phil who told me that Russell and Janice had been worried because they hadn't heard from Bobbye for a couple of days. Russell had decided to go over to the big house to make sure she was okay, and he'd found Tripp unconscious on the kitchen floor. He'd ridden in the ambulance with Tripp to Piedmont where the doctors had told him Tripp had overdosed and, in the process, burned his eyebrows, the end of his nose, and his fingertips.

"He's in the psychiatric ward on the fifth floor," Phil said. "I'm assuming Bobbye is with you because I've been calling both of you since yesterday. I called your boss because I knew he could get in touch with you. You guys better come home."

When I got back to the room, Bobbye was in the shower. I started packing up what little we'd brought and brushed my teeth and hair. I took a long time doing both while I tried to figure out the best way to tell Bobbye about Tripp. In the end, I decided to wait a while and see how she was doing before I said anything.

When she came out of the shower, I asked her how she was and she said, "Okay, I guess. I feel much better this morning than I did last night. A good night's sleep always helps, doesn't it? Thank God for valium."

She'd covered the fabric sling on her right arm with the plastic bag from the ice bucket and was wearing a shower cap to protect the bandage on the back of her head. I helped her take those off and get dressed. She wanted to put her hair in a ponytail and wear her Braves' ball cap, so I helped her with that, too.

Then I said, "I think you need to eat something, Bobbye, something nutritious. There's a little restaurant across the street where we'll be able to get a decent breakfast."

"I'm not hungry, Stacey," she whined. "I'll go with you and get some coffee."

The place was practically empty, but I went all the way to a booth in the back. And when a waitress brought mugs and a pot of coffee to the table, I told her we'd have the special…bacon and eggs with toast. Bobbye didn't eat all of hers, but I let her get most of it down before I said, "I need to tell you something."

She looked up from her plate and said, "Okay…so tell me."

"Tripp's in the hospital…Piedmont. Phil called and told me that your dad found Tripp lying on the floor of the kitchen last night and rode with him in the ambulance to the ER."

Bobbye sat very still for several moments, while her eyes darted around looking at everything but me. Finally, she said, "He's been doing all this crazy stuff and I guess it caught up with him."

I was so surprised at her response that I sat there stunned. I'd thought the moment she heard that her precious Tripp was in the hospital, she'd let out a wail. But she hadn't, so I said, "I guess you won't be going down to the boat...right?"

She touched her napkin to her lips and flung it down on the table. "I wish my dad hadn't taken Tripp to Piedmont," she fussed. "Now all my friends there will know."

Three hours later we arrived at the hospital and took the elevator up to the fifth floor. I'd never been in the psychiatric wing, but it was different from other areas of the hospital. The windows were larger making the room brighter. There were several open areas with tables and comfortable chairs through which a man in a tweed sport coat was making his way toward us. He looked at Bobbye and said, "Are you Mrs. MacAvoy?"

She nodded and asked how he knew. "Your husband has a picture of you in his wallet," he answered. "I'm Doctor Benson. Would you like to see your husband?"

Dr. Benson seemed not to notice Bobbye's swollen eye, the sling around her right arm, the yellow bruise that colored her cheek. I assumed he was used to such things because, in his job, perhaps he had to deal with them as a matter of routine.

He led us down a hallway to a closed door. "He's heavily sedated," he said, "and he may not know you. Before you go in, I want to tell you a little about his condition. Especially the way he looks. He suffered some burns on his face and hands. But when they're sufficiently healed, the plastic surgeons can help."

I wouldn't have known it was Tripp MacAvoy lying in that hospital bed if we'd not been told. The only recognizable thing about him was the tuft of golden hair that stuck out above the bandage that covered most of his forehead. Looking at his face, which was swollen twice normal size, was especially difficult. Patches of deep maroons and pinks covered most of the surface on the right side. The left was a sea of bubbling blisters.

Because he was breathing heavily, I assumed he was sleeping. But when Bobbye laid her hand on his arm, he moaned. Dr. Benson was immediately at her side. "Don't talk to him yet, Mrs. MacAvoy. The sound of your voice might produce more excitement than he needs just now. It's critical that he rest as much as possible now so the burns can begin to heal." He turned and nodded to a nurse who was sitting in a chair by the window.

We'd been in the room about three minutes when Dr. Benson suggested we leave. Once we were back in the hallway, he told us that Tripp would have nurses 'round the clock for the next forty-eight hours. Then a team of burn specialists would start the next phase of treatment. In the interim, they would continue to keep him sedated with morphine to help control the pain. Dr. Benson turned to Bobbye. "Perhaps in a couple of days you and I can meet and talk about treatment for his addictions."

Bobbye frowned. "Addictions? I know he has a problem with alcohol, Doctor Benson, but he's not an addict."

Dr. Benson cleared his throat. "When your husband was found unconscious, it was the result of a number of substances…illegal substances, Mrs. MacAvoy. He had a blood alcohol level of 0.34. And subsequent tests revealed there were amphetamines present, along with cocaine, and a new drug known on the street as PCP. We think PCP is what put him over the top. Since he was alone, we'll never know. But we think he tried to mix PCP in a bong with cocaine, but without any water. When he put a match to it, it exploded and burned his forehead, the end of his nose, and three of his fingers."

I took Bobbye by the hand and turned to Dr. Benson. "We've been away for a couple of days, doctor," I said, "so we knew nothing about what happened until early this morning. As you can see, *she* was the victim of Mr. MacAvoy's latest abuse. I need to take her home."

Dr. Benson nodded. "But before you go, could you join me in my office, Mrs. MacAvoy?" And Bobbye asked if I might come, too, saying, "Stacey is my closest friend and like a sister to me. I have no secrets from her."

Once inside, Dr. Benson closed the door and asked us to sit down. "Has Mr. MacAvoy ever been arrested?"

Bobbye shook her head and answered with an emphatic *no*, and I sat there amazed at the natural way her mouth had delivered that lie. Just prior to his infamous flight to parts unknown, Tripp had been arrested, fined, and had his driver's license revoked.

Dr. Benson's voice brought me back to the present. "Well, the police were called when your father dialed 911 to request an ambulance. They've searched your house but found nothing except the remains of the bong. Your husband isn't under arrest, Mrs. MacAvoy, but when the time comes, he must agree to a voluntary commitment. He'll have to appear before a magistrate in what is commonly called drug court. And that judge will be the person who decides your husband's fate…at least for the next year or so. Voluntary commitment means that he'll be confined to rehab in a facility run by the state, or in a private facility, for the next month or more depending on how well he responds to treatment. And if you bring assault charges against him, his situation will be more serious. Do you plan to file charges?"

Bobbye's hands began to shake as she struggled to speak. "I...I hadn't thought," she stammered. "I hadn't thought about it, doctor. But I don't want Tripp to go to prison."

"If you don't press charges, the judge will need assurance that Mr. MacAvoy is not a flight risk, that he'll go *immediately* from the hospital into drug rehab. You'll need to check out facilities in this area and select a few you think might work for him. Once he completes rehab, he'll have to continue treatment and he'll be on probation for a while."

Dr. Benson waited for Bobbye to respond, and when she nodded, he asked her to please call him so they could begin working on a plan for Tripp's recovery.

When we got to the big house, I called Janice and told her that she and Russell needed to come see their daughter. I wanted to be gone before they arrived, because I wanted Bobbye to be the one who told them why she looked the way she did. I said a quick good-bye, thankful that I had the excuse of having to get to work.

On Saturday I called my dad and told him about Tripp, how he'd overdosed and was in the psych unit at Piedmont. "I'm not surprised," he said, "It's been coming for years. How long do you think he'll be there?"

"Bobbye called yesterday and told me they'd moved him from critical care to a regular room. He's got some burns, Dad, on his forehead and face. No one knows exactly what happened, but his doctor told Bobbye and me they think he tried to mix some different stuff in a bong, and it backfired."

"Good lord... he's being treated for burns as well as addictions?"

"Bobbye told me she'd been looking into rehab places and she thinks the best one for Tripp is up near Rabun Gap because they treat patients like Tripp with multiple addictions. Bobbye said Dr. Benson thinks that by the end of this week Tripp's burns will be healed enough for him to go. He'll be taken in a hospital van because he's not allowed to see anyone—not Bobbye or anyone else—for the next two weeks."

"Hum… I didn't know people in drug rehab were not allowed to see their friends or family. Sounds kind of harsh to me. Did you know that?"

"Yeah. They say that being in rehab the first couple of weeks is like being quarantined. But it isn't that way the whole time. Dr. Benson told Bobbye Tripp might be up at this place, Stoneridge, for a month, maybe six weeks, depending on how he does. And if things go well, she could go up to see him around the Fourth of July. Sorry, Dad, but I gotta go. I'll call you again when I know more."

June was pretty normal that year, hot and muggy, with thunderstorms in the late afternoon. A big tropical storm hit Houston killing 22 people and we got loads of rain from it. I spent a couple of afternoons at fire stations helping pack trucks with food, nylon tents, and med supplies for Texans who'd been flooded out of their homes. Most days I sat in endless meetings listening to county commissioners and members of the city council fight over what to do with the remaining revenues left over from last year's budget. The first of July was looming, and they needed to spend that surplus before they approved budgets for the new fiscal year.

My dad and I decided to host another cook-out at his house on the Fourth of July, so I'd called and invited our usual crew—Phil and his parents, Janice, Russell, and Bobbye. But Bobbye said she couldn't come because she was going up to Stoneridge to visit Tripp. I told her how happy I was that she'd finally get to see him and promised to catch up with her when she got back. But late on the third of July she called and asked if she could come to the cook-out.

"They won't let me go tomorrow," she said. "A Doctor Shaw called to tell me that Tripp had had a little set-back and they thought it best if I didn't come now. He refused to go to group therapy and told Dr. Shaw he wasn't going to air his dirty laundry in front of a bunch of riff-raff and drug-heads. So, they sent him back to isolation. She's going to call me when she thinks he's ready to have a visitor. Am I still invited to the picnic?"

We went all out with patriotic decorations, and the food was delicious, but *party* is not a word I'd use to describe that evening. Despite an attempt at cheerfulness on the part of a couple of us (Phyllis Sanford and me), everyone there was sidelined, emotionally, by concerns about Tripp and Bobbye. Janice was especially quiet and kept her eye on her daughter the whole time. The wound on the back of Bobbye's head had healed and the scar there was no longer visible because her hair had grown back enough to cover it. The bruises on her neck and face had faded, and the doctor had removed the fabric sling from her arm, so there was no evidence of the physical assault she'd endured the night her husband had told her over and over that he was going to kill her.

The following week Bobbye called to let me know that Tripp's counselor, Dr. Shaw, had called to tell her she could come to Stoneridge on Friday. "I'm to be there at ten," she said, "so Dr. Shaw and I can talk before Tripp and I have lunch together in his room. Dr. Shaw said not to bring anything, and not to wear any perfume or flowery-smelling hair stuff. God, this is hard, Stacey. I'll bet when he comes home, he'll have a long-ass list of rules. I'll call you on Saturday morning and let you know how it went."

I was up early that Saturday when the phone rang. Bobbye came on and I knew immediately she was really down. "Oh, Stacey, he's so sad," she began. "He's not himself at all. He just sat there the whole time with this blank look on his face... and he didn't laugh, not even once. Dr. Shaw came in and asked Tripp how he was doing, and when he answered he sounded like a wind-up toy. He'd asked for shrimp for lunch because I like it. So, we had fried shrimp, but Tripp didn't eat any. When they brought in dessert, which was chocolate layer cake, he gobbled his piece down in seconds and asked for another, which they gave him. He has a bag of chocolate candy on the table beside his bed and he's in it constantly."

"Why does he eat all that candy? I don't understand."

"I asked Dr. Shaw and she told me it helps with his addictions, that the sugar helps assuage his cravings. Sugar is terribly addictive, but it's not anything like coke or meth and, evidently, recovering addicts eat candy all the time. Tripp will probably need it for the rest of his life and chocolate is really good for him because of all the caffeine."

I responded with something like *hum*, and asked, "How does he look, Bobbye? Is his face healing?"

"It's better," she said, "but it's still pretty bad. He's going to need some work, especially on his nose. His fingertips have healed and his left eyebrow, the one that got burned off, is beginning to grow back. But those places around his mouth, the places with third-degree burns, there's no feeling there because of nerve damage. So, when he eats, he's messy."

I hated to tell Bobbye I had to go, but I had a meeting at the paper's headquarters in Dunwoody and needed to get on the road.

On the last Monday morning in July, I was in the mayor's office interviewing him about a new road project that would cause problems for property owners in a high-end neighborhood. From my purse, I could hear my new phone buzzing and wondered who'd be calling me so early on a Monday morning. After I left City Hall, I went down the street to a bakery for a coffee and sat down at a table to find out. It was Bobbye who'd called, and I called her back. "Tripp's coming home," she said. "They're releasing him Wednesday morning."

I told her how relieved I was that Tripp would be coming home, how he needed to be with people who cared about him. "Well, that's one reason I called you, Stace. Dr. Shaw suggested I invite our little group over to welcome him home and give him encouragement for the days ahead. I know a clinical psychologist here in Atlanta whose specialty is addictions and I've arranged for Tripp to meet with her two mornings a week. That schedule's already in place. Plus, he has to attend AA meetings every day. Then there's the community service thing. Tripp asked if he could work in the city parks, so he needs to be at the maintenance offices downtown at seven. It looks like this coming weekend is the best time to get together. How about Friday evening? Would that work?"

I told her Friday was fine. "Maybe we can meet for lunch tomorrow and talk about it."

At noon the following day, Bobbye picked me up at the apartment and we headed to Round Man's Pizza. We ordered, and as soon as it arrived, began wolfing it down. "Gosh, this is good," Bobbye said, "and I'm so glad you suggested we do this because it's like old times when we still lived together."

"Yeah, it is," I said. "We had fun, didn't we, cooking together and raiding the thrift shops for things we needed for our little place. I sure do miss you."

Bobbye looked down at her lap and mumbled, "I miss you, too, Stace. I love Tripp, but I've never had a better friend than you."

When she said that, I decided it was now or never and plunged in. "Speaking of friendship," I began, "you've never told me about the night Tripp beat you. I've seen him angry, and I've been there when he's hit people. But, as far as I know, he's never hit you."

Bobbye's eyes begin to fill as she put the slice of pizza she'd been holding back on her plate. "I've been wanting to tell you about that, Stacey. But so much has been going on with Tripp that I haven't had a chance. But the main reason I haven't told you is I'm so ashamed."

"Why?" I asked, as the Christmas cover of **POINTS** Magazine popped in my head.

"Well...Tripp has become more, shall we say, more adventurous when it comes to sex. He wants to try new things like bondage and sex toys."

I just shook my head because none of that surprised me. Tripp had always been edgy when it came to sex and I knew he'd badgered Bobbye about it because I'd heard him do it. "Tell me what happened, Bobbye."

"We had a fight. We began fighting that day about the same thing he's been harping on for months...he wants me to give him enough money to open a restaurant...a hundred thousand dollars. By mid-afternoon, he'd had a lot to drink, and he kept at me. Then he started giving me the soft sell... you know, telling me how beautiful I looked and how much he loved me. He had a little stash of what he calls *red hots* in a bowl and he washed a couple of them down with bourbon.

I interrupted. "Red hots...amphetamines?"

Bobbye nodded. "They're potent and expensive...about a hundred a pop. And they were really working for him. We were in the kitchen and he tried to pin me, tried to wrap his arms around me, but I pushed him away and went around to the other side of the counter. I kept thinking if I got the chance, I'd run out and down the hall to the bathroom where I could lock the door. That works sometimes because if he passes out, I can come out of the bathroom. But that night he was acting really strange. He kept pointing at the ceiling and laughing. I looked at the ceiling but there was nothing there. He was just wild... bouncing around on the balls of his feet, breathing heavy, and sweating like crazy. He kept insisting that I come to him, and when I didn't, he balled up his fist and tried to punch me in the shoulder. But his punch went wide so I knew something was screwing up his hand-eye coordination...which is unusual for Tripp. He dragged me out from behind the counter and started pulling at my shorts, and the next thing I knew, he had them down around my thighs.

"I kept jumping away from him, but he wrenched my arm up behind my back and began kicking my ankles forcing me to walk up the hall with him to the bedroom. That's where he pushed me down inside his closet—pushed me way in the back of it. Then he sat down in front of me and started throwing stuff out... shoes, dirty socks, all his junk. When he started doing that, I tried to crawl over him, but he turned around and began hitting me. And he hit me over and over until I passed out. When I came to, he was sitting on top of me with a video tape in his hand."

She avoided my eyes looking off at something on the other side of the restaurant. "Do you remember when we went to the beach house our first year in college and had that party?"

I nodded. "Of course, I remember."

"Remember, my dad took us to the bus station in our station wagon...the one he calls Green Bean? Well, on his way back home that morning, the engine quit. So, he and my mom had no car. He had to buy a new engine plus pay the mechanic to install it, which cost almost three thousand dollars. That meant they didn't have any money to give me for school. When we got back to campus, I told Tripp about my dad's car and that I wouldn't be able to stay at school. He told me not to worry, he'd come up with whatever I needed. Then he invited Meredith and Hamp to go back to the beach with us the last weekend in January. And while we were there, we made a video of Meredith and me having sex."

I wasn't surprised, but I wasn't sure how to respond, so I said nothing. Bobbye took a sip of tea before she went on. "Tripp had kept all the costumes we'd worn at the New Year's party and we went back to that same store again and bought a Jackie mask for me, a Marilyn mask for Meredith, and a JFK mask for Tripp. Hamp did the camera work."

I pushed my empty plate to the side of the table. "I remember when the four of you went back down to the beach together, so Tripp must have had something in mind."

"Oh, he did. He told Meredith and Hamp and me that he knew he could sell copies of a video to his friends…that lots of guys he knew were looking for things like that to liven up fraternity parties. He felt sure he could sell dozens of copies at $500 a copy. But it had to be really good. What he meant was Meredith and I had to do some things that were… *unconventional.* I told him I wouldn't do anything without wearing the Jackie mask and Meredith agreed. So, we put the masks on and began by stripping to some music. Meredith stripped first, then I stripped. Then we did the usual stuff like oral sex on each other. Tripp put on the JFK mask and got in the bed and we did a threesome. We'd do a couple of things and Tripp would tell Hamp to turn the camera off and then he'd tell us what we were going to do next and put us in position for it. He wanted to have anal sex with me, but I refused." She looked at me as if she wanted my approval, so I nodded.

She hesitated for a moment, cleared her throat, and said, "But Meredith didn't. She agreed to do it for a price. They agreed that every Friday Tripp would buy a bag of coke from his supplier and give it to her. I don't know if you knew, Stacey, but Meredith became a big coke head. She was really unhappy for some reason, but I've never known why… and she got hooked on coke that spring. Anyway, the two of them sealed their bargain in an act that would have made

Hollywood jealous. Meredith ran her tongue all over Tripp and then she screamed and screamed while they did it and sweat was just pouring off her. We'd all taken a few hits of coke before we started filming, but I think Meredith had done more than the rest of us."

I sat there thinking about Meredith Reynolds and what a bad spring she'd had that year. I'd been with her in the rest room stall at Burger Boy. But what I hadn't known was how clever Bobbye had been in dealing with that business. She'd known all along that Tripp was the father of that baby, but she hadn't let that little piece of information interfere with her plans. In the end it was Meredith who'd slunk away, her very attractive tail between her legs, and Bobbye who'd come out on top.

"Tripp must have sold lots of copies of that tape," I prodded, "because you stayed right there with us in the dorm that whole semester." Bobbye nodded. "Tripp told me later he could have sold a hundred copies. But he made just enough copies to get the money I needed and to pay for the camera and film he'd bought with money from his allowance."

"Anyway, the night Tripp beat me in his closet, he waited until I came to, and then he stuck that tape in my face. And he told me if I didn't play Donkey Kong with him then and there, he was going to show that tape to my parents. He sank his fingers into the sides of my hips and tried to turn me over, but I kicked and kicked until he lost his grip. That's when I ran. My pocketbook was sitting under the bench in the foyer and I thought if I could just get it, I'd have my car keys. But he caught up with me there, threw me down, and banged the back of my head on that marble floor over and over until my skull cracked. That must have scared him because when he crawled off me, he had this funny look on his face like, *Oh God, what have I done?*

"That's when I had this burst of energy, Stacey. I don't know where it came from, but I forgot all about my wrist and my cracked head and flew out the door. He came after me, but he slipped and fell. That gave me a few seconds to put some distance between us. I've always been able to outrun Tripp and I went straight for the ditch. He kept hollering, 'I'm going to kill you, Bobbye Revels—he kept calling me Bobbye Revels—I'm going to kill you.' Oh, Stacey, I don't know what I'd have done if you hadn't come."

The scene she'd described made me impatient to go home, to snuggle down in bed with a good book, to try to forget what I'd just heard. But I knew I couldn't, so I said, "Why don't you leave him, Bobbye? Why don't you get a divorce?"

She cocked her head. "For better or worse, for richer or poorer."

"You sound like my Granny Edith. It's 2000, Bobbye, not 1850. And no court would deny you a divorce after what Tripp did to you."

Bobbye's face filled with the kind of determination she'd had on the pitching mound. Her upper teeth came down over her lower lip and she held them there for a moment before she said, "I can't leave him, Stacey. I promised Ed..."

"Ed?" I interrupted, "Ed's dead. He'll never know the difference."

"He might not, but I will. Ed and I spent a lot of time together when he was sick. Hours and hours. And over those long months he told me lots of things...things I suspect he'd never told anyone. And he talked about how he'd hoped Tripp would follow in his footsteps and run MacAvoy Enterprises. And how disappointed he was not only in Tripp, but in himself because he'd failed to save the company. *But you can save my son*, he told me one afternoon when we were sitting out on the terrace in the sunshine. He said he thought

Tripp loved me enough to do the right thing… that I could influence Tripp. Ed never knew I have no influence over Tripp. You and I know it was always the other way around. But I didn't tell Ed that because he was so sick, and I couldn't give him any more cause for worry."

We left the restaurant and I walked Bobbye to her car. As she got in, I said, "I wish there was something I could say or do that would make things easier for you."

She shook her head. "There isn't, but thanks for offering. I know Tripp can be difficult, but I can't leave him, Stacey. He's always talking about how he has no one now. And that's true in a way because he really has no one now but me… and you and Phil. And I owe it to Ed to do whatever I can to help him."

Tripp's homecoming the following Friday evening went more smoothly than I thought it might. About four, I went over to the birthday cake house to help Bobbye. When I got there, she was busy in the kitchen and Tripp was in the shower. They'd decided that Tripp would cook chicken on the grill, and Bobbye had made a sweet brown sugar barbeque sauce to go with it. The day before, she'd called all her guests and reminded them not to wear any perfume, hair spray, or anything with a flowery scent. She'd told Russell, who was a smoker, he must never again smoke around Tripp, that he had to shower and put on clean clothes every time they saw each other. "The first six months are critical," she'd told all of us, "and while these things may seem strange to us, they're important to Tripp's recovery."

When he walked into the kitchen, I worked hard to act as normal as possible because it was all I could do not to turn and run. His eyes were still bronze, but they were dull. His hair, once shimmering blonde, had lost its sheen and hung in lanky clumps around his shirt collar. But it was his face that almost did me in. Bobbye had told me the plastic surgeons hoped to begin reconstruction on his nose before Thanksgiving because they'd had to remove cartilage from the end of it, which left Tripp with the turned-up snout of a pig. On one side of his mangled nose, from the outer edge of his cheek down to his mouth, was a hatch work of tiny holes where the blisters I'd seen in the hospital had eaten away the top layer of his skin.

Ah, the strutting peacock, I thought, how vain you were. Now the peacock's teeth were gray, his eyes opaque, his strut the uncertain shuffle of a much older man. As I gave Tripp a hug, I was aware of the beefy flesh that had accumulated across his shoulders and around his middle. He held onto me and thanked me for coming. "I couldn't have done this without you, Stacey. I don't mean this dinner tonight. I mean what's happened over the last few weeks. I wouldn't be here tonight if it weren't for Bobbye and my friends."

Tripp's chicken was tender and delicious and, as he and Phil finished off the last two pieces, Phyllis offered to drive Tripp to his sessions with the psychologist two mornings a week. "That will take some of the pressure off you," she said to Bobbye. Russell told Tripp that over the next month, he'd pick him up in the evenings and take him to his AA meetings. And I volunteered to drive him to meet the grounds' crews at the city offices two mornings a week. Tripp thanked everyone for their help and said he was looking forward to working in the city parks because he was sure that would be the best part of his recovery.

During dinner, he drank several large glasses of Coke, spooned extra barbeque sauce on his chicken, and snatched handfuls of malted milk balls from a cereal bowl beside his plate. His hands trembled as he reached for them while he chattered away like a magpie, telling us over and over how he'd turned a corner, how important we were to him, how he'd never have gotten through without us. Barbeque sauce puddled in the cleft in his chin, chocolate dribbled from his lower lip and, every now and then, Bobbye reached out with her napkin to gently dab at his face... the same thing she'd done for Ed.

* * * * *

Bobbye called the following Wednesday to thank me for all I'd done to make Tripp's homecoming a success. "He's adjusting pretty well," she said. "And he told me he enjoyed working with the maintenance crew this morning... and he went to his first group meeting with AA yesterday. So, things are good on this end."

I could hear excitement in her voice when she told me that she and Tripp were working on a new project together. "He's always wanted a home movie theater, and he wants it to be downstairs on the main floor. So, we decided to tear out a wall of bookcases in the library and install it there. We have all these old books we need to get rid of, and I thought about you. Most of them were Patricia's, but some are much older. And there's all kinds of reference books, too, and collections of old magazines like *Look* and *Life*. Please tell me you'll come get some of this stuff, Stacey, because I can't bear the thought of taking it to the dump."

I thanked Bobbye and told her I'd come the next day after lunch.

"Well, Tripp and I won't be here" she said. "We're going to Roswell tomorrow to meet with the theater contractor and look at some plans. We'll be gone most of the afternoon, so that would be a good time for you to come. I've still got empty boxes from when I moved in here last April, and I'll leave some for you in the library...and the front door will be open. I think I told you my cousin Cammie is getting married, and my mom and dad and I are leaving Friday to drive up to Knoxville, but I'll call you when we get back so we can get together."

I'd forgotten that Bobbye was going to Tennessee that weekend for her cousin's wedding, but I acted like I hadn't. "Have a great time at Cammie's wedding," I said, "and be safe on the road. Thanks again for letting me have those books."

I hung up and went back to the article I'd been working on about the fight between city leaders and county commissioners over a new plan for annexation west of Marietta. Phil and I had made plans to have dinner that evening, but I hadn't told Bobbye because I'd hoped he and I could have that time alone.

The next afternoon when I got to the birthday cake house, I drove up the driveway and parked just outside the front door so I wouldn't have far to walk carrying books. I paused just inside the foyer, looked up at the portraits of Cogdill ancestors hanging there, and thought about the first time I'd seen them...the first time I'd met Caroline Cogdill MacAvoy...the first time Classie Dixon had invited me into her kitchen. It had been a while since I'd been in the living room, so I peeked in, curious to see if anything had changed. The baby grand was right where I remembered it and the photo of Tripp's Grandad Rand with JFK sat on the little table where it had always been, so I knew Lark hadn't changed a thing. The two matching sofas wore the same elegant fabric, the same bright chintz still covered the chairs, and I knew Caroline was alive and well in what had been *her* living room. I recalled the day, years before, when Tripp had taken Bobbye and me in there to show us the picture of his Grandad with JFK, the day Caroline had called Bobbye the *janitor's adopted daughter.* I stood gazing at the fancy Meissen vases on the mantel, wondering what she'd think if she knew the janitor's adopted daughter was now Mrs. James Edward MacAvoy III.

I trooped back across the foyer to the library and stood in the doorway admiring the wormy chestnut paneling, the beautiful magnolia-leaf clusters carved on the lintels above the windows, and the custom-made cabinets and shelves filled with priceless maps and cherished newspapers from the forties and fifties, their headlines faded, their stories lost to the ages. I thought about the last time I'd seen Ed MacAvoy alive and how upset he'd be knowing that part of the library he'd loved so dearly was being torn out and replaced by a giant movie screen...not to mention the addition of a stuffed armadillo sitting on a shelf, a blue-feathered parrot standing guard by the magazine rack, or Tripp's prized anaconda. All twenty feet of her were stretched across brackets above the double windows at the front of the room.

The library ladder had always stood in front of the bookcases on one side of the fireplace. I walked over, grabbed the sides, and moved it to the north-facing wall, the wall that was being torn out. After checking the rubber stays on the bottom of the feet, I started climbing, scanning titles as I went. I chose a half-dozen books by Hemingway, more by Cather, and four by Edith Wharton. I went up and down the ladder a dozen times hauling heavy books to the table that sat under the front windows.

Over the next hour or so, I covered the entire surface of that big table with piles of books and knew I had to stop. I opened the half-dozen boxes Bobbye had left for me, pushed the lids down inside a couple, and started filling them.

After I'd filled five boxes, I hauled them out to my car. When I went back in, I realized there was room for two more books in the last box. So, I went back up the ladder for a biography I'd seen by Goodwin and kept searching for another book, an illustrated copy of the first edition of *The Yearling.* As I checked the shelves again, it dawned on me that I'd already taken the Goodwin book down. I turned and looked toward the table to be sure it was there, and something caught my eye. What the hell was that? I thought. Curiosity got the best of me and I went down the ladder, hauled it across the room to the table, and went up again.

As soon as I was eye level with Tripp's souvenir, I scrunched down so I could see inside her mouth. Behind a double row of deadly fangs, I spotted something…something square and black. I got as close to that snake's gaping mouth as I dared and, as I looked up from under the side of her jaw, I saw something pink.

I went quickly down the ladder, sank into one of the wing chairs, and wracked my brain trying to figure why somebody would put a tape recorder in the mouth of a snake. I felt sure that the tape recorder I'd seen was mine and I knew I had a duty to file the information it contained in *the Constitution's* archives. So, back up the ladder I went. But when I came face to face with a double row of shiny, curved fangs, I froze. "Just do it," I said aloud, trying to convince myself I could. "Just put your hand in there and pull."

As a first step, I reached in with my right hand and pressed the tip of my index finger against the back of the recorder. Now, I said to myself, press the pad of your thumb against this end and pull. When I did, the recorder fell out and landed on the table with a thud. I all but fell from the ladder in my haste to get that tape recorder. I crammed it in my purse, snatched up the last box of books, and hurried out the door.

Back at my apartment, I took the stairs two at a time, fumbled with my key, and when I finally got inside, fell back against the door trying to catch my breath. My heart was pounding so hard I thought it would burst. Just breathe, I kept telling myself, you'll never have to face that goddam snake again. It took a couple of minutes, but I finally regained enough composure to pour myself a bourbon. I knocked it back in one gulp, reached in my purse, and brought out the tape recorder.

I sat down on the sofa so I could make sure there was a cassette in it....and there was. I pushed PLAY, heard some static, then Tripp's voice saying, *Wild things! wild things! Ride 'em cowgirl!* In the background, there was a faint buzzing like a bell ringing.

I played the recording again and there was no doubt it was Tripp's voice. But it took a moment or two for me to realize that what he was saying was the same thing Phil and I had heard him say when he and Bobbye were in the bedroom beside ours at Lake Toxaway. The ringing of the bell was familiar, too, but it took a little longer for me to realize that the bell I was hearing on the tape was the same bell I heard ringing every day from the school across the street from my apartment. I sat there as if I'd been struck dumb trying to get my head to accept the obvious: Tripp had deliberately made a tape using *my* tape recorder so Phil and I would think that he'd been in the cottage with us at Lake Toxaway.

I hit the PLAY button again and heard Tripp say, *I'm crazy all right, Bobbye. Crazy about you, girl!* More static followed with Tripp imitating a howling gorilla—something I'd heard him do dozens of times. Doubt continued to consume me, so I listened to the cassette a third time.

I didn't want to, but I knew I had to call Bax Dobson and tell him about the cassette tape and ask him what to do. But when I made the call, his secretary answered and told me Bax was out of town and wouldn't be back in the office until Monday.

I needed to call Phil because the two of us had made plans to go out to dinner, but suddenly that didn't seem like such a good idea. I knew when he heard the tape, Phil would hit the roof and I didn't want to be in a public place if that happened. Inside the fridge, I found a carton of barbeque and some slaw and put a box of hush puppy mix on the counter.

Then I called Phil. When he answered, he said, "Hi, I'm still at work, Stacey. I thought I was gonna pick you up at six-thirty. You sound funny. Are you okay?" And I told him he needed to come over right away.

Phil had always been the steady one in our little foursome and I'd never seen him so angry. As soon as I played the tape, his eyes got big. "God dammit!" he shouted at the top of his lungs while I hurried to the fridge for a couple of beers.

He guzzled down half of his before he asked, "Where'd you find your tape recorder?"

I told him that Tripp and Bobbye were tearing out a wall in the library for a home movie system and she'd told me to come get all the books I wanted...that they'd be gone to meet with the contractor. Then I explained how I'd discovered the tape recorder, where Tripp had hidden it, and how I'd just happened to see it because a ray of sunlight had struck the little piece of pink tape I'd put on it. "We need to talk with Bax Dobson," I said. "I won't be a part of this."

Phil shook his head. "Oh, but you are, Stacey," he said. "You *are* a part of this. And so am I. And no matter what happens, we'll never be free of it. I think we'd better slow down and give ourselves time to think this through." He paused to down the last of his beer. "Are we still going out to dinner?" I shook my head. "I've got a carton of barbecue and some slaw. And I can make some hush puppies if you want."

Phil nodded and asked, "Do you think Bobbye knew what Tripp was going to do?"

I thought about what Bobbye had told me about the night Tripp attacked her... the videotape they'd made at the beach house, the copies he'd sold, the money he'd given Bobbye. And creeping anxiety rolled in like a fog.

"I don't know," I said, trying to dodge. "Let's just figure out what we're gonna do about that tape. Why don't I make some hush puppies and as soon as they're ready, you can microwave the barbeque."

I mixed up the hush puppies, but when I started to put a spoonful of batter into the fry pan, my hand shook so badly I dropped it. I stooped down to clean up the mess I'd made and, before I knew it, was crying like a baby. Then Phil was beside me saying, "Oh, God, Stace, I'm so sorry. Forget about the hushpuppies. I'm not very hungry, so barbeque and slaw will be plenty. You need to calm down."

I slumped into a chair as Phil filled a dish with barbeque. "I just don't think I can do this," I began.

"Yeah, you can. And when it's over, we'll never have to see Tripp MacAvoy again."

We didn't say much while we ate, but when we finished, I reminded Phil that Bobbye was leaving the next day to go to Tennessee with Janice and Russell for her cousin's wedding and Tripp would be staying home by himself. "Want to go over there now?" I ventured. I'd meant it as a joke, but Phil didn't respond.

We cleaned up the dishes and went back to the sofa where we sat for the next two hours talking about the hearing in Brevard, about how Bobbye had told Judge Ragsdale that she'd slept on the sofa in the living room that night, about how both of us had lied, too, telling him Tripp was there with us. I'd never thought much about the word *alibi*, but I did that night and it spurred me on. "I don't mind calling the police chief," I said. "I think he'd help us."

But Phil thought it was too soon. "Right now, I could shoot Tripp MacAvoy...but what good would it do? He's been in that god-forsaken rehab for the last six weeks. I'm no psychiatrist, but in my opinion, he's still fucked up."

"Forget Tripp for now," I said. "The person we need is Bax. I tried to get him this afternoon, but his secretary told me he'll be out of town until Monday."

Phil got up. "I think you're right," he said, starting to the door. "But I wouldn't want to be in his shoes…he could be disbarred. My dad and I have our usual Saturday morning golf game tomorrow, thank God. Maybe it will help keep my mind off all of this. I'll call you Sunday after church and see where we are." He paused for a moment. "But you know everything we do from now on, Stacey, will depend on what Bax tells us on Monday."

He opened the door, and as he started down the stairs, he turned to look back at me. "I know it won't be easy but try to get some sleep."

* * * * *

I tried to sleep but didn't succeed. I just kept tossing and turning, remembering the smallest details about the cottage on Lake Toxaway where Tripp had made felons of Phil and me with the help of *my* tape recorder. I wondered if he and Bobbye had sneaked out of the cottage and gone to Balsam Peak Farm together…or if Tripp had gone alone. How had he gotten there? I hadn't heard the sound of a car, or truck, that night, but I knew it was too far for him to walk.

Amazingly, I slept until after ten the next morning. I drank more coffee than I should have but felt so shitty I didn't care. I needed to work on an article due at the paper on Monday, so I sat down at my computer. But I couldn't focus, couldn't get going. Six boxes of books sat on the floor in the living room, and I decided to give them my attention instead. After a quick lunch, I hopped in my car and began searching thrift shops in the area looking for bookshelves. All of them were crowded with Saturday shoppers and it took a while, but at the last shop, I found a matching pair. On the way home, I stopped at a grocery store. Then I called my dad and invited him for dinner. I told him about my new/old books and the pair of bookcases I'd bought because I knew he'd help me haul them up the steps into the apartment.

It was a long day. While I zipped around in my car, I'd played the radio really loud and sang along. When I was at home, I had the TV on. I did everything I could think of to keep the image of that tiny piece of neon tape winking at me, of putting my hand into the mouth of that monster snake, of Tripp's voice on that cassette tape as far away as possible. My dad came straight from afternoon bridge and helped me get the bookcases inside before dinner. I worked hard to pretend that everything was just peachy keen, that I hadn't a care in the world. I'd made his favorite casserole and I could tell that he was pleased. He'd asked about Phil, and about Bobbye, and I'd reminded him that she and her parents had left that morning for Tennessee to attend her cousin's wedding. "What about Tripp? Did he go with them?" he asked.

"Don't think so. Bobbye told me that Tripp wanted to stay home and work on ideas for his new movie system. I don't think Tripp is ready to be with people, Dad. He's so self-conscious about how he looks...which is understandable. Bobbye told me he has an appointment with a plastic surgeon next month."

My dad sat silent for a moment. "I think it's a damn crying shame. Tripp MacAvoy is far from being my favorite person, but I'm sorry about what happened to him." He folded his napkin and I waited for him to get up, but he didn't. "There's something I want to tell you, honey," he said, his voice suddenly quiet. "I'm seeing someone. Her name is Jessica Lynch, and I met her last spring at bridge club. I'd like to introduce you to her sometime."

I was out of my seat in a flash and around the table giving him a hug. "That's great, Dad! I'm so happy for you. Is it serious?"

"We'll see. She's really special, Stacey, and you'll like her. Thanks for that good meal...hit the spot. Now, I need to get out of here so you can arrange your new bookcases."

I unpacked two boxes of books. Then I read for a while. But when I went to bed, sleep eluded me. No matter how hard I tried, my eye lids wouldn't stay closed. From Mrs. Ferguson's hallway below, I heard the grandfather clock strike midnight, and must have drifted off after that.

A loud knocking woke me, and I looked at the clock on the bedside table. It was ten after three. I hurried into the living room and, when I opened the front door, Phil said, "Hurry up and get dressed. Tripp's house is on fire."

He took the shortest route racing down Ponce de Leon Avenue at an alarming speed while he told me what he knew. "About two o'clock, a neighbor saw flames on the hill above her house and called 911. She and her husband are friends of my parents, and she called my dad and told him she thought the MacAvoy house was on fire. My dad called me and asked if Bobbye and Tripp were in the house, and I told him that Bobbye was in Tennessee with her parents, and I didn't know if Tripp was in the house or not."

He glanced at me. "Do you think Tripp is there...there in the house?" The tires squealed as Phil took the turn onto Highland Avenue. "I'm not sure," I said. "But Bobbye told me he wasn't going to the wedding, so I expect he's there."

We heard a big sound like an explosion and, seconds later, a bright light flared across the windshield. I peered through it where a sheet of flames danced across the dark sky. At the turn onto Virginia Circle, two cops with big flashlights tried to send us the other way, but Phil hit the brakes and got out of the car. One of the officers told him to get back in his car and turn around. "Sorry, son," he said. "This street's full of fire and rescue vehicles. Unless you have a pass, you can't go up there."

Phil got back in the car and waited while I rummaged in my purse for my Press Pass. I leaned in front of him so I could show it to the cop. "I'm Stacey Parks," I said. "I'm a reporter for *the Constitution*."

The guy looked carefully at my pass, his lips moving as he silently read my name and that of the paper. He gave me a nod and looked back at Phil. "*And* who are you?" he asked. "Are you with the paper, too?"

Phil said, "No sir. I'm Phil Sanford." And the guy said, "Oh, okay. Your dad is up there on the front lawn with the fire chief. You can go up where they are, but you can't go any closer. Just leave your vehicle here."

Double and triple-span ladders were suspended above the six fire trucks that had been parked in a circle around the birthday cake house. Brock and Chief Simon Delbridge stood under a cluster of oaks in the side yard below the garage, which had miraculously escaped damage. As Phil and I headed toward them, it was all I could do to contain myself when I realized the third floor of the house was completely gone. Beneath it, the rooms on the second floor were blown like a war zone. Through the windows on the first, I watched as bright yellow demons feasted on wormy chestnut paneling inside the library. Around us, heavy smells like that of diesel and fire retardant fouled the air.

As soon as they saw us, Brock and Chief Delbridge came over. I reached out to shake the chief's hand and said, "Do you remember me, Chief Delbridge? I interviewed you a while back." The chief took a step toward me to get a better look. "Sure do," he said, smiling. "You're Stacey Parks... right? Thank you for that fine piece you did about me in *the Constitution*. I've been meaning to call you, but my days," he turned and raised his hand toward the conflagration behind him, "and my nights just seem to get away from me."

I assured him he had no need to thank me. Brock introduced Phil to the chief who, over the roar of the fire hoses, the crackling staccato of heart pine, and the constant rumble of falling joists and beams, told us his crew had removed a body from the second floor...that they'd found it lying in what must have been a small kitchen. "Not long after we got here, we discovered evidence of a gas leak in that room. My men are bringing the body out now," he said, straining to keep his voice above the din. "Mr. Sanford told me he thought the owner, Tripp MacAvoy, was in the house. Do you all know?"

I cupped my hands around my mouth and shouted, "I think he may have been. His wife, Bobbye, has gone to Tennessee with her parents and I'm sure he didn't go with them."

From about twenty yards away, I saw movement along the side of the house, and soon it was obvious that two men were coming toward us carrying a stretcher. They walked over to Chief Delbridge and one of them said, "We think these are the remains of a young man, chief, but his face and upper body are burned so badly we can't tell."

I sank to my knees and Phil's long arms wrapped around me and pulled me back up. Chief Delbridge looked over at Brock, then back at Phil and me. "I understand that you all were friends of Mr. MacAvoy. Someone will have to identify the body, of course, and I guess that will be his wife. God help her, what a damn awful homecoming. Do you know when she'll be back?"

"Tomorrow," I said. "She told me they'd be home by noon tomorrow."

The chief nodded. "Well, it would help if one of you could tell me anything that might...might assure us that the poor soul inside this plastic bag here is Tripp MacAvoy. There's already a backlog of cases at the morgue and the number of bodies there will only continue to grow through the weekend. If you're not a relative, you're not allowed to see the body, but I am. Can you think of anything—a birthmark or a tattoo—anything that will help identify Mr. MacAvoy?"

Phil looked at me, his eyes pleading. "He wears a ring," I began, "on his right hand... a gold signet ring that belonged to his father. It has the letter M engraved on it."

Chief Delbridge directed his men to lower the stretcher to the ground. Then he stooped down beside it and unzipped the bag. I watched as he gently drew out a hand, a hand covered with soot, a square hand with short fingers that ended in black stubs. Behind us an explosion sent a burst of cinders skyward and, as they fell like shooting stars around us, a glint of gold flashed on that blackened hand. The chief turned to look at me and I nodded.

Phil's arm tightened around my shoulder. "It's okay, Stace," he whispered. "You did what you had to. Come on, I'm taking you home."

Bobbye wanted to have a simple grave-side service as soon as possible. "I just want it to be over," she'd snapped when I'd ask her what I could do to help. I told her I thought Tripp would want the kind of service his mother had had—music and flowers, a church filled with mourners. But when I tried to talk to her about it, she'd flipped me off with a resounding NO and said she'd never enter The Sign of the Shepherd Episcopal Church again. Then she called the Rector there and arranged for a graveside service to be held two days later. But it had to be rescheduled because, when Bobbye called Tripp's Aunt Judith, she'd been in Chicago attending a merchandise show and told Bobbye she'd have to fly back home to Arizona to repack before she came to Atlanta.

Less than a year had passed since the day Lark had been buried when we gathered in the cemetery. I stood with Bobbye, Janice, and Phyllis while the Rector read the Twenty-Third Psalm over Tripp's remains. Afterward, he plucked a single yellow rose from the casket blanket and offered it to Bobbye. But she refused to take it. I felt sorry for him and leaned in to suggest he give it to another member of the family. So, he walked past the pall bearers—Brock, Phil, Russell, Bax Dobson, Jay Dubose, and my dad—and gave it to Tripp's Aunt Judith.

Back at the Warrens' house, the sideboard in the dining room had been laid with a buffet where my dad's death cake stood beside a meringue-topped pie. Leaves had been added to the table to accommodate the ten people Bobbye had invited for lunch.

Conversation was strained because people don't know what to say when a person dies in such horrible circumstances. None of us engaged in small talk, and no one mentioned the pile of rubble, still smoldering, at the top of the hill on Virginia Circle. The day before, Bobbye had hired a contractor to remove all traces of the birthday cake house. Then she'd signed a deed transferring the property to the City of Atlanta, along with a donation of a half a million to fund the building of an arboretum on the 22-acre site, the center of which would be a rose garden dedicated to the memory of Ed MacAvoy.

When the last cup of coffee had been drunk, and the last good-byes said, I looked at her and asked, "Is there anything I can do?"

"No, Stacey. You've done so much helping with Tripp's obituary and the service. Come on. I'll walk you out."

I grabbed my pocketbook and followed her out the front door. I'd been one of the last to arrive for lunch and had parked my car around back. I told Bobbye where I'd left it and the two of us headed up the driveway. The door to the garage was open and Russell's old station wagon, Green Bean, was parked inside. Beside it, leaning against the wall, I saw Tripp's black dirt bike. And in a flash, I experienced one of those rare *ah hah* moments when something cloudy becomes crystal clear. I turned to look at Bobbye. "Why'd you do it?"

"Why'd I do... *what?*" she snapped.

"Why'd you help Tripp make that tape? Why'd you cover for him that night at Lake Toxaway when he rode his dirt bike to Balsam Peak Farm?"

Bobbye eyes bore into mine and, for a moment, I thought she was going to slap me but she turned away. With her back to me, she said, "I don't know what you're talking about."

Caution left me and I reached out to touch her forearm. "*You* know exactly what I'm talking about, Bobbye Revels. You and Tripp stole *my* tape recorder and used it to make the tape *you* played in the bedroom at Lake Toxaway so Phil and I would think Tripp was in there with you. But he wasn't, was he?" An image of Meredith Reynolds dressed in a lime green bridesmaid's gown filled my head while her words, *You wouldn't know the real Bobbye Revels if she fell on you like a ton of bricks,* rang in my ears and I waited to hear what Bobbye had to say.

She leaned down and her face was so close I could smell the sour odor of red wine on her breath. "You're crazy," she hissed as she turned from me and began walking toward the back of the house. "But I'll say one thing for you, Stacey Parks. You're really good at making up stuff."

"I have no reason to make up anything," I insisted, hurrying to catch up with her. "The simple truth is you and

Tripp took my tape recorder and made that tape so you could cover for Tripp when he killed Lark."

"You know," she said, with her back to me, "you were never able to see your way clear when it came to Tripp. And that's always been a problem. I don't think I'd go so far as to call you delusional, but I think you have a hard time separating fact from fiction."

She turned to face me. "What can I say?" she demurred, shrugging her shoulders. "The coroner said Lark died of a heart attack. Tripp had nothing to do with it. I think you'd better leave."

I opened my mouth to protest, but just then the back door opened, and Janice stuck her head out. "What are you two doing?" she asked.

"Oh," Bobbye said, flashing her mom a smile. "I was just telling Stacey that you and Dad and I are cruising to Nova Scotia."

When she looked back at me, her smile was gone, her tone all business. "We're leaving tomorrow morning, Stacey, and we have to be on board "Mac the Knife" by ten. I've got a lot to do, so I'd better say good-bye. I'll see you when I get back." She ran up the steps and slammed the door on her way into the house.

I wanted so badly to run after her, to bang on the door, to open it and yell, *How could you? How could you? How could you?*

But, as I stood there on that span of gravel, all the energy that had fed my anger melted away. A feeling of lightness propelled me forward and I hurried off to my car. By the time I'd settled into the driver's seat, my hands, which had been shaking and damp just moments before, were dry and steady. I backed down the driveway, and as I drove slowly past the house, I made myself a promise. "Never again, Bobbye Revels MacAvoy," I vowed. "You'll never see me again.

EPILOGUE
October 8, 2019

From the deck, I watch a persimmon-colored sun spread its iridescent blanket across the azure waters of Hamilton Bay. I take a sip of Campari and lean forward to check the gang plank below. Soon, Bobbye will return from a meeting at one of the condo complexes she owns on the island of Bermuda.

From Trinidad, we've come north to take care of this last bit of business before we cruise south to spend a month with our folks in Atlanta. Bobbye has given Rosa and Enrique, Captain Ennis, and our engineer, Ned Gallaher, some time off. The six of us are a congenial lot and that's good because we spend months together aboard "Mac the Knife."

Rosa walks past me, an aqua cloth folded over her arm, a vase of tropical flowers in hand. She starts up the stairs to the foredeck to prepare a small dining table for Bobbye and me. We're celebrating our fourth anniversary tonight and Rosa will make sure everything is perfect. Soon, I'll need to get out of my damp bathing suit, shower, and put on something nice.

Back in 2008, when I was still renting Mrs. Ferguson's apartment, my dad married a woman named Jessica. They decided to live in her house and my dad gave me the house on Kentucky Avenue where I'd grown up. So, when Bobbye and I are in Atlanta, we spend time there when we're not staying with her parents in the beautiful new house she bought them in Lenox Hills.

In 2011, Phil met an attorney named Keri Blue and three months later, they were engaged. He called one day to say they were pregnant and getting married sooner than they'd thought. My invitation would arrive shortly. On the Friday night before the wedding, Brock and Phyllis would be hosting a dinner and I'd be invited to that, too. "You're like a sister to me, Stacey," he'd said, "and I can't get married without you. See you soon."

The years I'd spent with my Walkman eventually paid off and I'd lost weight. Then I let my hair grow out and a friend at work talked me into going to a colorist who turned it ash blonde. It took a while for me to get used to it, but I got so many compliments I learned to like it.

So, when I walked into the Saddlebrook Country Club on the night of Phil and Keri's rehearsal party, I felt really good about myself. The dinner was being held out on the terrace and I hurried along knowing I was late because of a detour on the way.

Phil and Keri greeted me with a hug and told me I was at table four—over to the right. I looked toward the table where I saw my dad and Jessica sitting in two of the chairs, and Bax Dobson and his wife in two others. On the far side, a woman with short black hair had her back to me while she talked with someone at another table. I slipped into the vacant chair beside her and when she turned around, both of us jumped. "Is that you, Stacey?" Bobbye said. "You look amazing!" Others at the table echoed her compliment and soon all of us were chatting away over dinner. When it was over, Bobbye invited me to the bar for a nightcap and that's where we began again.

I loved my years at *the Constitution*, loved my work and my colleagues. But those days are over, and I know I'll never work at a regular job with a regular boss and regular hours again. I do have a job, though. I take care of Roberta Revels MacAvoy, seeing to her wants and needs, her little whims and desires. Fortunately, it's a job that comes with considerable perks. Winter finds us in southern climes, cruising from one exotic port to another. In summer, we spend a couple of months at Bobbye's chalet in the cool green hills above Lucerne. In the fall and spring, we're at home with our folks.

This life is all about *now* because the past is something we avoid. After forgiving each other for past transgressions, we made a vow before we married to never speak of the things that had wrenched us apart. These days, we put our time and energy into making each other happy. This afternoon, I put Bobbye's favorite turquoise silk sheets on our bed and sprinkled them with fresh rose petals. Nearby, there's a bottle of her prized brut cooling on ice. A couple of days ago, I asked if there was anything she especially wanted for our anniversary dinner. She smiled and said, "Would you please make your dad's death cake?" And, of course, I did.

Elliot's Death Cake

1/3 cup water
2 (1-oz) squares unsweetened chocolate
2 sticks butter, softened
2 cups brown sugar
2 eggs

2 1/2 cups all-purpose flour
1 1/2 teaspoons baking soda
½ teaspoon salt
1 cup buttermilk
1 teaspoon vanilla extract

Combine water and chocolate in a small saucepan and cook over low heat, stirring constantly until the chocolate melts; remove from heat. Using mixer, cream butter in large bowl; gradually add sugar, beating well. Add eggs one at a time, beating well after each. In separate bowl, combine flour, baking soda, and salt. Add to creamed mixture alternately with buttermilk, beginning and ending with flour mixture. Add cooled chocolate and vanilla extract and mix until just blended. Pour batter into 3 greased and floured 9" round cake pans. Bake @ 350 for 15-18 minutes. Cool layers completely on wire racks. Ice with Marshmallow Frosting.

Marshmallow Frosting: Combine 1 ½ cups white sugar with 1 teaspoon cream of tartar, dash of salt, and ½ cup water. Cook over medium heat, stirring constantly, until clear. Cook without stirring to soft ball stage (240 degrees). Using mixer, beat 4 egg whites until stiff, and continue beating while you slowly add the hot syrup mixture. Beat until stiff peaks form. Cool completely and fold in 2 cups miniature marshmallows. Frost layers and sides of cake.

Also by Jeri Fitzgerald Board:
The Bed She Was Born In (2006)

Praise for The Bed She Was Born In:

"Jeri Fitzgerald Board has written a sweeping, important book which illuminates the lives of Southern women, black and white, as they struggle with the harsh realities of sex, race, class, and history. Yet this novel brims with life and love on every page. The Bed She Was Born In is a remarkable achievement—and a great read!"

—Lee Smith, Author of Fair and Tender Ladies and Family Linen

"Over the last few years, a new writing genre known as 'historical consciousness' has emerged, and Southern women have seized the baton in this arena. In The Bed She Was Born In, Jeri Fitzgerald Board gives us a tale of courage and endurance, but with a wry sense of humor, and a writing style so stripped of the superfluous that she moves action along as fast as Hemingway—and then clobbers you with a completely unexpected turn of events. This novel could be the companion piece to W.H. Auden's Any Girl, but it could also be the story of your wife, mother, sister, lover. It is not to be missed."

—John H. Roper, Historian, and Author of
Repairing the March of Mars:
The Civil War Diaries of a Steward in the Stonewall Brigade

"This is a book you could live in. This means even after you know how the story turns out, you'll want to read it again and again. Get a copy of The Bed She Was Born In. Read it. This is a book to live in."

—Schuyler Kaufman, Book Nook

Nominated for the Pulitzer Prize for Fiction, and for the PEN/Faulkner Award for Fiction; Finalist for the Southern Independent Booksellers Alliance Award for Fiction; and, the 2007 winner of the President's Award of the North Carolina Society of Historians.

The Bed She Was Born In is available on AMAZON.com

CPSIA information can be obtained
at www.ICGtesting.com
Printed in the USA
FSHW011834231121
86394FS